The GOLD

COTEAU
BOOKS

www.coteaubooks.com

A NOVEL

The GOLD

DAVID CARPENTER

The historical characters that come and go in this novel share the same fate as the ones I invented: they are subject to the whims of my imagination. The settlements of Lac Maria and Sangris (named respectively after a fish and a Dogrib chief) are not on any map, nor is the Burbidge-Riley claim. Go there at your peril.

Edited by Leona Theis
Cover designed by Jamie Olson
Typeset by Susan Buck
Printed and bound in Canada

Library and Archives Canada Cataloguing in Publication

Carpenter, David, 1941-, author
The gold / David Carpenter.

Issued in print and electronic formats.
ISBN 978-1-55050-909-0 (paperback).--ISBN 978-1-55050-910-6 (pdf).--
ISBN 978-1-55050-911-3 (epub).--ISBN 978-1-55050-912-0 (mobi)

I. Title.

PS8555.A76158G65 2017 C813'.54 C2016-907129-4
C2016-907130-8

COTEAU BOOKS

2517 Victoria Avenue
Regina, Saskatchewan
Canada S4P 0T2
www.coteaubooks.com

Available in Canada from:
Publishers Group Canada
2440 Viking Way
Richmond, British Columbia
Canada V6V 1N2

10 9 8 7 6 5 4 3 2

Coteau Books gratefully acknowledges the financial support of its publishing program by: the Saskatchewan Arts Board, The Canada Council for the Arts, the Government of Saskatchewan through Creative Saskatchewan, the City of Regina. We further acknowledge the [financial] support of the Government of Canada. Nous reconnaissons l'appui [financier] du gouvernement du Canada.

Saskatchewan Arts Board
Canada Council for the Arts Conseil des Arts du Canada
Canada
Saskatchewan Ministry of Tourism, Parks, Culture and Sport
Regina City of Regina

for Kever

To have gold is to be in fear, and to want it to be in sorrow.
—Samuel Johnson

Gold makes the ugly beautiful.
—Molière

Prologue

Ethel's Moment

She did the upstairs first. That went pretty slick because the Englishman's office was locked, and all she had to do was the master bedroom, the two bathrooms, and a sitting room they hardly ever used. She didn't do the third floor because there had been no guests for some time. She hit the downstairs running, and by three o'clock she was puffing and sweaty and dying for a cigarette. Her son was supposed to give her a hand today, but he was walking the Eggers' dog. And taking his sweet time about it. The only thing left to do was put away the dishes she had washed. Some went up high on either side of the sink, and the good ones went into the dining room cupboards and Mrs. Eggers' china cabinet.

She opened the pantry to put away the sugar bowl. Hanging at the back of the cupboard on a little hook was a key on a tiny brass chain. A skeleton key. She had never noticed it before but she thought it must be the one her boy had referred to. Sometimes Rennie was her little spy. But where the hell had he gotten to this afternoon?

The house was so quiet the kitchen clock sounded unnaturally loud. She plucked the key off the hook and tiptoed down the creaky hallway to the door of the Englishman's library. Unlike the office upstairs, the library was always locked, except when he was in there reading, or whatever he did.

There had been a phone call after lunch, and all of a sudden Mr. Eggers and his wife were up and rushing around. Mrs. Eggers had called out, *This may take some time, Ethel, but we'll be back before you're done.*

Ethel inserted the skeleton key and turned the lock. One little peek wouldn't hurt. She flipped a switch. Under the light of an old chandelier, the library came to life in all its dusty glory. Lord help us, the room had not been cleaned in months. There were hundreds of books on shelves, and many more in glassed-in cupboards or stacked up on long tables. How could anyone read all those books? Especially such a trampy-looking Charlie like Mr. Eggers.

She spotted a smallish metal bar lying on a window ledge. She picked it up to inspect it, and when she felt how heavy it was, her heart seemed to flip over and belch. The thing was scarcely bigger than a pencil box and it was burnished to a pale yellow lustre. She replaced it on the ledge and recoiled, stole back towards the door. She was about to turn off the light and flee when her heel brushed up against something hard. She looked down and nudged it with her shoe. It didn't budge. It was a brick. She got down on her knees and gave the thing a good push. It grated slowly across the hardwood, heavy like a gravestone. Mr. Eggers must have put it there to hold the door open. Her heart was thumping so loud she wondered if she'd be able to hear someone returning to the house. She leaned out the doorway to listen, and all she could hear was the rooster clock in the kitchen. She crept up to one of the bigger shelves, about nose high, stacked with big important-looking volumes even bigger than *The Book of Knowledge*, and she spied – *holy!* – another gold brick wedged in to make a book-end. And another down the row. And behind the second one, almost out of sight, was a third gold brick, somewhat smaller than the other bricks but much bigger than the bar on the window ledge.

She reached up, lifted it down, and took a deep breath. It was many times heavier than Mrs. Eggers' oversized steam iron. It caught the light from the chandelier, and it seemed to blink at her.

Part One

Age of the Hero

Chapter 1

The Sunshine Pit

At night the men march past the window clomp clomp clomp. They have made him be awake. He waddles in the dark past his sleeping brother to his mum and dad's bedroom waddle waddle see Joey waddle. They are asleep. He can hear Mum and Dad breathe. *Thigh*, he whispers to both of them. The men are marching up the road. Soon they will be gone. Why are they marching up the road?

"Thigh," he says, a little louder.

He grabs the blanket and tries to tug but no one moves.

"Thigh?"

He pulls the blanket again and it won't budge. Mum opens her eyes and closes them and opens them again. She takes him by the hand to go to the loo. Joey doesn't *want* to go pee-pee. She hauls him up to sleep between Mum and Dad. It is warm there. Between Mum and Dad.

Another night, the men wake him up marching past the window in the dark. It is wintertime. Joey totters out past his brother and into his mum and dad's room. He whispers, *Thide?* His mum just lies there on her stomach with her mouth open.

"Thide?"

He pulls the blanket until it starts to come away. His mum she gives him a look.

She says, "Joey go pee-pee?"

He whispers, "Thide."

Mum picks him up and settles him down. She tells him to go sleepy-bye. The men are gone, they are marching somewhere up the hill. He sucks his thumb. Joey does not want to wake up his dad. *Dad needs his sleep*, his mum always says. Joey puts his mouth to Mum's ear to whisper.

"Thide?"

Another time, it is the day, it is warm out. Mum takes Joey and Arthur for a stroll. She holds Joey's hand, he looks up at his mum. She smiles down at him.

He says, "Thide!"

Joey's mum, she looks around, she laughs and laughs.

OUTSIDE IN DAYTIME and outside at night. Outside at night the men march past the window in their clogs. They are heading for the mine. The mine is in Castleford. Castleford is in Yorkshire. Yorkshire is in England. England is in the rest of the world. Outside in daytime is best. Outside with Arthur. Arthur is his brother, he is six, he goes to school. Outside walking with his big brother Arthur and sometimes Joey's dad. Dad, he says *the great outdoors*. The great outdoors with the mountains. The mountains are not real ones. They are muck-tips, says Dad. They're only mounds, says Mum. Joey calls them mountains because mountains are to climb.

The old men march by the window and wake up Joey. It is dark out. It is always dark out when the men go marching to the mine. They go up the mountains and down again, that's what miners do. Why are they old? Joey tiptoes out of the bedroom. Arthur is asleep, little Wally is asleep, Joey can hear his mum and dad breathe, they sound different when they breathe. Mum she sighs up, she waits a long time and sighs down again. Dad he rattles his inside nose. Joey gets dressed, he puts his shoes on in the dark. He ties his laces in the dark. He goes outside. He trudges up the street to the mountain.

Joey walks up the mountain. He can see where he goes, he makes footprints. Sometimes he makes deep footprints. Joey falls into a hole, he climbs out of the hole, he walks more up the mountain. It's got the ashes, they make Joey sneeze. He walks up to the top of the mountain. Puff he goes puff like the old miners do. He can see other mountains. His dad says they are muck-tips. His mum says they are mounds. The book says they are slag heaps. There are no miners up here. There are no miners anywhere.

He goes back down the mountain. He walks around the big hole. He comes down to the street, he opens the door. He sneezes. His mum is tippy-toeing, she's doing their breakfast. But now her mouth is open. She says to Joey where has he been.

"I climbed up the mountain to see the old men."

"You're filthy!"

Mum slaps off the ashes, whack whack whack. Mum is mad at Joey. She turns him around and around.

"You just wandered up there in the dark? How did you get so filthy?"

"Why are all the miners old?"

"Joey, you must promise me. Never wander out of the house at night. Never, do you hear?"

He wants to tell his mum it isn't night any more. When Mum gets mad she has a soft voice. Her spanks never hurt. When Dad gets mad he has a loud voice, he spanks you on your bummy, harder than Mum does.

"Will you tell Dad?"

Mum, she says, "Shhh!"

THE SLAG HEAPS WERE about seventy feet high and a quarter of a mile long, each one a great pyramid of dross from the coal pits. They were made of unburnable rubbish. The children all got very dirty playing there, and some of them looked like small versions of their fathers who worked at the colliery.

Very early in the morning, the old men would go by the Burbidge flat, marching to work in their clogs, and Joseph would awaken to their clopping past the bedroom window until it faded away. Most of the young miners were gone to the War to fight the Kaiser. Why did the old miners walk to work in clogs? Were their feet too old to wear boots? Did they carry their boots with them? They never sounded ordinary, they always sounded like soldiers. Hours later, still in the dark, he and his brothers (Arthur older, Wallace younger) would walk to school past the mountain of slag at the end of the street, and they would arrive yawning just as morning began to leak through the fog and rain.

Joseph fought a lot, everyone did. The boys had to appear as tough as possible. At the Half-Acres Junior and Infants School a teacher taught the boys how to box. The boys circled each other, backs straight with their fists extended and their heads up, bouncing around the ring, feinting and jabbing, looking fierce like small soldiers. It would be keen some day to go and fight the Kaiser. That's what Arthur said so Joey said it too.

He was Joseph at school, Joseph Burbidge. His mother was Winnie. She was a parson's daughter and she talked proper. His father was Walter. He was born in Sewerby on the Yorkshire coast, where his own father had worked the coal docks. Joey's dad Walter didn't talk proper, he talked like the miners. Walter used to be a coal trimmer, and later a staith master. He explained to his boys what a coal trimmer did and what a staith master was, and how dark it got underground, but Joey forgot most of that. He found out that they never climbed mountains, so he forgot. Now Joey's dad was a boss in one of the mines.

Joey's mum had a funny name when she was young. She was Winnifred Bibbing. But now everyone called her Winnie. Every so often she liked to tell her boys where she came from and how she met Joey's dad. They met in the graveyard at Methley Church just outside of Castleford. He asked her if she was visiting the grave of a loved one. She told him that she was not. She liked the old cemetery because it was peaceful. Winnie had come with her family from a village called Slaidburn on the southern moors. It was just inside the Lancashire border, she told them. Her father, Parson Bibbing, rode on horseback from village to village to attend to his flock. Not a real flock but a bunch of people. He and his wife were from Maidstone. They read books all the time and they all talked proper. Winnie said it set them apart. She said it was sad that it set them apart. Joey never asked her what that meant.

After the war, each summer, Joseph, his older brother Arthur, his younger brother Wallace, and their little sister Angie were taken in the cart to Slaidburn for a fortnight with Winnie's family. As far as Joey was concerned, his mother's village was everything that Castleford was not. Slaidburn was so small it was almost not a real village. His mum said it was a place where two roads crossed and little more. People got around very little. His mum's sister Auntie Vi liked to say, *they kept the noiseless tenor of their ways.* Joey never asked her what that meant. But if someone went to Manchester or Preston, it became a community event. If someone went on a team of oxen forty miles or more, Joey's mum said, *he might be considered a fit client for the mental hospital.* The nearest railroad was nine miles away, so the village where Winnie and Vi grew up was as isolated as any village in England.

While Joey's parents laughed and chatted with Winnie's sister Vi and the elder Bibbings, the children ran out and played on the moors. It felt wonderful. In Castleford they were used to playing in caves and quarries, and climbing the muck-tips, of course, and they could go down to the slaughterhouse and watch the butcher and his men fell the cows and pigs and then bleed them, and that was smart good fun, but Castleford was nothing as good as Slaidburn. It wasn't beautiful and free like Slaidburn, where they could take bicycles and go fishing in the streams or go blackberrying or scare up the marsh birds and collect their eggs. They could ride the ponies from the farm next to the Bibbings' cottage and pretend they were cowboys and Indians, and they always never told Mum and Dad.

Everywhere they went it was beautiful, even the heavy fog was beautiful, and everything they did was somehow shot through with the summer light on the moors and the quiet little village, and when they became exhausted they would come home to the Bibbing house where their mum and Auntie Vi grew up and have their tea and fall asleep in the quiet old cottage. The back streets of Castleford were grimy from the ashes and the smog. But in Slaidburn they didn't even have back streets, just paths to run on, and no one hardly ever got filthy.

In Joey's opinion Castleford was a wintry place hemmed in by pit heaps and dirty fog. The town had all sorts of wounded men from the war with missing limbs, and sick men too. People called his father's colliery the Sunshine Pit, because every time it turned sunny, the men were allowed to go home and take a holiday. And since it was almost never sunny, this name was just a stupid joke.

Slaidburn was a summer place with wide open horizons and mostly sunny days. It was *thide* all over. Castleford meant early rising in the dark and school all day and homework on the kitchen table at night and being rocked out of sleep at four or five in the morning when the miners marched by in their clogs. Slaidburn meant sleeping in, and then devouring breakfast to hurry out into the moors to play all day. You had to worry about adders and getting lost and falling into the stream, but that made it all the more exciting.

If anyone at school ever asked young Joseph how the moors of Slaidburn differed from the vast moors around Castleford, he would say that the Slaidburn moors were summer ones, but the Castleford moors were winter ones. And besides, in Castleford they were so close to home the moors were ordinary. If anyone challenged Joey's little pronouncement, he would just scoff.

Joey thought he was closer to his father than his mother. She made them all go to church every Sunday and after, they stayed home and she read things to them. Joey and his sister and two brothers all spoke in a voice like their mother's, without the broad accent of their father, but Joey liked the way his father talked. *It's up in the mornin for school, me lads. Won't learn owt much under the covers.*

He was a hardworking man and strict with his family. He cracked the whip at work and he cracked the whip at home, but he was surprisingly easy to live with. He wanted his children to succeed in life, so he made sure they did their homework and that they were attentive at school. Joey's dad would come home at the end of his shift looking tired and surly, and he would sit in his easy chair and fall asleep, and the children were very careful not to wake him or to come too near to his chair. But when he had arisen to take his tea, he was eager to talk with the children.

As the three boys grew older, and their sister Angie followed them everywhere on their forays into the abandoned pits and excavated caves that ran deep into the hillsides, their father laid down the law – no more crawling around underground. A boy had been killed in a cave-in just outside the town. It was days before they found his body.

"We weren't born to burrow underground," he said. "We're not a boonch of rabbits."

"What about the miners?" said Joey. The miners were always going underground and they had a railroad train under there.

"Thank tha lucky stars tha's not one a them poor lads. And thank tha lucky stars there's places above ground for workin. Thee can go off and be barristers or wheelwrights or summat tha wants. Get tha's education. Get a good situation somewhere. Don't have to spend tha's whole life in Castleford."

That sounded good to Joey. He had always wanted to see the ocean. And the jungle, and maybe also the desert.

"If tha's to be a miner," Walter continued, "go to the wild Northwest or the Outback and prospect for gold."

"But Walter," said Winnie, "what good is gold for anyone?"

Joseph's sister Angie piped up. "Gold is for treasures."

"Where is that?" asked Joey.

"The wild Northwest is in Canada and the Outback is down

under in Australia."

Joey wanted to know which one was best.

"Best for what?" his father said. "Best for weather?"

"No," said Joey, "best for gold."

One night at the dinner table Joey's brother Arthur wanted to know what was wrong with working down in the coal mine. Arthur was thirteen and almost as tall as his father. "They make but one pound a week at the pithead," young Arthur said with much authority, "but down underground they make a better wage. And they give you a lantern for the dark."

His father raised his fork. "Lads, you erd Arthur's question? Well, I've got a story for you. When I were your age, Arthur, I used to work wi' ponies. They were used to pull tubs that held coal. They would haul down a string of empty tubs on a track and turn around and haul up the full uns from t'workins. I was a driver. Me job it was to walk beside me pony and urge him through't tunnels. Damned dangerous work for a boy," he said. "It was dangerous enough down there for a man."

"Look at you," said Arthur.

Joey would never challenge his father like that. Neither would Wally. But they both liked to argue with Arthur and get him mad.

His father brought up the fork again for silence. "Aye, look at me. I'm alive because I was lucky enough t'escape job of drivin ponies a thousand buggerin feet down under t'ground. Imagine it, Arthur."

Wally wanted to know what it was like, driving the ponies underground.

"Right. Picture this, lads. Ponies were fed early in't morning before shift. We fed them hay and grain. I were't driver for an old pony named Gudgeon. I'd pick him up at start of shift and take him back to't stable at the end of't. Gudgeon were near blind when I got him, it happens to all t'old uns. Light in tunnels is so poor because't oil lamps don't shine up owt much down there. To make matters worse, ponies were much overworked. We were supposed to use them for one shift and then take them back and rest them till't next day. Supposed to work shifts like miners did. But in our mine, ponies would be forced to do double shifts."

"That's not fair," said Angie.

"It's certainly not," said their mother. "Poor little Gudgeon."

"One day Gudgeon warn't up to it. I found out later he'd been on his third shift without a break. I walked beside him, see, and pushed on his arness collar to get him to pull, but he kept crowdin' me into t'walls of tunnel and tryin roll over on me, like. Made me scramble to keep from gettin pinned down beneath him. Went and found t'doggy, I did, and told him that Gudgeon was dyin. Doggy he came and checked out Gudgeon, who was lyin on floor of t'tunnel. *The bugger is sound asleep!* cried t'doggy, and he proceeded to kick t'poor animal awake. Well now, Gudgeon gave up on that vale of tears, didn't he. No, in a week or so they put him down and I always felt bad that I'd driven him."

"I'd never do that," said Arthur.

"Of course you wouldn't do that," said his father, "because you'd never be gormless enough to work underground. You 'ears about the Castleford men who die, don't you, by cave-ins and explosions and the black lung. But you 'ears nowt about them what gets hurt or sick and can't work no more. Young men, some of them too bloody crippled to walk to work. And right here, Arthur, right in these towns."

"Poor Gudgeon," said Angie.

"Joey," said his mum with a smile, "your mouth is wide open."

Joey's dad liked to tell stories about all sorts of things, but this was the first time he had ever told a story about what miners did. It was the first one and the last one. Not long after Joey had turned eleven, when the fall had gone rainy and dark outside, his dad went to bed and never woke up. On a stormy night in late October his heart gave out. Joey woke up to his groans, but he thought it must have been something else they did in there. On a quieter night Joey's mum might have heard Walter moaning, or fumbling for his glasses, or struggling to catch his breath, but in all the rush of rain, wind and thunder, she slept right through Walter's last moments. When she awakened to start breakfast for the family, he was already stiff and cold. She brought them all into the bedroom so they could say their goodbyes. She told them all that he had passed in his sleep, so that's what everyone said, but Joey didn't believe her.

His mum would stand by the stove, pale, unmoving, staring like a statue in the churchyard. Joey might say something to her and she would snap out of it and reply something cheerful. She threw herself into the daily chores of mothering as much as she ever had, getting Joey and the children fed and off to school in the dark, washing, shopping, cooking, mending and organizing her brood. She did everything she could to keep the grief away. That's how Joey remembered it later. The shopping trips she made to Queen's Park when the children were at school became a weekly respite. She would recount her travels to the children when they came home from school. By the edge of the park was Castleford's new library where the townsfolk could read newspapers and take out the latest books. She took Joey there sometimes to help carry things home. They would visit the library on their way home from shopping, lay down the grocery bags. She would gaze at the newspapers, check out the latest frocks and jumpers. She would dip in and out of the books and magazines as freely as she pleased until she felt rested enough to continue. She scarcely ever took a book home because it would merely add to the weight of their load.

The park had a bandstand where she took Joey and Wally and Angie. The bandstand was for the major events of the town, including the miners' rallies and the military concerts. Once in a while, she brought the children for a weekend picnic. People marveled at how well the family was doing, and Joey wished they would mind their own business.

Every Sunday she took the children to her church and sometimes she fell asleep during the sermon. Sometimes Angie or Wally would fall asleep as well, but Joey and Arthur never did. Sometimes at the end of the service they were given a basket of food to take home. Arthur always carried the basket.

Joey became his mother's confidante, and he learned things about her struggles that he kept to himself. She managed most days to exhaust herself with the chores of the household. She did this, she told Joey, so that she would sleep better at night. On a good night, she would fall asleep for several hours. Joey felt bad when he heard this, because most nights he could sleep all night long. Sometimes he woke up to hear her talking to his dad, and it felt as though his father's ghost was in their bedroom. Joey thought that was nice, but apparently her little talks with Joey's dad didn't do much good. She confessed to Joey that she feared his dad was cold where he lay, and that he needed warming.

One night in February, Joey showed up at her door.

"Arthur can't sleep," he said.

"Then tell him to come in here."

Joey fetched Arthur, who had been muttering angrily to himself. The two boys sat at the side of their mother's bed.

"It's no good," said Arthur. "Me noodle won't stop thinkin."

"And what about you, Joey?"

"I can't sleep neither."

"Well, you're the pair, aren't you."

"Mother," said Arthur, "I want to quit school and get a proper job."

"You what? Now?"

"Like Father did."

"Your father always said that you boys should get your education. Remember? He always said that. You can't get a proper situation if you don't finish school."

"I don't care," said Arthur.

"Come here," said Winnie. She lifted the blanket. "Both of you."

Arthur backed cautiously into his mother's bed. Winnie embraced him from behind and he began to cry. She turned to Joey. "What about your sister? Does she have trouble falling asleep?"

Joey went in to see how his sister was faring. He found her awake in Wallace's bed, and she too had been crying.

"Do you want to sleep with Mum?" he said.

To his surprise, both children answered yes and climbed out of the bed. At last all four of the children gathered around their mother like month-old puppies and sniffled their way to sleep.

Throughout the last weeks of winter their mother's bed became a sort of gathering place for young insomniacs, and when their need was greatest they would file in, sometimes all four of them. On the nights when Winnie's bed was most crowded, they each found a place under the sheets and blankets. Arthur stayed farthest from his mother and closest to the bedroom door so that he could rise first and set the morning fire. Wally slept between Arthur and his mother, Angie slept next to her mother's back on the other side, and Joey slept next to Angie on the edge of the bed nearest the window. The children could have their spats outside of Winnie's bedroom, but beneath the blankets of her bed there was a permanent state of peace.

Outside of his mum's bed, as Joey would remember it later on, the world dictated another sort of existence in which money ruled, or the absence of it. The miners' collective agreement allowed for pensions for their widows. If a miner was killed on the job, he would get the maximum pension allowable for his wages and his level of seniority. But if the employee passed away anywhere outside the mine, his widow was accorded a smaller pension. Winnie's pension was ample enough to pay the rent and the fuel, but she had to pay for most of the family's food and other necessities out of her husband's savings, and soon these savings dwindled and Winnie's worries mounted.

More than once Joey overheard her say to a friend, *However shall we manage?*

Winnie tried to keep her financial woes to herself but these worries began to infect her children. Her visions of their impoverished state seemed to seep into Joey's dreams. One night in March, in their mother's bed, they had a conversation about money.

"Mummy," said Angie, "why can't we go to Slaidburn?"

"Because it's not summertime yet," said Joey.

"It doesn't have to be summertime to go to Slaidburn," said Wallace.

"We can't just go to Slaidburn," said their mum. "We don't live there, and there's no longer a school there, and we can't afford to go there."

"We don't have enough money to go to Slaidburn?" asked Joey.

"But that's not fair," said Angie. "Why do we need money just to go to a place?"

"Such questions."

"We have to pay the man with the wagon," said Arthur.

"Then why don't we get a nicer driver?" said Angie.

Her mother chortled over that one. "The drivers need money to feed their oxen, Angie. And they need to feed their families. That's just the way things are."

"I don't think that's fair."

Arthur was perched on the side of the bed, slouched over like an old man. He was almost fifteen now and he was growing tall.

"I could get a job," he said. "I know I could get one."

"Arthur," said his mother, "get in bed with us. Come on. Snuggle up to us and we'll talk about it."

"I don't want to get into bed. I'm just saying that I could get a job."

"Where?"

"I could work at the grinding mill."

"How do other people get money?" said Angie. "Why don't people give us money like everybody else?"

"Just a minute, dear. Arthur, the grinding mill? That doesn't sound very healthy for a young man."

"It's healthier than working down in the mines."

"Arthur, you must promise me this, that you'll finish your year at school and then we'll talk about getting jobs. Will you promise me that?"

Arthur stood and made for the door.

"Where are you going? Arthur?"

"I'm going back to bed, Mother."

"Don't you want to sleep in here?"

"No," he said, "that's for the children."

Joey listened as Arthur walked away to sleep in his own bed. It seemed to Joey as though his older brother was drifting away from them, and that he'd never be their brother again. Arthur would be lost somewhere out there in the world if they let him go. He almost got out of his mother's bed to follow his brother, but everywhere outside his mother's bed was cold.

JOEY'S MUM HAD A LONG spell of mourning, during which Auntie Vi paid them a visit, around midsummer. She took up lodgings at a nearby inn called the Dog and Spud, and every day she walked over to visit her sister and the children. Auntie Vi had been living in Canada, where she was married to a Canadian man, a French Canadian man the neighbours said. Joey's mum and Auntie Vi did most of their talking in the kitchen when the children were outside playing with their friends, but one day Joey was reading one of his Doogy Hazard books and he fell asleep in the children's bedroom. He awoke to the sound of his mum's voice. *Absolutely not*, she declared, and Joey sat up.

"I think, Winnifred, that you are being very noble."

"I'm not being noble," Joey's mum replied. "I'm not the sort of person who goes from one love to another."

"Dear me," said Auntie Vi. "We must have read different novels when we were growing up."

Joey thought that perhaps he should get off the bed and join his mum and Auntie Vi, but something in their tone made him wait. He sat on the side of the bed so he could hear better.

"Seriously, Vi, if you lost your Bernard, God forbid, could you possibly consider marrying again?"

"Not immediately," said Auntie Vi. "But Winnifred, there are...how shall I say...better ways to make do than –"

"Perish the thought," said Winnie. "We're getting on just fine, thanks to you, and thanks to the congregation and people like–"

"Living in this tiny hovel?" said Auntie Vi. "Living hand to mouth in a two-room flat and little Angie –"

"We're getting a cot for Angie. She will sleep in my room."

There was a long silence and Joey strained to make sense of the huffing and gasping and murmurs that followed.

"I am only saying, my dear Winnifred, I am only saying...that you can endure anything, even poverty, even, God forbid, the disease and early decline that comes with poverty, but there are limits to what prayer can bring you, my dear, and you *can't defeat nature!*"

Joey's mother replied, "I have no idea what you are talking about."

Aunti Vi said, "Oh, yes you do."

Chapter 2

The Pebble

"HOWEVER DO YOU MANAGE with four children?" said Mr. Eggers.

Joey was sitting next to little Angie in the rumble seat and he was listening but he wasn't paying much attention. Because of the motorcar. A 1923 Austin Chummy with the top rolled up, because it was raining. Mr. Eggers drove them through Castleford *with a keen sense for the road.* That's how Doogy Hazard would put it. *Mr. Eggers drove the sleek new Chummy through the town at a jolly clip, and all the people of Castleford stopped to stare at Joey and his rubicund sister Angie.* Joey wondered what made a girl rubicund, because maybe his little sister wasn't rubicund at all. *And all the people of Castleford stopped to stare at Joey, his sister, and his mum, who rode with Mr. Eggers in the front seat. And who among the townspeople of Castleford would know that they weren't a family coming home from gymkhana and other such revels?*

"We manage," said Joey's mum.

Mr. Eggers was a solicitor and a property manager in Castleford. He bought and sold land along the northeast coast from Scarborough to Hartlepoole. One rainy day after church he was lingering in the same churchyard where he had buried his first wife, *many a year ago, and a sad time it was for all,* and there he spied Winnifred. Joey's mum was thirty-eight. Her skin was pale, her nose long and thin, *and her face was kindly and somehow more youthful than her years. Looking far off into the distance, she had a sweet sadness upon her brow. Her hair was sprinkled with white and her figure exceedingly neat. She was less than perfectly gowned, her clothing nondescript...*

"The older ones help the younger ones," Joey's mum added.

His mum had somehow made the most of herself. Because people said so. She had been walking through the graveyard with Joey and young Angie, remembering Joey's dad to them, when Mr. Eggers approached her. He offered them a lift in his motor-car, and they accepted. Angie remembered the talk that passed between Mr. Eggers and her mother, his booming voice and her scarcely audible responses. She remembered Mr. Eggers's jocular manners, the enthusiasm he had for every little sight along the way, and her mother's pleasure at the spectacle of Mr. Eggers' attentions. Angie told this to Joey.

Joey remembered the car, the plush seats, the novelty of riding in a chugging vehicle with no horses. They exchanged these contrasting memories a number of times in that first year, and Joey took possession of his little sister's version of things – how Mr. Eggers had begun to prattle in his great booming voice.

What was making him talk so loud? Where was all that enthusiasm coming from?

"Is that where you live?" said Mr. Eggers. "Don't those little flats get chilly at night? You must coom for tea at the house. Mrs. Watkins lays a fine table. Oh, she is a good Christian lady and she runs the house with an iron hand. Be lost without her, I daresay. I'm a widower meself."

"Mr. Eggers," Joey's mum said, "it's very kind of you to invite me to your home, but you see, I can't leave my children to fend for –"

"Bring them along, Mrs. Burbidge, bring the whole flock. It's a big empty house. Be quite jolly to have a boonch of children there for a change. Old Watkins will put on a feed."

He held an umbrella over their mum's head as she walked up to her door, hand in hand with Angie, and with Joey in the lead.

"Well," said Joey's mum on that rainy day, smiling sadly in her doorway, "perhaps I can rally my brood for a visit."

HUGO CALLED HIM JOSEPH. He took Joey to a racetrack south of town one afternoon to show him what men of leisure did in their spare time. He said to Joey that he'd always wanted a son. In his cups, Hugo was seldom discrete, nor his voice very low, and he lapsed back from time to time to blurt things out in his Yorky voice. Young Joey overheard Hugo talking to one of his chums at the racetrack about the first meeting with Joey's mother. *She was penniless, see, very much in the need of a man to take over an' all, but I could see she was a girl of soom quality. Brought out the gentility in meself like. Think I'm daft, do ye? Roomy boogger. But I couldn't do owt but propose to her.*

Joey's mum got married that same year in Methley Church, and suddenly Mr. Eggers had a houseful of Burbidges. At meals, and when he returned home from work, Mr. Eggers sometimes wore a bewildered look, as though he had forgotten that he had acquired a big family. Before he had gotten married to Joey's mum, Mr. Eggers had had what he referred to as various *gels* to keep him company. But, as Joey's mum told him, *that was all past now*, and Mr. Eggers would never be a lonely widower again. Yes. Just as Joey was adjusting to the new regime, and thinking that life in Mr. Eggers' huge house might be to his liking, Arthur moved out.

Arthur had recently become Joey's idol. He talked with Joey like a scoutmaster or a coach about all sorts of things, especially about how Joey should take charge of his life and get himself *ready*, whatever that meant. Ready for being a grownup? Ready for a job? A course of training? A career in the military? Arthur was never very specific about his plans for Joey. Maybe what it meant was just *ready*. Ready for his flight from Mr. Eggers' big house.

Arthur had announced that he wanted no part of the new regime, including Mrs. Watkins. She was a woman of few words, a tall unsmiling edifice who ruled her small staff, her house (Eggers' big house, that is) with unwavering authority. She regarded this new brood of Burbidges with the sort of vigilance one might have reserved for a party of the Kaiser's advance troops. Arthur took a job in the grinding mill and went to live in a dorm with the other apprentices.

Joseph was fourteen. With Arthur gone so suddenly, he was left with his younger brother, Wallace, who was nervously compliant with the new regime, and little Angie, who was only eight years old. She took a curious liking to her new father, who began to refer to her as "our little princess," and then "my little princess," and Angie managed to tolerate Mrs. Watkins better than anyone else in the family. Joseph's mother darted everywhere in a half-smiling daze, as though she could not believe the great providence her prayers had brought her. At other times she arose from her prayers in a half-grieving daze, as though providence were a great deal over-rated. On these occasions, she grew silent, fearful, waiting each day for news of her son in the mill. In all of this, Joey was her confidante.

"JOSEPH," HIS NEW FATHER said one evening in his study, "have you thought of where you'd like to go to school?"

Joseph confessed that he had not. They were facing each other across his great desk, having what Hugo referred to as a father-son conversation. To Joseph it felt more like an interview with the principal.

"Well now. Joseph. I know the chap who runs the grammar school in Shacklesbury. It's down in Derbyshire. Crotting's his name. He's the kind of headmaster the boys are inclined to mind. If you take my meaning, boy. He's an educator with standards, an' all. Young Wallace might not be quite up to Shacklesbury, but I think you'd be a good fit."

Joey pondered this eager wisdom for a moment. He had a question for Hugo, but after many months he still did not know how to address him. Hugo Eggers always seemed a bit distant, a bit formal. Dad or Father was out of the question.

"What do you think, boy?"

"Um, sir," he began, and he felt this too was the wrong word, but he stumbled on, "why is it, um, why is it, d'you think, that this school would not be a good fit for Wallace?"

Hugo bent forward eagerly, lowered his voice. "Confidentially, between you and I, me lad, between you and I, young Wallace is more of a Burbidge than an Eggers, if you see what I mean."

"Oh," said Joseph, and his mouth went dry with...what? Was it fear? No. Was it anger? No, not that either. Was it weariness then? Was he just weary of all these changes to his life? Missing his father, missing Arthur who was his favourite person to talk with? Dreading his own memories of happier times, was that it? Dreading the day when he would have to bid Wallace and Angie and his mother goodbye? And what did his new father mean about Burbidges and Eggers?

"I see," Joseph said.

"Shacklesbury would just break poor Wallace's spirit, Joseph. I think our Wallace might want to find himself an apprenticeship or a situation where he'd be useful and happy." Hugo eased back into his chair. "But you, young man, you would rise to the 'casion. You've got the fighting spirit of your older brother, Joseph, and you're right smart at the book learning. Better at it than I was, I'll tell you that. Hah! I warn't brought up, I wer punched up! Some of us get to read the books, and some of us have to put the baps on the table, if you see what I mean. You've got an opportunity, boy. You've got a new father who can pay your way. Me, that is. Think of it. Public school with all the young chaps striving to get up in the world. With good schooling you could make a name for yourself, Joseph."

Joey found himself nodding, wearily, towards this version of his future. He wasn't sure if Mr. Eggers was making any sense, but it didn't matter if he was making sense. It was impossible to contradict the man. Joseph thought it very likely that he would hate Shacklesbury.

Headmaster Heath Crotting was apparently jolly keen on flogging with ash sticks, and he held his housemasters, prefects, monitors, and the school Sergeant to the same high standard. A thrashing worth its salt was executed by taking a bit of a run at the kneeling culprit, and delivering such a blow that the stick would sometimes break. If you didn't break the odd stick now and then, you were soft on flogging, and if you were soft on flogging, well dash it, you'd be soft on damn near anything, including the criminal element and Bolshevism.

This was how the boys in Joey's dorm talked about old Crotting. One day one of Joey's teachers, Master Herron, told them about the school. The long aftermath of the Great War was still being felt all over England. It had diminished the pool of certified teachers for an entire decade. Of all the grammar schools in the region to feel this pinch, Shacklesbury was one of the hardest hit.

"This is how yours truly obtained his appointment," said Master Herron, who looked very old indeed. "They couldn't find a maths wizard for their school, so they did the next best thing and hired me."

Their facility had rudimentary plumbing, no electricity, no telephones. Shacklesbury had always been, at best, a middling to minor grammar school, but the teacher shortage meant that an elderly cricketer was teaching history, that old Master Herron had to be brought out of retirement to do logic and maths, and old standards such as Latin and Greek had to be replaced by subjects as diverse as Horesemanship, Civics, *and that old pedagogical standard, The Manly Art of Self-Defense*, Master Herron told them.

Joseph came to Shacklesbury with just the remnants of a northern accent, but he stuck out. He was one of only a handful of commoners at Shacklesbury, which made him self-conscious of his northern intonations. He began at once to try and mimic the less inflected voices of the other boys. No one called him a commoner or a Yorky to his face, but he felt this perception as soon as he arrived at the school, as though he had been carrying a mysterious, hitherto unknown deformity. The boys at Shacklesbury seemed to speak a code known only to insiders, whose entrance to the school had much to do with family. Hugo Eggers had apparently found a back door to the school for his newly acquired child and felt it prudent to donate a goodly sum to the school in order to secure a position for young Joseph.

Joseph became friends early on with a boy from down in Essex named Allan Benbow who shared his love for the outdoors and his distaste for the Crotting regime. Together they maintained a brotherly antipathy towards flogging, towards fagging for the older students, and towards all lordly persons (LPs). Allan was a better student in class than Joseph, calmer, more measured and articulate. When challenged by a master he could think on his feet. Joseph was better at hitting the books. One by one, as the term unfolded, he sifted through them. Science, literature, history, anything to do with geography. He read like a pirate, sacking each volume for the good stuff. He worked best on his own, but because he was slow at maths, good old Benbow had to enlighten him on occasion.

One day after the showers, they were comparing their wounds with some of the younger boys. Just that day, Joseph had received four of the best from Crotting himself for fighting on the rugby field. He had sustained a black eye from an older boy over an insult hurled his way. *Oh, there's Joseph, getting festive again.* Getting festive could mean almost anything at Shacklesbury – getting obnoxious, being a bore, comporting oneself in a romantic fashion towards another boy, or just having a good time. It all depended on the intonation, and Joseph did not like the intonations of James Watson-Bowes, an LP of the highest order.

"Why is Watson-Bowes such a blighter?" he asked his friend Benbow.

"Because," Allan replied, "he was born to pull his pud, he was raised by pud-pullers, and he surrounds himself with pud-pullers. They even *smell* like pud-pullers."

The boys fell silent and looked up and there was the devil himself, wearing a towel and sporting a cut lower lip. He was surrounded by other LPs, who towered over the boys.

"Oh, I say," said Watson-Bowes, "there's young Benbow getting *expressive* again."

"That was topping good, Benbow," said Gerald Winkle, Monitor, LP, PP (Pud Puller) First Class. "I'd say that from now on, you and your *festive* friend, Burbidge there, will need regular good ticklings, hm?"

Mr. Bevis Glow, pronounced gloo, the Third, LP, PP, son of Bevis Glow II, Honorary Colonel of a regiment from Cambridge, chimed in with his own appraisal of things: "I think that it would be simply bang-on if both of you did some fagging for us. What do you say to that, Benbow? Burbidge?"

Burbidge and Benbow, non-LPs, professed non-PPs, pretended to know their place and said nothing.

"What's this Burbidge nonsense?" said Watson-Bowes. "I have it on good authority that his name is Eggers. That right? Eggers, is it?"

Allan Benbow interposed himself before Joseph could even make a proper fist.

"My good friend Burbidge wants to thank you for your invitation to fag for you, but we both decline to mix with the lower orders."

Quite a few boys began to snicker over that one, and the snickers turned into belly laughs.

Watson-Bowes cuffed a boy on the head for laughing too loud, and the boy cried out as grievously as he could, and another boy grabbed Watson-Bowes's towel, thus exposing the Honourable Member from Goonhilly Downs, and the battle was on.

It led all the way, once more, to Crotting's office. He was so put out by the rough-housing that he lectured Watson-Bowes and his two friends on the need for boys from fine old families to show a good example. On the other hand, Benbow got his first flogging, and Joseph got another sample of Crotchy's finest, upping his personal record of whacks by two. Joseph had not fared any better in his second encounter with Watson-Bowes, who was not only a stalwart of the school's boxing club, but taller and bulkier than Joseph.

Joseph spent some time brooding over this latest encounter with Crotting justice and at last began to come around. He examined his bruises at bedtime, a black eye, a scraped jawbone, a swollen red nose, and a series of flogging marks, the old ones next to the new ones; they looked like military stripes, purple and yellow. He brought them to Benbow's attention.

"Alan, I've got more stripes than you have. Mine are spectacular and they're all over my haunches. How many whacks did Crotchy give you?"

"Only four. But we all have to start somewhere, Joseph."

"I got six."

"Well," said Benbow, philosophically, good loser to the end, "that's just you, Joseph. You are simply unbeatable."

JOSEPH WAS INVITED to visit his friend Benbow during a school holiday. They stayed at Allan's home, and Allan's parents were quite welcoming to Joseph. Allan's father had some family money, and he spent much of his time publishing a journal and writing and editing essays and manifestos. Because he was an eager conversationalist, he reminded Joseph of his own original father. Mrs. Benbow was an artist and a suffragette, and she reminded Joseph of his Auntie Vi. Mrs. Benbow was even more vocal on public issues than her husband, and she had bequeathed this distinction to her daughter. Allan introduced Joseph to his sister at tea.

"Joe, this is Buggy. She's a frightful flirt, so be wary of her."

Buggy shook hands with Joe with a restrained yet somehow mischievous smile.

"I am not a frightful flirt, I'm a spectacular flirt."

"Pleased to meet you, Buggy."

"We're trying to make you blush, Joe."

Joe obliged them all.

They retired to a living room around a coal fire and read and argued and teased one another. Allan had read something about flappers and the Great War. How was one connected to the other, he wondered out loud. His father skirted the question and quoted a bolshy chap who said that war was immoral. Mrs. Benbow picked up a book and read a pretty poem out loud about a falcon *(the achieve of, the mastery of the thing!)* that Joseph did not understand. Mrs. Benbow began to talk about this chap named Hopkins, but right then, sister Buggy challenged her father on several points about morality, or maybe she was challenging him on the subject of flappers, yes, and to get both wife and daughter going, Mr. Benbow said some sarky things about a writer chap named Lawrence, and, well, it didn't happen in *quite* that fashion, but that's all Joe could file away before he fell asleep. Hopkins, was that the poet or the bolshy chap? And what was a flapper anyway?

The boys went fishing almost every day, dunking worms for tench, bream and pike, or anything else that might bless them with its presence. They stood on the banks of a murky pond and reviewed their lives at school. After much talk they had a go at Joseph's tutor in maths, who doubled as their instructor in logic.

"What do you think of old Herron?"

"What do you mean what do I think?" said Benbow.

"Think he might be...you know...a bit expressive?"

"Herron? You must be joking. He's too bloody old to be expressive. This buggery, you know, Burbidge, it's a pretty vigorous business."

"How would you know, Benbow?"

"Haw haw, very good, Burbidge. You get off the odd good one now and then, I suppose."

"I catch m'self listening now and then. To Herron, I mean. He doesn't really fit in, does he."

"Well, Herron would be the only master you listen to then, Burbidge."

"This is spectacular," said Joe. "Haven't done this since we was in Slaidburn."

Allan had never even heard of Slaidburn. "Not very pukka, this."

"What's not very pukka?"

"This sort of fishing, Joe. Not the least bit pukka."

Joe had only the vaguest idea of what pukka was. "What's wrong with this here?"

"Well, Joe, I'm not going all toffy on you, but it's just coarse fish here. It's just three per cent better than going for eels."

"What's wrong with that?" Joe said, pointing to an expired pike of about three pounds with a head poking out of Allan's creel.

"Trout fishing," he said. "Salmon fishing. Legal or otherwise. That's pukka, Joe. Fishing with a fly rod. You've got to come back and we'll get my father to take us up for the trout."

"And that would be more pukka than this?" Joe said. "I've heard about flyfishing. Isn't that for Lordly Persons? And don't these LPs flog the water and go home empty-handed?"

"Sometimes," said Allan reflectively.

"Pukka is results, Benbow. Pukka is fish in the pan."

"I'll make a note of that, Burbidge. Always a pleasure."

"Boy, what is your name?"

The question came from Headmaster Crotting. He was a bald man with perfectly rounded, black-rimmed glasses and a moustache as fastidiously trimmed and squared-off as a toothbrush. He glowered at Joseph and Joseph peered back, relieved that the headmaster's desk was between them, and that Crotchy's flogging sticks were nowhere to be seen. The headmaster looked more perplexed than outraged this time.

"My name, sir?"

"Yes, boy. That is what I said."

"Joseph, sir."

"Joseph what?"

"Joseph Burbidge, sir."

"Not Joseph Eggers?"

Crotting thumped a plump finger on the register that sat on his desk.

"Me birth papers says Burbidge, sir. That was me father's name, sir."

"*My* birth papers and *my* father's name."

"My father's name."

"But your application says Joseph Eggers. I know your father, Joseph. He is your father is he not?"

"I don't know, sir. But I fancy it was his secretary sent in me letter."

"*My* letter."

"My letter."

"You don't know who's your bloody… Look here, boy, have you or have you not been adopted?"

"I don't know, sir. I don't even know how you get adopted. Is there a…"

"Is there a what, boy, speak up."

"Is there a ceremony like?"

Crotting turned his attention to an instrument on his desk.

"Do you know what this is, boy?"

"Looks like one of them telly-phones, sir."

"Right you are, boy, a brand new telephone, and we are going to use it. Because your current father has one at his office."

Once more, Crotting looked perplexed, as though he could not be sure that the instrument in question would obey his commands. He picked up the earphone and, remaining almost at arm's length from the machine, dialed something. Somebody answered, an operator person. He gave instructions to this person and beckoned

Joseph to come forward and face the telephone. It perched on the corner of Crotting's desk like a shiny black poodle. The headmaster held out the receiver for a moment of indecision and they both listened to what sounded like a goose honking.

"Hugo, that you?" cried the headmaster. "Crotting here. I'm fine. I'm fine, fit as a fiddle. And you, Hugo, how are things up there in the real world these days? Yes, yes, well, that's a question for another conversation, isn't it, Eggers old boy. Your son is here with me, and let's just say that he's in a bit of a muddle over his name. Seems to think he hasn't yet been adopted or something. Would you like to talk to him, straighten out this riddle for us, old boy? Very good, Eggers, here he is."

Crotting whispered slowly, as to an infant or a lad with a brain deficiency. "Ask, your, father, what, your, name, is."

"Hello, sir?" Joseph said. "Ah, Headmaster, sir, he needs to know what my real name is."

"Roobish. Your name is Joe Eggers. End of story."

"But my birth papers, they say it's Joseph Burbidge, don't they, and I only have the one."

"You only have the one what?"

"I only have the one birth certificate. Have you adopted me, sir? I mean, isn't there some sort of…of ceremony?"

"You want to get legal with me? You want to get legal with a solicitor? You want a ceremony, boy? You want an adoption ceremony? Repeat after me."

"Sir?"

"Repeat after me. I am."

"I am?"

"Joseph Eggers."

"I am…Joseph…"

"Eggers. Say Eggers."

"I am Joe Eggers."

"How's that for an adoption ceremony, hm? Full stop, end of sentence, good day to you."

When he returned the receiver to its cradle, Headmaster Crotting was smiling like a well-fed cannibal.

"Thank you, Joseph Eggers."

"YOU'VE BEEN BROODING quite a bit lately, my boy. Couldn't help noticing."

"Yes, sir."

"I hear you've had a run at Watson-Bowes, Joseph. A fortnight ago? Not once but twice. Was that two in one week or two in one day, Joseph?"

"I believe that was two in one day, sir."

"And how did you fare the second time, Joseph? A bit better?"

"No, sir, not so well. And I didn't mean…"

"Well, my boy, you can't be all that bad."

Joseph peered up at Master Herron. He spoke with a boggy, musical intonation that made each word sound important.

"Don't look surprised, son. I can say anything I want these days. I'm too old to know better. Hah."

The afternoon was monumentally cloudy, chilly, with a fitful wind and brief bursts of rain. They were standing at a deserted cricket pitch, and Master Herron was gazing past the fields of Shacklesbury to the wooded hills beyond. On a happier day with decent weather, it might have made a pretty sight.

Herron was an old Irishman with spikey silver hair that looked as though it might defy any hairbrush or barber in England. He was as bulky as a bullock, and he made Joseph feel small.

"Too old to hold my tongue," he said. "So, Joseph, how are you getting on here?"

He wanted to tell the old man that he was surviving, that things were looking up, but the words would not come. The words that did come were a surprise to him.

"I miss me mum."

"Well, Joseph, you'll see her pretty soon then, won't you. End of term in a week's time."

"I mean, I miss her the way she was when…"

"Ah, yes. I see."

The old man put an arm around Joseph's shoulder then, as naturally and unemphatically as if he had been the boy's uncle, and Joseph wept for the first time in years. He had not wept at any of his floggings (four so far), but now the tears came out with every choke and spasm of his breath.

"Miss your father too, I suppose."

"The first one, yes."

"Well, boy, if the world looks as bleak as all that, you'll just have to go back to the dorms and give our friend Watson-Bowes a real drubbing. When you're ready, of course."

Joseph chortled then, but the tears continued to flow as though there were no end to them. Old Herron handed him a nose rag, and Joseph dabbed his face dry.

"You must feel trapped here," said Herron. "Does it feel that way?"

Joe nodded.

"I suppose, then, it's not the right time for me to tell you that everything will be all right?"

"No, I 'spose not," said Joe. He had little idea what the old man was getting at.

"Every day I get a little older and more decrepit, boy, but every day *you* learn more and get a little stronger and grow you a set of wings."

"Wings, sir?"

"I don't mean angel wings, I mean the things every young fellow grows to get the blazes out of here. He gets strong enough that, one day, he wants to try them out. Goes trekking around the country, goes and joins the bloody foreign legion, has some adventures."

Joe shrugged. The old man ordered him to blow his nose and he obeyed.

"What I'm saying is this, Joseph. You might think you're

trapped here, that your whole path has been laid out from the start by some malignant drudge up in the sky, that your dreams are futile and the whole blooming world is against you, but a day will come – are you listening, Joseph? – a day will come when you'll walk away from all those limitations and you'll be ready to try out your wings."

Joseph looked up at the old man. "You said in class that we were all determined."

"Except?"

"Except…something about the time."

"Oh, for pity's sake."

"You said we was all…"

"Joseph, I asked you to explore the proposition that life was pre-determined, and that all of our choices were inevitable. And then, if you'll remember, I *also* invited you to explore the possibilities of free will."

"Yes, I know. Free will."

"And when might it be apparent that free will exists?"

"When you're young and you don't know any better?"

"No, young sir. Free will becomes a possibility in the present."

"Oh, right," said Joseph. "I understood all that."

Herron bent over, grunted and began to wheeze, picked up a pebble with his left hand. He tossed the pebble up into the air and caught it, tossed it and caught it.

"See this? See how nicely rounded it is? I am about to throw this pebble."

"Yes?"

"Joseph, where am I going to throw this pebble?"

"I don't know."

"Of course you don't know. Neither do I."

"Because you're determined?"

"No, boy. Because I haven't decided where I want to throw it. Because right now, you see, I have free will."

Joseph sniffled and nodded his accord.

"Which hand will I throw it with, Joseph?"

"Your left."

"Why would I do that, Joseph?"

"Because you're left-handed?"

Master Herron switched hands.

"No, Joseph, I think I'll throw it with my right hand."

"But you're just saying that to prove me wrong."

"No, Joseph, I'm saying that because I choose to throw the pebble with my right hand. I am free to do it."

Herron gazed at the cricket field, tossed and caught the pebble once more, reared back and heaved. It was clear to Joseph that he had once been a boy on a playing field. It was also clear to Joseph that old Herron was right-handed.

"There," said Herron. "I chose to throw the pebble over the pitch with my right hand."

"That's because you're right-handed, sir."

"In this, Joseph, you are absolutely right."

"Thank you, sir."

"But, Joseph, I didn't actually throw the pebble. See?"

Behold, the same rounded pebble lay in the palm of the old man's right hand. Herron transferred it to his left and lobbed it a good distance towards the masters' residence.

He smiled at Joseph. "You see, my boy? Isn't free will wonderful?"

"But what does that mean, sir?"

"Aha, we have come to the lesson of the day, Joseph. And this you will write on a piece of paper and paste to the mirror of the jakes wherever you go. Read it every time you look into the mirror."

"I'm ready, sir."

"Learn from the past and live in the present."

Joseph sighed mightily and looked up at his mentor.

"But sir, what does that mean?"

"It means that some day all the hard times you've endured

since the death of your father, Joseph, all the gloom of living as a first year boy in this bloody prison, all the grief of missing your mother as she was, of missing your father, the *weight* of it, son, will become lighter. And on that day, Joseph, mark my words, you will be ready to try your wings."

"Didn't you say last week, sir, that you were a determinist?"

"When it suits me. When I want to learn about the past. We can learn a lot from history, boy. Maybe even avoid making some stupid mistakes. But the past, Joseph, the memory of it, can have too much weight. And to awaken from all that, son, the present comes in pretty handy. The here and now, don't you see."

The rain began falling again, and they ambled back towards the old grey building in silence, old philosophers trying to figure things out. It was a companionable silence. Joseph wondered briefly if Master Herron had a love for the great outdoors, and if so would he fish with worms or flies.

"Have you noticed, Joseph, that Watson-Bowes jabs with his right hand? He does it to set up his left hand. Standard procedure for lefties."

"Yes sir."

"Makes it hard for a right-handed pugilist like yourself to throw a good punch, correct?"

"Yessir. And he punches down at me."

"Yes, yes, a regular Goliath. But Joseph, have you noticed that when he jabs down at you, he brings his right hand back…down here?"

"He does?"

"He brings his right hand back here, level to his chest, to cock it again, instead of bringing it up higher to cock it. See what I mean? If he brought his right hand up here, he could block your counter left. But he leaves the right side of his head wide open."

Herron stopped and confronted Joseph, as though they were about to spar together. With his right hand, the old man made a slow-motion jab in the direction of Joseph's head, and then he cocked this hand in the vicinity of his right nipple.

"You've got a split second here, Joseph, to throw your left hook. Practice that left hook, young man, practice it high and low, and good luck to you."

The old man ambled a few paces towards the masters' residence and spotted something in the grass. He stooped to pick it up, turned, and tossed it back to Joseph. It was his pebble.

THE SCHOOL YEAR ENDED, the boys returned home, and in the term report he presented to Hugo Eggers and his mother, Joseph had proved himself to be an average student. In the aggregates he was ninth in his class. Not much good in Civics, slow in Maths, not bad in Geology, History, not bad in Logic and English, and good in Chemistry. He had joined none of the school's societies.

In his second year at school, Joseph joined the rifle club and proved to be not a bad shot. He joined the boxing club, avoided sparring with Watson-Bowes, and practised setting up his left hook. He fished for trout with Benbow and Benbow's father but he maintained his allegiance to coarse fish and to the lowly worm. He did some cautious flirting with Benbow's sister Buggy. She had beautiful lips.

Arthur came home from an accident in the grinding mill wearing a leg brace. He had developed a stammer. For the first month or more at home, he seemed at a loss to do anything. He would not talk about his job at the mill, from which he was suspended. He didn't even rise to the bait when Joseph and Wallace tried to argue with him. He lay around a lot and smoked, sequestered in his gloom, as though he were waiting for something.

During Joey's holidays from school, his mum's spirits rose to see her children all together again. Sometimes Joe spoke with impatience to his mother, a Hamlet to her Gertrude. Young Angie maintained her allegiance to the new regime and waited hand and foot on her stepfather when he returned each day from work or later in the evening from the pub. Down in Castleford, people talked about the Great Depression, the scarcity of good jobs, the men out of work, but up in the House of Eggers, such talk was not encouraged.

When Joseph returned to Shacklesbury for his last go at school he was seventeen. He had grown to a height of almost six feet. He was as tall as Arthur now, taller than his own step-father, taller than his friend Benbow, and almost as tall as his perpetual foe, James Watson-Bowes, who was two years older and more than one stone heavier.

Good old James had chosen to remain at Shacklesbury, much to everyone's surprise, hanging around to double as junior tutor and School Sergeant. Winkle stayed on as well. Watson-Bowes felt compelled to offer excuses for his new post. *Crotting jolly well begged me to do it. Nobody else would. Impact of the economy and all that.* The rumour was that his father had insisted on it merely to keep the boy out of trouble, and especially out of London, where James and Winkle had had some drunken adventures.

The day came when Watson-Bowes needed a taller boy to spar with. He wanted to demonstrate to the boys in the club the virtues of standing tall and fighting out of the classic stance. The crouch was not on, not in Shacklesbury, not if Watson-Bowes had anything to do with it. Only the darkies favoured fighting out of the crouch, and it looked unmanly.

It was apparently Joseph's role to look unmanly. They did it first in slow motion.

"Look here, scuts, I am jabbing downward, you see, jabbing downward...downward. I say, Eggers old boy, that's right on, you must be jolly pally with the darkies, ha ha ha."

Joe noted that in the crouch, Watson-Bowes could not reach him with either glove without leaning in.

The boys looked on as the pantomime unfolded, and Watson-Bowes planted a slow-motion left cross on Joe's temple. Joe tottered back, also in slow-motion, eyes rolling heavenward, tongue lolling out like a dead sheep.

"Right. Jolly good. Don't overdo it, Eggers. Now, shall we spar a bit and show these neophites how it works?"

"You want me to spar with you?"

"Of course, Eggers. Are you trembling, is that it? Shall I go easy on you, hm?"

"No, Jamie, I just thought, you know, I could..."

"Eggers, old boy, let me do the thinking, will you? And to you I am James. James Watson-Bowes, not Jamie, not Jimmy. Have you got that, Eggers? Right. Now then, give us a bell will you, Winkle?"

Leaning on the ropes, Joe peered around the gymnasium to see if perhaps Allan Benbow or old Herron were watching, but neither was there among the crowd of boys and teachers who had gathered. Winkle clanged the bell and the boys circled one another. Joseph flew at Watson-Bowes in a blind rush and caught a nice right jab on his mouth. As Watson-Bowes moved in on him, he lowered his right hand, cocked it, smirked, and Joseph remembered the one thing he'd been preparing for: *the left, you ninny, the left.* Joe spat out some blood and Watson-Bowes planted another painful jab on his forehead. Again, the bigger boy kept his right glove chest-high and cocked it for another jab. Joseph circled right and set his feet, took a breath. Watson-Bowes homed in on his head once more, and just as Joseph went into the crouch, James whistled a nice right jab over Joseph's head. Back went the dreaded right hand and, winding up his own left, Joseph drove forward and launched it with all his weight, the gospel of Master Herron faintly ringing in his brain.

Something like this – in each moment of our lives, the past proclaims itself like a song we want to forget. But we must learn from this tedious song if only to silence it for a while. Give history its choruses now and then and get on with your life. History tells us things about how nations muddle into war, or muddle into depression, or how they rise up against the Goliath of aggression.

Memory tells us about a lost paradise on the moors, a new father who dismisses the deceased one, a school that favours LPs, defames the family name, and a maths and logic master whose wisdom comes in handy; yes, a wisdom that propels the left hand towards the chin of the oppressor, and this propulsion, the discipline, the speed of it, the youthful power, this is what propels you from the sometimes dreary truth of the past into the present: the crunch of it, the achieve of, the mastery of the thing, the flight that ensues.

Chapter 3

Rolland's Riches

THREE CALAMITIES HAD DESCENDED on Joe and his family. First, at a meeting of the Shacklesbury Board of Trustees, it was decided that decking the School Sergeant during a demonstration of pugilism was not on. It was thought to be insubordinate, unmanly, and all around bad form. Joseph was characterized as a ruffian, a leader of rebellious boys, and he was expelled. His stepfather and his gentle mother were not pleased, but Joseph could not have cared less. He would get a job in Castleford, save some money, forget about climbing Hugo's ladder to success, and leave home forever. Joe could not escape the insistent whisper that adventure was calling. He told no one about this new awareness, these almost daily eruptions of excitement. But he did test the waters by mentioning to his mother and to Eggers that he might try life abroad for a while.

"You seem to be plotting your own disasters, my boy," said Hugo. "Why not carry on elsewhere? Your prospects in this part of the world are not worth a bloozy pen'orth."

Eggers may have been right. But then there arrived the second calamity, at which Joe and his older brother Arthur could only shake their heads. During a visit to the flat of one of his lady friends one night, Eggers took a great tumble down a staircase and broke his neck. He died at the bottom of the stairs.

Hugo Eggers, solicitor and man of affairs, should have known better, but he left two wills behind, only one of them dated. In what Joseph assumed to be the most recent will, the house and a sum of money were to go to Joseph's mother, another sum to a very special lady friend in Hartlepoole, and another sum to a not so special lady friend, who may or may not have birthed a child by Hugo. None of Winnifred's brood had been adopted by Hugo, which prompted a lawyer to call attention to this lapse. Joe did not think of it as a lapse. He was working for a pittance in his original father's old office by the colliery, and all he knew for sure was that if he and his family did not manage to come up with some money, his mother, his sister, and his brothers might sink back into poverty.

The third calamity was the Great Depression. It hit the industrial North very hard, and one by one, among the four colliery towns, the mines slowed, the crews became smaller, there was massive unemployment among the miners, and town life for Joe and his family went from bearable to dreary to desolate. Joe discovered a lot of drinking-to-forget chaps down at the Blackberry. That's where older brother Arthur would go, as though he belonged more to the Blackberry than he did to the Eggers house.

Joe and brother Arthur were at the pub one night, and thank God, at last they were having an argument.

"I want," said Joseph, "to abandon our family for a while without feeling like a perfect lout. Ungrateful son and all that. My clerking job is not going to last much longer, and besides, I don't make enough to make a difference at home. Mother gets a pittance from me, here and there."

"Joey, spit it out. What kind of nonsense are you up to?"

"I want to go off to the goldfields and make me fortune, Arthur. You can laugh if you want, but it's all I can think of to help us all out of this rut. What would you do, Arthur? We can't even retain a decent lawyer."

"You'd make more wages in the mill, Joey. But I suppose that isn't adventurous enough for you."

Arthur was slumped at the table staring around at his mates, shaking his head the way their father used to do. Arthur's body had mended and he was back at his job. This bit of good luck seemed to bring no joy to Arthur.

He turned at last to Joseph. "The bloody goldfields, is that what you said?"

"In Canada, in the Northwest, where Auntie Vi lives."

Arthur shot his brother an older-brother look. "Auntie Vi?"

TWO YEARS AFTER the onset of the Depression, one year after Hugo Eggers had tumbled down to his final resting place, and not long after Joseph had given his notice at the colliery paymaster's office, Joseph took a last walk past rows and rows of miners' homes to the flat where he was born. He stood by what was once his bedroom window, stood on the road where the miners used to march by in their clogs. The flat seemed too tiny for any family to grow up in. He waited to see if he could sense the lively spirit of his father and the caring spirit of his mother. He waited for a small whiff of nostalgia or regret or loss. Nothing.

"Well," he whispered with a mixture of glee and guilt, "that's it for you lot."

He bade a silent farewell to the monthly routine of work, home, rest, pub on Friday nights, occasional picnics with the family at Queen's Park, occasional appointments with the family lawyer, occasional jaunts to church with his mother. He bade goodbye to heaving up hymns like *We are Climbing Jacob's Ladder* in a voice too weary to climb a scale. He worked his last shift, and one week later, he withdrew his savings from the bank.

With all appropriate apologies and farewells, Joe made his move. He could spend his savings on a great liner in tourist class, have a jolly time, and if the ship didn't do a Titanic, he would arrive in Canada hung-over and more or less broke. Capital plan. Or, he could spend fewer quid on a cheaper passage, suffer a bit of seasickness on the stormy Atlantic, and arrive with enough money to get him by train to the great Northwest where Auntie Vi lived, perhaps even to the Yukon. Perhaps he would gain employment as a bookkeeper or a bank teller, like the writer chap, Robert Service, had done. Or maybe he could work on a cattle ranch as a cowboy. He remembered fondly riding the ponies when he was a boy at Slaidburn, and he liked the idea of working with horses. He could start out slowly by earning his keep and do his prospecting on the side. Did they do prospecting in ranch country? Did they raise cows in prospecting country?

Rolland's Riches was a tern schooner out of Blackpool, and like her crew of seven, she had seen better days. She was a one hundred and twenty-five ton square-rigged vessel that ran cargo up and down the English coast. Once in a while, however, as she had done in earlier days, she ran cargo and passengers across the pond. Captain Silver Foddy, his crew, his passengers, might all shake their heads in moments of lapsed faith, but their ship still managed on occasion to sail to Halifax and back again at a good clip. Because it was a schooner, *Rolland's Riches* looked pretty sleek to Joseph. No engine, oldfashioned rigging. Trim, fast, ancient, adventurous, a three-master with a crew of old salts. Worthy of a Jack London novel. And this was a boat that Joe Burbidge could afford.

Shortly after Christmas, 1931, the schooner ventured out into the Atlantic. The seas were predictably, though not unseasonably, rough. *Rolland's Riches* went through the swells groaning like a slow freight train, and in the heavy seas when the wind was up, she rolled and pitched to histrionic extremes, drenching everyone above decks. The little tern remained sea-worthy all the way to Witless Bay off the coast of Newfoundland, and then the fog enveloped them.

Joe went above to the deck because he loved the fog. It was melodramatically gloomy and it seemed to be conducive to thinking. His old friend Benbow had given him a lift from Castleford to the docks, and he had asked Joe a question. *Supposing you could do it all over. Instead of fighting with good old Jamie, you turned the other cheek, wrote your last exams, passed with flying colours. Would you opt for appeasement rather than resistance?*

For Joey it was not a question of appeasement or resistance. *It's resistance or murder the sodding lot of them.*

Benbow nodded, perhaps with a trace of sadness. *Very good, Burbidge. You have only one door to go through.*

Captain Foddy appeared out of the fog.

"We're in for a bit of a blow," he said to Joseph, which could have meant anything as far as Joe was concerned.

"You mean *another* great blow?"

Foddy shook his head.

"No, lad. I mean you better get below decks and stay there."

Joe's sailing anxieties had floated away once the Rolland had crossed the Atlantic. They were a bloody stone's throw away from Canadian waters. Surely there was no need to take the captain's words as ominous. Foddy's course was obvious: head south for Cape Race and stay off the rocks, then head west past Trepassey Bay and sail for Halifax. A stiff breeze whistled from the southeast, but nothing for Foddy to worry about, right? The fog was something else, of course, but fortunately the old Captain knew just what to do. Any fool could tell you the same thing – get far enough south to miss the rocks, and then, and only then, make the big ninety degree turn for Canada. Good old boring, safe Canada.

The rocks in question lay off Cape Race and they remained a menace all the way down to Mistaken Point. The Cape is a prominent headland that draws the attention of seafaring men from a long way off, a rocky monument worthy of saluting, but on a foggy night with a big blow on and a heavy sea, as Joey was about to learn, it is the last place a sailor wants to be. The tides that curl around this corner of Newfoundland are so ornery they can pull a befuddled ship straight into the rocks.

On the night of Foddy's big turn westward, the sound of a mighty horn pierced the night. Eggers thought it was a passing ship. So did the captain and so did the crew, because surely a fog horn this far out was simply…it was simply out of the…

When the *Rolland's Riches* cracked into the rocks, the schooner rebounded from the impact, and Joseph was tossed out of his bunk. He was already dressed, so he grabbed his bill-fold, his passport, tossed a few more things into his haversack, and ran up to the deck. He gathered with four other passengers just as the lifeboat went over the side. In the pounding surf and the high tide the lifeboat drifted away from the schooner, and most of them had to plunge in and swim for the boat. The water was achingly cold, enough to shrivel the coddies on the Ram of Darby. With five passengers aboard, plus crew and captain, there remained one last problem. Where the hell were they? Foddy's crew rowed with the surf, trying to angle away from the worst of the rocks while the Captain squinted through the fog at the shoreline.

"Lord have mercy, boys, we're just off the Drook."

Joseph groaned with the other passengers because they were shivering to death and they didn't have a clue what a drook was.

"It's over there," the Captain said, and they rowed past the waves that exploded onto the rocks and angled into a small cove as their ship foundered behind them like a great doomed animal. By morning *Rolland's Riches* would be smashed to pieces.

On their way in, they passed a dory going out, and the men in the dory seemed very hearty indeed. People greeted them and helped them off the dock, up the steep path, and through the woods to the village. People brought out blankets and warm clothes and they were all taken care of by the friendliest, most hospitable, nocturnal strangers Joe had ever met. Many of the travelers and the crew drank rum with the locals and stayed up all night. Joe began to enjoy himself. There was a sort of enchantment to the foggy night and the friendly people. They all sounded Irish to Joe.

He commended the jollity of their hosts to Captain Foddy.

"Salvagers," the Captain said, "are always happy."

JOE HAD MANAGED TO SALVAGE and dry out his currency, his passport (Burbidge), his birth certificate (Burbidge), his grammar school records (Eggers), his employment card (Eggers), and an operator's license (also Eggers). He thought he might solve this confusion by changing his name to George the Fifth. Just to impress the Canadians.

It took the crew and passengers a week to get a ship to Halifax, but at least his passage was free. It took Eggers another week to reach Edmonton, Alberta by train. He wobbled out of a CNR coach and got some directions from the station master. He walked south from the train station towards the North Saskatchewan River, where he would locate LeMarchand Mansion and the flat where his Auntie Vi was living. He had scarcely any luggage or clothes, only a small knapsack. As he stomped over the new-fallen snow, he could hear the squeaking of his boots. Joseph had never heard that squeaking sound before. He had never before felt his nose hairs freeze to his nostrils. As the cold began to penetrate from his skin to the marrow of his bones, he resolved to buy a winter coat. He squeaked and crunched his way south, found the river, headed west, and eventually located the building, not a mansion at all but what appeared to be a stately red brick hotel overlooking a frozen river.

A doorman let him in where he waited, shivering, in a grand and gloomy lobby. *I am twenty years old*, he reflected, *and I am in bloody Canada without a coat in the perishing bloody winter, begging hospitality from my auntie like young bloody Copperfield so I won't bloody freeze to death, and I haven't seen her since I was a little boy.*

And she appeared, Auntie Vi, in a belted powder blue robe and men's shoes, and a doleful tender smile. It was a horsey sort of smile with a few too many teeth, a smile somehow angelic and oddly beautiful.

"You must be Joseph," she said in a low, soft voice, looking away up into his face and taking both of his hands in hers. "Well now, you have come along very nicely, I'd say. How's my sister, still in mourning? Your hands are frightfully cold, you poor man. And you had a shipwreck? Dear dear. Were the meals in the dining coach *quite* to your liking?"

Joseph tried to respond but he could not stop shivering, and the shivering made him stutter and stammer like a chimpanzee. He smiled down at Auntie Vi, and his big smile must have sent some sort of message to the lady, perhaps the relief a trapper bloke might feel upon snowshoeing to town and finding a saloon open on a winter's night in the Yukon.

She bade the doorman a good night, and bearing a squat candle in a saucer, she led Joseph up the stairs and through a gloomy, sumptuous hallway to her flat.

"Mr. Lefebvre will bring your luggage up presently… You may not know, but my husband has just passed away…has Winnie told you…? No, no, of course you don't have any luggage, do you, what was I thinking… We are all very sad around here… Poor Bernard." Bear-NARR, she pronounced it. "He always seemed so robust…watch that bump there, no one ever sees it…I've always enjoyed walking with a candle, gives me a sort of beatific quality don't you think…here we are, watch out for Désirée, she might just maul you when you step inside – I do hope you can stay with us long enough to get acquainted, your mother extolled you to the…"

Auntie Vi opened the door to her flat and a big tabby ran out and disappeared down the hallway.

"Did you say your husband has just passed away?"

She nodded.

"I'm so sorry to hear. This can't be the best time for you to receive a visit from a complete…"

There was a large coffin on a long table in the hallway.

"Is this…? Is this…?"

"Bernard, poor thing. He was, what would one say, a chronic enthusiast. Never slept more than three hours a night. Never still, always up and doing. Spoiled his patients rotten. Always here when he wanted to be there and there when he... Can I pour you a whisky, you look as though you could..."

Joseph nodded to the offer of a whisky and, strolling around the flat in his over-ripe socks, gazing at the pictures and figurines, he began to regain control over his shivers and his stammering voice. The walls of the front hallway were covered in paintings of all sizes. The living room walls were similarly plastered with them. Portraits, misty landscapes of the old country, starkly outlined landscapes of Canadian mountains and rolling fields with wheat stooks, a good dash of nudes here and there, some ripping nice girls wearing bed sheets or bathing together in the buff, village sketches from the continent, Indian chiefs. Statuettes of girls dancing in the corners of the room. More in the parlour, and drawings and family photographs. A photo of all the Burbidges at Slaidburn, posing grave and self-possessed from the door of the cottage. What a serious young boy I was, he thought. Serious little Joey.

Auntie Vi showed Joe to his bedroom, where he finished his whisky, undressed, yawned mightily, and burrowed under the quilt. The last thing he was aware of was a conversation from the hallway, and he thanked God for whoever it was out there, keeping company with poor Auntie Vi through the long winter night. When Joseph awakened the next morning, Désirée the tabby was wrapped around his neck asleep. He crawled out from under the quilt and found himself listening to the very same conversation, a muted exchange full of consoling sounds.

He threw on his rancid clothes, lumbered out to the hallway and beheld Auntie Vi, her arms folded, murmuring to the man in an open casket.

"Ne t'enquiète pas, Bernard. Best not to think about it. And I will do my utmost to make sure that – oh, dear, Joseph, you must think I'm daft –saying a few farewells, you know. Last things and all that. A bit of domestic eschatol..."

Auntie Vi began to founder, and Joseph caught her before she hit the floor. She was light as a blanket. He carried her to the nearest sofa and put a pillow beneath her head.

She seemed to come out of it for a moment.

"You reek in those clothes, Joseph. You'll need to have a bath and change them. In our bedroom, Bernard's closet. Take whatever suits you. I'll just lie here for a…"

Auntie Vi was fast asleep.

BERNARD CLOUTIER, MD, had been a big man, perhaps as tall as Joseph, who was just under six feet. Bernard had been heavier, but thanks to a pair of suspenders, Joe managed to float around in the good doctor's clothes and his overcoat each day as he explored Edmonton's riverbank path and its downtown establishments. The agreement was to stay out of Auntie Vi's way while she made the arrangements for Bernard's funeral. She had plenty of help, and the only help she requested from Joseph (he was Joseph now) was to carry tables and chairs from a storage area in the basement up to her flat to accommodate her guests after the funeral.

He wandered for three days. Owing to something called a chinook the weather warmed up, and he found the whole downtown area to his liking, found it pretty lively in a new world sort of way, with plenty of streetcars and Model Ts to dodge. He found all the newspapers and tobacco he wanted at Mike's Newsstand on Jasper Avenue. He found a congenial nook for late breakfast and coffee at the King Edward Hotel. He spent several hours a day at the public library reading up on geology, and he found a good bookstore where he bought a reputedly smutty book by an Irishman (Benbow's recommendation). But in the geology reading room at the University of Alberta, amid an abundance of glittering rock samples, he began to encounter the mysteries of gold-bearing formations, geological surveys and quartz mining regulations. He bought his first miner's license at a government office for five dollars.

Auntie Vi's reception after the funeral was a surprisingly convivial affair. The medical fraternity and the nurses were well represented in Vi's living room. A gathering of artists showed up, some of whom Vi and Bernard had supported for years. There was a northern contingent, mostly mining people, because in Bernard's early days as a general practitioner, he did fly-in emergency work up north. There was a strong French-Canadian presence and a scattering of British and Scottish friends of Bernard and Vi.

One of her guests was a tall, sturdy fellow twenty years or so older than Joseph. He had arrived on a motorcycle as though it were the heart of summer. Joseph had been playing doorman in Mr. Lefebvre's absence, and he let the fellow in. He was wearing a tweed suit, bowler hat, but no overcoat.

"Can't bloody afford one," he confided. "My last penny went into that little monster." He nodded in the direction of his motorcycle and held out his hand.

"Tom Payne," he said. "Vi wrote me about you. Said you wanted to try some prospecting up in the Yukon?"

"Quite the transportation," said Joe.

"Not the easiest machine to start on a winter's morn, I'll tell you."

The two men ambled up to Auntie Vi's flat, and in that short time, Joseph learned that Payne had grown up in Essex, the son of a doctor. He was living a rootless existence, working wherever he could find employment from Fort Smith to Great Bear Lake. The man crackled with such high energy that he seemed to give off heat. To Joseph's great delight, Tom had done some prospecting for gold up north.

"Wouldn't go up to the Yukon if I were you, Joseph. No, no. Too many prospectors, too few un-staked claims. Not as much gold up there any more, unless you own a big dredge the size of this building."

Joseph asked the man where he should go.

"You seem pretty keen, Burbidge. Ready to freeze your bones and sleep on the ice floes and all that? Ready to work like a navvy? I'd go straight north if I were you. Good bit of country just opening up in the Territories. Keep on going till you run out of Alberta. I'm just down from Great Bear Lake, Cameron Bay. Lots of new prospecting going on up there. I have a friend who runs horses up north named Stinky Riley. Montana chap. You should write this down. That's right, that's his real name. He's been running cattle and horses up there for a while. Barges won't take them any more. Stinky likes to prospect on the side. You could hire on with him, work your way for free up there. He could be your boss and your mentor. Always thought I might join him, but I think I can make better money running a Cat around Great Slave Lake."

Joseph took down some particulars from Tom Payne, who promised to write a note of introduction to Stinky Riley, and then both men joined the funeral reception. Later on in the afternoon, Payne came over and gave Joe his current address in a rooming house on Ninety-fifth Street. "Pop over to my hovel soon as you can. I don't have a telephone. Let's talk some more about your plans. I'll be flying north in a week or two."

Payne's last words were, "Don't drop dead from surprise, Burbidge, if you bump into me some day, lugging a gold pan. You see a little gold in your hand, you always want to see more."

AFTER BERNARD CLOUTIER was buried, Joseph stayed on with Auntie Vi through to the end of January, running errands, rearranging furniture, and doing a bit of carpentry to set up a living space for Vi's new tenants. They were two young women hunting for jobs in Edmonton, Maisy Lippscott and Peggy Broderick, whose parents had known the Cloutiers. The girls would live with Auntie Vi for an indeterminate stretch.

Joe moved out in early February, secured a job at the King Edward Hotel, and the two girls moved in with Auntie Vi. Shortly after the move, they came down to the hotel to bring Joe some lunch before his shift. They were worried about Vi.

"She's not eating enough," said Peggy.

"She wanders around all night talking to Bernard," said Maisy.

"She's still a delight," said Peggy, "but she's sad."

"And we thought we should throw her a party," said Maisy. "She loves parties."

"So we're having a party this Saturday, and we want you to come," said Peggy.

"We're worried there won't be enough fellas," said Maisy.

"What if there were lots of blokes?" said Joe. "Would you still want me to come?"

"Aww," said Peggy.

"Aww," said Maisy.

Joe was more or less in love with both of them and pretended otherwise. Peggy embraced the last exhausted tatters of flapperdom as though it were still the twenties because dammit she wanted to have a good time and raise some H. E. Double Toothpicks. Maisy was perhaps more bohemian than her friend. She drifted happily through the new freedoms and the parties and all the privations of the Depression as though this was all a pleasant route to somewhere better.

After only a few days' looking, they both got jobs at a music store. Auntie Vi's big flat was perfect for them. They lived less than a mile from work and walked to the music store to save on streetcar fare.

"You must come," said Maisy.

"Ditto," said Peggy.

Joe couldn't help feeling that he would enjoy himself more if Tom Payne were also at the party. He couldn't get Tom Payne out of his mind. Friendly chap, energetic. And a fellow Brit. He'd make a great man to partner with up north. Auntie Vi said that he could fix anything, and he had that keen look about him when Joe brought up the subject of gold. He rifled through his pockets for the slip of paper Tom had handed to him, bearing the address of his rooming house, but he couldn't find it.

On a cold Saturday night, Joe strode into Auntie Vi's flat in a borrowed Bernard suit and found himself surrounded by revelers he'd never met before. It didn't seem to matter, with all that heartening glitter of rhinestones, crimson lips and bare shoulders. Auntie Vi floated through the party, serene and tiddly, smiling mysteriously at all she beheld, pouring drinks and cranking up the gramophone. She announced to some of the younger guests that she was a libertarian, to others that she was a Fabian socialist, and to Joseph that she was a charming fake. She put on an aura of regal disapproval of all things North American, beneath a tolerant, giving nature. She was no longer the aunt he never quite got to know in his boyhood; it seemed to Joe that she had earned her title as local eccentric.

Some young people began to sing around Vi's piano, a song about a girl named Frivolous Sal. They were dressed as though they were all going to different parties, the men in tuxes, suits, or casual clothes, varsity sweaters and khaki pants; and the young women in jumpers and skimpier gowns that bared their shoulders and arms or little skirts that revealed some foreleg. The roaring twenties were over and no one seemed to know how to dress for Vi's place, and no one seemed to care. Everywhere Joseph looked, there were young men better turned out and clearly more confident than he was, hovering around Maisy and Peggy like hornets in a ripe orchard. A bloke named Schuman, a skinny sort with buck teeth, seemed to get most of Maisy's attention, but he was obviously no threat.

Maisy preferred not to sing. She sort of wanted to dance. She looked entirely vivacious in a black fringy skirt, legs kicking in a half-engaged sort of way, holding her drink and talking while she danced. She sort of wanted to flirt. She never seemed to finish a dance or a drink, leaving everything unfinished, including conversations, for others to continue. Joe moved in on her but her chatter seemed to keep him at arm's length. She grabbed the

Schuman chap as he was wandering by and begged him to dance with her. He said he didn't know how to dance.

Someone asked Maisy how her Saturday shift had gone.

"Same old thing," she said.

"Oh, that's too bad, Maisy," Peggy said, "because just as I was ringing up a sale, who should walk into the store but Paul Whiteman."

"Oh, him again," said Maisy. "Well, kiddo, I forgot to mention it, but I had the nicest conversation with John Barrymore."

"Like fun you did. John Barrymore? Is he stuck up like they say?"

"Oh, not at all," said Maisy. "He was just swell. He asked me out to lunch but I told him I was having lunch with you. He looked awful disappointed. How was Paul Whiteman?"

"Well," said Peggy, "at least he was an improvement on whutzisname, the Prime Minister."

"Oh, not him again. You wouldn't mean Mr. Bennett, would you?"

"Yeah, that's the one. Kinda snooty."

On and on they went, dream-struck, smart, sassy. Maisy's hair was even darker than Joe had remembered. It was almost black. She wore it short, with curls bunched up over the ears, and bangs like Louise Brooks or some such movie star.

Maisy was having another go at the homely chap, Schuman, teaching him the foxtrot, and Joseph surmised she must have felt sorry for him. Maisy had a heart of gold, that was it. Someone lifted the needle on the gramophone and a middle-aged chap with a green plaid bowtie announced a game for the guests, something Vi had dreamed up for all to play. Two lists were hung over the fireplace. The first had twenty quotations.

1) England expects that every man this day will do his duty.
2) There is time to finish the game and beat the Spaniards too.
3) Honi swat qui mal y pense.

"Honi Swat? What's that?"

"That's when yer honey gives you a swat."

"Yeah, but who said it first?"

"The guy that wrote it, dumbbell."

"Yeah, but who wrote it?"

"When in doubt always say George Bernard Shaw."

"Who's he when he's at home?"

"An Irishman or something. Ask Vi."

"Dear me, one might have thought that this could have been edifying. I'll give you all a hint."

"No, Auntie Vi. No hints. Elliot, who said that stuff in Latin?"

"Abraham Lincoln?"

"Maisy. Dear. You've spelled it wrong."

"Not Abraham Lincoln? I coulda swore it was Abraham Lincoln."

"No, but look, that word there. It is spelled S-O-I-T, dear, and it was first uttered by a king."

"That's gotta be King Tut."

"You people, you are beyond the pale."

"That's not so bad, Auntie Vi. I thought you was gunna say we was hopeless."

Joseph was tipsy. He asked Maisy for a kiss and she politely declined. He asked Peggy for a kiss, and she pecked him on the cheek. Auntie Vi came over and gave him a hug.

"King Kong, it's gotta be King Kong."

"King Edward the Third, you ninnies."

"I was just gunna say that."

"Not *gunna.* Please."

Joseph wandered over to a corner of the room, leaned on the piano and gazed at the partiers. He felt like a tourist at Aunty Vi's, not that he minded. But just as he was set to go into a state of invisibility, one of the girls whose name he was trying to remember came up to him, and then another who called herself Lady Barbara, and then Maisy herself. They gathered around him and teased him, insisted on calling him Joe, not Joseph, but Joe, and carried on with their banter to one another, and he just stood there like a gardener in a flower bed.

February 28, 1932.

Benbow, old scout, I believe I am in your debt. You were one of the only people to urge me to come out to Canada. Wonderful land. I am in Edmonton, the capital of Alberta, a province with mountains in the west, farms and ranches in the south, and some small bits of prosperity if you know where to look. It's still the Roaring Twenties here, or a drab Thirties version of the Roaring Twenties.

My Auntie Vi has been a most congenial host. Her husband has just passed away, but even in her state of mourning, she is always taking in waifs and hopeless cases, blokes like yours truly, and she can't do enough for us. I've been supplanted now by two lovely girls from around here. Both of them eye me with unfettered lust and I believe my virtue is in danger of...bla bla...you don't want to hear about it, I'm sure. But they are both nineteen, love to dance, devil in their eyes. I've told them all about you, that you're no slouch in the romancing department.

Had a fun crossing on the good ship Rolland's Riches, *a little schooner out of Blackpool. We slammed into the rocks somewhere off Newfoundland and we had to row ashore to a village. Atlantic wet and very cold, don't try it in the fog. Don't know who Rolland is, or how he got his riches, but likely not as a seafaring man.*

Anyway, I am currently living in a tiny closet in the King Edward Hotel as a combination bellman, bar porter and bouncer. I roll beer kegs up from the cellar and carry luggage for men down from the North better able to do it themselves. I bounced my first tearaway this week. If the chap had been sober he would have ground me into the floorboards. Good old left hook.

Bless old Herron. Learn from the past and live in the present. Herron must still be with us, don't you think?

This hotel is the preferred gathering place for all sorts of adventurous types from up north in Eskimo Land. Prospectors and trappers and remittance blokes. Ever heard of John Hornby? You must have. He's the toff from over in Cheshire who roamed all over the Barrens. Froze to death a few years ago. He used to stay in this hotel. They say his ghost and the ghost of his partner, military chap, walk the corridors here at night.

My best to all your family. I'll be here in Edmonton till the spring, at which time I hope to go northward in search of (not a word of a lie) a venerable wrangler (horse chap) named Stinky Riley. He apparently knows everything there is to know about panning for gold. Will proceed from there to vast riches, surpassing those of Rolland, poor chap, and return to England for extended debauch.

Yrs trly, Cowboy Joe Burbidge.

He had gone from England to Canada, from Eggers back to Burbidge, from Joseph to Joe, from Yorkshire to Alberta. The minute he dropped his letter to Benbow down the hotel mail slot, he felt as though he had walked through a door that allowed no backward glances. He said he would do it and now he had to do it. When spring arrived, he would leave the comfort of a big town, the warmth of Auntie Vi's parties, climb aboard a coach on the Northern Alberta Railway and head to the end of the line. He would be much farther north than John O' Groat, and he would ride even farther north on a horse. A horse, for God's sake. Riding into a northern summer with some cows and a man who went by the name of Stinky Riley, and Joe Burbidge would never be Joseph Eggers again.

Chapter 4

Canada

His bedroll consisted of a feather pillow, two large woolen blankets, and two full-sized soogans. The blankets had been washed recently, and they retained a trace of campfire smoke from years of wrangling down on the prairies. The soogans hung from the rafters, airing out from the beams of Riley's make-shift barn. When they were folded double, lengthwise, one on top of the other, their goose-down filling made for a half-decent mattress.

Following the instructions of Stinky Riley, who hovered above him as he knelt, Joe unfurled a canvas tarp on the ground and spread it out, fourteen feet square, then placed the soogans, then the blankets, in the centre of the tarp. He folded the two sides of the tarp over his bundle. One side had rings and the other side had snaps.

"Don't forget that there pillow."

He unfolded the top part and put the pillow in place. There was something else he had to do, but with Stinky looking over his shoulder, he couldn't concentrate.

"There's where you put yer stuff."

"Right. I know."

"Sure. Course you know."

Inside a war bag he had packed a new pair of denims, a couple of shirts, a heavy wool muffler, some underwear and wool socks, a wool sweater, his shaving kit and razor, his unread smutty novel, a skinning knife, a couple of twists of tobacco and makings, one of Auntie Vi's big squat candles, a roll of fool's cap, and a couple of pencils.

"Now, Joe, just fold in the head of the tarp like I done, and roll up the whole shebang, head to foot."

"Yes, Stinky."

He bound up the bedroll into a neat bundle with two leather straps and jammed a rain slicker between the bundle and the straps.

"Yiz can bounce that off a bull's head and let him maul it all mornin and she'll stay neat and solid. Carry that on the cantle of your saddle for a week or two and lie in it every night, it'll unroll each and every time, nice and ready for sleep. You think I'm some old know-it-all, but by the Jesus, you'll thank me down the trail."

"Sure, Stinky."

On this chilly May morning Joe had pulled on his long johns; his new and stiff pair of denims, pants that would wear like leather for weeks on the trail; a thick wool plaid shirt; a new pair of riding boots purchased in Edmonton; a canvas coat, lined with raw wool; and a big stetson with a pointed peak, a wider version of what the Mounties wore. Very Canadian, they had assured him down at the livery store.

He took in a deep breath, and with it a waft of sweat from the horses' backs, a whiff of oats and hay, of cow patties and horse turds, of worn ropes and leather, stale tobacco and man smell. The long, halting train ride ahead, from Indian village to Indian village to Fort MacKay, was forgotten. Edmonton was forgotten. Smelling was believing. As far as beginning rituals were concerned, smelling the Riley barn for the first time was like smelling salt, kelp and cod guts the day he first walked up the plank of the *Rolland's Riches*.

Not quite forgotten were Auntie Vi and her two new flat-mates, who had all three seen him off at the train. A kiss from Auntie Vi, a hug and a peck from Maisy Lipscott, and a big hug and a smacker from Peggy Broderick. He gave her his scarf and she tied it around her hips and danced away with it.

He had become one of their favourites and he tried not to

count the days till he returned to Edmonton. Triumphant return, leap off the train in his cowboy duds, sack of nuggets in his duffel bag. Guitar slung around his neck (note: buy guitar, learn how to pluck the thing), outdoorish glow to his skin, newly acquired northern Canuck accent, bag of tanned fox pelts. *Peggy, my darlin! Maisy, my sweet! Auntie Vi, pour us a drink for oldtime's sake.*

A wiry halfbreed boy named Charlie was helping Stinky to load up the chuckwagon. Like most things in Stinky's outfit, the wagon came from the ranchlands to the south. This one had some northern adaptations, including attachable skis in case the spring reverted to winter and sent a blizzard their way. Young Charlie worked quietly, lugging supplies from a shed to the wagon. He had a classic bowl-on-the-head haircut, with the back and sides of his head shaved bald. He was leaner and smaller than Joe, but he carried heavier loads than either Joe or Riley, and he spoke not a word throughout the morning.

"Charlie's not what you'd call a talker," said Riley, with Charlie close by, as though the boy were deaf. "He's a young pup but he's already makin a name for hisself on the northern rodeo circuit. Bronco buster and a good roper. Girls up here, they just won't leave him alone. Hey, Charlie?"

Charlie looked away as though he had remembered something.

Loading the wagon was cheerful work, the prelude to their ride north into the boreal forest towards the Treaty Eight country south of Great Slave Lake. A sack each of beans and rice, the usual bags of sugar, flour, salt, coffee and tea. A tin each of molasses and hardtack, a tub of butter, a gallon of honey, tub of lard, cans of milk, jam, corn syrup, a bag of pepper, some cans of fruit and bags of dried prunes and apricots. Vegetables from the root cellar, onions, carrots, beets, potatoes, turnips and cabbage. A slab of sow belly and a box of smoked jackfish. Some small bags of nuts, and last of all, Stinky's two-gallon earthen crock, which he used to mix his sourdough starter with flour, sugar and water for pancakes.

With all the food on board, Joe could see something young and vital in Stinky's eyes, as though the job of range boss and camp cook were a God-given vocation. Young Charlie and an older man named Isidore harnessed and hooked up four horses to the wagon, and Stinky called out instructions with great authority. He seemed to know which horse went where, according to size and experience.

Big Joe Burbidge, outrider first class, surveyed the scene. One wagon with six horses, some extra horses for the trail or for sale up north, twenty-five steers for meat and ten heifers for milk and breeding, five calves, one sleepy-eyed old bull, and four men.

Stinky and Isidore were arguing gleefully about the relative merits of oxen and horses. Stinky came down heavily on the horsey side of things. He was bigboned and beefy from top to bottom. He had been lumbering all morning from barn to wagon like a much older man. But suddenly the great strength within Stinky's body began to re-assert itself, and he seemed to regress to about half of his forty-seven years. He pulled his stetson down tight, climbed up on the spring seat of the wagon, picked up the reins, and stomped hard on the brakes to check the horses, for they seemed ready to gallop out of the pasture and fly past the herd like the firey steeds of Revelation, and all their mounts, even Joe's old mare, were trembling in their bridles. With a few clicks of Stinky's tongue, they were off, the chuckwagon bouncing so violently that Joe could only wonder if his trail boss would manage to hang on to his teeth. Stinky's rosy complexion turned beefy red as the morning unfolded.

Joe rode north on Shanghai Lil. She wasn't much good for herding, too old for roping and hard riding, which was just as well. She was trail-wise and reliable, the perfect horse to break Joe in. Stinky used her as a night horse sometimes, because she was so sure-footed, and because she had ridden the trail to Fitzgerald half a dozen times in the last two years. By mid-morning she had slowed, plodding behind Stinky's cattle in a rhythm of resigned boredom that was welcome to Joe. Galloping could come later. Preferably next year.

Joe and Riley clopped side-by-side up the trail, Joe looking down from the heights of Shanghai Lil's back and Riley talking non-stop from the wagon.

"I gotta tell you, Joe, this is not my cup a tea, not by a long stretch. I'm from the open prairies where you can see stuff for miles off. I useta drive cattle for the Texas Rose Land and Cattle Company. Big outfit from San Antonio. Done all my work for them down to Montana and up in Southern Saskatchewan, down and back every year. But them buggers up and sold out their entire northern range clear to Montana. Here I am sellin a handful a cows to a fly-by-night operator name of Buster Krahn. No more big cattle drives in southern Saskatchewan. Period. The goddam Depression rules everything. Hired myself out to do farm labour for a while in the Red Deer Valley. One step from the rockin chair. Not my cup a tea neither."

"What if something else came along? Other than driving cattle, I mean. What would that be if you had a choice?"

"That's easy," said Stinky. "Number one, I wouldn't work for a skin-flint sonofabitch like Buster Krahn. And number two, I'd go fly one a them airo planes."

"You'd be a pilot?"

"Sure I would. I can already drive a truck. I can drive Buster Krahn's tractor. How hard could it be? Maybe take that license course they got, up by Red Deer. Get down the finer points. Nothin to it. Couple a months, I'm airborn."

"You'd get a license and fly your own plane?"

"Maybe to the first and no to the second. Might be able to afford the course and the license, but I couldn't afford no airo plane." Stinky went quiet long enough to spit, wipe his chin, and gaze into the woods. "Hell, who would hire me to fly a damn plane? These days I just take what I can get. Few years ago I got the call to come up here and run my own outfit. Buster Krahn, up at the portage." Stinky nodded two hundred miles or so in a northerly direction. "He wants to grow a herd up there, feed the crews comin through. Horses, another bull, cows for breedin, the whole bit. The sonofabitch is my best customer. Ever since this goddam Depression."

"Is that young chap up there with Isodore from the south too?"

"Yep. He's Isidore's son. He's even younger than you. Good with horses. *Ease up you son of a bitch!* Good roper too. Got a girlfriend workin up at Fitzgerald. Isidore is a halfbreed Cree from way over in northeastern Saskatchewan, used to break in the broncos for us, work our cattle with the Texas Rose. *I said ease up!* Brought his son Charlie along to work for me. But there's not too many halfbreed Cree families up here. Dog-ribs. Chipewyans. Speak a different language. None too friendly with the Cree up here."

"How do you know Tom Payne? Was he ever down at your cattle drives?"

"Everybody in this country knows Tommy. Toss the man in a junkyard he'd drive out with a new tractor in two days."

"He tells me he'd like to have a go at panning for gold up here."

"Oh, he'll get to it. I met him on a ranch down in Hughton, Saskatchewan. I was bunkin with some cowhands. We was waitin to collect some cattle to take down to the Landing, up comes Tommy and a friend with a bottle a home brew. Shared our bunkhouse. Not bad brew neither. Leastwise it didn't kill no one."

"Did he ever include his address in that reference letter he sent? I'd like to drop him a note when we get to Fitzgerald."

"Somewheres in Edmonton. I got the letter in my war bag. Right under there. Help yerself."

"Horses and ranches and cowboys. Heady stuff, Stinky. Now I'm a British cowboy. Speaking of which, did you ever run into a famous Brit named John Hornby?"

"Did I hear you say *cowboys?* You don't never use that word around here. Wrangler, yes, cowhand, yes. Cow-puncher, bronco buster. Saddle tramp, maybe. But this ain't boys' work, fella. Another thing. Don't never say *raunches* if you know what's good for ya. Ain't no such animal around here as *raunches*."

"I'll make a note of it, Stinky."

"Cowboys," muttered Riley. "Sheee-it."

"Stinky, you should hire yourself out as a language tutor for British immigrants. Good pay and it's safer than driving cattle or flying planes."

"Hornby, you say? I seen him once up at the Portage. Little feller. Lotsa heart but no compass. They say he could carry the load a two grown men."

ON THE FIRST DAY of the drive, Isidore was good for a half hour of conversation, young Charlie seemed to have been born without a voice, but Riley was good for about sixteen hours of straight gabbing.

"Like I say, Joe, this ain't my idea of a cattle drive, no sir. I like the wide-open spaces. Mind you, a blizzard blows up around here, you don't git the wind." He gestured to the trees around him, thick stands of jackpine, black spruce and tamarack, small stands of birch and some occasional aspen, and willows thick around the boggy sloughs and streams. "It's like these trees is here for our protection, you might say."

They camped in a clearing with a small cabin and a makeshift corral. Charlie and Isidore drove the cattle into the corral and fed them some grain. Stinky and Joe unhitched the horses, Stinky in instructor mode, and they both rubbed the horses down, fed and hobbled them. Joe finished up these chores while Stinky got a fire going in the cabin and built a larger fire outside for cooking beans, sowbelly and biscuits.

They pulled up logs and sat by the fire and ate their supper, listening to the call of…

"Stinky, would that be the coyotes?"

"Wolves," he said. "A few of em out there."

"Wolves? Would they ever get after our animals?"

"No," said Stinky. "They just go for human flesh. More fat in a human body, more tender too."

"I see," Joe muttered.

"They's particular fond of English flesh," said Stinky. "What you got to do is lather yerself in horse piss so's they don't like yer smell."

"Da cowshit, ah? Do a better job of it," said Isidore.

"Speaking of which," said Joe, "me cowshit measure is reading pretty high about now. Think I've had it with you lot."

Stinky looked Joe's way. "Okay, this here is a serious proposition, Joe. You heard tell a night-hawkin? No? I want you to be our night-hawk. We need a man to keep a eye on the horses and cattle. All you do is climb up on Lil and plod around the corral once in a while, check out the horses, keep your eyes open. You see anythin ain't right, why you just give us a whistle, we'll be out there in a flash."

"When do I sleep?"

"Oh, you can get Charlie to relieve you about four in the mornin. Kip out till breakfast. Few days from now, Isidore or Charlie can be the nighthawk and you can get your beauty sleep. You *British chaps*, you know how to shoot a rifle?"

SHANGHAI LIL MOVED sluggish and surefooted around the corral and stopped to graze with the horses hobbled in the grass next to the cabin. The stars were out in great multitudes, more than he had ever seen, pulsing and twinkling, embedded by the millions in the Milky Way like…luminiscent frogspawn…no, like sublunar grains of…like countless little fragments of phosphorous…

The wolves had stopped howling and all he could hear was the munching of horses, the occasional moaning of a cow, and snoring from at least one of the men. Probably Stinky. *Dear Benbow, I have become familiar with solitude and with the absence of decent beer and the King's English. No such thing as a bloke out here. And never call a cowboy a cowboy. Tonight I am on wolf patrol with orders to shoot anything that moves, unless it's wearing a big hat. There are no darling buds of May up here, just millions of trees and cold bloody nights and promiscuously farting cows...*

He dismounted and led Lil back to the fire. The logs were smoldering, so he kicked at the un-burnt butts until they caught fire and he threw in another couple of logs. He sat with his back to the fire until he could feel his backside go from chilly to frying hot, then he turned around to warm his front and yawned his way into a slow doze until his chin was drooping into his sternum. Shanghai Lil woke him up with a soft nicker, a slow shifting of her hooves, and he heard something, a stealthy sound. Something big out there moving through the trees. He was up and stumbling towards the rifle before he knew anything was amiss. He slipped Riley's thirty/thirty out of the leather case and crept away from the coals and waited till his eyes began to readjust to the dark. A half-moon was up and the woods were silent, and the horses had stopped munching by the side of the cabin, heads up, ears shifting. Something round and black drifted up to the edge of the clearing, its back edged in silver from the moon. It moved from the bush to the clearing and stopped to take in the air. A bear as big as a lion.

He brought back the hammer, took aim at the animal and squeezed the trigger. The rifle cracked like thunder overhead, and the animal seemed to leap up in the air in defiance of its great bulk. It ran crashing into the trees, a fading black colossus, and it was gone. The cattle were bawling. In the cabin the men arose, confused and cussing.

"It's all right!" he cried to the men inside, to the milling cattle in the corral, "It's all right! Just a bear!"

"You just shot a bear?" said Stinky, crouching over his long legs and hitching up his pants.

"Think I hit him, scared him off."

"You mean he ran off?"

"I guess so," Joe cried. "Yes. He seemed to jump like he was hit. But maybe I just scared him off. He's gone."

Isidore came around the side of the corral with a rifle in his hands.

"You kill da bear?" he said.

"Go back to bed," Joe cried. "Sorry to disappoint you all. No dead bear for brekky."

"You okay, kid?" said Stinky.

"Couldn't feel better. It's the most exhilarating thing I've done since I swam fully clothed in the Atlantic. Now go back to bed."

"Dat bear still out dere, him," Isidored whispered. "He's maybe hurt big. Dat's not good. You soot at dah bear, you gots to kill im dead."

"Isidore's right, Joe. Wounded bear in the bush, that's no good at all."

Charlie had appeared from another direction. Isidore handed him a rifle. Isidore and his son went slowly into the woods where Joe was pointing. He had an urge to go along with Isidore and Charlie, but Stinky was blocking the way.

"These boys," he said, "they know what to do."

They stood there in silence for a few minutes until two explosions a second apart rocked the forest clearing. Riley and Joe seemed to exhale at the same time.

"You ever et a bear steak?" said Stinky.

For the next week, as they moved further north on the trail, they camped in clearings, and because the mosquitoes and blackflies had not yet emerged, they slept in their bedrolls, without netting, over a stretched canvas. During each stop they had to mend the corrals with rope and haywire. Then it was young Charlie's turn to be the night-hawk, and Joe slept as soundly as a dog. He slept next to Stinky, who snored loud enough to scare off any bear in the country. It was a strangely comforting sound.

One evening by the fire he pulled out his novel and read a dozen pages before Stinky broke the silence. Riley had been sitting on a log, sucking meditatively on a cigarette.

"That there's a pretty thick book, Burbidge," he said.

Joe nodded and kept on reading. He couldn't decide if he liked the story. It seemed rather...what was the word? Literary?

A minute later, Riley said, "What's it called?"

Joe held out the book and Stinky squinted hard at the cover.

"Why'd anyone want to write a whole book on molasses?"

Joe gave Stinky his vexed expression.

"I'm serious. I mean, you taste it once, try it on your beans an bread, what's more to be said?"

"It's not molasses, Stinky. Put on your spectacles. It's *Ulysses.* That's the name of the novel."

Joe went back to his book, which was about a couple of young Irish blokes living in a tower. The main chap had lost his mother and he seemed pretty sulky. Joe kept reminding himself how much it had cost him and how impressed Auntie Vi would be with his taste in modern literature. And hadn't it been Alan Benbow who'd recommended the book in the first place? With the promise that it was eminently smutty? The bastard.

"What's that?" said Stinky.

"What's what?"

"Ulysses. That a fella's name?"

"Yes."

"What kinda name is that? Foreign name?"

"I think it might be Greek."

"You're readin about a Greek fella?"

"Well, no, not exactly."

"Them Greeks. I hear tell they go at their women every which-a-way but sidewise. I hear they do the wildest things to their women. Bad buggers? Wowie. Orgies?"

"Are you through, Stinky?" Joe replied. "You don't mind if I continue?"

"They actually eat live chickens. Did you know that?"

"No, Stinky, I didn't."

Stinky was smiling at Isidore. "Do me a favour, Joe? Underline the smutty bits for me?"

"What if I were to tell you, Stinky, that so far there aren't any smutty bits? Not a trace of dirt."

"Just you mark my words, Burbidge," he said with a yawn. "If it ain't smutty, it ain't Greek. If it ain't smutty, it ain't even foreign."

"So far, Stinky, there aren't even any Greeks in it."

"No Greeks at all, eh?"

"It's Irishmen, mostly."

"Then why in the hell does he name his book Greek?"

"I don't know, Stinky. Maybe it's a figure of speech or something."

"A figure of speech. Huh. Now I'm really confused."

"Stinky, how the hell am I supposed to know? The book is over seven hundred pages and I'm only on page twenty-seven. Blame it on your compatriots."

Riley acquired a bumptious look. He was shaking his head as though perhaps the whole act of reading was a questionable enterprise.

"My compatriots? I'm from Montana. I'm as American as the day is long."

"I'll tell you one thing, Stinky, the bookseller had to have this book smuggled out of Europe. It's been banned all over the place."

"You don't say," said Stinky, and his interest seemed to revive. He sat up straight. "And no smut yet?"

"None."

"I was to write a book that long, Joe, I'd want to get in a fair bit a smut right off. Grab yer attention, see?"

Joe could see that his reading was over for the evening. Stinky was too stimulated by his own literary theories to allow him to continue. Presently, Stinky arose, ambled over to his wagon, sorted through a pile of clothes in a duffle bag and picked out a dime novel. He returned to his log by the fire and held up a paperback entitled *The Altar of Fallen Flesh* by Jackson Steele. He pointed to the cover of the book, licked a finger, opened it, and mumbled his way down the page.

"Here," he said, clearing his throat. "Yeah. 'Stag Bullard hitched up his pants and walked across the barroom floor. He looked down on Fell-sheeah…Fellikia…'"

"Felicia?"

"Felicia, yeah. 'A sal-dor-nic…a sal-donic'…

"Would that be sardonic?" said Joe.

" 'A sardonic smile crossed his rugged features. With less than a second's hesitation, he poked at the flimsy garment that sheathed her heaving…'"

Joe waved a hand in quiet surrender. "Okay, Stinky, you've made your point."

"Page four, Joe. Page four."

Riley closed the book, cast a snooty glance first in Charlie's and then in Joe's direction, nodded to Isidore, nodded to the horses whose heads were raised to look back in apparent wonder at him, and headed for his bedroll. Oh, but Stinky looked smug.

One afternoon the herd crossed a shallow creek, one of many they had driven through.

Joe asked Stinky, "Why not try there?"

They were following a trail that wound its way beside the Athabasca River and headed towards Claire Lake. They would soon be riding between Claire Lake and the western shore of Lake Athabasca and heading for the final leg of their journey.

"Ain't the right colour," said Stinky. He had already dismissed several creeks that day. *Ain't got no gravel. Ain't got the right rocks.*

Ain't got no quartz. Don't look right to me. No rubble an shit, no goddam prospects.

"What do you mean, not the right colour?"

"Wrong colour, that's what I mean."

"But what is the right colour?"

"I'll show ya, Joe. I'll show ya when I see it."

"So, how do you...pan for it?"

"That part's easy. Just get a grub pan from the wagon and gouge out some gravel and water. Shake the hell out of it. Good way a cleanin the pan. Get the water flowin over the gravel, shake er up, and let the gold fall to the bottom. Heavy stuff goes to the bottom. That's all there is to it. And don't go pannin where there ain't no gold."

THAT EVENING, at the eighth camp they had made on the trail to Fitzgerald, when the sun was at least another hour from setting, Riley pulled out a small canvas poke and tapped some gold fragments and dust out onto his hand. He tapped the little sack again with his index finger and a small nugget fell out. He stretched his hand outside the canopy and held it in the sunlight.

"Is that solid –"

"Damn rights. That's the real McCoy. Go ahead. Pick er up."

"What if I drop it?" said Joe.

"Pick er up."

He held the nugget in the palm of his hand so that the sun picked up the pale yellow glint of it, a nugget about the diameter of a shirt button. Joe couldn't help but feel the weight of it. The men gathered around.

"Stinky," said Isidore, "you gonna sell dat gold?"

"Nope."

"What you gonna do wid dat gold, you?"

"Nothin."

"You gonna carry aroun dat gold for nothin?"

"Yep."

"How much gold you got dere?"

"Ounce or two."

"Why you do dat, Stinky, carry it aroun? You could buy a new hat and boots."

"Already got a hat and boots."

"I could buy dat gold from you," said Isidore. "Me, I could pay you ten bucks and a bearskin."

"What would you do with it, Isidore?"

Isidore thought for a moment. "I tink I juss carry it aroun for a while."

The men all laughed at that one, even young Charlie.

"Den me, I sell it back to you, Stinky."

"Same price, Isidore?"

"Oh, no, Stinky. Man's gotta make a livin."

While Isidore spread open the little poke, Riley poured back the gold fragments and the nugget, brushing dust from his hand with an index finger, doing so with all the delicacy of an apothecary at his bench. He gave the poke a few shakes, twisted it closed and retied the drawstring.

That night as the sun sank below the treeline, a vast glow remained well into the night, as though the gold itself had lent its gleam and majesty to the sky, and as the men yawned their way into their separate dreams, and as young Charlie stood watch by the fire, the wolves moved in close and howled well into the night, sending skyward their musky vapours and calling down mournful judgements, it seemed to Joe as he dozed into his pillow, from the very heavens.

THEY WERE IN Treaty Eight country now, where the Northern Cree, the South Slaveys, the Dogrib and the Chipewyans hunted, fished, trapped, traded furs, competed and fought. Fitzgerald was a straggle of cabins, dugouts, boat-houses, shacks, sheds and tractors, all scattered on the shores of the Peace River around a large, extended wharf where the barges came in with cargos of heavy machinery and staples, labourers and prospecting crews.

Buster Krahn and an Indian crew had thrown together the beginnings of a small ranch just outside the settlement, with a corral and a Jerry-built house that smelled of creamed corn, or at other times of rotten milk. It was part dugout, part sod shack, part storage shed, and part log cabin. Krahn had always done his business down south, a hotel here, a beer joint there, but this was the first time that he'd ventured north. He'd grown up on a ranch near Hanna, a dusty town on the Eastern Alberta prairies. When he was in his mid-teens he ran off to the city and worked as a flunky at various hotels and establishments of ill-repute. Since then he'd risen in the world, and now he owned an equally infamous hotel in Fitzgerald.

Stinky had gone to some lengths to prepare Joe for his first encounter with Buster Krahn. Buster had grown into a rank edifice of a man who smelled, as far as Joe could tell, of resentment. He walked bowlegged and bullheaded, heaving his body forward one big ham at a time like the front half of a bull elephant, indifferent to anything or anyone underfoot. He smiled a lot and his smile made people feel uneasy. They said that in his drive for fast money he was a bottomless pit and counted every penny. As Stinky liked to say, *Krahn is tighter'n a mare's arse goin up a hill.*

Krahn had paid Stinky and the men for the drive. Joe had wandered down to the general store where a post office was installed. He sent letters to his mother, to Auntie Vi, and another one to Tom Payne's address. On his way back he encountered young Charlie coming fast down the trail.

"Where are you heading, Charlie?"

"Dunno," said Charlie with a shy smile.

"Charlie, you are blushing! Could it be that you're meeting with your sweet-heart?"

Charlie looked away.

"You can tell your old friend Joe. I will say nothing to the men." Joe crossed his heart and smiled at the young fellow. Charlie looked at his boots, shook his head, and continued swiftly down the trail. "Go get her, Charlie!"

Joe advanced slowly up the trail to Buster Krahn's cluttered yard and his sprawling cabin. Krahn was standing near the entrance to the house with his hands in his jeans pockets and his weight on one boot, not talking to Stinky. Stinky was doing likewise. Many were the minutes they passed this way, and Joe did his best to emulate their taciturn composure.

"So," said Krahn, perhaps to Stinky, perhaps to anyone at all, as if to sum up everything he knew of the unforgiving bush and the fallen world.

Stinky moved up and leaned against a post closer to where Krahn was taking in the sun.

"So."

Stinky wanted to know when his next drive might be put together.

"Depends," said Krahn.

"On what?" said Riley.

"Lotta things. Where'd that injun go?"

"Isidore?"

"The young buck."

"What do you care, Buster?"

"He's got his eye on one a my workin girls."

"You wouldn't mean his girlfriend by any chance?"

Through his twitching snout Buster made a scoffing sound.

The gulls were screaming down by the wharf and the geese were coming over in high waves, cackling in falsetto. Somewhere a man sawed wood as a tractor chugged off a barge. Joe leaned against the log wall within the shade of the front porch, glad for the rest.

"Well, Buster, me and the boys are ready for a day off, so why don't you just think about our next drive and I'll ask you again."

Krahn glanced over at Joe and back at Riley and shrugged.

"Yiz goin fishin?"

"Me and the boys gonna do some pannin."

"Which creek?"

"The one with the gold in it."

"You ain't got no idea, have you," said Krahn.

"We'll just see, won't we."

"You should learn to lay around a bit, Stinky. Take it easy. A man of your years."

"Too much to do, Beezer. Maybe next year."

"The name is Buster."

"Plumb forgot."

"Suit yourself, Stinky. You boys lay over a day or so, then give me a hand with them steers. And maybe we'll need some feed up here before too long."

"Feed? You can get feed off them barges."

"They charge too much. Can't say as we need any more cattle, Stinky."

"Judgin from the traffic on this river, Buster, I'd say you need a hell of a lot more cattle."

"Nope. I'm not made a money. See how she goes this year and then decide. Right now it's all up to my bull and them heifers."

"Suit yerself."

"What we need up here, Stinky, is a Chink laundry."

"What's that got ta do with me?"

"We need a very special kind a Chink laundry up here, Stinky. A family of my acqaintance in Edmonton could do the job, but they would need special transportation."

"What's wrong with them barges?"

"Too many curious types."

"You're not talkin about no Chink laundry, are you Buster."

"I'm talkin about a special type a laundry, Stinky."

"You're talkin about a hop house. And you want me to be your setup guy. Haul in the girlies, haul in the opium and whisky. Hell,

Buster, why don't I just bribe a few cops, bribe a judge or two? You and me and Joey here, we can all become gangsters."

"Man has to make a buck, Stinky."

"I run cattle."

"You work for me, Stinky, you run what I need. You got that?"

RILEY AND JOE RETURNED to the last creek they had crossed before ending their drive at Buster Krahn's place. Unlike the other ones they had seen, Riley's choice was a fast-moving stream on a big slope that appeared to come from a high series of cliffs and eskers with snow still melting on their upper ledges. The creek bed looked like a washout, a mountain creek, with scrawny trees uprooted on both sides.

They pulled out their pans from their saddlebags and sloshed away in the gravel for some time.

"He thinks some day I'm gonna break down and kiss his ass," said Stinky.

"Who?"

"That bugger Krahn. He's thinks I'll be his goddam slave. He thinks we're just putty in his hands. He knows goddam well I drive cattle, not prostitutes or opium."

"And you pan for gold."

"Yes, by God, let's pan some gold."

Charlie showed up with a distant smile on his face. To Joe he looked younger somehow, perhaps more innocent. He and Isidore came together, and they had both brought tin plates. They all went at it above and below the trail until they were puffing and heaving. Stinky Riley was the only one to keep his clothes dry.

About an hour after they had begun, he roared, "You girlies come over here!"

Still breathing hard, they gathered around Riley to look at a small accumulation of black sand at the bottom of his pan. Joe noticed something sparkling up at him. Stinky poked a twig at a tiny bright pebble.

"Don't block out the sun, boys. Looka this here."

The remaining sand was flecked with pale yellow and the pebble was a fragment of gold scarcely bigger than a buckshot.

"Dat's da stuff, ah?" whispered young Charlie.

This was more English chatter Joe had heard from Charlie in more than two weeks of travel.

"The real McCoy," said Stinky.

The men all returned to their pans, gathering gravel, shaking and sluicing it around, letting the stream carry it away in small measures, poking at the remains at the bottom of the pan. They exhausted themselves. Joe focused on a ten-foot stretch of creek in the fast water where grayling held in the current beneath the shadow of a boulder. Isidore spent his time upstream from the others, and he was the only one besides Riley to find a trace of gold. It was no bigger than the fragment that Stinky had found.

"We have to have another go at this, Stinky," said Joe.

"Lotta work for liddl bit gold, ah?" said Charlie. He had become a bona fide, potential chatter-box.

"I done okay in this water last time I was up here," Stinky said. "If you girlies wasn't so tired, I believe I'd pan here some more."

He scraped some gold particles into the poke and tied the drawstring, smiling all the while. He shoved the poke down into his jeans pocket so that it made a bulge beside the other one between his legs.

"But I guess we better get back to the camp, get you boys fed and tucked in for the night."

Riley and Joe bunked down on the floor of Buster's shack next to the stove, and Isidore and his son disappeared for the night. Father and son had been whispering back and forth in brief fragments of Cree. They seemed to be arguing or planning something, and it made Joe uneasy. The floor of Buster's shack was as smelly as any other part of his make-shift cabin. Joe would try to fall asleep and the smell would catch up with him and declare itself without quite proclaiming its source.

"I'm leavin early with Isidore and Charlie," Stinky whispered. "I got no yearnin to hang about here."

"We could go panning, Stinky."

"Some other time, Joe. I gotta take Charlie and Isidore home. I'm through here, Joe. If I can't drive no more cattle up here or down south, I got to set down somewheres and figure things out. Got friends down in the Red Deer Valley. They'll need help with the crop again. Someone to mind the cattle and help fix things around the place."

"Does this rancher have a daughter, Stinky?"

"Nope, but I've got my eye on the gal who runs the hotel up the road." Stinky had turned reflective in the dark. "Anyways, I need a pleasant place to stay while I figure out the next move. Wind up the business and suchlike. Talk with the boys at that hangar up by Red Deer."

"Where's this ranch?"

"You heard tell a Patricia? Little village in the Red Deer Valley? Not too far from the river."

"Stinky, I need to give this gold panning thing a decent try."

"Course you do. Stay with Buster for a while, give him a hand and he'll let you stay. But I need to take Shanghai Lil with me. You're on your own legs up here. I'll be wrappin things up at the barn. You find a gold mine, write me care a the post office in Patricia. I'll want fifty percent right off the top."

Riley yawned, farted and sighed. The end of a perfect day.

JOE AWAKENED WITH a frown. Someone's voice was rasping, hissing like a big snake. It cut right through the profound whicker from deep in Stinky's adenoids. The smell was back. He sat up, sniffed, and tried to locate it, but like some ghost announcing its presence by wandering in and out of nostrils, the smell had drifted away. He peered through the gloom to see where he could possibly be, and he wondered why there was no smell of tent canvas. The cabin. Buster's smelly cabin. And the sound of two men talking in explosive whispers.

"Where is she?"

"She's gone, that's where. Now get the hell outa here and let me get some sleep."

"Where is she?"

"None a yer goddam business. She left of her own accord and she ain't comin back."

"Dat's a long answer. How bout a short one?"

"Short answer? Get the fuck off my property."

"Where is she?"

They were just outside the cabin. There was a noise like the sound of a great animal hoofing the gravel, a thump and some grunting and something fell over and crashed on the ground. And then more grunting and then there was silence. And the sound of someone trudging off into the dark. In the morning Joe noticed an ugly scrape on Buster's cheek.

JOE WALKED THE TRAILS into the hills for longer outings, panned for gold all day and slept in a tent cabin Krahn had erected for cowhands and bargemen. Two or three days a week he did chores for Krahn, who let him stay there and eat one supper a day in Krahn's cabin, but Joe found Krahn to be bleak company at the best of times. He missed his tiny part of England, he missed Auntie Vi's sumptuous flat in Edmonton, he missed his little room in the King Edward Hotel, he missed Auntie Vi's vivacious flatmates, Peggy and Maisy. Or was it Maisy and Peggy? He hadn't got the ranking straight yet. Most of all, he missed his conversations with Stinky Riley.

In his letter to Tom Payne Joe had mentioned the traces of gold that Stinky had found. Now he hoped this letter might entice Tom to come up to this nowhere place and keep him company.

The valley in early June turned windy, and one evening a great surge of foul weather moved in from the west. The clouds ran dark purple with bulging white highlights and they stampeded through the entire valley. The precipitation hung down from the clouds in tatters like worn rags and cobwebs. The wind struck and then the hail, bombarding the canvas on his tent cabin. The rain followed the hail, the roof above his bunk bellied downwards and began to leak. Joe enclosed himself within the folds of his big tarp and listened to the uproar of wind, thunder, cracking trees, and something else that sounded like flooding or mudslides or shifting gravel. The ruckus persisted all through the night. The sun came out around breakfast time. Joe arose and heated up some smoked bear meat that Isidore had left him, made coffee, and dug out biscuits from his food box. He sloshed his way along the south trail to the creek that Stinky had first taken him to. The trail was littered with hailstones the size of big marbles, and the rain had left the trail in such a mess that it took him an extra twenty minutes to get there. When he arrived at the creek, the sun was warm and the light was bouncing brightly off the rocks and the water. Already the stream was flowing half-clear again, and the treacherous levels of silty water had mostly abated. Joe looked around for a place to dip his pan, and he could not find his favourite boulder. The fish and their staging pool were gone as well. The storm had created a great slide, and Joe's constant boulder was gone like a great molar ripped from the mouth of a snoring giant. But it had left a modest crater behind in the middle of the stream, and once more the stream ran clear.

He waded nearly up to the tops of his wellies and scooped out a panful of gravel from the newly created basin. He came up with sand and pebbles that were white, greyish green, solid black, or freckled with rust-red granite. He trudged over to the slower-moving water and sluiced the gravel around in the current, shaking the clay and root particles out of it, letting the lighter material flow out of the pan. He was so absorbed in this labour that he was almost immune to the aching cold of the water. Up came the pan with some of the gravel washed away. The larger lumps of clay Joe broke apart with his fingers. He tossed out some of the larger rocks. Then he held the pan almost horizontal, tilted slightly downwards and away from his body, so the silty material flowed out from the lip of the pan. Joe repeated this process, filling his pan with clear creek water, rotating it gently again and again until the lighter gravel had been reduced. He picked out a dozen or so small rocks and colourful pebbles. Glinting in the sunlight in the midst of a residue of black sand were the first particles of gold he had ever lifted from a stream. Some of them were too small to be called gold fragments, too big to constitute mere grains of gold dust.

As carefully as Stinky would have done, Joe tweezed and scraped the gold into his new poke, a canvas pepper sack from the supply wagon. He poured the water out of his wellies and waded back into the stream and thanked God that at least the sun was warm on his back. He rolled up his sleeves and burrowed into the crater's gravel again and repeated the process, holding the pan not quite parallel to the ground to perform his mambo swirl of gravel and water, shaking the pan to loosen its contents. This time he found a ragged nugget as big around as his thumbnail.

He worked the gravel as quickly as he dared, as slowly as he could contain himself. Each time he came back to render down the sand and gravel he found particles of gold and sometimes a tiny nugget roughly the size of a saskatoon berry. He was shivering from the cold, so he lay on the stream bank and let the blood pump through his veins and the sun warm his body. He tried panning directly upstream and down from the crater and found nothing.

He had enough strength and energy for one more immersion, but this time he left his pan on the shore, waded in, hovered over the crater as the silt moved around, and he stared into the shallow basin the boulder had left behind. The last clouds of silt drifted away, and the sun penetrated the flowing water and picked out an enticing beacon of glinting light. Joe plunged his hand into the water and plucked out a white rock the size of a well-crumpled sheet of stationery, a chunk of quartz that was so infused with gold that it seemed to weigh heavy in his hand.

In Joe's hand. In Joe Burbidge's hand.

He waded to the edge of the stream, chattering and laughing in a high squawk that had little to do with joy and much to do with frenzy.

Bring on the shipwrecks, bring on the saddle sores and the howling wolves and the bloody bears, bring on the hailstorms and the blackflies and mosquitoes, bring on the frigid water that made him stammer like a ninny, bring on the Christly elements, bring on the blizzards, bring on the unbearable Buster Krahn, bring it all on, the whole amalgamated welter of crap, whatever it was called. Canada, yes Canada, by Christ, Canada, I loves ya. Do you hear that? *Joe Burbidge loves you!*

Chapter 5

Isidore's Tripod

THE TIME HAD COME for Joe to leave Buster Krahn's joyless little outpost. He had staked his first claim, and now he would sell it. What a strange thing to do. Find the good gravel, pan it, work it till you're exhausted, and then sell it as fast as you can. Pack up your bedroll, Joe, he said to Joe. Everything you can carry to Fitzgerald. If you want to prospect further north, you need to walk to town and get on a barge.

Since staking his claim, Joe had been camping alone in the bush for three days. He wasn't merely trying to escape Buster Krahn's company; he was looking for some placer gold in another stream. It made good sense to do this, but he had no luck at all, nothing like the claim on what he referred to as Boulder Creek. And the black flies were out and the mosquitoes were forming their squadrons. At last he'd made it back to Krahn's outfit to get his things together to catch his barge north. His dread of the North, the loneliness, the ranging emptiness of it, was giving way to fascination. He almost loved the desolation of the North. It appealed to the restless imp inside him.

Thide, it said to him. *Thide.*

Krahn lumbered up to Joe with business on his mind. Joe wanted to ask him about the scrape on the side of his face. It had scabbed up and soon it would be gone.

"You're back."

"Not for long, Buster."

On that day, Krahn seemed to think that Joe was worthy of some respect, and the aura of menace and resentment appeared to have receded. Joe Burbidge was no longer an insufferable limey whiner but a man to be reckoned with, a man with gold in his poke. Buster had taken one look at the gold and offered Joe five hundred dollars for his claim on Boulder Creek. Joe accepted the offer, cash on the barrel-head. Krahn also bought some of the gold in Joe's poke for thirty dollars.

"Feller was lookin for you. Name a Tom Payne?"

"Tom Payne was here?"

"Yeah, he left for a barge around noon. Bugger couldn't wait. Said he had to get north. Had a job up on Great Slave somewheres. Great Slave? No, maybe Great Bear. I dunno."

Joe shook his head and summoned an oath from deep down in his chest. If he hadn't gone into the bush on a wild goose chase, he would have been here when Tom came to see him. Christ.

"Here," Krahn said to Joe, and handed him a wad of bills.

The transfer would be called the Boulder Creek Claim. They signed a piece of paper with the stub of a pencil and shook on it. Buster's hand was huge, meaty, padded, moist. He lumbered off with a mildly contemptuous look, as though Joe had no idea what he was giving up for five hundred dollars. Joe did not have the equipment or the time to go down to the bedrock and see what the claim was really good for, but he knew he was finished with it. The more he'd gouged up the gravel, the less colour he'd found. Besides, the fun was in *finding* some colour, not mining it. He thought he should wish Krahn good luck on the claim, but he couldn't heave up the words. He had come to feel towards Buster Krahn the way Stinky Riley had, the way Isidore and his son Charlie had. He loathed the resentful creamed-corn smell of his breath.

Joe counted his money and stuffed it into his pants pocket. He gazed over at Krahn's corral and wondered if he was too tired to haul his bundles to town. He could ask Krahn if he could borrow a horse, but…

There, by the corral gate, like a memory become flesh, was

Isidore Chartrand, muttering to the horses. Where the hell…

"Isidore! What are you doing here?"

"I hear you got some of dat gold, Joe."

"Aren't you supposed to be down south?"

"Not so good down dere, Joe. No more work wit Stinky. Hard to fine work at Fort MacKay. I come back to here, me. Try da per-spectin, ah?"

"How did you get back here so quickly?" said Joe.

"On da barge."

"Where's Charlie?"

"He's off ta fine his girl, Charlie. He don't wan ta look for no gold."

That set-to in the night outside Krahn's cabin. Charlie's hike down to Buster's rowdy hotel. The scrape on Buster's face. Joe decided to change the subject. "What about your wife and family?"

"See's putty smart, Loney. Plenny smart an plenny tough. See's okay, got some of her famly down dere."

Isidore was giving Joe his bemused look, an expression Joe never really understood.

"Hey Joe, I seen Buster up at your crick, ah?"

"I sold my claim to him."

"He says you sell him yer gold, Joe."

"I did. He bought some of it. I haven't figured out why."

"Maybe he juss like to have it."

"He paid me a decent price for the claim."

Joe had more wealth on his person than he'd ever had in his life. He had been paid in cash by Stinky Riley, he had Buster Krahn's wad of bills in his jeans pocket, and, at twenty dollars an ounce, he still had about thirty dollars worth of gold left in his pepper sack. With Isidore there before him, Joe's outlook was verging on cheerful.

"Where you gonna go, Joe?"

"Where the gold is."

Isidore looked away, nodding towards the north, and said, almost inaudibly, "Me, I gotta nidear where da gold is."

"You know where to find the gold? Isidore?"

"Me, I talk to a fella."

JOE NEVER FOUND OUT Isidore Chartrand's age because Isidore would never tell him. Isidore walked younger than he stood. Through muskeg or deep snow, mushing dogs or breaking trail with his long legs, Isidore was as tireless as a man of thirty years. As far as Joe could find out, Isidore was a halfbreed Cree from Domremy, a village southwest of the forks of the North and the South Saskatchewan Rivers. And if he was ageless and tireless on the trail he was inexhaustible around a campsite, moving hunched and restless among his blackened pots, setting up the tent, feeding the fire, feeding the stove, doing the carpentry for their wintering cabin, and muttering in his bedroll all through the long nights in snatches of Cree and village English, then up before first light to feed the dogs and the fire again. Joe had to assert himself to help him with the chores. Isidore's camp cooking was not delectable like Stinky's meals were, but it was fast and palatable. Stews, soups, beans and fried balony, and anything they could hook, trap or shoot. Anything short of ravens, lynx meat or beavertails.

"These are the only meats I will not consume," he said to Isidore one day.

"You never tried lynx? Not so bad, Joe."

"I don't care. We Burbidges do not eat cats. Or skunks, Isidore. Can we agree? No cats and no skunks?"

"No skunks up here, Joe."

"But just in case one wanders into camp some day. A lost skunk, say. I couldn't live with myself if I ever ate a skunk."

From the hour they walked off Krahn's corral hoping to catch a barge, the two men had started making plans to winter at Great Bear Lake. A mining explorations boss down at the docks named

Pep Glauser intercepted them and hired them on the spot to prospect for an Edmonton syndicate. They had never met the man before this, they never even signed a contract, but his syndicate grubstaked the two of them, which meant a free plane trip in a Bellanca Pacemaker rather than a slow trip by barge. This was a fair deal in the middle of the Depression. Glauser paid for a few supplies for the men to build a cabin, a wall tent, a wood stove and some grub. He added a small stipend for the men to buy either a dog team or a boat up at Great Bear. He was tightfisted and tough to bargain with, but he opened the door for Joe and Isidore to begin their lives as northern prospectors.

"If you find some colour or some good minerals on company time," said Glauser, "we have the rights to them. Gentleman's agreement. But if you fellas find something on your own, we split sixty-forty. My sixty, your forty."

"On our own?"

"Yeah, day off or something. If you do, you are duty bound to give us first refusal on the claim. Is that clear?"

Joe shook on the offer for both Isidore and himself. No one else was available to back them. Whatever else they needed, Joe had to pay for it, and he was happy to do it with Buster Krahn's money. It felt good to be free of Krahn and it felt good to have money. Isidore thought of Joe as a supremely wealthy man.

THE PROSPECTING AROUND Great Bear did not go well in the late summer and fall. The North Slaveys in Déline were not friendly with the Northern Cree, and some of them must have assumed that Isidore was one of the enemy. Joe and Isidore could not get very far down the lake on foot beyond where the locals and fly-ins had already prospected, so they decided to prepare for the winter.

Joe and Isidore selected their logs in the forest, seeking out the largest trees they could find. The trees were stunted, regardless of what kind they were or where they grew. The men tagged the best ones, chopped them down, lopped and limbed them. They carried them out with the help of a neighbour and his dog team. From this meagre beginning, with logs scarcely bigger than hiking staves, Joe and Isidore threw up a small cabin.

Owing to the diminutive size of these trees, their cabin was only six by eight feet, a structure that came with a guarantee of unintended intimacy. Joe and Isidore chopped up a derelict boat and salvaged some planks for the floor. They fit them across a row of poplar saplings that they had laid in lengthwise. The cabin had no door, only an entrance-way that looked like a window. The entrance had a shutter door, and it started one foot up from the floor of the cabin and terminated at around Joe's breastbone. A man did not walk into the cabin, he climbed in. The cabin was little more than a den but it warmed tolerably soon after the stove was lit. Their space allowed for two small cots on either side, and the wood stove in the corner. Isidore thought that Joe should sleep closest to the stove.

All through the winter Joe kept his dollar bills rolled up in a pants pocket and his poke from the Fitzgerald find in the other front pocket. He scarcely ever took them out; the weight of one and the feel of the other were sufficient comfort to him. Several times Joe asked Isidore about the gold formations at Great Bear. Each time Isidore said roughly the same thing.

"Da gold's all over da place, Joe. Jus no one aroun ta stake it, ah?"

"Who told you that the gold was everywhere? Buster Krahn?"

"Scotch guy wit a blanket. Blanket wit a hole for da head, ah? Forget da name, dat guy. He tol me we gotta get up here before yudder guys, dat man. Stay all winner, out on da rocks in da spring. Walk aroun take a looksee."

From what they'd seen in late August and September, he knew that this bounty of gold prospects could hardly be true, but during the long nights of his first winter in the tiny cabin, he teased himself with the possibility that *some* of it might be true, and that they just hadn't looked far enough down the massive lake.

During the slow passage of winter, the near-perpetual dark, he often wondered where Tom Payne was working. They would have made a great team. They would have chatted long hours about geology and reminisced about life on the old sod and (Joe liked to think) speak in complete sentences. He expected to meet the man every time he walked into Déline. But Tom only showed up when you least expected him and he would be gone the next day. Some barge men had talked about him on the docks in Fitzgerald. Tom had apparently just managed to bring up a sunken barge and rescue its contents. Some surveyors out of Norman Wells had spoken with Joe about him at their work camp. They said he'd been there around Christmas time. Apparently Tom was headed south on a dog team, heading for Hottah Lake. A mining company needed him to repair and maintain heavy machinery.

Staying all winter in the cabin was the syndicate's idea. It meant merely that Pep Glauser's outfit would save the cost of flying the men home and bringing them back in the spring. It also meant that the men would have to harvest their own meat and learn how to pass the many dark hours. Sometimes the night sky, with its uncountable panoply of stars and its pulsing aurora, set Joe's eyes to gander and gaze for the length of a long piss, but never longer.

Joe and Isidore talked about gold. They had to catch fish through the ice to get enough food for themselves and their neighbour's dogs, but even in the thick of it, netting fish and freezing their fingers, they talked about gold.

Perhaps around the tenth time Isidore had repeated what the *Scotch guy wit a blanket* had told him about the abundance of gold at Great Bear, April had arrived. Each afternoon the temperature rose to about ten degrees below freezing, and the light began to return. Isidore, Joe, and their neighbour, an old Slavey man named Freddy Nadzo, had been running the dog team up beyond the river to Freddy's trapline. They shared their take with the old man, and he was as friendly to Isidore as he was to Joe. Isidore and Joe had acquired a modest stack of marten, fox and mink hides lying in a shed that they had cobbled together.

"This time we might need a boat, Isidore."

"Doan need no boat ta walk aroun. Use Freddy's dogs."

"A boat would give us a bigger advantage, Isidore. We could go farther up the lake, where the others wouldn't go. We could go up the lake and camp and we wouldn't have to feed any dogs. Let Freddy feed his own dogs."

"Maybe."

Isidore seemed to be meditating. He began to hum to himself, on and off, on and off, in a beelike monotone. With Isidore, Joe had to be patient.

"Da white guy's got two boats, him. Near da town."

Isidore's white man, in this case, was living just outside of Déline, a trapper named Ed Bueckert. He lived with a North Slavey woman in a cabin on the Great Bear River a mile down from Joe and Isidore's place. There were other white men in Déline and Fort Norman, but they were mostly new arrivals. Every day in the spring, Joe would take a walk past Bueckert's place for something to do, but he never saw any boats. In late April they paid the man a visit and discovered that he had two boats buried in the snow, a sturdy canoe he had bartered for with a man from Norman Wells, and a big dory he ran up and down the river with a kicker. They decided on the canoe. They gave the man all of their furs, a gold nugget from Joe's poke, forty dollars, and a Riley crusher for grinding small loads of ore. No relation to Stinky Riley. Joe was anything but pleased at the transaction.

"Isidore, we could have bloody well used that crusher."

"You got da yudder ting."

Isidore was referring to Joe's mortar and pestle.

"That's not the point. If you didn't throw that toy into the bargain, we could have gotten the canoe and the paddles and kept my crusher."

The toy in question was a surveyor's tripod with long, adjustable, metal legs but without a transit. Isidore's logic in rebuttal, however, was hard to refute.

"Hang da pot from dat, Joe."

"We never had a problem hanging pots before this."

"Can't hang a pot from dat rock crusser."

Soon it was warm enough to cook outside the cabin, and Isidore never lost a chance to demonstrate the virtues of his tripod, which he mounted over a small fire each day from which to boil water and cook stews. The legs of the tripod blackened as the spring progressed, and gradually the tripod lost any resemblance to a piece of surveyors' equipment. When the ice was more than half melted from the lake, they loaded the canoe for their first big exploration, and Isidore brought along his tripod.

They paddled down the river and into the vast lake, and although the big canoe was seaworthy, to avoid squalls they stayed close to the southern shore, heading east, and checked out the rock formations along the way. By the end of June they had found traces of copper and a variety of rocks run through with oxidized minerals, enticingly tinted oroide and some cobalt, but nothing worth bagging for their syndicate. In August they went farther down the lake and both Joe and Isidore came to appreciate what a huge territory they had chosen for prospecting. *It's just too much*, Joe kept muttering. And each time Joe said it, Isidore replied, *Nex spring, Joe, we gonna have a good spring.*

THEY WINTERED BACK in their cabin once more and widened their circle of friends. When Glauser's plane came back in the spring of 1934, they had very few samples to show him and his pilot, but they renewed their agreement for the year and agreed to meet the plane in late summer.

When the ice was out again, they loaded up their canoe and headed out once more. This time they kept paddling east along the southern shore of Great Bear and camped their way a good sixty miles from Déline. One day they arrived at a wooded peninsula where they pulled in for a rest. They came upon an old campsite down by the water. It offered a nicely protected spot on the windward side, it faced south, and it lay right below an enticing bank of horizontally stratified rock.

On the first day after setting up camp, they climbed a game trail to the top of the peninsula, and almost immediately Joe found some crystallized minerals set in coarse-grained granite that appeared to be a deposit of pitchblende. They bagged some samples and spent the rest of the day hunting for ptarmigan. Two days later, walking west of their campsite on the same slope, they found several closely spaced patches of silver-bearing ore. It was embedded in pitchblende and had a weathered brown texture. Again they hacked away and bagged some samples. They marked both spots and paddled back to their cabin over a stretch of two days to get supplies and meet once again with Pep Glauser or his pilot.

The pilot was waiting for them, alone at the dock, to take back their samples. He seemed pleased with the pitchblende samples, and he told them that he would return in the early autumn when the pitchblende and the other ore had been assayed.

"This might not be silver, you know."

They nodded.

"It might be zinc or lead or nickel. Or something else. But Krahn also wants gold from you guys, so keep your eyes peeled."

Joe's heart sank, and he wondered if he'd heard the pilot correctly.

"Krahn? You mean Buster Krahn?"

The pilot nodded.

"I thought you worked for Pep Glauser."

"Pep, he sold out to Krahn around last Christmas. Buster wants to concentrate up here at Great Bear."

"Then you, Isidore, and me, we're all working for Buster Krahn."

"You got it, buddy. Your free-lancing days are over."

"Jesus."

Working for Buster Krahn meant what? Legal enslavement? No more weekend prospecting on their own? Glauser had given Joe and Isidore that option. But with Buster Krahn's outfit, things were different. The prospectors down in Yellowknife had all claimed that the man owned your soul.

ALL THROUGH THE SUMMER when the flies and mosquitoes were at their worst, the two men prospected for gold. They found some sizeable veins of white and blue quartz but no visible gold. They decided to return to their original campsite, where the silver deposits and the pitchblende were, and they set up around the old campfire. On top of the ridge above the campsite, walking up and down the peninsula was easy.

One day in early August when the wind was blowing off the rocks and the mosquitoes and flies had at last left the men alone, Isidore came running. He had found some traces of surface gold in a patch of blue quartz. They scraped away moss from the rocks, scrubbed the lichen with sodium hydroxide and took their hammers to Isidore's find. Very soon they uncovered a narrow vein of gold in the quartz that seemed to widen and flow down into the dark weathered basalt that surrounded the quartz.

Taking turns with a pry bar, they hand-steeled a little trench for blasting. When they could pry no more, Isidore laid a charge one foot into the bedrock, and Joe stumbled down the slope and squatted in the trees. He hated dynamite. He didn't trust it, and he didn't trust Isidore with it, especially if the charges looked as old and greasy as these did.

Isidore loved dynamite, new or old. He blew a hole in their trench and they returned to a modest new pit that went more than three feet down. And the fun began. Joe found his way to some scrap gold and Isidore hammered out several chunks of blue quartz flecked through with it.

"You gonna keep summa dat, Joe?"

"Souvenir," said Joe. "Find yourself some nice bits."

"Hoo boy."

Some of the rock was rotten, which was a good sign. They pawed through the rubble and took their hammers to the walls of the pit and gathered a pile of samples. In a couple of days' hard work they had managed to enlarge the pit by chopping and digging it out. This work yielded several more bags of sample rock and a few pea-sized nuggets for each of them to squirrel away.

Joe was grinning at their take by the campfire, examining a handful of small fragments of gold. It never looked ordinary. It never looked anything but beautiful.

"Isidore, should we be doing this?"

"Joe, if you feelin bad, you can gimme your nuggets, ah? No trouble wit dat. Gotta raise my famly, me."

"I've got a family too," he said. "Back in England. Haven't sent them any money since I left Fitzgerald. But if we come down from here laden with gold, I'll send them a nice fat cheque."

In the spirit of fair play, they decided to relinquish a number of the small gold fragments for the sample bags. The larger fragments they kept for themselves.

They broke camp and paddled sixty miles back to the cabin, laden with eleven bags of ore. Joe spent his days grinding up rocks with his mortar and pestle and panning out the gold from the ground-up gravel. They knew the plane was coming and they wanted to be ready.

When the Pacemaker returned, they paddled down to the village with the sample bags and some gold dust, and there to greet them at the main dock, smiling like a bull walrus through a newly sprouted moustache, was Buster Krahn. They reported their gold find to Krahn, first Joe and then Isidore, and Krahn peered at them the way a sapper looks for booby traps.

"A lotta colour or just bits an pieces? Hey, Isidore? How wide is that vein at its widest? Two, three inches? If I paddled up the lake to your claim, is that what I'd find?"

"Yup."

"You lyin sons a bitches," he said. He was smiling at Joe. "You mean I'd find a claim like the one you flogged off on me? Not enough gold to fill a Mosquito's arsehole?"

Joe smiled back at him. "I'll bet you sold that claim. I'll bet you used the gold from my poke to sell it."

"Bullshit."

"Come on, Beezer."

"Buster."

"Are you telling me you haven't sold the Boulder Creek claim yet? I'll find out when I get down there."

Krahn turned to Isidore with a grin and an admonitory index finger. "Ain't he the touchy one, Injun? Joe tends to forget who he's workin for."

No one said a word.

"Anyway, your pitchblende turned out okay. Pitchblende is still a hot commodity down south these days. If you guys could stake that out before the snow flies, I think I could sell that claim."

Krahn's appearance was an ongoing source of fascination for Joe. He kept noticing the man's physical presence. He had a bald lump of a head that reminded Joe of a huge peeled potato, about as white and rounded as one and just about as expressive. He had a big slab of a body. When you put the slab and the potato together it stood about five foot ten and weighed in well over two hundred pounds. Even with the new moustache, he didn't *look* like a walrus, but every time Joe turned his eyes away from Krahn, he retained the aspect of one.

"You stake out that silver too, okay? Showed not bad. Not bad. Might sell that too."

Isidore nodded and allowed his eyes to crinkle agreeably.

"And stake this gold as far as it stretches, then cover your tracks, fill up that little trench. No fuggen traces, you hear?"

Joe said, "We might have to hurry."

"You got that right, pal."

"You want this before the winter sets in?"

"You bet." Krahn raised a fat fist and pounded the air as though he held a hammer. "Everything staked and ready by October one. We'll pick you up and we'll all fly home."

"By October the first?" Joe said.

Krahn flashed his long incisors and his creamed corn breath drifted past their noses. "And remember, Limey. Everything you stake is the property of the syndicate." He sidled up to Joe, smiling playfully, smiling balefully. Joe could not tell which.

"I'm not absolutely sure we can –"

"Joseph, you wanna get paid, don't you? Wanna get flown back home, don't you?"

Krahn took out his lens and pawed through a bag of samples with his pilot. He held their bagged-up gold dust in his pudgy hand, as though to weigh it. Isidore and Joe were silent, and Joe was glad that they had both pocketed some of the more sumptuous gold fragments. At this moment his latest gleanings were in the poke in his right pants pocket. It was getting reassuringly heavy. By now it would run to about three ounces.

"I like your rocks, boys. I gotta feelin about them. By the time our plane gets back up here, I'll have this shit assayed and we can all go home. You think we got a mine here, Joseph?"

Joe shrugged. "We might."

Joe went off to sit on a log and take in the sun. There were more than a dozen men on the pier.

Krahn hauled some bags down to his pilot and they began to load them into the Pacemaker. Joe decided not to volunteer to help him. It was too nice a day.

Isidore had meandered down the pier in the other direction, his bent-over long-legged frame still recognizable from two hundred yards. He was in conversation with one of the fly-ins. Joe gazed back in the direction of Krahn and his pilot. A peeled potato on a side of beef. The man talked too much. He smiled too much and he seethed with rancour. Rancour and creamed corn. If Joe ever knocked the man down he would hit the ground with a big yellow squelch.

By the time the sun began to head for the horizon, the planes had flown out and the pier was deserted.

"Who was that?"

"Dat guy."

"What guy?"

"Dat Scotch guy I tol you about."

"What Scottish guy?"

"Guy wore a blanket, ah? He tol me where da gold was at, him."

They sat on the bench gazing at the beginnings of a sunset. Already the air had lost some of its warmth. Soon they would have to paddle back upstream to their cabin.

"Wish I could have talked to him. Does he have a name?"

"Me, I doan member it. He's a guy like you, Joe. Everbody knows dat guy."

"You don't mean mean Tom Payne, do you?"

"Yup."

"That was Tom Payne?"

"Dat's da guy."

"You said he was Scottish. I distinctly remember you saying the fellow was Scottish."

"Yup."

"But he's English, you ninny."

"Yup. Seen im wear a blanket wid a hole in da neck. Keep warm dat way."

Isidore gave Joe his bemused look. He released a soft belch into the waning light and began to roll a smoke.

"We need to get paddlin up da river, Joe."

He wanted to ream out his friend, and talk about the vast differences between the Scots and the English, but the absence of mosquitoes, and the absence of Buster Krahn, and the late August sun had felt so good, he was too content for recriminations.

In early September Isidore and Joe packed up their canoe for the sixty-mile trip east. The wind blew cold from the west as they paddled away from Déline, but it was at their backs and they made good headway for two days. As long as they kept moving they didn't feel the cold. They put up the tent in the woods at their old campsite at the foot of the peninsula. This time they had brought a large canister that Isidore fashioned into a heating stove for their tent.

They could choose from plenty of trees to use as stakes. The sun was out each morning after breakfast, the wind was down, so all the signs were positive. There was no evidence that other prospectors had been there, and even the reconnaissance planes that flew over the great lake from time to time had stopped buzzing up and down the shores. The two men worked fast, anchoring their posts and recording locations, the pitchblende find first, the silver ore second, the gold pit last of all.

"Did you hear what that bastard said last week?"

"Nope."

"He said, *if we wanted to get paid.* He said, *if we wanted a flight home.* We have to do all this bloody work and we can't even post our own claims."

"Dat Buster. Yup."

"I'd rather work for bloody Glauser. At least he doesn't talk too much. Isidore, does nothing ever bother you?"

Isidore smiled. "Dey womans, dey like to bodder me."

By the end of the third day they had finished staking the first two claims, and that left their basalt pit with the blue quartz. The sun had vanished behind a drift of light grey clouds, and as the temperature dropped, the two men piled on the clothes. They climbed up to the top of the peninsula where the land flattened out all around them.

"We got frens up here, Joe."

"You mean skunks, Isidore? Beavers? Remember, we don't eat varmints."

Isidore was pointing towards their blasted-out trench. A few feet from the trench was an impressive pile of bear dung, filled with seeds, berries, some unidentifiable hair, and dark green vegetable matter. Farther away was another bear dump but Isidore was focused on the nearest one.

"Putty fress, dat."

"Pretty damn big too."

They'd brought their equipment but they had left the rifles down at the campsite. Isidore volunteered to get the rifles and Joe began to chop and dig at the edges of their pit. It did not take him long to come to the end of the quartz; it had simply played out at a depth of less than five feet. The vein they had been pursuing had widened, narrowed, and then given out. There was nothing more.

"Good news," cried Joe with a big smile.

Isidore was propping up the rifles on a fallen tree stump.

"Howcome?"

"We can stake the claim right here and forget about extending it. There's no more quartz, there's no bloody mine here. The gold was all near the surface. We can pack our bags."

"Tomorrow, paddle for home, ah?"

"Let's finish up."

All through the waning afternoon of the fourth day they chopped down small trees, crowbarred holes in the basalt, measured off their distances, and drove in their newly fashioned stakes. Because they were up on a flat area, pacing off the steps went easily. While there was still enough light, Joe lowered himself into the pit and inspected the quartz one last time.

Isidore had gone for a piss in the bushes and now he was mumbling something, likely in Cree and likely to himself, the way he sometimes mumbled in his sleep. *Macik'* he announced, like a preacher. In the gathering gloom of the afternoon there was enough light to see tiny traces of gold in the quartz, but there was precious little. And this would be Krahn's problem, not theirs.

Something about the sound of Isidore's voice made Joe look up from the pit. Isidore had tucked himself in and he was slowly retrieving his rifle, staring off at some bushes, and no longer muttering, but calling.

"Naha. Maskwa okimaw, iyako ci?"

Joe sat half-in and half-out of the pit. He pushed himself to his feet and climbed out. The hair on his head and all down the back of his neck began to bristle. Scarcely twenty yards from where Isidore was standing, a large brown bear had emerged from the trees. Isidore dangled his rifle by the end of the barrel.

"Tanwisi etwiyan anohc ka-kisikak?"

The bear lumbered slowly forward, the hair on its big hump rising, and it pawed the ground with both forelegs. It was a nicely fattened animal, two shades of brown, a young grizzly in no mood to trifle with men. Joe scanned the work site to see where Isidore had left the other rifle. He might have to finish this business himself but he couldn't see his rifle.

"Ikyiohkiyan oma tipiyahk. Ikiya sikisi, Maskwa okimaw."

Isidore continued his apostrophe to the bear, his voice soft but audible. The great muscles around the bear's neck and shoulders seemed to ripple forward, it moved closer, and still Isidore did not raise his rifle. At last Joe spotted his weapon ten feet away, leaning on a fallen log. Isidore raised his own rifle slowly, and instead of pointing the weapon at the bear, he merely cradled it in his arms.

"Kikiskeyimitin," Isidore whispered, more than once.

His voice continued at length, as though he were laying down a legal argument to an invisible jury, and the bear paused, then gathered and tensed its limbs, hesitated, swaying head and neck left and right, and at last it emitted a high whine.

"Kikiskeyimitin."

The bear turned and padded away into the woods, stopped abruptly to look back, and plunged down the hill on the far side of the peninsula. Perhaps the animal would stay on that side and away from their tent. Joe was too rattled to think much about the alternative.

"Boss Bear," said Isidore with a smile, "he wants to have a sleep, him. Maybe sleep in dat pit we got."

"Why didn't you shoot him? He might come back tonight."

Isidore shrugged. He sported a far-off grin on his old face.

"What did you tell him?"

"I tell him, da closer he get da better I can soot. Me, I tell him who's da boss. I say doan come roun our tent tonight, ah. Get yourself shot in da bee-hine."

They set their rifles leaning on the log and began cleaning up the site. Drops of rain started to fall and by the time the work was done, the raindrops had turned into stinging pellets of ice and snow. They hiked and slid down to the campsite, built a big fire, and Isidore warmed up a pot of stew and suspended it over the coals from his tripod. They gobbled down bowl after bowl and retired to their tent for a long night's rest. They brought their rifles inside, which allowed Joe to relax on the subject of their resident grizzly.

In the morning the sky had partially cleared and the wind had fallen to a steady breeze and shifted to the northeast. For their first day of paddling home, the wind would be angling from the right into their backs. Isidore and Joe broke camp in record time and packed the canoe. Joe got in and Isidore took the stern.

"Joe," he said, "let's go like hell, ah?"

Joe and Isidore paddled like hell.

They did not stop for lunch. A wooly range of clouds had rolled up and the wind descended on them in the early afternoon. The waves whipped up into whitecaps, and then bigger whitecaps that glided past them, splashing icy water into their canoe. At last the snow arrived and descended on them.

Joe spotted a small inlet by a shallow stream and they headed for shore. They pulled the boat into the stream and dragged it up to their campsite. In a screaming wind, Joe unraveled their tent, and, as the snow intensified all around them, Isidore ran for the canoe. He overturned it and stowed the paddles and bags underneath as the flurries exploded all around them. Joe could scarcely see his friend. Seconds later he couldn't see Isidore at all.

"Over here, Joe! Over here!"

He had never heard Isidore's voice at such a demanding pitch.

"Bring da tent, Joe!"

He dragged the big unraveled tent in the direction of Isidore's voice. The wind knifed through Joe's coat and the snow pelted them with renewed fury. Joe stumbled at Isidore's feet and Isidore ordered him to squat beneath the legs of his tripod. He had drawn up the metal legs to their fullest extent, flattened and widened their reach.

And then it dawned on Joe what Isidore was doing. He handed Isidore a corner of the tent.

"Hang on, Joe. Doan let go!"

As Joe crouched on the ground inside the three legs of the tripod, Isidore wrapped the great tent, top to bottom, then crept in under the canvas, dragging something behind him. It was a bedroll. He spread it out on the ground, canvas wrapper down, soogans on top. Joe's ears were freezing and filled with the roar of the wind and the driving snow. When his eyes had adjusted to the dark of their tiny tipi, he located Isidore's face less than a foot in front of his own. He was hunched over, his arms crossed like a sculpture of himself, his hands tucked into his armpits and his eyes closed against the storm. Joe adjusted his body to match Isidore in every aspect, and he too closed his eyes against the storm. Without cease, the wind shrieked with demented fury.

"Isidore?"

"Yuh."

"What if it gets colder tonight?"

"No fire tonight, Joe."

"But what if it gets colder."

"You ever pray, Joe?"

"I'm not a believer, Isidore."

"Den you got to preten, Joe."

"Pretend."

"You got to preten you believe on some ting."

And later, when night had fallen and the wind was still howling around them, and both men were dozing from a sitting position, Joe recalled something.

"Isidore, remember when you and your guy were talking? Tom Payne? It was just before he flew back south."

"Yuh."

"What did he tell you?"

"He tell me where ta go for da gold. He say go fudder sout. He say roun Slave Lake, ah?"

"Further south?"

"Yuh."

The wind rose and fell, shrieked and whispered, singing mortality, hurling down Wiccan lullabies and fierce judgements in a tremolo too old for human speech. How could you pray to something like that? Joe found a big towel from inside the bedroll and he wrapped it around his shoulders and shivered.

"Me, I doan belong up here, Joe. Too far nort. Not a frennly place for me, Joe."

"Neither do I belong here, my friend. When that plane comes back, I'll be happy to go."

"What plane?"

"Krahn's plane."

Isidore did not reply and they sat there as the snow banked up outside the tripod. Bit by bit the snow gathered higher around the canvas, forming an outer crust, and it seemed to insulate their bodies from the wind. At last Joe stopped shivering.

"Forget about dat plane, Joe. It's a whadayou call. It's a sitsuasun now, ah?"

"What?"

"It's a type a sitsuasun, Joe. Can't fly da pontoons up here. Not now."

"Why not?"

"Because. Might freeze like hell, Joe. Dey got liddle bit ice on da lake. You'll see putty soon. Can't fly da skis up here."

"Why not?"

"Because same ting. Dey got liddle bit ice on da lake."

The men dozed and the wind tapered off to a whisper, and before too long they were awake again.

"But after that, Isidore. After."

"Might not come, Joe. Dat Buster, he doan have to. He can come nex spring if he want to."

"Isidore, why do you talk to me in English and talk to the bear in Cree?"

He looked at Joe for a moment. "Joe, you speak da ingliss."

"I know I speak English, but Isidore, listen. Why do you speak Cree to the bear?"

"Joe, you a smart guy, ah? You bin aroun?"

"Yes."

"How many time you hear a bear who knows da ingliss, ah?"

Joe erupted in laughter. He could not make out his friend's features in the dark, so close to his face, but he guessed that Isidore would be giving him his bemused look.

Chapter 6

The Rock

By Joe's reckoning, Krahn's plane was seven months late, and when he mentioned this to the pilot, shouted it, actually, there were excuses but no apologies. At their request, the man flew Joe and Isidore south to Great Slave Lake, and when they landed in Yellowknife Bay, he paid them their wages.

During that same week, Joe felt himself awakening, like a creature from hibernation, to a sense of new possibilities. At first he thought this awakening might just be his response to the warmer weather, or the magnificent views from the unnamed hills around Yellowknife Bay. But Isidore too seemed to be showing new energy, revived curiosity. They liked what they saw. The two men lived in their wall tent, bought for them courtesy of Pep Glauser's outfit. Joe bought a large Indian canoe from a Dene hunter, and through the spring and summer of 1935, Joe and Isidore managed several excursions down the long North Arm of Great Slave Lake. They explored the bays and inlets, the small islands and outcrops. They learned to avoid the vast formations of granite and favoured the dark fields of greenstone. The quartz looked enticing. The oxidized patches of minerals looked enticing. The fault zones looked enticing. The gold was just around the corner in some volcanic crevasse or other. Or it was lying beneath the igneous formations further inland. Or it was buried right there, or there, just below that gossan patch. The gold seemed to whisper to Joe in his sleep. He found himself entangled some nights in an interminable reverie of pursuit. Each day, further and further along the North Arm, he and Isidore paddled near the shore and gazed obsessively at the rock formations. The summer passed quickly for them, and the men turned their thoughts to wintering.

Prospectors referred to Yellowknife as The Rock. By the spring of 1935 there were still almost no buildings in Yellowknife. It scarcely existed as a settlement, except in the warmer months. Almost the only cabins Joe encountered were in the Dogrib village of Detah, which lay on a point a few miles south of Yellowknife. Joe and Isidore threw up another small shack, not quite as small as their quarters near Great Bear Lake, but on the same model. Other prospectors lived in tents and left in the fall. Joe and Isidore's little shack was a nice exception to the rule. They wintered in Yellowknife because they wanted to try things out. They wanted to be ahead of the competition from the syndicates that could afford to buy or rent bush planes. By the summer of 1935 they had found a few small veins of gold, and they decided to stay. Thus began a three-year stretch of hard work, rising expectations, and the sort of wilderness adventure Joe might have dreamed of as a boy in Castleford.

Yellowknife certainly had its down side. Buster Krahn had decided to stay there. He had formed a company now, Hanna Prospects, and he went public with the three claims that Joe and Isidore had staked at Great Bear in 1934. They held little promise for commercial mines, but mineral fever, and gold fever in particular, were running high in the North. Krahn registered the three claims and had them sold by summer. Selling stocks for rocks, Joe called it.

Joe and Isidore passed the summer prospecting up and down the North Arm of Great Slave Lake, returning each month to Yellowknife for supplies. Because they were unsyndicated, with no one to grubstake them, they had to pay for their supplies themselves. If they found some interesting mineral deposits, they would stake and sell the claims. If they managed to pry or blast some gold from the rock, they would gather what they could and sell it back in Yellowknife. And there was always Joe's savings to fall back on if their prospecting drew a blank. It felt good to be unsyndicated at last, but it also felt precarious for both of them.

In a cautiously hopeful way Joe and Isidore embraced the climate and the growing settlement. The differences in the weather between Great Bear and Great Slave Lake were subtle but discernible. Their first two winters in Yellowknife were numbingly cold, but Great Slave Lake was farther south and had more sun, and its stunted trees were more profuse and offered better logs for their new cabin. The Canadian Geological Survey began in earnest, and Yellowknife began to pop out of the granite and greenstone like a scattering of mushrooms. By the spring of 1937, it had swarmed into a ramshackle clutter of canvas tents, wall tents, tarpaper shacks, countless privies, and a few cabins, all built on a rock surrounded on three sides by the lake.

Living right in Yellowknife had unexpected advantages for Joe and Isidore, because now everything was a short walk or a short paddle away. A man could jump into his canoe and buy a jar of home brew from Pete Racine on Jolliffe Island. He could open up an account at the Bank of Commerce, which was located in a tent just up from Chummy Plummer's pool hall. There was a primitive mail service, which allowed Joe to send letters and money to his family in Britain. He could pay for a bath and a shave now and then, buy a hot meal at the Wildcat Café. At times he was tempted to pay for the company of a woman. Except, of course, his money would go straight to Buster Krahn. That was the reason many a prospector, like Joe, avoided Buster's new hop-house.

Yellowknife was rough, lusty and loud, and to Joe, life in the midst of this unholy rabble was surprisingly tolerable. For the most part, the prospectors got along; they were all more or less hard up for cash and following the same carrot in front of their noses. Drinking home brew at the crude hotel on Latham Island was nothing at all like having a pint in the Blackberry. To his great surprise, Joe discovered that he preferred the drinking life in his new home.

The biggest surprise for Joe, however, was the arrival of Stinky Riley in the spring of 1937. He bought a cabin on Jolliffe Island, where he anchored his new plane, an aging all-metal Junkers two-seater. He did not yet own the plane, but his customers paid him handsomely to fly them all over the back country beyond Slave Lake. He preferred not to speak of himself as a wrangler or an aspiring rancher; he was now a bush pilot, and he scarcely ever missed out on a chance to publicize the fact. In his first few months in Yellowknife, the re-invented Riley acquired a good reputation as a northern flyer. He did mail deliveries, medical flights, he sometimes flew investors up from Edmonton and back again, and he partnered in a couple of decent finds northwest of Yellowknife.

Joe and Isidore had also acquired a solid reputation among the prospectors, and whenever they could, they freely shared and gathered information on finds and on rumours of promising territory. Joe and Isidore moved their wall tent into the shadow of Hearne Hill and went everywhere with their ears open for prospects around the northwestern shores of Great Slave Lake. By the spring of 1938, they had a bit of money in the bank, they were slightly more than paying the bills, and they would never again allow themselves to become part of a syndicate.

On a bright morning in late May of 1938, Joe and Isidore were coming from Weave and Devore's emporium with two big wooden wheelbarrows full of supplies. Joe was forming an argument for Isidore on the subject of bringing his beloved utensil. There simply was no room for a christly big tripod. They had enough supplies to sink their canoe, enough to last them six or seven weeks. His list of his supplies had been filled.

48 lbs flour
20 lbs sugar
8 lbs dried milk powder
2 lbs salt

10 lbs butter
5 lbs lard
3 lbs tea
5 lbs coffee
4 dozen eggs
1 side bacon
25 assorted meats (small cans)
5 lbs macaroni
5 lbs cheese
1 dozen Oxo cubes
10 lbs dried fruits
2 cartons wooden matches
50 lbs potatoes
20 tins assorted veg
4 lbs baking powder
2 lbs powdered egg
12 lbs jam, syrup, honey
2 small cans pickles
5 lbs fresh veg
3 boxes corn flakes
4 lbs Sunnyboy cereal
5 lbs white beans
5 lbs rice
6 packages Jello

JUST AS JOE AND ISIDORE were wheeling these supplies up to their canoe, a photographer from God knows what city walked by, stopped, and scrutinized them. She was tall and striking. Fashionable, that was the word. She was wearing...not riding breeks, exactly, but men's trousers. No no, they looked too fetching to be men's trousers. She was tall and beautiful and wearing trousers, and by her side was a small citified young man assisting her. As the two strangers approached, Joe glanced at Isidore, whose mouth was open.

"Say there," the woman cried out in a jaunty voice, "we would like to take your picksha. Would you boys be okay wit dat?"

They both nodded, as speechless men tend to do.

The young assistant asked Joe and Isidore if they would pose by the loading dock. He showed the men a card that proclaimed they were from *Life* Magazine. It felt like an interruption to Joe, but a welcome interruption, a reminder that there was a world of wonders south of Yellowknife. The woman's lipstick was as brazenly red as anything he had seen at Auntie Vi's soirées. And right there, in plain sight, she flicked her tongue over her lips, and her tongue was a sizzling dark pink. Jesus have mercy.

Isidore was not quite as smitten as Joe, perhaps, but he was all curiosity. He'd never heard of *Life* Magazine, but he couldn't get enough of the two cameras wielded by this fashionable lady and her assistant.

When the lady was ready, Joe played it to the hilt. Northern Joe and his native companion. Eyes on the northern horizon. Eyes on the conquest and all that. Eyes on the photographer and her sleek, sensual, citified looks. Her manner of flinging her hair back over her shoulders in mock irritation. Northern Joe was swollen with expectation. Ahem. Manly smile, touch of arrogance. Snap. Loading the canoe with a practiced and easy confidence. Snap. Isidore with his boot on top of the wheelbarrow. Snap. Long grey hair, silver moustache, wide-brimmed hat, beaded belt. Snap. Old as the hills was Isidore, but always the handsome devil. Snap.

Joe Burbidge with his jacket open and his arms stretched back along the railing, easy smile. Snap. One more for the road. Give her the old Ronald Coleman, give her a flare of the old nostrils. Snap.

"What's *Life* doing away up here?" Joe asked the lady.

She was writing down their names.

"You'd be surprised how many reports we get about Yellowknife," she said. "A gold rush, right? All these planes buzzing around? This brand new settlement? This place is news,

Mr. Burbidge."

"Miss," said Joe, "you are a sight for sore eyes."

"You flatta me," she said with a smile. "You're a fine hunk y'self, Mr. Burbidge. You and your friend there. Isidore? Did I get that right? This camera? It adores you two guys."

"What's your name?" said Joe.

"What's my name? Say, Charlie, when's the last time you saw a city gal?"

"Good question."

"Not many da womens up here to live," said Isidore. "Mebbe dat's gonna change, ah?"

The photographer gave Isidore a warm smile. He would appear to be her favourite of the two.

"The one person we haven't managed to run down yet is Tom Payne," said the assistant. "Do you know him?"

Joe groaned. "He's the sort of chap who shows up at a gathering. You don't actually see him, but you talk to people who claim they saw him, or claim they saw someone leave the Wildcat Café who looked like Tom Payne."

"Have you actually met the fella?" said the woman.

"I have. And if he's in town right now, you might find him at Chummy Plumber's. They say that's the first place to look."

"The gent with the pool hall?"

"That's the one. And if you see the blighter, tell him that Joe Burbidge wants to speak with him."

Two years earlier Tom Payne had made a big find near the settlement by re-staking a claim hours after it had expired. It was all the town would talk about, a rags to riches story complete with heroes and villains. The syndicates sought in vain for news of his whereabouts, and every down-and-out prospector talked about Tom as though he was their best friend, or as though he lived two tents down from their camp. There were times when Joe felt he wanted to *be* Tom Payne.

"Have you interviewed Vicky Lepine yet?" said Joe to the lady.

She wouldn't meet his glance; she was fiddling with her equipment.

"Who's she when she's at home?"

"Vicky is the first female prospector in Yellowknife."

"You know," said the lady, handing her camera to her assistant, "I think I've got her on the list. Vicky Lepine. Yeah."

On and on Joe bantered with her. Her name was Miriam Goldman (*the* Miriam Goldman, the celebrated photographer). Joe would never see her again. She was more elusive than Tom Payne. The prospectors she photographed in Yellowknife all adored her, and many claimed that she had favoured them most of all. Among her many charms, Joe mused, was her last name.

All through July of 1938, as they prospected on an unnamed island south of Detah, they drew Miriam Goldman into their conversations. They named their site Goldman Island, and the flirtatious and chatty spirit of Miriam Goldman approved of the name. At last they abandoned their island, paddled back to Yellowknife, and Miriam's visiting spirit drifted south, along with her body, to New York City.

Happily, Miriam Goldman wasn't the only unattached female in town. Along with some ladies of the night, not all of them working in Buster's hop-house, there were waitresses, nurses, water taxi women, a female lawyer, a couple of school teachers.

One night, drinking in the Wildcat with Joe, Isidore had turned uncharacteristically gloomy. He had received a letter from Loney that hinted at some bad news. Joe could never quite pin down Isidore's relationship with his wife. He assumed that they had separated when he and his son Charlie headed north on the cattle drive with Stinky. Whether their parting was official or temporary or permanent, Joe couldn't tell. Sometimes Isidore referred to Loney as if he were still married to her. Isidore was always either tight-lipped or jocular about his private life, and particularly evasive about his feelings for Loney.

"I tink I gotta go home, Joe."

"I thought this was your home, Isidore."

"Here?" he said, and gave Joe his bemused look, which always seemed to speak volumes and communicate nothing.

"You have problems back south, Isidore?"

"I tink I gotta go see Loney, me."

"But Isidore, we haven't made our fortune yet. And I need a good partner."

"You make a fortune, Joe. Maybe you gotta fine a woman too, Joe. Me, I gotta go home. Maybe talk to Charlie. See Loney, talk to Charlie."

Old Master Herron used to tell his students about the oracle Proteus. If you wanted a prophecy from him, you had to track him down, and when you tracked him down, he would change shapes and disappear on you. Sometimes talking with Isidore was like wringing the truth out of Proteus. Isidore took the next barge out of Yellowknife and left Joe at loose ends, alone in his cabin.

ONE AFTERNOON, during an irresolute stretch, sitting around the camp, Joe conceived a resolve to spruce up his life. He decided that it was time to treat himself to a little holiday. A good sleep in a real bed, and a chance to clean himself up. This meant a visit to the Ingraham Hotel, where he could have a meal, a shave and a haircut, and a good scrubbing. Joe had no energy for prospecting, no appetite for going through the rigours by himself, no desire to find a new partner. He considered Isidore irreplaceable. So off he went, with money in his pocket, to the newly appointed Ingraham. After a good night's sleep, perhaps he could paddle over to Jolliffe and have a jar or two with Stinky.

He registered in the hotel lobby and took a small room for two nights. His first real bath in ages felt very much to his liking. He visited a barber shop next to the lobby, and he watched as his hair and whiskers piled up on the floor. He took a walk down to Weave and Devore's emporium and bought a new shirt and a decent pair of trousers, some socks and underwear, and a pair of oxfords. He returned to his hotel room and stared at Joe Burbidge in the mirror. He looked quite fit, but the sun and wind and the sheer labour of prospecting, living in a shack, and camping all over the North, had taken their toll on him. His complexion had acquired a bushy glow, a ruddiness that made him look considerably older than his twenty-six years.

Joe returned to the lobby to seek out the chap who had registered him on the previous day. He wanted to pay his bill in advance because he feared that, in his current irresolute state, he might forget to pay. He stepped behind the registration booth to look for a pencil and some paper so that he might write a note to the fellow. He was just finishing his note when someone walked up to the desk.

She said, "I'm just off the barge and I need some help with my boxes."

Joe looked up and saw her for the first time. He said, "I'll be right with you."

"What's your name," she said.

"Joe Burbidge."

"Joe what?"

"Burbidge. What's your name?"

"I'm Lucy."

Lucy Castaway. Force of nature. School marm with a degree, newly arrived from somewhere else in the North. A vision with a troubled smile. Nobody's fool.

WHEN SHE WAS eleven years old Lucy Castaway had been carried off to a residential school. The year before, her mother and father had managed to protect her by hiding her in the gutting shed, underneath an upturned galvanized tub. They had also hidden Lucille's older brother and told the government man that he had died of the cholera. They pointed to a gravesite where they had recently buried their Kokum and told the man it was Lucille's brother who was buried there, so the government man went away. But the following summer the man from the government came again for Lucille, and he found her hiding out in the gutting shed and took her away. She had grown too tall for the tub to cover her entirely.

Her parents could read and write in a rudimentary fashion, and they wanted Lucille to get an education, but they could not stand the thought of losing her to the school, so they grieved at her departure.

Lucy knew a bit of English, and she was a good learner, but she hated one of the nuns who patrolled her corridor at night. Sister St. David was lame in one leg and carried a cane, which she used freely on the girls when her temper got the best of her. Every night after prayers she would stand outside the washroom holding a bowl of salt for the girls to clean their teeth with, but there was never any salt on the table for meals. And Lucy hated the old prinicpal, who hired some of the older girls to clean his rooms and then tried to jump them. Also he wouldn't let her talk to anyone unless she spoke English, and she didn't feel like speaking English. It was a stupid language.

One of the nuns befriended her and tried to protect her and some of the other girls too. She taught Lucy to read Bible stories, and she taught her some songs in English about Jesus, and how to skate on the frozen lake, how to crochet and skip rope. But by the time Lucy had entered her teens, that sister had been sent away and they never saw her again.

One November night, when Lucy was fifteen, the prinicpal chose her to clean his rooms. She decided that rather than fall into this trap, she would run away and go home to her parents in Fort Smith. Other kids had tried to run away, but the school was on a large island in the middle of a lake, a lake so big that when you looked south to where the road was supposed to be, you couldn't even see the far shore. Usually at this time of the year, if a kid was to try to run for it, they could easily be spotted or tracked down in the snow. However, this year the ice had formed on the lake before the snow had come. You could skate on the ice near shore and see the fish swimming below.

When everyone was asleep, Lucy snuck into the kitchen and grabbed some food and a bottle of milk and put it in a pillow case. She went to the laundry room and stole some socks, a pair of long johns and two nuns' habits, because it was cold outside and all she had for the winter was her mitts, a thin jacket and a sweater with holes in the elbows. She stole a pair of skates belonging to one of the nuns, a pair that wasn't too big for her feet. The moon was out as she skated straight for another island that lay several miles south of the school. Before the sun rose she had reached this island and was resting in the bushes. When she had stopped puffing, she ate some bread and cheese and drank from her bottle of milk. The sun was up. She looked to the south and saw another island. It might have been ten miles away, maybe even more.

"You must have been bloody cold," Joe said.

"Nah," she said. "It was day. I was heated up from the skating."

She went back to her story, back to the island on the vast frozen lake. She finished her snack and skated for the second island. It started to snow and the wind came up and her outer habit flapped like the wings of a crow. She could see well enough to go in the right direction, and she got to the second island and ate some more bread and cheese and rested on a log until she wasn't panting any more. The snow stopped falling. Off to the south, or maybe the southwest, she could see another island, bigger than the first two but even farther away. By now everyone would know she was missing. They might take the truck over the ice road and start to look for her. They might send messages to the Mounties, but there would be no footprints in the snow, so where would they start to look?

She was too tired to go on, so she decided to stay overnight on the second island. There was an old boat lying upside-down on the rocks and a pile of old fishing nets, and as the sky faded she made a place for herself, stuffing the dry nets underneath the boat. She crawled in and tried to fall asleep. It was too cold to take off her skates so she left them on. It was a bad night for sleeping. It was better than making beds in the principal's room, and maybe fending him off with a kitchen knife, but it was a bad night for sleeping.

In the morning she was nearly paralyzed from the cold. She roused herself, had a snack and a small drink of milk. She'd slept with the food in the pillow case next to her body but the milk was still partly frozen. Her feet were numb and blistered and she had the beginnings of a cold, so her progress over the snowy ice towards the distant island was slow. The sun came up, she began to feel her body return to life, and she felt a surge of desperate energy. By the time the sun had returned to the horizon, she had made it to the third island. She was exhausted, coughing and sweating, and she thought she was going to die.

She skated right up to the shore and collapsed by a fallen tree. Her legs did not seem to work right any more. It grew darker and she ate the rest of her food and drank the last of the milk. The wind made her shiver. She got scared and thought she heard a wolf howling. Then more howling somewhere off in the night.

"My God, you must have been frightened."

"I guess so. And cold, eh? I couldn't feel one of my feet."

She was sure that this was it for her, that she would die alone on this cold island. She managed to stand up and stagger on her skates into the trees to escape the wind. Just over a small rise in the centre of the island she spotted something square that looked like a huge rock. She skittered towards it guessing correctly that it was in fact a small cabin. She lurched all around it and peeked into a window but there were no footprints outside and no sign of anyone inside. She picked up a big rock to smash the window, but decided to try the door first. She limped over to the entrance, turned the knob, and the door opened, just like that. She clattered inside, and in the last faint light to fall through the window, she spotted a box of matches. She lit a match and looked around, lit a second match, and spotted an old green candle about the length of her hand. She lit the candle, scuttled over to the door and closed it. And then she sat on a small cot and took off her skates.

"Was there a wood stove?" asked Joe. "Was there any food?"

She nodded. "Some rice I boiled up. Maybe half a box of soda crackers. And some raisins. I only stayed there that one night and part of the next morning."

"Why? You were safe and warm there, weren't you?"

"I was scared somebody would see smoke coming from the stack. I grabbed some stuff and put it in a knapsack the next morning and I took off. I could see the shore. A long way off. I just skated until I hit the shore. I was so afraid they would catch me that I forgot to be afraid of the real danger, eh? But I had the cabin guy's rubber boots in the knapsack, so I just pulled off the skates and pulled on the boots. I left the skates right there on the shore. I always wondered if someone would find them. A pair of ladies' skates, eh? Where the heck did these come from?"

Joe chuckled where he lay. She shifted in the bed and raised up her leg to admire it. He could see the outline of her leg against the moonlight that came in through the window. She was vain that way. It was her left leg, with the foot that had only four toes. If he was Shakespeare he could write a sonnet about that leg.

"Keep going. How'd you get from there to…"

"Oh, Mr. Burbidge, you ask a lot of questions."

She brought up her other leg and did some slow kicks and flexed her ankles.

"I couldn't find nothing. No road. But I found a path and it led to a bigger path. You know, the bigger path lead to a bigger one, a wagon trail, and the wagon trail lead to a road? And this guy picked me up…" She was chortling now as she kicked both legs up at the ceiling. "He says, *Sister, are you lost or what?* And I was so dumb, I'd forgotten what I was wearing."

"Dumb or exhausted?"

"Hey, I was sick by then. This guy drove a truck, a nice warm truck, and he drove me all the way down to Fitzgerald. He was a German guy. Even when he realized I wasn't a nun, he drove me all the way to a medical clinic in Fitzgerald. They said I had pneumonia and they shipped me down south on a plane to Lac la Biche, and this guy he came with me on the plane! He got a car from someone in Lac la Biche and we kept going through these little towns, you know, with the Pool elevators? Me wearing my nun's clothes? And I could read, and I thought they were signs for swimming pools. And I kept wishing he would stop so I could go swimming in a nice warm pool, eh?"

"Poor thing," he said.

"I'd heard about swimming pools. Anyway, by the time we hit Edmonton I think I was halfway out of my head. I was hackin away and I had a fever, and he took me straight to the hospital. Pretty good for a white man, eh?"

"Pretty good for a white man. Did he fancy you?"

She began to laugh again. "Did he *fancy* me?"

"Did he take a shine to you?"

"Jesus."

"Did he get fresh with you?"

"You know, to this day, I wish I could thank him? But I didn't even get the guy's name, or if I did I didn't remember it. A little German guy with a heart of gold. You know the good Samaritan, eh? That's who he was, the good Samaritan. Not a lusty old dog like you." She gave him an elbow in the ribs. "Mr. Burbidge."

"Sometimes you don't speak like a school marm."

"Men are such beasts."

"Mea culpa."

"You know," she declared, "that's where I actually began to learn English? I could read it but I couldn't speak it very good. And I was in that hospital for a long time and all they spoke was English. They were nice to me. They didn't know I was a runaway. I just told them that when I got better I'd write to my mom and dad and they'd come and get me, and the nurses believed me. They asked me what was I doing in a nun's habit. *Two* nun's habits. And I said, *It was cold out, whadya think?"*

Now they were both laughing.

"You know my parents, especially my dad, they were dead set against white men. When I went off to do the Normal School, I was eighteen, they thought I was going to hell. But I found out at the hospital white people weren't so bad after all. As long as I didn't have to go back to that damn school on the island, I was okay with white people."

They both fell asleep and when he woke up she had some coffee on. She was looking out the hotel window, peering at nothing, perhaps lost in the past. It bothered him to imagine what she might be remembering.

"I think, last year, I read an article about you in a copy of *The Edmonton Bulletin*," he declared, and she turned and smiled absentmindedly.

"It said you were the first Indian woman to teach public school in the North. Nice picture too."

"Yeah. Well."

"Well what?"

She turned back to the window and he reached for his trousers.

"When you meet her, don't talk her head off."

"I won't. I promise. Why not?"

"And remember, this is not me taking you home to meet the parents, okay? It's not like that, so don't get scared and run out the door. I just want you to meet her."

"Okay."

Lucy's mother lived in the same shack she'd lived in since she married John Castaway several decades before. The community was a mile inland from Great Slave on the Rae-Edzo Trail, a Northern Cree and mixed-blood settlement on the shores of Lac

Maria, named after a fish that fed on the bottom of the lake. This community was located near the southern hunting grounds of the Chipewyans, but, all things considered, a friendly enough place for a widow who had some years left in her. Still, her bad lungs, her arthritis, and her incipient blindness were all catching up to her, and she spent much of her time in the cabin in a rocking chair that Lucy had brought from Yellowknife in someone else's truck.

"Whiteman, you gonna break her heart?"

"She's already broken mine," he said, and Lucy laughed but the old lady did not.

"You gonna break my dodder's heart?" she said.

"Mum, he's a good man. He's not gonna break my goddam heart, okay? Jesus, Mum."

"I was not talkin to you, Lucy."

He followed mother and daughter outside, and the old lady stayed in front of the cabin while Joe brought in an armful of wood and then brought in some kindling.

"How long you tink dat wood gonna last, Whiteman?"

He went out and brought in another armful. Lucy stood behind her mother and gave him an apologetic shrug. The more conflicted her smile, the more striking Lucy looked to him. She had a saucy, mock-despairing way about her. She referred to him as Mr. Burbidge to anyone they met, but if she called him that when they were alone, it was only to tease him. During intimate moments, he became Burby. He had never before enjoyed, quite so much, the gift of a nickname.

The old lady sat in her rocker, and her face took on the gravity of a stone carving. She stared ahead. He could not tell just how blind she was, or just how deep her resentment might run.

"White men come up here and they smile and they stay all summer and make friends wit us. They want the fish, they want the timber, they take the rocks down to the south. Never come back, maybe leave a bit of money. Leave a baby and never come back."

"I see," he said, and brought in a third load of wood.

On their second visit to the old woman's cabin he noticed the rock. It rested on a table near the curtain that marked the entrance to the shaded side of the cabin where the old woman's bed was. The rock anchored a long curling strip of flypaper. He picked up the rock and held it to the light from the window.

"You like my rock, Whiteman?"

She wasn't even looking his way.

"Yes," he said, "I like your rock."

He placed it back on the table so that the rock re-anchored the long strip of flypaper. Dozens of dead flies studded the orange strip.

"The flies love it too," he said.

"Dat's a nice pretty rock."

"Yes," he said, swallowing, and hoping that she didn't hear that he was swallowing, "it's a very pretty rock."

It was heavy, larger than his hand, a rusty amalgam of porphyry crystals, stained quartz and gleaming pyrite, with glints of free gold scattered like stardust all over the quartz. Right in the middle of the rock, larger across than a thimble, a long nugget was encased, and not like the nuggets he had found in streams, not an actual nugget, but a vein that ran right through to the darker side of the rock. He turned it over and over in his hand and placed it back once again on the table to anchor the flypaper. He brought his memory of the rock's russet wonders back outside. Lucy was in the smaller cabin, behind her mother's, packing some personal items for the drive back to Yellowknife.

"I've seen that look before," she said.

"On me?"

"No. Other guys."

"Other white guys?"

"She never tells them."

"Tells them what?"

"What do you think, Mr. Burbidge?"

Lucy had to go back the next day, so they packed up his borrowed jeep and drove the wagon trail out to the gravel road that ran east to Yellowknife. She was silent for a long time, staring at the road, and he knew something had changed. The summer was over. She was almost a schoolmarm again, with all the business and the respectability that involved. She had things to do, meetings, people to see. Already he felt like a cast-off sweetheart and they weren't even halfway to Yellowknife.

"I need a favour," she said.

"Anything."

"I need to see if she's all right before the lake starts to freeze. Before Thanksgiving, I mean. But I can't just come up here on a two-day weekend. Even if I had a car. I got stuff to do, eh, and I need a big...a real big...favour."

He nodded, because he knew what she was going to ask.

"You can stay in that smaller cabin," she said. "Maybe for ten days? Go off and do your prospecting, go fishing, eh, you don't have to be with her night and day. But if her lungs are bad you give her some steam and maybe some gum to chew. If she needs wood, eh, you chop it up, and a lot shorter than the stuff you gave her back there. She needs it shorter so she can close her stove door."

"Aye-aye. What about the winter up there? Who'll take care of her then?"

"My brother will be back for the trapping, him and his family. It'll be their turn to be with her."

"Does she ever talk about going back?"

"Never. She doesn't want to be stuck on a reserve, she wants to be near to her kids. She likes her cabin. But she needs stuff, and that's a big favour I'm asking you."

"It will cost you, my dear."

"And Burby," she said, "you can't just drop in for visits at night. Not in Yellowknife, not now. Where I live, everyone in town knows who goes there. You know? I could get fired."

"Aye-aye."

"Don't just..." She stopped herself and reached over to place her hand on his right wrist. "I don't know what to do with you," she said. "I can't afford to get fired, Burby. We have to put the damper on."

"The what?"

"You know what I mean. We can't just see each other and hope for the best. We have to stop for a while."

As the jeep lurched and clattered down the ragged road they were quiet again. He tried to wait her out.

"I'm not saying hit the road, okay?"

The dust behind the car was so thick that the road in the rearview mirror was invisible; but the road in front, and the black spruce and lodgepole pines, the beaver dams and the great hulking eskers, seemed to spring forth in all their sunlit clarity. The aspens were approaching the peak of their colour and they made him think of gold.

"Okay?" she said.

He was thinking of the rock.

"Okay."

HE SAW THE OLD LADY every morning. She would boss him around and then clam up. He would check her supply of wood, carry in some water from the lake, and if the stove was cold, he would shovel out the ashes and dump them outside. She was not entirely crippled, she could shuffle around her cabin and rinse the odd dish, but she was too old to get around much beyond the daily trips to the loo and the odd time she spent standing on the front stoop, looking out at the lake. Looking? Was that what she was doing?

He always asked her how she was feeling, whether she slept well, and she always grunted something back at him that aimed for neither insult nor civility, nor even information. Sometimes he went behind her to examine the rock, to memorize its rusty glittering texture and imagine the vein of gold that, long ago, must have flowed through it. His daily visits with the rock seemed to energize his trips into the bush with his hammer and his magnifying glass, but no matter how far afield he walked, he could never find any of the faults, the shear zones, the screes or the quartz beds flowing through the basalt and the iron deposits where gold might be found.

He yearned to go hunting for fresh meat but he had given Isidore his rifle as a parting gift.

One day she said, "Whiteman, I make a deal wit you."

"What kind of a deal?"

"You do me a favour, I'll tell you where I got dat rock."

He didn't believe her because she came off as...what? Cold? Conniving, was that it? But he couldn't quite resist her offer. He'd been a fool for other things, her daughter, for example, so why not a fool for gold? A man should never fear his capacity for foolishness, should he, or he wouldn't learn anything.

"Okay."

"You fix my door so it closes, ah. You fix my stovepipe too."

The door had moose-hide hinges that were partly worn through, and the old lady's stovepipes leaked smoke into the cabin. They were hanging together with a couple of nails and some rusted wire.

"I'd have to drive down south to get you a new stove pipe," he said. "How would you do without me?"

"Get me some wood before you go," she said.

Towards the end of September on a windy Saturday he drove back to Yellowknife and got the old lady a new stovepipe and a set of hinges and screws for the door. The same day, he paid a visit to Lucy's tarpaper shack near the school, but Lucy wasn't home. He left her a note and drove back west in the dark. All things considered, it was a pretty glum trip.

He spent the following day fixing the door and reassembling the stove pipe while the old lady sat in her rocker wrapped up in a blanket, calling out instructions. His control over his language was exemplary.

"I got it for a decoration," she said.

"The stove pipe?"

"Dat rock. I got it up there for a decoration."

"Up where?"

"Where we useta come from," she said.

"Up at Behchoko? That way?"

"You thought I got it close ta here, ah?"

"Yes I did."

"You want it too bad."

"Your rock?"

"Da gold. You want it too bad."

"We call it gold fever," he said.

"So do we."

He remained patient and stood looking out the window at the lake. With the old lady, silence worked better than chatter.

"If I do a map for you, Whiteman, you got to promise you gonna treat my dodder good, ah. Make a ninjun promise not a white man promise."

"Of course I'll treat her good. She's a good person."

"She's tough as a rubber ball."

He laughed and she gave him a crooked grin that curled around her cigarette. Then he handed her his pencil and she drew the map, and even then, he couldn't quite tell how much sight remained in her old eyes.

"What's that?" he said. "Up there."

"Dat's a bad place wit no trees."

"All that area?"

"Long place away from Detah," she said. "Chipewyan country. Long place away from Lutsel K'e. Nort a McLeod Bay. Ten days wit da dogs. Need a boat, Whiteman. Maybe nairplane."

She had to mean the Barrens. He'd flown over them but he'd never wanted to touch down there. Who could possibly live up in the Barrens if there weren't any trees? Not even John Hornby could do that. The Barrens was hard on Englishmen.

"What's that down there by the lake?"

"Fissin camp. Where da white guys go. You don't go to da big lake, you go to da little lake."

"Does this lake have a name?"

"Maybe they call it Wolf Lake."

"The little one?"

"No, da big one."

And that was it. A map by a blind woman as fanciful and spare of detail as a child's drawing.

"Did you actually travel up there? That far from here?"

"I went wit my husbin up there. Hunting party. He got da rock right there. He said it was a present to me. I brought it down here for a decoration."

"It's quite a decoration."

"I forgot your name, Whiteman."

"Joe. Joe Burbidge."

"You be good to my dodder, Joe. She need a good man to settle her down, ah?"

"WHERE IN HELL *you* been to?"

"I met a lady."

"You marry her?"

"No, I didn't marry her. She broke my heart."

"You gonna bring in them violins over the goddam telephone?"

"I'll spare you the violins, Stinky."

Joe was telling the truth. He had finished his last shift with the old lady and driven down to Yellowknife. It was dark when he arrived, dark the way September can be when it ambushes you with harbingers of leafless October and stormy November. Not even the *weather* up here was civilized. He parked a discrete distance from Lucy's tarpaper shack and he'd been about to knock on her door when he heard some dance music from a gramophone, and over that, a man's voice, and then a phrase from Lucy, something she would say if she were horizontal and in the dark. *Men are such beasts*.

True enough, he supposed, but he'd begun to think that *he* was her beast, not this other chap. The fellow turned out to be the northern superintendent, Tim Hutchinson, an old beau from the time when she was hired. A man she'd been engaged to and then broken up with. Obviously he was back.

"Stinky? What are you doing down there?"

"I'm windin things down. Hang on. Some goddam kid's out there foolin with the truck."

"Isidore's kid?"

"No," he said, "Isidore and his lot are up an gone. Makes no sense to me, but they're gone."

A stream of profanity flowed all the way from a small hotel near Patricia, Alberta to the only decent hotel in Yellowknife. When Stinky had stopped hollering at the kid, he blessed Joe with his presence on the phone once again. It was not always easy to communicate with Stinky Riley, let alone admit to Stinky that his heart had been broken.

"You're hard to keep track of, Stinky. I take it you're coming back to Yellowknife?"

"Course I'm comin back. There's nothing cookin down here."

"Stinky, do you have one more adventure in you before the snow flies?"

"What sorta adventure?"

"Treasure hunt. One week tops. Need a plane and a man who can fly it."

More profanity, this time directed at Joe, a gentler brand of cussing that Stinky always reserved for his friends. Joe was phoning from the hotel bar, sipping a whisky and squinting at the old lady's map. He'd begun to annotate each figure on the map, each river or lake big enough for the old lady to remember, each reference or fragment of speech that might have an equivalent on the survey maps for the country north and east of Great Slave Lake.

"Might give er a whirl," Stinky said.He sounded aimless, perhaps even depressed. He was ruminating out loud. "They don't need me around here. Why not, eh? Why not go on one a Joey Burbidge's wild goose chases? Freeze my arse off an have a good time."

"Stinky, did you break up with your lady again? Is that what you're doing down there?"

"I got no truck with that romantical nonsense. That's your department."

"Where's the Junkers?"

"In the pasture. I just run er up to the gravel an away we go."

"Might be some money in it for you, this time."

"What, real money or your kinda money?"

"You never know, Stinky."

"Yer goddam rights."

Chapter 7

The Stakes

"I'M LOOKIN," said Stinky.

"So am I," said Joe.

"Nice day for a spin."

They were flying low over the Barrens, a long day's run out of Yellowknife, Stinky grumbling at the controls. They kept the tree-line always in view to the south, because Wolf Lake lay somewhere between the undulating dry plain and the forest's northernmost reach on a line north and east of Yellowknife. That much they knew, or hoped they knew. Gravelly eskers winding like eels on their left. Endless sparse and stunted forest on their right. They had little else to guide them. A sportfishing camp that might not be in use any more. A small nameless lake next to a larger one. A place where Cree and Chipewyan hunters from the south and Dogrib and Slavey hunters from the north found themselves fighting for the same caribou. Well north of Slave Lake but south of the Thelon River Valley. The needle was small, the haystack immense.

Their day began to wane, and the plane's shadow moved up beside them and then ahead of them, as though, in the midst of the men's bewilderment, the shadow was now leading the way and the plane following.

This flight felt to Joe like the culmination of something. Up here, a couple of hundred feet or so above the trees, it felt as though his teacher, old Herron, the beloved Irishman, had been right all along. *Learn from the past and live in the present,* and by God, Joe was doing both. Or he hoped he was.

But Stinky was cursing at what he saw. They were flying over a nearly treeless land the colour of deer-hide dominated by sandy eskers and hundreds – no, thousands – of small lakes lying before them, many of which could be what the old lady referred to as Wolf Lake.

"Jesus, Joey, throw me a bone here. When was the last time this gal come up here?"

"The last time?"

Joe did not have the courage to tell Stinky that Lucy's mother had only been there once, and that was a very long time ago. No doubt her memory leaked like a sieve, and besides, it was her late husband who had found the rock.

"Well, Stinky, I'm not sure. A while back."

"A while back. You don't think maybe she's havin a good laugh at us about now?"

"No Stinky, she was on the level."

Thus enticed, they persisted.

Stinky turned from cranky to mean. He shifted his curses from the lake-stippled Barrens back to Joe, who was shivering in the cockpit as the wind whistled through the windscreen and the sun moved closer to the horizon. *Real pretty country, Joe. Lotsa lakes. Sure is fun gawkin, eh?* Joe was wondering where Stinky might hope to put down the plane for the night when he saw what looked to be a strip of concrete on top of a ridge. Greyish pale ice or concrete.

"What're you lookin at?" Stinky growled over the high drone of the motor.

"Thought I saw a landing strip. You know, that light grey concrete you see back in…"

Stinky began to bank the plane, and suddenly they were heading back west.

"Where the hell are you going? I didn't mean a *real* landing strip, I meant a –"

"Light grey? Maybe a dirty white?"

"Yes. Oh, my God."

And there it was below them, a great chalk-coloured mound, longer than it was wide, that rose like a snowy slope above two lakes, a large one and a small one.

"Can you land there?" said Joe, gripping the frame of his seat.

"I can land on the big lake, no trouble. Hell, why not try the little one, eh Joe? She's closer."

"Stinky, for Christ's sake, you'll never make it!"

"Just kiddin, Joey."

THEY CAMPED ON the shore of the larger body of water, which may or may not have been Wolf Lake. There was wolf scat on the game trails, and a pair of lanky grey ones showed up at their campsite the first evening and peered at them from a safe distance. Lean wolves, hungry looking. That was good enough for Joe. The men were not, technically, on the Barrens but slightly south of them, into the sparse and spindly trees and bushes.

On the first day they hiked through berry bushes, dwarf birch and stunted knee-high spruce over to the smaller lake and up to the top of the off-white mound Joe had spotted from the plane. They hammered a few samples from the rock. It was solid quartz, milky blue to dirty white, with scraps of snow white, more quartz than Joe had ever seen, but it revealed no rusty patches or other signs of mineralized rock. They wandered over the top of the mound and returned to the shore of the smaller lake along a hog's back that was striped here and there in a zebra pattern with wide veins of quartz. They made their way down through the bush to a small stream that flowed through an iron-bearing fault zone. Some of the quartz down here was white, some dark blue, and some dark grey, enclosing big crystals of feldspar. The kaleidoscope of minerals caught and held Joe's attention like no other prospect he could remember.

Stinky was groaning about how much he loathed walking, that

on the ranchlands where he came from if a man walked very much at all it was looked upon as a sign of deficient intelligence. The worst thing about prospecting for gold was the absence of horses and saddles.

"I'd give up breakfast an lunch for a trail horse right now."

Joe was squinting at a rusty patch in the quartz, a place where dark grey, white, and blue quartz came together under the smallest of several shear zones. Stinky came closer and they stared, spotting tiny flecks of colour, gawking suddenly, like art lovers before a masterpiece, and they nodded their approval in unison. Joe brought out his glass and squinted up and down, side to side at the formation.

Colour. Free gold. Enough tiny glints to hold his gaze. They had both spotted traces of free gold near Yellowknife a number of times before, but this had a more abundant look to it.

They fell to hammering till the rock chips and the larger hunks began to pile up around their boots. Sidecutting with hammers. Perhaps it was like that for the Yorkshiremen in the coal mines, except a thousand feet down in the dark, where there wasn't a scrap of gold in the bargain. Sometimes in the gossan patches the rock ground into sand in Joe's fingers, twinkling with pale yellow flecks.

"Stinky, we could pan some of this rotten material. We've got the stream right here. We could set up camp and hammer away and pan through this rusty stuff."

Stinky was sweating and panting, his face redder than usual. He looked older than his fifty-two years.

"Jesus, Joey, think about this for a goddam minute. Just how far away is our gear?" It was the closest Stinky ever came to a rhetorical question. "Hell, I don't even remember if I packed our pans. No one uses them things up here."

"I packed them."

"Hell," said Stinky, looking out over the small lake.

His breath continued to whistle and heave. He pulled out his tobacco pouch and rolled a thin smoke, and gradually he took on a thoughtful frown.

"You know we can't land no plane on this little christer of a lake, right? And Joe, there is no way under the great northern lights I'm gonna pack in our gear. Not even the half of it."

Joe nodded.

"But there's a bigger stream up there flowin in."

Stinky pointed up the lake and then he pointed down the lake. "Another good-sized stream flowin out, hey? You notice that? Joey, my friend? My young friend? How would you like to go an git the dynamite?"

"What are you up to?"

"You'll see."

"You're going to make me carry explosives all the way from the bloody plane? You want me to haul in the drills as well? Why not the tent and the cookstove and the ..."

"Just git the dynamite, Joey. An a couple a shovels. I'm gonna try somethin."

STINKY RE-PACKED some of the charges that Joe had fetched in his knapsack along with some caps and fuses. He walked down the shore with his shovel and his knapsack and disappeared into the bush. *Time to set the table, Joey.* He would first lay out the dynamite by various crevasses and next to boulders that loomed on a slope above the outlet stream. He would muse a while above his sites, then attach the caps and fuses, ease the dynamite into the various recesses, and shovel as much sand and rubble as he could find on top of the various charges. Then Stinky would light the fuses, one after another, take cover and plug his ears.

Joe was to stay back at the dig. He would wedge and hammer in search of a vein, and he would watch at intervals to see if the water was coming up. His checking point was a flat island in the middle of their small lake. If the water rose appreciably, the island would begin to diminish, and Joe would grab a shovel, run down and assist Riley in finishing off his dam.

The plan was a dubious project, but Stinky had his teeth into this one and he could not be turned away. Every so often Joe would hear a dull *whump* and feel the force of it through his boots. Each *whump* meant that Stinky was still alive. The water did not seem to be moving up, so at last Joe started down the lake to see how Stinky was doing. What if Stinky overworked himself and had a heart attack? They'd be marooned out here with no one to fly their plane back home.

Another *whump* and the rumble of sliding rock.

Joe stopped in his tracks. There was a long silence. He hunkered down and waited for five, six minutes, and he tried not to think about how many tons of rock Stinky might be lying under. Against Riley's orders, he wandered over to the rocky slope, where his partner was busy shovelling rock chips and sand into a pile of rubble that lay over the outlet stream. His face was beefy red.

"You're alive," he said.

"Thought you was sposeta watch that there water."

"I got bored, Stinky."

"Whadya think, Joe?"

Riley pointed to his growing pile of rubble as though it were a cathedral he was constructing. The outlet stream was roiling around the rocks and sand in search of some escape. The water was rising.

"Grab a shovel, young feller."

They both shoveled gravel and rocks from the slope until they were streaming with sweat.

"Stinky, you made me miss all the fun, didn't you. Admit it."

"You find any more colour up there?"

"No I didn't, and don't change the subject. You thought I'd blow myself up."

"Occurred to me. This here dynamite ain't for amateurs."

When they returned to their original dig by the lake, they

looked over at the island. Joe brought out his binoculars. About a third of the island had disappeared beneath the rising water, and many of the protruding rocks on the far shore had disappeared completely.

"Joey, I think I'm gonna give er a try."

"Good luck to you, Stinky."

"Luck," he said, all smiles and camaraderie, "has nothin to do with it."

THE JUNKERS CAME IN low and flat over the lake and it pitched in light, as great northern geese and pelicans do. When Riley had secured his plane out from the shallows, he unloaded their equipment into the rubber dinghy and shoved it shoreward where Joe waited to unload. Their campsite was close to the little stream and next to their dig, and midway between the inlet stream and the dammed-up stream at the outlet. The much smaller stream that ran past their shear zones gurgled peacefully into the lake. Its rusty water reminded Joe of whisky, and Stinky of beer. It was mid-afternoon when the men finished the job of unloading and setting up, and the shadow from the great esker that loomed above them was growing longer. The men unfolded two wooden chairs, broke out the rum, and glassed their little lake and the island across the water from their camp. Stinky was holding the binoculars.

"Joey, when you was waitin for me to blow them charges, are you sayin you didn't find no vein back there?"

"I found a bit more free gold but no vein. I still think we've found something pretty special. One gold fiend to another."

"Okay. Whadya say, Joey? Feel like gettin snockered?"

"A bit late for that, Stinky. I've had one rum and I'm ready to fly your plane."

"You're ready t'fly all right."

"I am master of all that I command. I am Joe Burbidge and I

am King of the North. Along with my partner and pilot, of course. The legendary Stinky Riley."

"I got a feelin, Joey. If that patch a quartz and shit shows some decent colour, by the Jesus, some feller's gonna write a book about us some day."

"I might have to set him straight on the facts, Stinky."

"Never let the facts get in the way of a good story."

Stinky paused, sipped his rum, lingered over his drink. A gathering of wolves began to howl off in the distance.

"Just listen to that," said Joe.

"They's pore hungry critters, Joey. Hungry as hell. Ain't seen no caribou since we flew over McLeod Bay. Did you see any, Eagle-eye?"

"No."

"Nothin around here bigger than a rabbit. Them wolves must be lookin for the big migration." Stinky stared at his half-filled glass of rum. "Say, did that there old gal with the rock say anything about a big christly mound a quartz?"

"Don't think so."

"I got a feelin about our little patch here, Joey. I got one powerful hunch. All because a you an your goddam pathetic map."

The plane was anchored just offshore between the island and their campsite. An arresting sight, the all-metal Junkers on the calm lake. The autumn had advanced up here, the leaves had turned and most of them had fallen, but the weather was fine. The mosquitoes were gone and the black flies were scarce. The second rum was almost as good as the first one. The work tomorrow would be...

"What are we doing tomorrow, Stinky?"

"First thing, we should go do some serious hammerin. Hammerin, trenchin, blastin. Pile up the best samples an bag em. Then we come back here an pan that there gravelly shit for gold dust. First feller to find a vein anywheres around here gets to buy the beer."

"Stinky, back before I met you, did you ever find a property that produced enough for a mine? Even a small mine?"

"Never. Not once. Panned some good gravel, made a bit of cash to pay the bills, just like you. Found a good surface vein or two, made some more money. Staked some so-so properties and sold em for a good buck now and then. Paid off that there plane this year with cash dollars. But I'm like you, Joey, I got nothin in the bank."

"Hmm. I plan to change all that, you know."

"Jolly good," said Stinky, in the worst imitation of a British accent Joe had ever heard.

Don't count on your luck, he warned himself. Optimism was for fools. Work hard and live in the present. Let the chips fall, etcetera. No no. Learn from the past and live in the present. Beware the gold fever, Burbidge me boy. Don't worry about tomorrow's prospects. Don't even think about them. You are not immune...

"I am not immune to the inevitable."

"What are you goin on about?"

"I was pondering something, Stinky. That we are not immune to the inevitable."

"You talkin about the clap or what?"

Joe smiled, shook his head, and released a rum-sweet belch into the vermillion sun. Good time for an epiphany, snockered or not. Something inspired that old Herron might appreciate. Something about how you live your life. If you live in the presence of free will, live in the shining moment of right now, did that not mean that in fact...another belch...that in fact you *are* immune to the inevitable? No, because that made you vulnerable, didn't it? Forever chasing the gold. Like those blokes chasing the maidens around the Grecian urn. Never quite get there, do they? Happy as the day when a soldier gets his pay. With the gold just out of touch. Why did this all have to be so complicated?

"I'd say just take yer precautions, Joey. I prefer to use them lamb skins myself."

"One more snifter, if you please."

Stinky Riley poured the rum. The end of a perfect day. When they ate their pork and beans over an open fire they were both perilously close to sober again. That night, during a fraught conversation Joe was having with Lucy, or was it her mother, the wolves howled him awake.

Joe and Riley were up well before the sun. They inhaled their breakfast of fried spuds, eggs, prunes and dense, boiled coffee. They took a slow walk on opposite sides of the rusty little stream. The morning light brought out every crystal, bump and contour in the rocks. On Stinky's side, the grey zone was rusted over in places, and large veins of greyish quartz fingered their way through the russet patches. Riley beckoned Joe to his side of the stream, and the men gazed approvingly.

They took their hammers to the russet rock, and then they got the larger picks, and they hacked and pounded their way into some faceted cubes of pyrite that showed pale and brassy in the sun. The quartz was marked with parallel seams, hunks of dark sulphides. The rubble accumulated like gravel around their boots. The seams they uncovered were glittering with the oxidized surfaces of bornite and various pyrites that shone forth in rainbows of colour, as though the feathers of ancient peacocks had been hurled up in the magma through layers of earth and ocean.

"Stinky, how in the hell do we choose?"

"Beats me. Just look for colour."

They picked through a great excess of samples, spotted enticing glints of gold, and hauled the smallest and best ones back to camp in canvas bags for the assay office.

Visible gold glittered here and there. Stinky was clearly excited and pretending otherwise. He rowed these first sample bags out to the plane and stowed them at the back of the fuselage. There would be more later.

Joe panned from the pile of rusty sand and gravel they had dislodged, shaking the silty mix in the stream, and the stream carried away each cloud of roughage. He had to command himself to slow down, go at it methodically, but his work was sloppy as he rushed to render down the gravel. After ten or fifteen minutes of this, Joe held the pan up to the sun, gave it a good perusal with his glass, inhaled mightily. He brought the pan over to his partner.

"Didn't want to ruin yer day," said Stinky, offering up a chunk of quartz for Joe to glass.

He handed his pan to Stinky and brought Riley's quartz up to the magnifying glass. It was mostly grey and milky blue, but poking out of the jagged surfaces on one side of the rock was a yellow protuberance the size of a sparrow's beak. It was solid gold.

"Check the pan," he said to Stinky, and he turned the piece of quartz around in his hand. There were ample flecks of free gold on one side of the rock, but nothing as bounteous as the little beak.

"Glory hallelujah," said Joe.

"Yeah, well. Some of us got the Midas touch, young feller."

"Now, Stinky, please. Check the bloody pan."

Stinky tilted the pan to the sun and blinked at the contents gathered into a discrete pile. It was something close to the colour of corn, glittering like wedding rings in a jewelry store. Stinky took his eye-piece to it. Perhaps half an ounce of gold particles were gathered there, including some fragments of free gold about the size of barley seeds.

"Joey, you little bastard."

Joe scraped the gold into his poke and Stinky pocketed his piece of quartz. Joe burst into a smile as though he were about to sing a music hall ditty.

"Uh uh," said Stinky, shaking his head. "Now now. Don't git yer goddam hopes up."

Stinky chopped away at the spot where he'd found the gold-bearing quartz, at first straight down with great crushing blows, then with measured blows angling into the rock. He followed through with some light chipping. Stinky was smiling.

"Like I say, Joey..."

"Let me see that."

"Don't get yer hopes up."

"Out of the way you old fornicator."

And there it lay, glinting up through the grey quartz, a vein of brazen yellow like the fillings in a rich man's mouth. They took turns having a go at the quartz until they thought they might see the trajectory of the gold. The vein went wide and deep into the rock. They hacked out shards of quartz heavy with gold and only stopped when Stinky called a halt for grub, and they left the gold lying wherever it fell. Limping and lurching sore and stiff back to camp, they couldn't stop grinning at the ground, pounding each other on the shoulders, chuckling like men emerging from a bar.

THEY WERE EATING bread smeared with lard and hunks of cold baloney, lounging in the wood and canvas chairs, when they heard the drone of a plane, a big Noorduyn Norseman as it turned out, big enough to hold an entire crew. It circled the small lake entirely, wings dipping left and right, left and right, like a vulture descending through the thermals, then it disappeared over the esker behind them and roared back low for a landing. A logo on the cargo door read *Hanna Resources*. Even before the men emerged from the Norseman to haul it up to the edge of the island and unload, Riley had heaved himself out of the chair and grabbed his axe.

"Joey, I'd say we got some real fast work to do. I believe these sons a bitches might just drop in for tea."

Riley hauled his axe and a shovel to the hole where the first four corner posts would be driven in. He handed the axe to Joe, and Riley began to dig. Joe started chopping down aspens for the posts. He peeled and squared them off at the tops as quickly as he could, leaving enough bared wood to scribble down his location notices. Riley used his compass and paced off the distances, fifteen hundred feet in each of the four directions, while Joe held the end of the tape. With an axe and a machete the two men cut and blazed the boundary lines.

"Who the hell is Hanna Resources?"

"You're not going to like this, Stinky."

"You don't mean Krahn," Stinky muttered softly, as if the new arrivals had already stationed themselves behind the nearest boulders to listen in.

"I do."

"They musta heard we was comin this way."

"How could they know?"

"I told the fella back in Yellowknife, that short fella at the assay office. The one with the little square moustache? Just in case the Mounties couldn't read our goddam excuse for a flight plan."

"You told him we'd be out here?"

"Not exactly here. But I always tell someone, Joey. You know that."

They were just finishing up on the second claim line.

"Looks like maybe I told the wrong son of a bitch. It's just like Buster to foller us out to a claim. He's done this before. If he likes what he sees, he'll stake all around us in every direction. He doesn't fool around with hard work, that butter-ass bastard."

The axe and the machete rose and fell and the aspens and birch came down, each one at a single swipe. Their claim lines grew, and more corner posts were sunk, and as the afternoon sun beat down on their backs, they piled the rocks around their stakes. The last job was to gather the best and last of the ore samples and to cover up their vein and its quartz with the largest rocks they could wield and hope that no one would spot it.

Back at the campfire, they showed off their blisters to each other. They kept glassing the big Norseman, which remained tethered fast to the edge of the small island so that the crew could go in and out of the plane to get their supplies.

"Well, Joey, they won't camp on shore with the likes of us. I'd call that snooty."

A shot rang out from somewhere beyond the island, and then two more from the same direction.

"Was that a rifle?"

"Shotgun. Rabbits or ptarmigan be my guess."

The men on the island were a noisy crew, and liquored-up by the sound of it. Two of them had been pumping a rubber dinghy on the near shore of the island, a larger boat than Stinky's by the looks of it. Everything the Hanna Resources bunch had brought north with them would be larger than Joe and Stinky's equipment. The two men paddled over in the dinghy, hauled it up on shore and stood there for a moment.

"Jesus," said one of them, "what is that awful smell?"

"Smells like a Yank and a Limey."

The two men came up from their dinghy and emerged from the shadows, a podgy man and a tall and lean one, who remained just behind his boss. Joe and Stinky continued to sit.

"Beezer Krahn, I believe," said Joe. "What a delightful surprise."

"So," said Krahn, checking out the campsite.

The big man heaved his body right up to the fire and exhaled mightily. He looked around the campsite in a proprietary manner, as though he were in charge of the whole operation, puffing and smiling.

"So. Knaaker, this here is Stinky Riley and this fella over here is Joe Burbidge."

The tall man nodded at Joe. He remained just inside the glow of the fire, gaunt, unsmiling. Krahn exhaled a familiar mix of whisky, rancor and creamed corn. The big smile returned. Either the man had too many incisors or excessively long ones. The right ear on his great potato of a head had vanished. Only a purple lobe remained. A lobe and a scar.

"You gonna offer us a shot of rum, Stinky?"

"No, I'm not, Buster. Think I'll turn in shortly, if you don't mind."

"Not very hospitable, Stinky. Burbidge, you wouldn't mind if I look around?"

Another shot rang out, this one from right on the island. It was followed by some whooping and yelling that sounded like a rodeo in full swing. Joe and Stinky remained squatting by the fire.

"Yes, Buster, I would mind."

Krahn turned to the quiet man behind him. "Joseph and me go back a few years, Knaaker. I think he disapproves of my boorsome ways."

"Beezer, whatever happened to your ear? Were you eating from a can of corn again?"

Joe noticed that Stinky had brought the .22 up next to his boot. Joe let his arms hang down from his lap. Slowly he grappled around in the dark and found himself clutching one of his rejected samples on the ground, a rock big enough to do some damage at close range.

Still puffing, Krahn beamed his oleaginous grin, first at Stinky, then at Joe. He did not seem fazed by their greeting. He offered a resonant fart and flashed his abundant teeth in the light of the fire.

"Joe, while you and Stinky here was diggin holes back upstream, madly stakin away, I was right here. Ha. And I checked out where you was hammerin rocks right over there. Oh, I seen some mighty interesting rocks there, Stinky. I believe you might be into some colour, you lucky cocksuckers. We're pretty partial to that stuff. Never mind. Me and Knaaker here, we'll discuss your good fortune with the boys back on the island. I'm guessin they'll be pretty excited about your find. Yiz haven't been here long enough to stake out the whole territory, have you? I know that for a fact. So there should be lots more for the rest of us, eh?"

Riley smiled at Krahn. "I'm wishin you all the best a luck. Just stay the hell outa our claim."

When the men had gone, Stinky ambled back to the campfire.

The night had turned cool and he tossed some sticks onto the fire. Joe watched as he unloaded the twenty-two, ejecting some tiny shells. He reloaded it with a handful of long-rifle rounds from his knapsack.

"Don't git excited, Joey. And don't mind me. I don't expect it'll come to no shootin, but up here a unloaded rifle ain't much use."

"Where's your thirty-thirty?"

"In Patricia."

"Why is it in Patricia?"

"Where's your rifle, you young nimrod?"

"I gave it to Isidore as a parting gift."

"Generous of you, Joey."

"I thought so."

"Never mind."

"I wonder who might have bitten off Krahn's ear. The chap should get a medal."

Riley clicked on the safety of his twenty-two. "I'd pay a dollar to have that ear pickled in a jar. Make a nice ornament."

"At least his companion is a jolly sort."

Using the twenty-two as a stave, Stinky rose grunting from his spot by the fire.

"Joey, we gotta fly outa here an goddammed soon, hey?"

"What?"

"We need to register this here claim. Before Krahn's boys find out how rich this ore is. They do and they'll rip up our stakes and replace them with their own markers. They'll do it, because they've got a faster plane. They could rip out our stakes and beat us back to the assay office in three, four hours. It'll be their word against ours and that's roughly eight sworn statements to two. I don't like them odds. And if we brought up charges, hey? Ol Buster, he'd fly a Edmonton lawyer up here as fast as you can whistle. His outfit has the dough."

"Slow down, Stinky. You mean we fly out of here when Buster's crew is off somewhere in the field? We get a good head start?"

Stinky took in a long breath and exhaled.

"I don't know what I mean. Wish we'd planned this here trip a little better. Heh. Wish we'd brung a proper rifle."

Riley leaned his twenty-two on a big rock next to the tent. He was biting his lower lip.

"But we gotta move real fast or we're gonna lose maybe the best claim we ever seen. An I do not think Buster's gonna find much to write home about around here. Gold, I mean. Not this late in the season. Because it could be anywhere. If it's lyin around between these two lakes it'll take him too long to find it. Too late t'do any serious prospectin, and this here trigger-happy crew of his, Jesus. They look like a bunch a claim jumpers to me."

"You never know, Stinky."

Riley pointed towards the source of their little stream. "I almost hope Buster does find colour somewheres back there. Who knows what's back there? I also know what he is capable of doin and he will bugger us up if we let him."

"What you're saying, Stinky, is if we abandon our own stakes, Krahn and his boys would simply come over and re-stake the claim with their own markers. Then fly straight to Yellowknife and beat us to the punch."

Riley drooped over the campfire and gazed at the coals for a moment.

"Yeah, Joey, he'd do that and worse. But if we stay put and guard the claim, these buggers can just bide their time. They're better set up than we are, more food and whatnot. Then what? Wait till all them sons a bitches storm our camp or sabotage our plane? We're buggered if we stay and buggered if we fly to Yellowknife."

The discussion circled around for a while until Stinky came up with an idea. It all depended on Buster and his drunken crew sleeping through the night.

"Here's the iffy part, Joey. When the time is right, I'll row out to the Junkers, gas up and take off."

"You mean I stay here?"

"Yeah." He was peering at Joe out of the corner of his eye. "Hell, Joey, we gotta die some time. May as well do er in the saddle, eh?"

"I stay here alone? I guard our bloody claim all by meself? While you lark around in Yellowknife?"

"I'll give ya the twenny-two." After a silence, Riley added, "Joey, this here is decision time. You been lookin for gold how long? Six, seven years? You wanna be a prospector bum all your life? You wanna be one a them guys down south ridin the rails? You wanna join the lineup at the soup kitchens? Or do you wanna be a rich man? Help out that family of yours? What do you wanna be when you grow up?"

Joe glared over at the small rifle that rested against the rock and answered his partner with silence. His bowels began to rumble.

"Joey, just think about them guys boozin it up down in Yellowknife. Young dreamers all over the goddam North. Always talkin about the next grubstake, the next big discovery, the next payoff. Flat broke and talkin about the day when they'll strike it rich. Fill their pockets with nuggets and all that bullshit. Well, Joey, this claim ain't no next time. We've finally hit paydirt. This here claim could turn into a real, actual goddam goldmine. We could sell it to a big outfit and you could live in the goddam MacDonald Hotel for the rest a your life. You could have a butler and a shitload a fancy women. I could go south and buy my own ranch. But right now, you need a goddam pilot and I need a partner to step up to the plate. What's it gonna be, buddy?"

THEY LAY ON THEIR bedrolls and Joe did not sleep. From the sound of his breathing, neither did Riley.

Around three in the morning the men in Krahn's camp had fallen silent. Joe and Riley crawled out of their tent and stood side by side for the morning piss. In the distance there came rumbles from an approaching storm, and the sky lit up continuously all across the western horizon. The thunder and lightning continued but the rain held off, and they made it safely up to the dam with their knapsacks, part one of Stinky's plan. They buried the dynamite as quietly as they could, as deep as they could, and Stinky lit a ten foot fuse. The two men waited behind a huge boulder. The concussion came with a dusty rush of air and broken rock like a bolt of lightning. The air turned sharp from a drift of cordite, and the water tumbled out of the lake.

Joe wondered out loud how that explosion might have sounded to the men in their tents almost a mile away.

When they returned to their own tent, however, and Stinky glassed the rival camp, there was no sign of movement. If Krahn's men had awakened from the sound of the blast for even a moment, they might have thought it was thunder, which was booming closer and closer as the wind rose. The weather was looming like a bad spirit over the north.

Joe glassed the Krahn site while Riley rowed his loaded dinghy out to the Junkers and then filled up his tank for the long flight. He rowed back and they had some breakfast around a fire and watched as the lightning approached and the water slowly drained away from the island across the bay. And then the big Norseman seemed to tilt its wings and ever so slowly list to one side.

Stinky Riley broke into a brilliant smile. "She's grounded, Joey. And I think I've got just enough water to take off."

Their own plane was moored in a deep channel, a one-minute row in the dinghy. Riley whispered a promise to Joe that he would fly back in a day or two. Three days at most. He reached the plane, unloaded their last samples from the dinghy, and shoved it shorewards for Joe to drag in. Soon Stinky was revving his engine. It throbbed out a high impudent roar that echoed off the opposite shore like something reborn from the Triassic era.

Buster Krahn was the first man out of his tent, hopping

around barefoot in his longjohns and a toque pulled down almost to his nose. He stared at the Junkers with the dismay of a man who had bet on the wrong horse. Then the rest of the men piled out of their tents, half a dozen of them, pulling on sweaters, rubbing the sleep from their eyes to witness the Junkers bumping over the waves, and then suddenly airborn. Stinky did a fly-by past the Krahn camp, and it seemed to Joe that even Stinky's plane was smiling.

Joe smiled too and waved at the men on the island.

Chapter 8

Wolf

AT FIRST HE ALMOST enjoyed himself, glassing Krahn's boys as they tried to move their big plane off the island in the receding water and the rain. They set up a great howl, yelling orders and warnings at each other, as hung-over men are wont to do.

Later, from up on the esker, Joe gazed down on them as they made their way across in the dinghy, three at a time, and then marched past his own tent to the dynamited slope to rebuild the dam, boulder by boulder. It had taken someone in Krahn's crew about two hours to figure it out. A couple of the men spotted him perched on the esker next to a boulder, holding his rifle, and they glared at him. But the men had a job to do. At first they worked together with the gloomy resignation of prisoners on a road crew. The silent one called Knaaker came back to their dinghy to row to the island for some shovels and crow bars and to pick up the last man. The whole crew scrambled through the rain and hove-to for several hours until at last the dam was re-built and the lake began to rise. Joe could not help but be impressed with the speed of their recovery.

He clambered down to his tent to re-light the fire, nibble on bits of food, and warm up. As he grew drowsy, his thoughts burped out of him in little puffs. *Krahn's boys. Nearly finished. Getting Norseman loaded. Good. Stinky, five hours head-start. Maybe six or seven by the time they get loaded. Joe feeling tired and crabby. Poor Joe, cold and wet. Tent. Food. And the noble Buster? What if he stays behind? Raises hell with me.*

What would his apelike visage look like atop the sights of my twenty-two?

I am Joey Burbidge and I have just had a thought in a complete sentence.

In his noctambular state, he drifted off and shook himself to return to the present. Drifted off again and again, drifted off to the Atlantic and England and Yorkshire, when his family and his mates used to converse in complete sentences; long, articulate sentences replete with cheeky wit and silliness. When he used to *think* in sentences. Now, only in fragments. No use for wit, that's elitist. No use for modifiers. Irony? For sissies. Think like the animals. Once upon a time. Wolf tracks. Going that way. Rabbit carcass. Dead two days, maybe three. Wolf scat. More tracks. Hmm. Lots of wolf scat. Mystery solved. Oldest narrative in the world. No letters, no words. Animal tracks, dung, bones. These his letters and words. And lo, humanity's first class in reading. Humanity's first whodunnit. Wolves done it.

Joe leaned sideways into a doze.

His dreams were drummed away by a mind-rattling roar, and he crawled out of the tent and limped down to the water's edge in his bare feet. The rain was still falling, the wind was up and the sun sat fuzzy behind a nimbus of cloud. But he could see clearly that the small island was deserted. The Norseman coasted up the lake, turned around and sped over the waves past his campsite and cleared the water. It was cold as hell. He waved to the plane, shivered, limped back to his tent.

"Alone at last."

HE AWOKE IN THE HALF-DARK morning to the high-pitched *howk! howk!* of hundreds of snow geese heading south. The rain had come and gone and the buffeting wind was colder than ever. He had a terrible thought. Why would Buster head for Yellowknife before he had exchanged his own stakes with Joe and Stinky's? *Oh, Christ.* Joe threw on his clothes and an extra sweater and a fur cap with big ear flaps that Stinky had left behind. The wracking wind and flapping canvas were the only sounds, and he pulled down the flaps so that he didn't have to listen.

In the returning light he glanced over at the island one last time to be sure that indeed it was abandoned, and then he pulled on his wellies and went to work. He began by checking his stakes to reassure himself that they had been left unaltered. Then he began picking through the remains of shattered grey quartz that lay at the base of their big find. He found a dozen or more rocks rich in gold from their vein and he bagged them. He stuffed the sample bag away between two boulders.

Joe strapped on his canteen, wrapped his rifle in his rain slicker and picked up his gold pan. He ambled up the russet-coloured stream a hundred yards or more from his campsite, sat for a moment on a boulder to regain his energy. He arose from his boulder and began to pan the loose and rusty sand and gravel their picks had dislodged, and this warmed him up, all but his hands. It was vigorous work, and almost every time he rendered down the gravel he was left with a nice residue of gold particles, more gold than he had ever panned. The presence of gold energized him. He scooped it out of the pan with a teaspoon and into his poke, and by the time he was ready for his midday baloney sandwich, he had an entire poke cinched up full of gold. Late afternoon, when the rain returned, he had more than half-filled Stinky's old tobacco pouch as well. More raw gold than he had ever seen.

This…what was it…happiness? This happiness, frenzy, whatever it was, it was exhausting. Joe put one poke in the right pocket of his winter coat and one in the left pocket, and they weighed his coat down like lead sinkers. Thus laden, once again he lumbered downstream and back to the campsite.

His tent was gone.

He stowed the two pokes in a crevasse, threw on the rain slicker over his coat, picked up his rifle, and wandered off in search of his tent. He tied his ear flaps up and the first thing he heard over the wind's constant moaning was the howl of a wolf. He lumbered to the top of the esker and poked around until he found his tent, stuffed away beneath a leaning slab of rock. The tent had been shredded. Buster bloody Krahn, hiding somewhere, waiting for Joe to freeze to death. Joe could almost smell the creamed corn on the man's breath.

It was late afternoon and getting dark when he brought the ruined tent down to his camp and threw it on the ground. Amid the pounding of his heart and the patter of the rain he checked to see if his gear was still around. His bag of rich ore samples was missing, but the two pokes were still tucked away in their crevasse. Underneath the rubber dinghy, he found his gear untouched, his demijohn still full of drinking water and his dry wood intact. He tossed most of the wood into the fire pit. He dumped some petrol on it, set it blazing, loaded on some wet wood and soon enough it all caught fire.

He took up his gun and waited till the fire got hot and he realized that his heart was pounding to a different rhythm. The fear coursing through his veins had turned to anger. Lupine, vengeful, sly.

The anger made him hungry. He tore open the food box and found some baloney and a raw spud in the flickering dark and he wolfed them down. He poured some rum into a tin cup and sipped it until it proclaimed itself in his belly and all through his chest.

"Buster! Bloody! Krahn!" He roared it, he boomed it like a declaration over the lake. "You must join me for a cup of tea! Bring your friends! Bring a pack of wolves for all I care!"

He wanted an echo but he couldn't get one. The wind and the rain drowned it out.

"I'm going to knock on your door!" he roared. "Very soon, d'you see? I hope you have a cozy sleep, Buster!"

Joe was stumbling around and almost asleep on his feet. But that didn't matter, did it. He lurched over to the dinghy, crawled under it cradling the twenty-two, sprawled on the shredded tent, and curled up like a wolf.

When he crawled out blue-lipped and shivering from under the dinghy, he saw that the ground was covered with snow, the whole murky world aglow with it. There were no tracks around his camp. Which meant that Buster too had gotten some sleep. Joe brought out the petrol can and the rest of his wood and got a fire going. He kicked up the charred logs from last night's fire, nudged them into the blaze, hunkered down to warm his hands. He sliced and fried some baloney and heated up a can of beans and spooned it all down.

The sky had been a gunmetal gray when he'd crawled out from under the dinghy, and he thought it might be merely the gray light of dawn, but as the morning came on, the sky's low ceiling seemed to darken with a new front of great ragged clouds, which meant more snow was on the way. A delicate lens of ice had formed at the edge of the lake.

What would Isidore do? Joe had no tent, there was not enough snow for a kwinzhee, or wood enough or sod or dry grass for a debris hut, and God knows he didn't have a tripod.

He would have to do what wolves did.

He grabbed the nearest spade, walked over to the foot of the esker, and he began to climb, rifle in one hand, shovel in the other. Half way up the esker, he found a brushy alcove, a sandy recessed area about six feet wide, and there he began to dig. He had spent much of his boyhood digging caves in Castleford and here he was at it again. The ground was not yet frozen, so the sand and gravel came out easily enough. In half an hour his body was warming. He rested frequently. In little more than an hour, he had the beginnings of a cave. Soon he would have a place where he could sleep the night and bide his time until Stinky came back. Because of the steep slope, he could not be ambushed from above at the top of the esker. He could only be approached from below, and because of the profusion of bushes around his cave, he could not easily be spotted inside. But when Krahn returned to pillage his campsite or to pull up his stakes, Joe would spot him from the mouth of his cave.

He leaned on the shovel and rested, then he trudged to the top of the esker and evacuated his bowels. He fumbled through his coat pocket, found some flagging and wiped himself. He walked the spine of the esker looking for footprints in the snow. Nothing. Krahn would be holed up somewhere down by the lake, perhaps where the stunted trees and bushes were thickest. Probably, he would be waiting till nightfall.

The snow began to blow in. He returned to his digging until he had managed to hollow out a half-decent cave. It went in six or seven feet, and it was big enough for him to sit down in and big enough for him to stow some of his supplies. Toting his rifle, he ambled down the esker, re-lit the fire, and put on the kettle for tea.

He fancied for a moment that he was slowly turning into a wolf, but he still craved his cup of tea, so he must still be an Englishman. He was still Joe Burbidge.

At last he plucked his shredded tent off some bushes and noted that it had dried somewhat in the wind. Good. It could be used either for the floor of the cave or as a curtain at the entrance to keep the cold out. He looked under the dinghy and he checked what was left of his supplies. Stinky's bedroll, some of Stinky's clothes, a smaller shovel, two picks, a second box of food as yet unopened, his demijohn of drinking water. Coiled next to his gas can were fifty feet of hose that Stinky had thought they might use with their pump for sluicing the gravel.

Fifty feet of hose.

Late in the afternoon, the snow had drifted off to the south and left him with three inches of fresh powder. The small lake was freezing up and down the shoreline and the ice was reaching out into the leeward bays. No footprints to be found. Buster Krahn had not yet roused himself. He would want Joe to come looking for him, but there would be no telltale footprints in the new snow for Joe to follow. This would be to Krahn's advantage. He would wait with his rifle for Joe to come through the bush. So Joe would wait him out. Krahn would catnap throughout the day and return in the night to do his dirty work. The great one-eared ape returns to hunt the wolf.

A rising surge of fear returned to him, and once again he wandered off and emptied his bowels.

"Stinky Riley," he growled softly. "Wherever you are. Get the hell back here before Burbidge goes barmy."

IN THE LAST GRAY LIGHT of dusk he dozed in his cave. What with the layers of tent underneath him and blankets around him, and two round, heated rocks wrapped in Stinky's clothes, he was tolerably warm.

He awakened in the night and the fear returned. He nosed out of his cave and shouldered a war bag, picked up his rifle. He had to flash his torch for seconds at a time to get his bearings. He climbed as slowly as he had ever moved, up the esker to the top. He crouched down at the peak of the esker and wrapped himself up in Stinky's bedroll. It had a sour musty tobacco smell to it. The fresh snow gave off a sub-lunar glow that brought out the edges of things. He lay on his belly and peered down at the dinghy, at his campsite, at where the small stream ran beneath the snow where the stakes were poking up. He rolled around and brought out a gas funnel from his packsack and worked it into the open end of the hose. The other end of the hose was buried fifty feet down the esker. He had driven the long handle of his spade through the roof of his cave and cranked it around to make a hole about two inches in diameter. He had eased the hose down three or four feet until it protruded from the ceiling of the cave. Then he suspended the tent to cover up the entrance to the cave. His footprints should lead Krahn to his den, and this was what he wanted.

But what if Krahn was already up on the esker, somewhere

close behind him? Peering through his binoculars. Peering through the telescope of his rifle. Hopping around in the snow in his underwear. Eating a banana. He should turn around in the bedroll and take a peek. Behind him. He should really…because the ape was out there somewhere, scratching his armpits. Swinging from branch to branch. He tried to open his eyes but he could see just fine with his…with his. Eyes closed.

You comin out t'play? No, thank you, Stinky, I'm not coming out today. You comin out t'play or do I let fly? A second or two to blink the eyes awake. A second or two more to realize that the voice had nothing to do with his dream. The voice was somewhere down the hill, and it wasn't Stinky Riley. A man with a rifle was moving erratically on the slope below him, bouncing up and down like a puppet. Why was the man dancing? Joe drew the funnel up to his mouth. It smelled of petrol.

He said into the funnel, "No, I'm not coming out."

"You not comin out?" sang the man, rocking back and forth, easing off his knapsack, laying down his rifle.

"It's too cold out," Joe said. "Go away."

"You want me to go away?" said the man. "You like livin in a hole?"

He had taken something from the knapsack. He continued his ungainly dance and released an ecstatic little cry. Perhaps he was just hopping around to keep warm. He did not look like Buster Krahn, so he must have been one of Krahn's men. He was tall and very lean. He spoke in a high monotone with a slight accent, a matter-of-fact voice, but Joe could not trace the accent or gather anything else from the voice.

"Who are you?" Joe said.

"I'm your friend," chirped the man. "Come out or I'll cut your nose off."

"You'll cut off my nose?" he said into the funnel. "Why would you want to cut off my nose?"

"See you bleed."

"Go to hell."

The man stooped down as though to tie his boot-lace, but after a moment or two, Joe could guess that he was up to something more complicated. Joe brought the rifle forward and pulled back the spring bolt. There was a spark or two from the man's hands, and a stealthy movement, and then the man leapt away from the entrance to the cave and crabbed backwards down the hill like a great spider.

With a profound *whump* the cave erupted, blew out the tent and all its debris onto the snow. As though the cave had been alive, an eructating monster. The tall man laboured back up the hill and peered into the cave.

"That was a mistake," Joe said into the funnel.

The man leapt back and at last he looked up in Joe's direction. It was the man named Knaaker, and in the light offered up by the glowing snow, his face had somehow emerged from behind the blank mask, the brow furrowed and the mouth now open. He spread his arms to either side, as though he were testing for rain. A plea for mercy? In his right hand was a skinning knife. Joe – or rather, someone inside of Joe – squeezed the trigger.

At the bark of the rifle Knaaker flinched only enough to blink his eyes, and for a second or two he looked as though he had been struck by an idea. The idea seemed to fade, his entire long body seemed to relax, and he fell backwards and rolled wobble-jointed over and over down the slope.

JOE NEEDED WOOD. There was a corpse lying at the edge of his claim, he was shaken to the core of his being, he knew that even if he survived this episode in his life he would never be the same again, but goddam it, Joe needed wood. He needed to get warm and he needed to burn a man's body and dispose of it.

The largest stands were up the shore to his left a few hundred yards from his campfire. He followed a trail carved by the runners of a sled and Knaaker's partially snowed-in tracks back to a large thicket, and he found Knaaker's campsite, his tent, and the supplies that Buster had left for Knaaker. He also found his own bag of ore samples. The thicket had some dead aspen bigger than the trees around Joe and Riley's campsite. Joe wrestled a dozen of them to the ground and dragged several back to his own fire pit. He chopped and stomped the trees into two-or three-foot lengths and went back for more.

Wait a bloody minute. If he burned Knaaker's body and disposed of Knaaker's bones, there would be half a dozen sworn statements to the effect that he must have murdered Knaaker and replaced Knaaker's stakes with his own. They would say that the claim was theirs and he killed Knaaker for it.

And Stinky Riley could not afford a good lawyer.

Didn't matter. Joe still needed lots of wood. His brains were addled with the cold.

A horrific idea bubbled up, an idea he had to combat with all his might. He carried the rest of the dead trees back to his camp in stages, and this necessity helped him to circle his idea, cast doubt on it, dismiss it, and when it slunk once more into his temporal lobe, he could pepper it with logic, ridicule it, and send it howling back to the abyss. He began to think that he was winning the battle against his horrific idea, because the grey matter in his brain, the good stuff in his frontal lobes, spoke reason to fear.

Master Herron seemed to agree: *You will confess your crime to your friend Riley when he picks you up, and he will fly you to the detachment in Yellowknife. Right. Young Burbidge, are you listening? Good. You will plead self-defense, of course, but if Mr. Krahn and his lawyers cast doubt on your motives in court, you will take your medicine like a man. Remember, you chose to shoot this chap. You were free not to kill the man. You could even have shot to wing the fellow in the leg.*

Young Burbidge: *In rebuttal, sir. Look, you don't understand. He wanted to kill me. He shredded my tent. I couldn't aim for his bloody leg. I had to…I had to destroy him so that he could never come back at me again.*

Master Herron: *This is just fear talking, Burbidge. You were afraid and you shot the man dead. Period.*

Burbidge: *Your goddam bloody rights I was afraid.*

Joseph's mother: *You don't need to use that language, Joey. You never used that language when you lived at home. If your father could only hear you.*

Burbidge: *Which father are you referring to? Would that be the one who loved us or the one who dismissed us?*

Auntie Vi: *There is no need to talk like that to your mother. We are all deeply disappointed in you, Joseph.*

Joseph's mother: *Chasing after gold. And where does it get you? The first man who tries to take it away and you shoot him.*

Burbidge: *Mother, for Heaven's sake, it had nothing to do with gold. Nothing. He was ordered by his imbecile boss to kill me.*

Stinky Riley: *Don't pay them women no mind. Never pays to argue with a woman. Try not to think about it. That's my advice, Joey. Don't lose no sleep over it. Another thing, Joey. Hide that bastard's body. Cops come up here and find him shot, you'll get life sure's yer born. Life, Joey. They got money, you and me got one half a two thirds a sweet bugger-all. They find that body, Joey, you are a goner.*

Burbidge: *So what do I do?*

There was no answer from Stinky, but the voices in Joe's brain began to gain insistence and to rise higher on the scale. They could not agree, they could only babble, and their words disappeared in the bubbled welter of their voices. Knaaker hunched his way into their midst, without a stitch on, wielding his skinning knife.

Knaaker: *Why am I naked? What kinda screwball would kill me and take off my clothes?*

Burbidge: *I'm going to dress you up, my friend. Don't worry.*

KNAAKER'S BODY WAS STRETCHED out on the snowy ground. One long arm lay across his stomach. His body had paled from bluish gray to white with a dark small patch on his abdomen from the pooling blood inside. His clothes, right down to his worn and frowzy longjohns, lay next to him on the woodpile. Knaaker seemed to be staring in puzzlement at the snowladen clouds above. The bullet had entered his head just above the left eyebrow and must have lodged itself somewhere in Knaaker's brain.

If Buster Krahn and his crew came back before Stinky could, that would be bad luck. He would have to run for the forest. The fear was winning, it was rampaging through his body once again, Joe's undressed body.

Impelled by the force of his horrific idea – no, his ingenious – no, his horrific idea, Joe had stripped himself as naked as poor Knaaker. Shivering by the fire, he hopped into Knaaker's long underwear. Then his stiff woolen socks. His patched and stained canvas pants. His sour old rubber boots. A moment of terrible sadness pulsed into the picture, a plea from the enlightened circuits in the grey matter. Sadness for Knaaker's old rubber boots and his rank, worn-out clothing. Joe had just killed a poor man. A nasty man, yes, but a poor one. An unfeeling man who would serve his master like a dog, but a man just the same. A man who danced like a puppet when he was excited.

He finished dressing himself in Knaaker's clothes, and then he yanked, coaxed, grunted away at the unpleasant task of dressing Knaaker in his own clothes. He even gave Knaaker his wallet with a few ones in it and placed some personal items in his knapsack. He was careful to keep all the Eggers papers, and to keep nothing that would identify him as Joe Burbidge. He wrestled his own wellies onto Knaaker's feet, because his own boots would be no good in the snow and he needed to counterfeit his victim in every way possible. Knaaker's rubber boots were a size or two larger than Joe's, but they had felt inner soles. Joe would make do with two pairs of socks.

"There, my friend. Well, not exactly my friend, are you? There, my enemy. Is that better? Never been so well turned out in all your life, have you? What else do you want, you haggard old bugger? You've turned me into a bloody killer, you and your demented boss. See where it gets you, Knaaker? See what a mess we've made? If the whole world acted this way we'd be at each other's throats, wouldn't we? Don't deny it. I may be a killer but I'm right, aren't I?"

Knaaker was silent on the question.

"May the Lord God commend thy bones to the – may flights of angels fly thee off to–may the good Lord take a liking–ashes to ashes, amen."

Joe's first funeral oration.

"Good bye, Knaaker."

He would leave the knapsack with the Burbidge ID a few feet away from Knaaker's body, and he would hope the wolves didn't take a shine to the knapsack. It wasn't edible, couldn't smell edible, could it? He tried to make up his mind what to leave and what to haul. He comforted himself with the bush wisdom that wolves loved to eat the brains of their prey. One of them might even swallow that slug. Hah.

"Isn't this what murderers do?" he said to the trees. "Rob their victims and slink off into the woods? Live like animals in a den?"

Knaaker seemed to be weighing both sides of the question.

"Oh, go to hell," he replied to himself. "Eggers can't be choosers."

He peered down at Knaaker, whose eyes held the glazed look of an insomniac, and who clearly did not appreciate the joke.

But God, that was a good one. Joe began to laugh and he couldn't seem to stop. His laughter became alarmingly loud until it racked its way up from his guts and turned to weeping, then howling with anguish, uncontrolled at first, and then softer as he began to pile on more wood.

IN THE MORNING Joe came out of his re-excavated cave half frozen to death. He was stumbling down the esker to light a fire when he heard the droning of a small plane. It roared over the lake and circled. Stinky's trusty all-metal Junkers. To be more accurate, it roared over a thin sheet of ice that rendered the plane's pontoons useless.

The larger lake they had first landed on would be the same. Stinky could not find enough water to land on. And the ice would be too thin for skiis. Stinky did another loop away from the small lake, turned about, and flew past, dropping a large bundle just above the near shore. Joe waved to Stinky but Stinky just stared at him from the cockpit, as though he had never known him, as though they had never been partners. And then he flew away.

"It's me, you silly sod! Me! Don't you know Burbidge when you see him?"

He was numb with the cold and he was getting colder. His

cave was not working. As the sound of Riley's engine faded, Joe emptied the last of his petrol on some kindling and re-lit the campfire.

"Burbidge? Is that what you just said? It's not Burbidge, me boy." Burbidge was as dead as bloody Knaaker.

He had found a small flat sled behind Knaaker's campsite, and he used it to haul equipment back and forth. He spent the day going through the bundle Stinky Riley had dropped from the sky and what Knaaker had left at his campsite. He took only what he could carry on Knaaker's two-by-five-foot sled. Both pokes of gold dust. Warm clothing. The unopened box of food. Knaaker's bush rifle. A small boxboard carton containing nineteen shells for Knaaker's rifle. Some wooden matches and a cigarette lighter. Knaaker's axe. A sturdy canister of rum and a small box of cigars courtesy of Stinky. A canvas-bound military sleeping bag stuffed with goose down. Knaaker's tent and cooking pots. Two squat candles that reminded him of Auntie Vi. His dog-eared copy of *Ulysses* for starting fires. His *Geological Survey of Canada, Series #7, 3rd Edition*. More paper in that one.

He contemplated the stolen sack of rich ore samples. It was heavy with the stuff. He emptied the sack of rocks on the ground and bundled his extra clothing inside. He stuffed Knaaker's wallet into his own pants' pocket.

He dreaded the moment when Buster and his men would return in the Noorduyn Norseman. Or would they? He dreaded the moment when he would have to leave his campfire. Head out from the Barrens in Knaaker's enhanced rubber boots.

When the sled was packed, Joe saw the last of his choices fall away. Neither Stinky nor Buster could land on this ice with pontoons. Neither pilot was stupid enough to risk a landing on the larger lake, for if it weren't already covered with a thin sheet of ice, it soon would be. He might fly in but he wouldn't get out. And there wasn't nearly enough snow on the ground for a plane to land on skis. There were no fields or roads, just endless eskers, scattered boulders. A graveyard of protruding rocks just waiting to knock off anything that stuck out on a bush plane. And if Joe risked another week on the windy Barrens, living in Knaaker's tent, he would probably freeze to death from exposure. He needed to get out of the wind and stay in the woods. The thicker the better. The further south the better.

And then what?

He hauled his sled up the esker, and holding out his compass and using a map of Stinky's, he charted a course roughly to the south of the small lake. He would head south but he would have to stay east of the stream that fed into a chain of lakes to the southwest of him. The ice would be too thin to cross. About two miles away was a long line of fir trees that grew darker and thicker the farther south he gazed. He would walk into the trees, set up his tent and hope that the wind and the snow would do their work quickly and erase his tracks. He looked up at the glowering sky, the drifting clouds, and he started down the esker. Given all the twists and loops in his journey, including a wide berth around MacLeod Bay, it was, he reckoned, probably less than two hundred and fifty miles southwest to Fort Resolution. If he could shoot an animal or two, and supplement his food supply, he could cover ten miles a day, could he not? Why not? One day per week to rest up? In these conditions, he could make it to Fort Resolution by early December. There were scarcely three inches of snow on the ground.

I am Knaaker Johanson, and I have killed an Englishman. Beware.

Camped in a straggle of small trees and bushes, lying at last in his new down bag, Joe listened to the wolves howling well into the night. At times they voiced a lunatic's approximation of human words. Crazed perhaps, but human. What a feast they must be having.

"Eat up, me hearties," he said to the roof of his tent. "Just as good as caribou. Seconds all around, don't be shy."

The howling faded and returned in a series of mournful canine utterances, faded and returned, rising from low sepulchral moans to hair-raising heights. It was an impressive conversation they were having.

"I shall go mad," he said to no one.

Chapter 9

Knocker Walks

HIS FEAR CAME LIKE a second shadow along for the hike, watching him through the day and night, tramping south beside him as he hauled his sled and prayed for snow to cover up his manifold sins. Finally the fear slumbered long enough for him to start organizing his equipment, resume his regular compass checks, notice the changes in terrain as he moved farther away from the Barrens. The trees appeared somewhat more profuse and perhaps even larger than they had at the place where he first entered them. Some were taller than he was. Didn't Stinky always say that this was a good thing? That the trees protected you from the wind and weather? That you couldn't get lost in valleys and trees if you used your compass? So why should he fear the trees? Isidore would not fear the trees.

Joe had had a shivery night of it at his first campsite. Isidore would have done a better job of making camp. Joe hadn't placed enough of a barrier between the snow and the bottom of his tent, and between the bottom of his tent and his down bag. He had let his fear distract him. He'd climbed into his down bag thinking that he would be insulated from the snow beneath his tent, but halfway through the howling night, he had awakened, perishing to the core of his being, as though the frozen tundra had headed up through the canvas of his tent, through the down in his sleeping bag, and crawled into him. He dozed and awakened, chattering, muttering, for the rest of the night.

This night would be different. First he gathered some thin twigs, dry weeds, bark and grass, and he placed them on top of two swept logs like a bird's nest a few inches from the ground. He lit a fire on top of the two logs with Knaaker's cigarette lighter. With great delicacy he leaned some sticks, branches and then the larger wood over the fire until it caught and gave off some heat. He had found some high ground in the midst of bush and stunted fir trees. He took his axe to the trees and laid down a springy layer of branches about ten feet from the campfire. He pitched his tent on top of the branches and laid a tarp on the floor. Over the tarp he laid down all the extra clothing he had, and a large towel and his only blanket. When he had eaten his fill and had his tea, he added his own coat to the pile of clothing beneath his down bag. He fashioned a candle-holder from a tin cup and lit one of his large candles. He placed the cup on a tin plate and let it burn in the corner of the tent as he prepared to slip into his sleeping bag. He fell asleep gazing at the candle, as Lucy Castaway might have done years ago, and it burned all through the night down to a three-inch stub. This time he slept without waking.

The next morning he moved on again, south and slightly west. The clumps of trees and bushy thickets seemed to be slightly more plentiful. The dirt beneath the thin layer of snow seemed to be sandy and dry. Best of all, there were no large lakes or rivers to block his passage south. Once more he camped and slept again without waking.

Perhaps it was the vast amount of brown sugar he had thrown on his boiled oats and raisins the next morning, but he was visited by a brief burst of hope. He had stopped shivering and his fear had once more abated. He was alive. The wolves had very probably chosen to dine on his little offering. Soon they would return to clean up the scraps but probably they would not pursue him. In any case he had Knaaker's bush gun. His body was warm. He was heading south for McLeod Bay.

And then he was loaded and pulling the sled over the snow, and he began to think about what it might be like to travel over an entire foot of snow, two feet of snow. Four feet of snow. And even if he managed to walk two hundred miles and more, how in the hell could he ever hope to hit Fort Resolution?

The fear acted as a goad to him and for a while he walked rapidly through the sparse woods, checking his compass every few minutes, getting overheated. And then he found himself humming a tune, as though something in the moaning wind were humming *him*. A slow, plodding song from his boyhood summers in Slaidburn, something they used to sing in his mother's tiny church.

We are climbing Jacob's Ladder,
We are climbing Jacob's ladder,
We are climbing Jacob's ladder...

It came out of him slowly, to the rhythm of his walking, settling his panic, so he muttered it out loud and off key, and louder, and finally on key, and as the morning wore on, he found himself praying to the great cloudy void soughing above him, *Move me forward, please move me forward. Keep me moving forward. Every day. I'm sorry I've taken your name in vain. Sorry I shot that murderous bastard. Just keep this bloody sinner moving. Two hundred and fifty miles more or less.*

Every rung goes higher and higher,
Every rung goes higher...higher.

He reached a small meadow, checked the horizon, and spotted what appeared to be smoke rising from a distant fire. It was many miles off, but it felt like a gift, so he followed it. His guess was that he had spotted either an Indian lodge set up for caribou hunting or a trapper's cabin. He walked faster. Every time he went down into a depression in the sparse and spindly woods, he lost sight of the rising smoke. He began to work up a bad sweat with a clammy feel to it. He was sick and he knew it, and he wondered if the smoke rising from the chimney was a mirage, and he wondered if he would fall before he arrived at the chimney, the mirage chimney or the real one, and if he fell and didn't get up, would his body ever be found, or would the wolves find it.

He reached the top of a barren rise and there was the smoke again, too distinct for any mirage. He staggered ahead for more than a mile.

It began snowing steadily, a profusion of big flakes in slow descent, a fabric so dense that he could scarcely see the cabin. It sat in a clearing above a recently frozen lake. Owing to some frost bite and some blisters he had acquired from Knaaker's rubber boots, he approached the cabin with a pronounced limp. Yes, a log cabin. Large enough to sleep a big family or two, the sort of well made cabin one dreams of when one is currently lost in the far North and trying to sleep each night in a tent.

Below the clearing where the cabin perched was a large boat shed and a fleet of beached rowboats covered with tarpaulins topped with snow. Off to one side about fifty feet from the edge of the lake stood a string of tiny cabins banged together from ship-lap and painted white with red trim.

He approached the door of the big cabin. His breath was whistling, his lungs aching. He either did or did not open the door of the cabin, walk inside and say hello to a man who sat in an easy chair facing a woodstove. He must have done, but somehow, later on, the memory of it seemed manufactured. The man was reading a book. Without looking up from his book the man called out a hearty greeting.

"Close the goddam door."

"I'm Knaaker Johanson."

"Well, Knocker, you ever heard a knockin?"

The man put the book down and turned to face his visitor.

"You the law?"

"No."

"You come here to make trouble?"

"I came in here because I'm tired. And it's bloody cold out there."

"You got a Swede moniker and a limey accent. You bring a rifle into my cabin, what the bleedin Christ am I sposed to think?"

"Welcome to you too," he said, and leaned Knaaker's rifle against the wall.

The man arose from his chair, strode towards him, a lean old battler, balding, unshaven, sporting the curled lip of a guard dog. A man who didn't seem to belong here. Fists clenched by his side. The man made straight for Joe and he was not going to stop.

Joe hit him square in the temple and he went down rattling like a huge golf bag. He lay on the rug for a moment with a dazed look, then strained to raise his head.

"What's your name?" he said to the man.

"Rusty Regan."

"I'm not a Swede," said Joe. "I'm not a limey either. Family's Norwegian actually but I'm not anybody. Just a traveler looking to warm up."

Rusty Regan came slowly to his knees. "Why didn't ya say so? Jeez."

Regan either did or did not bring Joe a plate of cold chicken, cold baked potatoes and a scattering of canned peas.

"Rusty," he said, "you'll pardon the observation, all due respect, but you seem to be all alone up here." He swallowed a glorious mouthful of chicken. He was going to live. "Are you in hiding from the authorities?"

Regan's mouth took on a painful twist that might, in other circles, have passed for a smile.

"Hiding from the authorities? I just love the way you guys talk. No, I'm not hidin from the cops, I'm guardin this place from them goddam Dogribs. The bastards come up to hunt, they break into the cabins, leave a mess behind."

Joe looked down at Regan's book, a brand new hardback by a chap named Chandler.

"Who owns this fishing camp?"

"Couple a brothers from California. I work for them. Hey, you walkin around out there in rubber boots? Don't be offended, pal, but no one walks around here in rubber boots."

"I flew in on a bush plane. Had no idea I'd be tracking all over the tundra."

"North is hard on you Brits, Knocker."

"I'm not British, you ninny. I *shoot* Englishmen. Ever hear of Joseph Burbidge, hm? No? I shot him in cold blood and fed him to the wolves."

"Yeah?"

"Don't worry. My blood was up. I'm all right now. Nothing to worry about. Sorry for the knock on the head, Rusty."

Joe either stood up and fainted, or he took himself and his rifle to the nearest bed and fell asleep. He remembered conversations with all sorts of Englishmen, most of them dead. Hornby and Critchell-Bullock. And those two young chaps who followed Hornby up to the Barrens, said their names were Harold and Edgar. And Sir John Franklin of course. Then a brief exchange with Robert Service, the writer chap. Either Joe was in the grip of his fever or these gentlemen were all in the room with him. Either he was hallucinating or he was communing with wandering spirits.

Knaaker, he kept telling them. *The name is Knaaker Johanson.*

I say, said one of the men, how *do you like the weather up here?*

Critchell-Bullock opined that he'd rather be back in the bloody Palestine desert or back with the Bengal bloody Lancers, that's how much he liked the weather up here. *My advice, Mr. Knocker, is get the hell out of the North and never come back.*

Either he had divested himself of his coat and rubber boots or Regan had performed this service. He rolled and tossed in his bed and he awoke (or did not awaken) damp from his own sweat or from the ocean spray. He thought perhaps he was back in the tern schooner *Rolland's Riches*. The writer chap, Service, had his notebook out. So did Rusty Regan. They were both scribbling down his words by his bedside.

You killed a guy because your blood was up? said Rusty. *Is that what you said, pal?*

Shot the poor bastard right in the head. Bang.

Spoken by Knocker Johanson on this the ninth day of November 1938, Wolf Lake.

Service put his notebook away and began to read one of his poems about a bunch of miners trudging up the Chilkoot Pass. Never was seen such an army, blah blah blah and unfit; *Never was seen such a blah blah blah full of courage and grit; Never was seen such a cohort something something and bold, As surged to the raggedy something or other, urged by the beauty? The purity? The lure of the Gold!*

Tom Payne was there too. He seemed to be enjoying the reading, and he applauded heartily with the rest of them. Not once did he glance in Joe's direction.

"DID I HEAR HIM SAY Wolf Lake?" he said one morning to Rusty. "That's this place?"

"Who?"

"The Klondike chap. Service. Did he say Wolf Lake?"

"This is it, pal. Wolf Lake. And I'm all there is. We're all alone up here. Now drink your tea. Gotta drink lotsa liquids."

"But the old lady, Lucy's mother," said Joe. "The old Indian lady said it was a bad place with no trees."

"It's no picnic, I'll tell you that. And you just head north couple a dozen miles, you got yer no-trees, bub. You're up in the goddam Barrens."

"Is there a…a smaller lake nearby?"

"Just over the ridge and down the other side. Why are you so curious about this place all of a sudden?"

"Actually," said Joe, "there might be some gold here."

"Gold?"

Joe began to babble about the presence of quartz lenses in basalt, he couldn't seem to stop, and how the grey quartz seemed richer in mineralized...

Regan raised a finger. "Wait a minute, fella. Right here? Gold right here?"

"All the gold you ever wanted, my friend. Get me cured of this bloody...whatever I've got, and I'll show you how to find it."

"That's Jake-aloo with me, pal. You got yourself a deal."

"Sorry about that rap on the head."

"Don't mention it, Knocker. Just lay off the weird stuff, okay?"

"What weird stuff?"

"These conversations you been havin with other guys, you got it? Ain't nobody here but us chickens."

ONE DAY WHEN the wind was down and the sun had returned for a few hours, Rusty took Joe out for a walk. Joe's blisters were healing and he went gingerly along in the melted snow. Rusty pointed the way to a path, and they scrambled up to a ridge above the main lake and surveyed the other side. A small lake lay perhaps three hundred yards down the trail beneath the ridge. When Joe stopped puffing, he paced up and down the ridge with Rusty peering bleakly in all directions. This height of land looked almost alpine.

"This is the only small lake around here?" said Joe.

"You got it, pal."

"Well well," said Joe, pointing to a long rocky slope recently melted and exposed to the sun.

"Well what? Knocker? I don't see nothin."

"I'll show you."

They left the ridge and descended about one third of the way down to the lake and stopped at a scree that lay at the base of a cliff.

"See over there, Rusty? Where the rock looks black?"

"Yeah?"

"It's greenstone."

"That makes sense," said Rusty. "It's black so they call it greenstone."

They picked their way along the base of the scree until they were directly under the wall of the cliff.

"Look again," said Joe. "Where the sun strikes the boulder? It's not really black is it. See a greenish tinge to it?"

"If you say so, Knocker."

"Igneous rock, Regan. Volcanic. Good sign."

Regan walked ahead, and whenever he spotted large boulders or deposits of greenstone he squinted at them, frowning, as though something beneath them had recently died.

"This black stuff," said Regan. "I mean green stuff. Is it s'poseta be where the gold is found?"

Joe was squinting at the far end of the cliff face.

"It's a good sign," said Joe. "Around here you avoid the granite slopes and look for the igneous formations. Might lead to something."

"Like what?"

Joe summoned Rusty to stand beside him. He pointed to a long dark recessed area among the rocks about a hundred yards ahead.

"Like that," he said. "Let's have a look."

The recessed area was apparently a fault zone where the edge of the cliff seemed to be cloven from its larger body in a long straight line. They walked right up to the fault and gazed at the path it had created between the dark cliff and the massive, broken-off fragment.

"Have you ever walked through there?" said Joe.

"Why would I walk into a thing like that? It's goddam spooky, it's like a rockslide waitin to happen. And who knows, you might find a bear at the other end."

"But Rusty, you might find something better."

They trudged their way slowly down the fault zone checking

the walls on both sides. Joe glanced right and left, noticed some stringers of white quartz but no real vein. He noticed a dark reddish patch level with his shins.

"What're we lookin for?" said Rusty in a low whisper.

"Mineral deposits," said Joe. "See this russet material? Here, look. That's called a gossan patch. Oxidized material. Not big enough to bother with, but a good sign."

"A good sign of gold?"

"A good sign of minerals," said Joe.

"Say, Knocker. Stop for a sec. I'm talkin to ya. Why are you so certain there's gold around here? Who sez?"

"The man I work for. Buster Krahn. Years ago he found a nugget in here that would choke a horse."

"And this Krahn jasper, he knows gold from granite? You trust him?"

Joe was thinking fondly of Lucy's mother and he smiled.

"With my life."

Cautiously, slowly, they picked their way down the corridor of dark rock until they were completely shadowed in. The fault widened up ahead and they moved into a bright slash of sun. At this point down the corridor the fault narrowed considerably and then disappeared.

"At last," said Rusty. "We can get the hell outa here."

Something down at knee level caught Joe's attention and he stooped to peer at a light-coloured patch of rock. It was mostly quartz, about two feet wide, and it lay like a long funnel of snow within the rock.

"What?"

"Look, right here and over there."

They got down on their knees and peered at the quartz vein, poking at it.

"Rusty, see the edge of the quartz? See the shearing of the rock wall? Right there and along there?"

Rusty squinted fiercely side to side.

"This is what you call a sheer zone. This is what you want."

"I don't see no gold, pal."

They stood again and trudged back through the crack in the fault zone, Joe babbling about porphyry crystals, pyrites, oxidized minerals, shearing, and Rusty nodding behind him. By the time they reached the big cabin, the sun was low on the horizon and they were both tired.

Rusty poured them both a shot of rum.

"Just be ready in the spring," said Joe. "When the snow is gone. You don't need a rock hammer. A pick will do just fine."

"Enough," said Rusty.

"And you don't need dynamite to be a prospector. All you need is –"

"Enough. Knocker, enough. I promise, I'll give it a try."

Regan stoked the fireplace and Joe stoked the stove. They drank their rum and had another and lounged like tourists in their easy chairs.

"You tryin to disappear?"

Joe looked up. "Me?"

"Yeah, you. Wanna disappear from the cops and start over? Is that your game, Knocker?"

"Something like that."

"I'm not pryin, I'm just sayin. Sometimes a fella needs to disappear. He's got his reasons."

"You too, Rusty?"

Regan shrugged. "Maybe. But if I did it, Knocker, I wouldn't go around braggin about shootin no limey. I'd get the hell outa here and find a new life. See, pal, I'd disappear and leave no traces. I got friends on the East Coast so when this little caper is over I get a bush plane down to Edmonton. I know people there. I can slip over the line and shazam, I'm a gone goose."

Rusty gazed at the fireplace and sipped his second rum with a tranquility Joe had not seen in him before.

"But you, Knocker. You got a different thing goin on, right? You work for this Buster character. Will he send you off somewhere? Help you disappear? What do you do for him?"

"I'm a trouble shooter, you might say."

Joe liked that expression. It gave him an aura of mastery and a hint of danger.

"Right, so this Buster fella. He's gonna take care of you? Hey? No? Right, so you gotta disappear yourself."

"How would you do it?"

"Hell, I'd change my name, get some identity papers and sign up. Join the army. Get assigned somewhere across the pond. They're always lookin for recruits. Then they're payin you to disappear."

Joe nodded dolefully at the fireplace. He had been nursing the dream of moving in with Stinky Riley, or with Isidore down south, laying low and working with horses and cattle till the investigation had faded. The search for Knaaker. The murderer of Joseph Burbidge. He wondered if a man could forget who he was. It made him weary to think about it.

Chapter 10

History

ONE DAY LATE IN NOVEMBER, Joe bid goodbye to Rusty Regan. Joe was sporting a well-greased pair of leather boots. Not exactly a perfect fit, but much better than Knaaker's rubber boots with the felt liners. His blisters had healed up nicely at last. He picked up his rifle, walked to the door, took a deep breath, and left the cabin.

He looked back only once, and Regan was standing in the doorway, watching Joe's progress and smoking a cigarette.

After almost three hours' walk, Joe began to tire. Over the past few weeks the snow had become almost a foot deep. He came puffing into a shallow depression and a frozen creek bed, and he found a place to camp out of the wind. He stayed there the following day, rested up, studied his map and reorganized his equipment. He would have to bear southeast to avoid McLeod Bay with its thin and treacherous ice. Then he would round the bay and immediately head southwest for Fort Resolution.

The following morning, Joe was ready to go in earnest. Just as he was packing up his sled he spotted some caribou moving in single file on the far side of the creek. He hadn't seen a single caribou in the Barrens, not even from Stinky's plane, but here they were, moving towards him, less than a hundred yards away. He brought Knaaker's rifle to his shoulder and dropped a young bull, walked up to the struggling animal and finished it off. Before he could begin to dress the caribou, another smallish bull came his way, followed by two cows and a calf. He brought down the second bull and it died right there on the spot. A long string of caribou, a hundred or more, split up and trotted by him on both sides as though he were no more threatening than a mosquito.

Joe had a few hours left of daylight, so he strung the first animal up by the tendons of its hind legs from the largest tree he could find. Isidore's style for all large animals. He lit a fire nearby where he could warm himself from time to time, and he gutted the first young bull and skinned it out. The work was slow but the nearby fire was a comfort. He had just strung up the second animal when he heard a sound behind him. He turned, and there stood a young Indian boy. A minute or so later a young woman lumbered up beside him. She was round and husky, unsmiling, circumspect, perhaps in her late teens. She was bigger than Joe. The skin on her face, the tone of it, the texture, was lovely in a way that he had never seen before.

He laid down his skinning knife and smiled at the two young people. They had to be from a settlement or a bigger party of hunters, perhaps the Dogribs that Regan had been complaining about. Perhaps they had been drawn to his gunfire that morning, but if so, how long had they been following him? Joe beckoned to his gutted and skinned caribou and tapped his chest. He went over to the second animal, which was swaying upside down from a second tree. He slapped it on the haunch and gestured to the two Indians.

"Yours," he said, and walked backwards to the first bull.

"Thanks, Mister," said the boy.

Smiles all around. In perfect silence he drew out the guts of the second bull, knelt by the fire and rubbed snow all over his bloodied hands. The young woman took his skinning knife and began at once to skin out the second carcass.

"Are you Dogrib?" he said to the boy.

"Yep," said his sister.

"Does everyone in your tribe speak English?"

"Nope," said the boy.

"Now," said the young woman, impassively, "you come with us. To da camp?"

He packed up his gear and bound the two carcasses to the sled, and the two young people pulled the sled and Joe walked behind. They took him two or three miles south to a lodge that the hunters had thrown together, a long rounded hut made of saplings and spruce boughs with caribou skins all over the ground and a wood stove at one end made from what looked like an old fuel barrel. Their lodge was surprisingly big and comfy.

The men were off hunting, so when the three of them arrived with the sled, only a few women and one old man remained in the lodge. Apparently the hunting had not gone well. From what Joe could gather, the men had not yet intercepted the caribou migration, part of which Joe had simply stumbled upon. When the hunters returned empty-handed, a feast awaited them, and Joe was regarded as a guest of honour. Most of the hunters were relatively old or middle-aged men, friendly to Joe, and they spoke a little English. But three of them were perhaps in their twenties and spoke no English at all. The young boy told them where Joe had downed the two caribou, and the boy and his sister took seven or eight hunters there the following day. They took all the dogs with them, and three days later they brought back the skinned carcasses of eighteen caribou.

After another feast, the hunters decided to pack up and head south for a small settlement Joe had never heard of named Sangris. Joe, or rather Knaaker, was invited to come with them. He told the men he was grateful to travel with them, but that he could probably not keep up with them on account of his feet. They were frost-bitten and there was little feeling in his toes. They had turned yellow, edged with black, and two of his fingers were similarly discoloured. The leather boots were a poor fit. They had failed to keep his feet warm. One of the women volunteered to make him a pair of mukluks out of caribou hide, and very soon he was up and walking with less pain. The Dogribs could not use their sleds for transporting people, because they had to be used for the caribou carcasses. The dogs hauled most of the meat, the men hauled the excess bundles, and Joe walked among them, pulling his sled, limping away in his new mukluks. The going was bearable for Joe because the younger men broke trail.

They arrived at the village of Sangris in early December. The people lived in cabins and tarpaper shacks that were scattered near the shore of a narrow lake. A big hill rose behind the settlement with a tipi on top. It was a ceremonial structure and no one seemed to sleep there. Just beyond the circle of cabins a short way into the bush a barnlike lodge stood in a state of rough repair where the people gathered.

The boys and men had a game where they gambled for sticks. When the game was over, the sticks were discarded, and no one ever owed anyone else. (The gamblers in Yellowknife, Joe recalled, had been less forgiving.) But these men, the older ones and the young boys together, they all had a part to play. The oldest men were musicians who would drum and sing while the game went on. The younger ones, the boys, broke up into two teams, lined up four or five to a side, facing each other on their knees.

Joe suspected that they were putting on a show for his benefit. He saw them do the entire game only once. On that night he noticed a number of much older men and more than a dozen boys, but very few young men. The young women outnumbered them vastly. At first it looked as though a generation of men was missing from the tribe. Perhaps the missing ones had gone off hunting.

The young boy who had first discovered Joe dressing the caribou was named Eddy. He was designated to start the game. He held out a stone so that the other team could see it. He tossed it from hand to hand and waved it around in the air and thrust both hands down between his legs and brought them out again. The stone had disappeared in the process. The other team had to guess where it was. The lead boy on the other team pointed down at Eddy's crotch but the stone wasn't down there; it was in the crick of Eddy's elbow, so Eddy won a stick from them. He did his routine once more with a similar result. He did it a third time, and the lead boy pointed to Eddy's crotch again, and this time the stone was spotted beneath Eddy's rump, so he had to give back one of his sticks, and it was the other team's turn. With the drummers drumming and the old men singing and the boys gesticulating and the girls and women laughing in the crowd, it was a lively affair. In another lifetime, Joe might have been caught up in the merriment.

He spotted an old white man standing near the door, smiling somberly. Joe had heard from Eddy that a priest was living with them, and that he had taught English to some of the children. The small man by the door wasn't dressed like a priest. He seemed to hold himself at some distance from the lively game. Perhaps, like Joe, he was weary. Perhaps, like Joe, he had seen too much of life in the North.

THE NIGHTS TURNED starkly cold. Joe had set up his tent in a clearing not far from the tarpaper shacks where he was sheltered from the wind, but no matter how carefully he laid down boughs and insulated his body from the snow, he shivered his way to sleep night after night. The priest was the first to notice his predicament. He was indeed the man Joe had spotted standing at the door of the lodge. Father Francis was a small, snowy-haired chap in his early seventies. He had retired from his vocation, turned his back on the Church, and thrown his lot in with the Dogribs. He came to Joe's tent one night and offered to share his cabin with Joe for a while.

"You'll find it small, but comfortable enough. We can set up a cot for you by the kitchen stove. It will be a lot warmer than your tent."

He told Francis that he would soon be heading for Fort Resolution.

"Why there?"

"I'm making my way back south," he said. "Bit by bit."

"Mr. Johansen, I'm not sure there is anyone living at Fort Resolution. Not at this time of year. Maybe a few trappers in the area, that's all. You'll get the boats and the planes coming in during the warmer months, because of course the commerce gets going then. So why leave us now?"

He could not tell Francis the truth, that sooner or later the Mounties would be looking for Knaaker Johansen. Or maybe a few of Krahn's boys. He was tired of being Knaaker. He looked forward to the day when he could be Joe Eggers.

"Perhaps I can stay for a while, Francis. Never stayed with a priest before. You might learn some frightful language from me."

"Oh, I daresay I could match you word for word, Mr. Johansen."

"Call me ..." He almost said Joe. "Call me Knaaker."

"Knaaker it is then."

His sickness returned, bringing on aches, night sweats, coughing spells, but no blood. The people stayed away from him. Francis explained that they were afraid of all manner of white men's diseases, but Joe still felt it odd. He rested a great deal through December and January, and gradually a few of the Dogribs got to know him. Young Eddy came by now and then. The boy managed a few shy exchanges with Joe but his colossus of a sister remained silent in his presence. Her name was Heraldene. On occasion, she would stare at him impassively from across the clearing. He wondered why she stared so.

One night in the chief's cabin Joe and Francis joined a few of the men for a smoke. It seemed to Joe that at last he was declared safe to approach. Joe brought out some cigars and passed them around. The chief was a trapper and a hunter by the name of Jimmy Norn. Jimmy wanted to know more about Joe, so he asked him where he worked.

"I'm a prospector," he told the chief. "I work for a man named Buster Krahn."

"What kind prospector, Knocker?"

"Gold."

"Do you ever go for dat Kweh Kha?"

The chief could see that Joe was confused. He turned to an old man who sat quietly in the corner of the cabin and they had a brief exchange. The old man spoke slowly, methodically, to him. They all spoke slowly because nobody seemed to be in a hurry.

"Kweh kha," he said again. "The rock fat, do you see? Do you prospect for dat rock fat, Knocker?"

Joe turned to Francis.

"I think he means pitchblende," said the former priest. "They call it rock fat because it looks like bone marrow. With the white rock inside?"

Francis glanced at Jimmy Norn and the chief smiled back his thanks.

Joe turned to Jimmy Norn. "Not any more," he said. "We found some of that rock up at Great Bear Lake."

"Ah," said the chief.

"Sahtu," said Francis to the chief.

"Ah."

"I've heard," Joe continued, "I've heard that it is dangerous for men to handle."

"Dat is what we have heard," said the chief. "Dis man you work for, dis Buster Krahn. We know of him. Did he tell you dat de Kweh Kha was dangerous?"

"I suppose he did," said Joe. "I don't remember."

"Do you like to work for dis Krahn?" said the chief.

"Oh, he's all right. He's got some nice equipment. Nice planes and tools and such. Big crew."

The old man emerged from his quiet corner and joined them at the table. He had a compelling, handsome old face. He was Jimmy Norn's uncle from Fort Rae, and reputed to be a shaman. His name was Mayday Medzin.

Francis did the introductions. He smiled at the old man. "Mayday knows bear medicine," he told Joe. "Mayday is a fine healer. I came to have a bad fever. I started to turn yellow like a

Chinaman and Mayday fixed me up." Francis pounded on his chest and looked very hearty indeed.

The old healer whispered something to the chief and Norn started nodding.

"Mayday wants to know if your fellow Krahn still hires da Dene."

The question seemed to be loaded with some vague implication, so Joe shrugged and said he didn't know.

"You don't know," said the chief.

He turned to Mayday Medzin. "He said he don't know. Do you understand?"

Mayday Medzin nodded his fine old head.

Francis spoke to Joe in a low voice so that only Joe could hear. "Knaaker, you don't bullshit the chief. Or Mayday. You can bullshit me or any of the others, but not these two."

"I was just saying," said Joe, and the chief interrupted his conversation with Francis.

"Does your boss, dis Krahn, does he still hire..." Norn turned to Francis.

"Indians," said Francis to the chief. "Say Indians."

Norn turned to Joe again. "Does your nice boss still hire Indians?"

"Oh, yes," said Joe. "He still does. Yes."

"And Knocker," the chief continued, "does your nice boss still mine after de Kweh Kha?"

The cabin had gone silent.

"Yes," said Joe. "But I think he is more interested in finding gold."

"I understand dat," said Jimmy Norn. "Do you understand dat, Francis?"

"Yes," said Francis. "I understand that."

"Mayday, you understand dat too?" said the chief.

"I too," said Mayday Medzin.

"The Kweh Kha brings him less money," said Joe. "The gold

brings him more money."

"Ah," said the chief. "Not because it is dangerous to handle? The Kweh Kha?"

"Oh," said Joe, "that too."

"You like our women?" said Mayday Medzin. "You like dem?"

"Your women are very fine."

Mayday said, "I ask you dis, Knocker. I ask you dis. We have a lotta women here. No husbins."

"They are very fine," Joe said again.

"The reason they have no husbins," said Jimmy Norn, "is because some of our young men useta work for your nice boss."

"They did?"

"They useta work for your man Buster. They are dead now."

"Dead?"

"They were hired by your nice boss to carry out dis Kweh Kha. At Sahtu, where you were working. To carry it in their canoes and then to carry it on their backs. Carry it on their backs so dat da Rock Man could see it up close through a glass. Carry it to da Rock Man all the way to Yellowknife. Three young men. And two more before dat. And they all lose weight, they all get tired, their hairs fall out and two die da following winter. Then tree more the nex winter. Francis brings dat doctor, him, by plane. Tell us to never carry da Kweh Kha. But dat is too late, Knocker. Because they die. We got tree more in da hospital in Yellowknife. Verrrry sick like da udders."

Joe walked back with Francis to the cabin. He could hear drumming from the big lodge in the bush, loud drumming and male voices singing. They howled like wolves, starting low and going away up into falsetto and back down again. Outside the door of the cabin, the old priest looked up to Joe and tapped his finger on Joe's chest.

"Get out of here. Don't tell anyone. Pack your sled and leave as silently as you can."

"You think I'm in danger?"

"You work for the wrong man, Knaaker. They can't get to this fellow Krahn but they can get to his henchman."

"What do you mean henchman? I just worked for him"

"Working for your nice boss, this Krahn character. That does not go well for you."

"But how," Joe persisted, "do you know I was Krahn's?"

"You talk at night."

"What do I talk about?"

"Maybe several things. You talk about shooting. You talk about sending a man back to Hell. You shoot this man many nights. Maybe you've shot more than one man?"

They entered the cabin in silence. They prepared for sleep at opposite ends of the cabin, and Joe found himself fidgeting. He glared at Francis but the old priest would not return his look.

"Can I tell you something?" said Joe.

"Never mind that. Can you get your boss to compensate all the widows and their children?"

"I need to tell you something, Francis."

"Why do I smell bullshit coming on?"

"I shot someone. He was coming for me and I killed him."

"I don't care," said Francis. "I don't do confessions any more. Even if they're not bullshit. This is between you and your conscience."

Joe began to pace. He had almost forgotten where he was. He looked up and saw the old priest beside his cot, whispering a prayer on his knees. When Francis had finished he stood beside the cot and gazed at Joe.

Joe said, "I thought you were through with that stuff."

"There are many of us former men of the cloth who do not stop praying. We can leave the church behind but we don't stop talking to God. I don't miss my church very much. I don't miss doing their work with these people. It didn't always make sense to me. I can say goodbye to all of that, but I can't say goodbye to God."

"Never could pray meself. Did I ever say the name of the man I shot?"

"I don't know. It sounded like…Garbage? Something like that."

Joe looked at the old man and the old man gazed back at Joe. It was a long, meditative look, as though he were re-evaluating the man to whom he had offered his hospitality.

"The honeymoon is over, my friend. The young men, the hunters, they will talk to Mayday, and he will tell them. You've got to leave as soon as you can pack your sled. Leave tomorrow morning if you feel strong enough."

"What's the village south of here?"

"Lutsel K'e. They speak Chipewyan."

"Those drums we heard here tonight. What did they mean?"

Francis stared at the floor.

"You know what they mean, don't you."

"Knaaker, I can't make it any clearer than this. Make up your mind to leave tomorrow. Leave early. Don't waste your time or your time will be up. I can pray for you but I can't protect you."

The following morning after breakfast Francis told him to head southwest until he came to the headwaters of the LaLoche River. Cross the river, he said, and continue southwest to Fort Resolution.

"You can walk from there all the way to Hay River. If you can't pray, Knaaker, think about your sins. If you don't feel like thinking about your sins, think about those young men and their widows and their children, and how your nice boss can compensate them."

AT FIRST LIGHT Joe packed up his sled. He had a hurried breakfast, said goodbye to the priest and headed south past the larger village of Lutsel K'e to the headwaters of the LaLoche River. It wasn't hard to cross the river, pulling his sled behind, and because the wind was up, he kept to a path along the river and headed southwest by the compass. Once again, the trees sheltered him. Not once did he think of his sins or pray to the god of Father Francis or any other god. Nor did he call upon the wisdom of his logic teacher of long ago, to learn from the past and live in the present, because all he wanted to do was get the hell south. His fear had begun to shadow him once again.

They found him the following morning, four young men and two older ones. He was camped in a grove of black spruce and some old birch by the frozen river. If he hadn't dallied over his fire at breakfast, they might not have caught him there. He might have slipped away under cover of the snowstorm that was gathering to the north. He recognized these men from his time in Sangris and from the hunting party further north, but he knew none of their names. They had all stuck together and moved in and out of the community according to the needs of their trap-lines or their need to pursue the caribou. Only one of them spoke some English, but they all seemed to know enough about Knaaker to despise him.

They came upon him quite suddenly and circled him as though in jest and yelled at him in their own language. They pushed him, knocked him down, and bound his hands behind his back.

"White men like to hang da bad guys, hey Knocker?"

"I'm not a bad guy," he said to the young man.

"We know a bad guy when we smell one."

While the others held him, the young man tossed a rope through the crotch of the largest birch tree around, pulled a noose over Joe's parka hood and tightened it around his neck.

"So, this is how it ends," he said to one of them. "And I'm not even your man, your Knaaker." They wrestled him closer to the old birch so that he stood teetering on a raised root. "I'm completely innocent," he said, and he thought of Francis, who would say *bullshit.* "All right, I killed a man. I shot poor Knaaker. And I've been locked…"

He stared at the tallest young man, the one who spoke the most English. He had a jagged scar on his forehead, and he may have been their leader.

"I've been locked in selfish pursuit. Gold fever and all that. I killed for it. I am a sinner before God."

He was weeping, trying to speak to a bunch of young men who couldn't understand his language. But nothing could stop him from confessing to them.

"I'm a sinner! I'm a bloody no-good sinner! I let myself turn into a wolf and I killed a man! There! Does that satisfy you? Do you want me to go down on my knees? Jesus Christ!"

A shouting match broke out among the young men and the two older ones. The shouting turned into shoving, but he couldn't tell what they were yelling about. Two of them grabbed Joe at the base of the tree and pushed him stumbling over to his own sled, forced him to stand there on top of his bundles while they shortened the rope above him. Their work was clumsy and distracted and some of the others continued to push and yell at each other. The loop of rope around his neck loosened and Joe worked one side of his chin into it, but someone pushed him hard to put an end to the debate, and at last he was swinging by his neck, and the blood welled up in his head and he could feel his eyes bulge. As the angry voices faded, and his tongue crawled swollen out of his mouth, he was at last turning free of the Earth.

HE AWAKENED TO THE sensation of someone molesting his body, someone who wanted to bugger him or draw and quarter him like a dead caribou. He wanted to tell his parents that he was sorry, but he couldn't speak. Someone had his head between Joe's legs. *Yes*, he said to himself, *I am still Joe.* And through the throttling pain, he realized that his breath was once more whistling through his wind-pipe, and that he was no longer swinging through the air on his way to eternal silence. But the place down by his crotch where they were going to draw and quarter him, that place felt no pain. He had shit himself down there. Only his neck was in pain, and his jaw, and his shoulders. And then he was rising up inch by inch and the rope felt looser and he drew a full, icy breath.

Someone said, "I can't reach da goddam rope."

"Uhhhhhh," he replied.

"I got you," the person said.

It was a woman. Her head was between his thighs and his hams rested on her shoulders. A woman.

"Uhhh," he said.

"Take da rope off yer neck."

"Can't. Hands tied."

"I'll let you dangle again. I'll untie da rope on your hands."

"No no no no no no."

"Have it your way," she grunted.

The sound of her voice hummed up through his bowels, up through his guts to his throat. Her shoulders felt strong and soft and massive. She began to weave drunkenly beneath him. She was going to fall.

"Hey, I can't stay dish way forever."

"A jacknife. In my coat pocket."

She swore at him, told him she couldn't reach his knife without letting him dangle.

"What's your name?" he said.

"Heraldene."

"Of course, Heraldene. I'm Joseph."

"Joseph Knocker?"

"No, I'm just Joseph."

"Knocker or Joseph," she said, "you smell like shit."

There was a long silence. Her great body seemed to give off heat. The sensation of riding on her shoulders was almost pleasurable, like riding Shanghai Lil. The silence lasted until her young brother came into the clearing. He stared at his sister.

Eddy said, "What da hell you doin?"

"I'm playin wit myself," she said. "What in da fuck does it look like?"

Heraldene tried to swear gently. She told her brother to get the man's fuckin knife out of his fuckin pocket and cut the fuckin rope on his hands.

"Why?"

She swore at young Eddy again, but this time not so gently. She alluded to Father Francis' orders and threatened hell-fire for her brother, and at last Eddy got it. He hopped behind them and began to pull himself up his sister's back. He clung to the soft leather of her jacket, tearing it in the process, and shinnied up higher. Teetering on her shoulders, he fished the knife out of Joe's parka, opened the blade and slashed the rawhide that bound his wrists.

Joe could scarcely feel his own arms, but he reached up, eased the rope off his neck, looked out at the spinning snowbound woods, and slumped forward under the weight of a vision. In the failing light, for the briefest second before gravity brought the three of them crashing to the ground, they must have looked like a triad of figures in soapstone, a sculptor's approximation, perhaps, of Canadian history.

Part Two

End of Story

Chapter 11

Women

He stopped to glance at the entrance to the building, remembering the first time he'd come there. How many years had it been? Was it seven? Almost exactly seven years, because when he arrived at Auntie Vi's door he was twenty years old. Joe had arrived shivering in the dark with no luggage. He remembered the casket just inside the door of Auntie Vi's suite. Her paintings and photographs.

He was shivering this time too, owing as much to his infirmities as to the January weather. He went inside and hailed the doorman. Shivering and clammy from a sudden sweat. He was wearing someone's cast-off shoes and a new pair of longjohns, Knaaker's pair of oft-mended heavy trousers, a shirt and a sweater that a railroad conductor had given him on the train ride from Peace River, and a torn and whiffy winter coat, a borrowed one that smelled of engine oil, axle grease, and the sweat of labour in the North. His garments hung from his bones. He was unshaven, unwashed, emaciated, and losing teeth at the rate of one per month. The pink scar on his neck had become infected yet again, and it was raging. In his pants pocket he had a pepper bag half full of gold fragments and small nuggets, but in his wallet no money at all.

He was surprised to see the same doorman, Mr. Lefebvre, but the poor old fellow had become near-sighted and he failed to recognize Joe.

"Here to see Vi Cloutier."

"She expecting you?"

"No, I'd like to surprise her."

"Don't go much for surprises these days, fella. Who shall I say is calling?"

"Joseph," he said. "Just tell her Joseph."

Auntie Vi had aged in the last seven years. When she opened the door to her suite she appeared hunched over and oddly suspicious.

"Yes?"

"Auntie Vi, it's me." He paused while she looked him over. "Don't tell me you don't recognize me."

"Recognize you? No, I can't say I do. Are you the fellow who does the electrical…the electrical whatnots?"

"No."

"Then, sir, why are we speaking at this time of night?"

"I'm…I'm Joseph."

"That's what Mr. Lefebvre said."

She stood in her doorway unmoored and tottering in her dressing gown. She came closer and reached up and touched both of his cheeks, touched the angry pink scar on his throat.

"You're…"

"Joseph."

"Oh, my…"

"I'm not dead, Auntie Vi. I…didn't die. People only thought –"

"You're my sister's boy? You're Joseph Burbidge?"

"Yes, I am. How is my mother doing, by the way? I haven't –"

"Don't let's talk in the hallway. Come in, come in."

She closed the door, locked it, and checked him out from top to bottom, smiling distractedly. She touched him on the chest.

"You haven't become one of those opium people, have you?"

"No, of course not."

"I've been reading about them. They call them drug addicts. Terrible habit. You'll be needing some more of Bernard's clothes."

"Bless you, Auntie Vi."

Just as she had done in the winter of 1932, she poured him a whisky, and after some brief bits of conversation, she ordered him to take a bath.

"You'll find Bernard's razor, brush and shaving mug in the cabinet. Couldn't bear to throw them out."

"Nothing wrong with a bit of sentiment," he said.

"Sentiment, rubbish. They're too good to throw out, Joseph."

He had his bath, a glorious sacrament of a bath that warmed him to the marrow, and he shaved his face all the way down to the infected scar that lay like a huge pink leech on his throat. He dressed in Bernard Cloutier's undershorts, his socks, his slacks and a nice white cotton shirt. A new look for 1939.

"Well, my boy, your name has been in the news. But that won't surprise you, I suppose?"

"Yes," he said.

They sat facing each other at Vi's kitchen table. He wondered where he might start and how much he could hold back from her.

"Your funeral, I have read, was something of an occasion in Yellowknife. A bunch of your fellow prospectors put on quite a show on your behalf. I do hope you were able to attend."

"No," he said. "I had another engagement."

"Joseph, you are a fountain of information. We must chat more often."

"Auntie Vi, as you may have guessed, well, I've been to hell and back."

"I haven't the slightest doubt, my boy. You look simply dreadful. May we now send a telegram to your mother? I think she might be quite heartened to find that her son is alive and kicking."

"I'd rather not, if you don't mind. Not immediately, I mean. If you don't mind."

Her cheeks rose, eyes scrunched skeptically, as though an atrocity or a sneeze were impending. Joe's many enthusiastic and contrary opinions had previously produced this effect on Auntie Vi's features. It only occurred to him now that he might have been a bit of a trial to his aunt.

"Well then. Your mother believes, as did I, that you were the victim of a murder. There was, I recall, a manhunt up there, and there is still, I think, an active investigation. Bravo for that. Joseph, what exactly have you been up to? Why have you decided to come back from the grave?"

"I can explain that," he said, looking down at the floor, but he wondered if he could.

"If you are now a fugitive," she said, "why have you come to see me? Do you need a lawyer, is that it?"

"No no. It's nothing like that."

"Well, Joseph? Emerge."

"I've had a hell of a time, Vi. The trek down to Fort Resolution. Went badly. No caribou. I got by somehow. An Indian girl and her brother took care of me. I took the train on the last leg, the good old Northern Alberta Railway."

"But Joseph, there is no train from Fort Resolution. How on earth did you..."

"Oh, Vi, I've had some bad…I've wandered a long way from young, you know, young Joseph Burbidge. If you see what I mean. I scarcely know that young man any more. But when I was up there, Vi, I never forgot your kindness. Your soirées with Maisie and…and…"

"Peggy. Both married. Continue."

"There were times when I could conjure you up, and this lovely flat of yours, and all the merriment. You sort of connected me." He felt his throat swelling and he was unable to speak.

"I connected you?"

He held up his hand and she waited.

"Yes, connected me. To everything I had left behind. To a part of myself who just wanted to be around people and have a good time. To my country, don't you see? The old one and this one both. That's why I'm here. To get something back that I lost up there. Something unrelated to the bloody…the bloody gold. You gave me the only social life I ever had."

"Do you need money?"

"No. Absolutely not."

She thrust a handkerchief at his face, which he accepted, and glared at him with what might have been impatience or curiosity, or perhaps even outright disapproval.

"Are you looking for a place to stay, Joseph?"

"No, Aunt Vi. No. A bed for the night perhaps? Thank you. But I've got to be off in the morning."

"Joseph, you look like an old man."

He nodded.

"What have you done to yourself?"

He told her bits of his tale. How they'd found some gold, how Riley had flown off to file the claim, how Knaaker was left behind to jump the claim and much worse, how Joe had shot Knaaker and disguised the body as his own. He skipped the cabin near Wolf Lake and went straight to the day the Dogribs had found him, befriended him, how some of the young hunters had nearly hanged him, and how once again he had been saved. How he, young Heraldene, and her brother had descended from Fort Resolution by dog sled to Fort Smith. How they had nearly starved on the final leg of their journey along the Little Buffalo River. At Fort Smith, he had cashed in more than half of his remaining gold and given most of the money to Heraldene and Eddy.

"A priest had sent her to find me," he said, and more of the story came back to him. "Heraldene and her little brother, they were like angels, I suppose you could say."

"So you said, my boy. How lovely for you. That thing on your neck, that scar, it's hideous."

"Yes."

He pulled out his poke and showed Aunty Vi a nugget. She held the nugget in her hand and glowered at it as though it were a slug recovered from a corpse. Joe let out a great yawn and smiled at his aunt.

"So now you're a prospector, Joe. And a northern adventurer, and a fugitive. And you have taken a man's life in – what was it –

self-defense, I suppose. And bully for you Joe, you even found some nuggets. Your mother's health is uncertain, I can vouch for that, your siblings need to get word from you, but you found some gold nuggets."

"I'm just glad I survived," he said.

"And now, my boy, it is time for bed."

"I'm going, yes," he said, yawning, and he staggered to his feet.

"This way, my boy. That's it, slow and steady. Time to tuck you in."

HE TRIED TO GET OUT of bed the following morning but he couldn't manage it. Vi phoned for an ambulance and Joe (Mr. Joseph Eggers) was off to the Royal Alec emergency in an ambulance. He was diagnosed with scurvy, with advanced malnutrition, and with a bacterial infection on his neck. Later they told him that he also had pneumonia. The attendants woke him up at all hours to fondle and poke, give him needles and enemas, bathe him with rags soaked in warm water, offer him ciggies and change his bedclothes. *Naughty boy, you are,* said one of them in the voice of Buggy Benbow. *Time for some muggledeepoo. Come along now.*

There was much chittering all around him, as though a house full of of demons had descended. An angel may have come to visit, a tired old chap with a downcast look, and he brought along a good whiff of body odour. From a certain angle, he looked like Knaaker Johansen. The poor fellow could not stop yawning but at last he seemed to pull himself together.

"My guess," said the angel, shaking angel-down and coal dust from his frowzy wings, "is that by morning you'll be dead as a doornail. Can we at least agree on that?"

"What? Are you serious? This is my life you're talking about."

"Excuse me," said the angel, yawning again. "I thought it was your death."

"Sod off."

"But can we agree?" said the angel. Tired though he was he had a determined way about him. "Can we just die and get on with it? I need some co-operation here."

The angel seemed to shift into the shadows and remain just out of sight. "He even stole my longjohns," he muttered to someone.

A policeman stood by his bed, clearing his throat.

"Raise your right hand," he said.

"I, Joseph Burbidge do solemnly swear."

"I, Joe Burbidge, do solemnly swear."

"To get on't business of dyin as–"

"No," he said to the policeman. "I do not agree. I take umbrage, do you hear me? I take umbrage."

"Oombrage? Wha's tha'?" said the policeman.

"Umbrage. I haven't the faintest...umbrage. It's just...just something that you take when you...Oh, for God's sake can't all of you just leave me alone? Am I under arrest?"

He was really stuck on that one. Umbrage. The policeman had caught him red-handed. Surely they couldn't use that against him, could they?

The demons were nattering again.

"Tha's had a nasty bit o' luck, lad."

"Sir. Officer. Excuse me but aren't you my father?"

"Dear me," said a merciful lady with a lamp and a familiar smile. "Poor darling, you're sweating like a work horse. And you're just too far gone to sleep here any more. Now off you go, quick like a bunny."

"Is that my fault? It's not my fault that I sweat like a work horse."

"I'll get you dried up in a shake," she said.

"It's just that with all these people coming in and out, I can't quite concentrate on...on..."

"All these people?" she said. "What people? You should have seen it the night before. We were run off our feet. Now, Mr. Eggers, give us a deep breath."

"Am I…am I, you know, going to prison?" he said to the lady.

"I don't think so. You should try to avoid those places. Try harder, now, that's it. A deeeep breath."

"Still can't see you."

"You can't see me? Don't bother. Nothing to look at."

"Was my father here just now?"

"Shhh," she whispered. "There, there, Mr. Eggers. It was only a dream."

The policeman had faded, the smelly angel had faded, the demons had gone, everyone was disappearing, all but the lady with the lamp, and now she had no lamp. She placed her cool fingers on his forehead and he sank slowly into a wondrous blue lake.

Chapter 12

Home

"STINKY?"

Joe sat on a hotel bed and he became aware that he was holding his breath. His hands were clammy and the bed smelled remotely of stale chicken, cigarette smoke and caustic soda. The piece of paper with Stinky's phone number on it, in Vi's meticulous handwriting, was shaking like a leaf in October.

"It's me."

"You gotten sprung yet?"

"You don't sound surprised to hear my voice."

"I just found out. That there old gal, she rung me up. I near shit myself."

"So you've met my Auntie Vi. I gave her your new number."

"She phoned me more than once. She's tryin to figger out what to tell the cops about you. In case word gets out. She's some old bird, that one. Don't think she approves of me."

"Stinky, can we get together?"

"Kin you walk?"

"A little. Auntie Vi gave me her late husband's cane."

Not that he wanted to admit this to Stinky, but Joe was a crumbling bloody wreck. He had no strength, no appetite, no colour in his cheeks. The doctors and nurses at the Royal Alec had quite possibly saved his life. As had Isidore, at least once, saved his life. As had Rusty Regan saved his life. As had Heraldene saved his life. And maybe Auntie Vi? He couldn't help but wonder how many lives he had left.

"If you only knew what I gone through to find your sorry arse.

Joey, you son of a bitch."

"But Stinky, can we get together? Soon?"

"You come out here. We'll have a drink, talk about old times."

"I don't have a car."

"Joey, you don't need no car. Call a goddam cab. You may not know it, buddy, but you can afford one." Riley paused a moment. "Oh, hell, I'll come an get yiz myself."

THE TWO MEN SAT in the kitchen of a renovated farmhouse a little more than a mile north of Edmonton. The house lay on a hundred and sixty acres of pasture and parkland. Stinky had a cow and he kept several of his old saddle horses, including Shanghai Lil. He was flying out of the municipal airport now and he was making decent money. He had two bush pilots working under him and a hangar all his own. It took Stinky about five minutes to drive south to Stony Plain Road to shop for essentials – fresh bread from Turner's Bakery, groceries from a small store called DeeBee's, cigars from Sprague's Drugs. It took him twenty minutes to drive to work. He had never in his life had to drive a car to work, but it was worth it just to live outside the city.

"You haven't told me, Stinky. How did you manage all this?"

"Don't go leapin down my throat now."

"You can do no wrong, my friend. Tell all."

"It's a long story. When the ice was safe, me an this Mountie Langfeldt, we landed the plane. Found the remains. Heh, we found *your* remains, you sneaky bastard."

"Joseph Burbidge. Rest in peace."

"I went pokin around our campsite, made sure them stakes hadn't bin fiddled with. Found some sample rocks next to the fire pit. Bagged em up."

"I think those were the samples I dumped ..."

Stinky waved off Joe and continued with his narrative.

"Well sir. I kept lookin for you. Between flights up to the

Barrens to find you, I run into a old client a mine? Big shot? Armstrong's his name. Decent guy. Geologist. Useta fly him up north to check claims and poke around. Told him you and me had found somethin good. Give him that bag a samples. He took er in to the University and had it assayed like we done with the first samples. I was hopin for two ounces per ton, eh? Come back fourteen ounces, can you believe that? Fourteen ounces a ton. Hell, as soon as the assay results come back I sold our claim to Armstrong's outfit for nine hunnerd thousand dollars and a pile a stock in Armstrong's company. Half a that belongs to you, Joey. How's that for a quick buck?"

"Who advised you?"

"Me? Who advised me? I done it on my own. No one advised me."

"I'm amazed, Stinky. You never had any patience with businessmen."

"Oh, hell, I mighta had a few words with Tommy Payne."

If Joe could have summoned the energy, he would have had a good laugh. But he barely had the energy to keep interrogating his friend.

"You say you flew up to the Barrens more than once?"

"I had a hunch. The evidence was that you was dead but if Buster's boy done you in, why didn't he change them stakes? Another thing didn't set right with me. Bit a hair I picked off a piece of the skull. Blond hair? Never showed the Mountie that bit a hair. He was too busy takin pitchers. But that bit a hair sewed it up for me. Knew for sure that was not your bones that fed them wolves. So I kept lookin. Flew up again with Isidore and we checked around. No footprints nowhere. Too much snow had fallen. Just some equipment here and there and that there cave you dug. But otherwise not a trace, you young weasel. Not a goddam trace."

Joe tried to summon his feelings about it all. He had expected to feel the thrill of new wealth, but all he could feel was his own fatigue. He was a rich man. He could send money to his mother.

Anonymously. Or perhaps he could find a way to tell her that he was still alive. Perhaps he might go to England and tell her. That's what wealthy men did.

"You know, Joey, I think Buster Krahn meant to leave ol Knaaker behind. Let him die up there after he done his dirty work. Leave no witnesses, sorta thing."

Joe gazed across the room at the immortal Stinky Riley, who was pacing back and forth between the coffee pot and the pantry. His partner looked anything but exultant. He looked as though someone had shot his cow.

"Stinky, settle down. Stop pacing. This is all good news, is it not?"

"When someone spots you," Stinky replied, pulling at his nose as though to make it longer, "reckanizes you, like." Here he took out his hanky and gave it both barrels. "One a them boys you knew up in Yellowknife, say, drinkin down here at the King Eddy. Or someone livin down here. Tommy Payne or one a them snooty friends of your auntie. When this happens, Joey, who you gonna be? Joey's twin brother?"

If there was one question that had rankled throughout his life more than any other, it was this one. *Who you gonna be?* He glowered at Stinky, who was sloughing off his winter coat, still puffing from the rigours of his morning chores. As usual, he could not answer Stinky's question. He had scattered most of the articles up north, strategically, that might identify him as either Knaaker Johansen or the corpse of Joseph Burbidge, and he had brought with him the remainder of his British ID: an operator's license, a union card, library card, a school transcript from Shacklesbury, all bearing the name of Joseph Eggers. The only people who knew of his need to bury the old name were Stinky Riley and Auntie Vi. Joe was growing his very first moustache, something the old Joe would have preferred not to do.

"I'm Joe Eggers. It's official because I can prove it. Perhaps I'll take a ship back to England, reintroduce meself to the family, pick up a passport over there. Good plan, do you think?"

"I've got a better one, Joey. How bout you get healthy again? Stay here till you've got some meat on them bones."

"Might be gloomy company."

"Me too, Joey. Couple a rich grumpy bastards."

My dear Mother, I daresay you have heard the odd rumour or read somewhere that I am dead. Well, I have a new address (enclosed) but it is not up beyond the pearly gates–or in that other place either! I am safely back from the North, living in Edmonton, and never more to roam. Sorry to have waited this long to write to you and the family, but you see, up where I was in the Territories, there was no mail service.

JOE SLUMPED IN HIS CHAIR, staring at the ink well on Stinky Riley's desk. What exactly was he doing here? Might not someone in his family, or a friend of the family, telephone these glad tidings to a newspaper? Would the news of his miraculous return to life make its way back here? Why not? The papers always jumped at the chance to print a David Livingstone story. *Yorkshire Prospector Comes Back from Oblivion.* Could he possibly ask his mother and brothers and sister to keep his news quiet? What would they think?

He wandered into his room and placed his unwritten letter in a dresser drawer.

Joe was wintering on the outskirts of Edmonton on Stinky Riley's quarter section. The two men had signed some papers at a lawyer's office, and Joseph Eggers went officially from pauper to rich man with the stroke of a pen. He turned over the lion's share of his newfound wealth to a young broker named Hamish Hamilton.

Occasionally Joe and Stinky would drive into town to a drinking establishment that was suitably down-scale. Beer only for Joe, no whisky. The Royal Hotel was a few blocks north of Jasper Avenue and a few blocks east of 101st Street, where hookers, scrappers, grifters, ne'er-do-wells, yeggs and ex-cons gathered. On these few occasions, hiding behind his new moustache, he would dress down, wear an old fedora, talk in low tones so that his faded Brit accent would draw no curiosity. The effect of these *sotto voce* conversations with Stinky was to make them both look appropriately shady for the bar in the Royal Hotel. Riley yearned for southern pastures, cattle country, and Joe wanted his body back. He wanted to feel strong enough to go for walks and do some dancing. Drinking with Riley at the Royal was a start in the right direction but for the most part it was a desolate pleasure.

Sometimes Joseph would get drunk. On one occasion, late in the afternoon, he phoned the office of Buster Krahn. *This is Knaaker Johansen*, he whispered to Krahn's secretary. *I'm back in town and I need to have a little talk with Buster.* The poor woman's voice began to stammer, and she explained to him that Mr. Krahn was away for an extended period of time. *That's all right*, he whispered. *I'll keep watch on his house.* A few days later, drunk again, he phoned again, this time pretending to be a lawyer. *I'll put him right on*, the secretary said, and Joe hung up before Krahn could come to the phone. Joe's body was shaking with a fury he had not expected.

"YOU DID WHAT?"

"I was drunk, Stinky. Don't worry, I hung up. Won't happen again. Cross my heart."

"You wanna git stupid with Krahn, Joey, you do it on your own time. Jesus."

"I said–"

"Cops can't get him because there ain't enough evidence. They found a twenny-two slug near the skull, but that might mean that Joey Burbidge committed suicide. Me and that Mountie found the twenny-two just a few feet away from the body. And you can't get

Buster, Joey, because you'd blow your cover. Stay the Christ away from him, do you hear?"

"What do we do, Stinky? Just fade away? I mean, how do you forget something like that?"

"I figure you either shoot Krahn dead and be done with it. Go on the lam. Or you forget the son of a bitch and move on."

"You could do that? Forget him?"

"Look, Joey. We beat him. We got the claim and he didn't. And you took out his favourite thug. I say two ta nothin for the good guys."

"What if I can't forget him?"

"Give it a while. Take some time away from here. Go see the world. Go where no one'll reckanize ya. You're what, thirty-five?"

"I am almost twenty-eight years old, Stinky. I'm always twenty-six years younger than you. And Stinky, for the moment, I have no plans to travel."

"Didn't mean to rush ya, Joey."

Mother, I beg you not to speak about this to anyone outside the family. I want my return to England to be a surprise to everyone. Can't wait to see all of you. Hope to book passage for the summer, but we'll see. But Mother, as they say over here, mum's the word. I could get into a bit of trouble if it got out that I was only playing possum! Nothing to worry about, but there are some individuals over here who might want to locate me if they found out that I was still alive. If you take my meaning!

Mother, under no circumstances can you or the family speak about my return from the dead. Period. Full stop. Is that clear? And when you answer this letter, be sure to address it to Joseph Eggers and not our former name. The walls have ears, if you take my meaning.

Back to the dresser drawer went Joe's fragments to his mother. He stewed over the letter to England for a week, and one day he simply picked up the phone and dialed the number of the Eggers house in Castleford.

"Is Mrs. Eggers there?" he said to a man.

"What would this be concerning?" said the man.

"I have some news for her," Joe replied. "Put her on for me, would you?"

"And who would this be?" said the man.

"Ahhh," Joe replied, "perhaps you could put Angie on the line?"

"She's off to town. How do you know Angie?"

"If Angie's not available, then put Wallace on, would you?"

"Who is this?" said the man.

"If I wanted to identify myself, I would have done so. Who the hell are you?"

"Don't have to get all stroppy," said the man, and the line went dead.

> *My dearest Mother, how have you been all this time? Do you still make it out to Methley Church every week? Does the family still have picnics down at Queen's Park? Is our Angie still giving the lawyers a hard time? (On that subject, please see enclosed cheque in pounds sterling.) Is Arthur still at the Mill? How about our old reliable Wally? How I miss bantering with him! How I yearn for the sight of all of you!*

WELL AFTER MIDNIGHT, in a great purging of tears, he finished his letter. When he re-read it in the morning he nearly broke down once again. After breakfast with Stinky, he grabbed the letter and drove into town. He did not want to be spotted by someone who might recognize him, so he chose the smallest post office he could find, one on Twenty-fourth and Stony Plain Road. There was a lineup at the wicket, so he did a furtive check on each customer and bided his time gawping out the window and reading notices at the rear of the room. He could not stop wondering who the strange man was on the telephone. His first thought was a man from Scotland Yard, but he dismissed that as nothing but his own paranoia. Could he be a boyfriend of Angie? A husband perhaps? But why was he shielding Joe's mother from callers?

Joe found himself gazing at the air between his eyes and the poster board. And then at the posters on the board. And then at one poster in particular with a faded black and white photograph of a man so faintly reproduced that he looked like a ghost. It was a WANTED poster. The man who looked back at him from the poster was Knaaker Johansen.

FINALLY JOE MAILED THE LETTER home to his mother, but all day long he wallowed in despair. Home? There wasn't a place in England where he could feel at home. He had made himself a stranger to his homeland, and his letter, with its implications of surreptitious activities, police investigations, might very well break their hearts. He should not have sent the letter.

Home. Be it ever so ungenteel, home was Canada for Joe Eggers. Edmonton, Alberta, gateway to the North and gateway to northern people like Heraldene. And Lucy and her mother. And Mayday Medzin. And Edmonton was where Stinky had his house and his business. Where Auntie Vi still lived. Where the possibility of a social life for Joe still existed, however surreptitious that might have to be. Where Isidore had settled, a three-hour drive to the south. Soon he would tell all to Isidore. And Edmonton was where his money and his broker were. The newly minted Joseph Eggers could meet prospectors down at the Royal and buy up their nuggets and gold dust. He could take this raw gold to a friend of Stinky's with a small foundry and have it poured into a bar or even a brick. All hush-hush of course. This would be his little hobby. Edmonton was the only place in the world where he would not feel perpetually lonely. If he continued from time to time to be visited by guilt, Edmonton was as good a place as any to wallow in it. But now he wanted a place of his own.

Riley was of mixed sentiments on Joe's quest for a home in Edmonton. He had become bored and depressed with his own life on the outskirts of town. The city was beginning to encroach on his property. Stinky was rich and he didn't need to fly up north any more. He could shut down his business, sell his Junkers, pick up stakes and move north to St. Albert and buy a new and cheaper quarter section, but that wasn't what he thought of as *horse* country. It was *farmer* country. Stinky's intention, still vague but growing, was to head back south for the Red Deer River valley, and settle in ranching country. Stinky was still sweet on the woman who ran the hotel in Patricia, and she appeared to tolerate his occasional visits. He just wasn't sure if it was the visits she liked or the "occasional" part.

"Stinky," Joe said one afternoon at the Royal, "why did you start up your bush pilot business in Edmonton?"

"Why the hell not? I wanted to fly."

"More than you wanted to ranch?"

"Maybe."

"You hired two other pilots, Stinky. You were stuck behind a desk most of the time, right?"

"Okay, Joey. Yer the doc. Why did I start a flyin business?"

"Oh, never mind."

Joe had his own theory and he was not about to expose it to Stinky's rebuttals. His friend had hung a shingle from the Edmonton Municipal Airport so that he could try and keep tabs on what had happened to his old partner. This was the only way Riley could conceive of to find his friend. Period. And Stinky Riley was damned if he'd admit to anything sloppy-hearted like that.

Joe changed the subject. "Stinky, I might need to take a drive into town. Check a few For Sale signs."

"To buy a house? Good for you, Joey. But what happens when someone spots you? What the hell you gonna tell them?"

"Stinky, I don't much look like meself any more."

"Still."

"If it happens, Stinky, it happens. I'll fess up and retire early. Get me stripes and become a man of leisure."

Joe glared back at Stinky, stared bleakly at the newspaper, turned to the real estate ads, glowered at a sink full of dirty dishes (mostly Stinky's, he was convinced), scowled at the stormy March sky, which scowled back at him through Stinky's picture window, and glared once more at his friend.

Could that be true? That he *wanted* to confess and atone in a jail cell?

"We are no longer meant for this life, Stinky. Living in a hideout at the edge of town."

"Don't avoid the question."

"No one's going to recognize me. I will go in disguise. I'm a businessman. I'm Joe Eggers now."

"Isidore thinks you're dead. He's down there on the Red Deer, back with his ol lady. I just talked to him yestiddy on the phone. What do I tell Isidore?"

"Tell Isidore I'm fine. I'll phone him meself. We can trust him. I just need to get my own place. Now that you've made me a rich man."

"Why not go to South America? Some place nice an hot where they don't have no newspapers. Or one a them islands in the Pacific where the women don't wear no clothes? Hell, I'd visit you."

For the better part of a month now, he had been asking himself why he stayed here, bunking like an outlaw with Stinky Riley on the northern outskirts of Edmonton. He had always thought that being wealthy should be fun, but by his most recent reckoning, it was no fun at all. 1939 had turned out to be a dismal year. Live in the present, old Herron would say. But how did you live in the present if the present no longer beckoned you?

Could it be that he remained lurking around Edmonton

because he was trying in some way to stay in touch with his old genial self? Perhaps. Or was it revenge he wanted? Revenge followed by a full atonement? He had no answers, just a vague prod in his gut that hinted at unfinished business.

And the recurrent fantasy of a lovely old house by the river, a bit of old England. With a quiet neighbourhood devoid of busybodies. His rationalization for this particular fantasy was that he could come and go as he liked, consort with a woman or two. Sweet personality, full of rascality, that sort of thing. Joseph Eggers could live the life of a secret agent and do it as graciously as he could afford without calling attention to himself. He could make the three-hour drive south now and then to visit old Isidore. And if Stinky moved down there in ranching country, as he kept saying he would, perhaps later on Joe could join them, build a summer place on the Red Deer River. They could all go hunting together, drinking together.

"By my reckonin you need either a shady place or a snooty place."

"I don't follow you."

"In a shady place, everybody's got somethin to hide. Hotel on the wrong side a the tracks. The Royal or some such place. The sort of establishment that has its long-term customers, eh. No one talks to the cops, Joey. All part a the code."

"And a snooty place?"

"Them guys down at the Edmonton Club? I useta fly some a them guys around up north. Chamber a Mines meetins, shit like that. Nobody tells nothin about themselves. Hush hush, insiders only. Skeletons stay in the closet."

"Not keen on joining any clubs."

"Still."

He missed the North. He missed Lucy Castaway and even her merciless mother. He missed the Dogribs up at Sangris, the ones who didn't want to hang him. Or rather, he missed who he was when he was with them, a wide-eyed visitor who liked the humour of their stories and their easy ways. Besides, he had other reasons to return there. But as Stinky kept saying, *Who ya gonna be, Joey? What's yer goddam story?*

Could he be Knaaker again? No. Because Knaaker was persona non grata up there. *No no, my friends, you've got it all wrong. I'm really Joe Eggers and I never worked for Buster Krahn. It was just one of my shaggy dog stories.*

If ever there was a place where he had to stay dead it was up north, especially around Yellowknife, where he had been buried, apparently, in an Anglican graveyard. The thought of Knaaker's bones in his grave sent him spinning into a depression, and Stinky had to promise him that they would go to the bar that afternoon. In return, he had to promise never again to phone Krahn's office. If Joe Burbidge had to stay dead, Knaaker Johanson had to stay forever in the shadows.

ONE NIGHT AUNTIE VI phoned him out at Riley's. She sounded positively vibrant. She wanted to have some people in for supper.

"You say you're drinking, Joseph? Oh, you men are such asses. Well, Joseph, if you get yourself half seas over, you can sleep in the guest room and go back in the morning. How settled are you, dear boy? Does civilization appeal? No? Are you at wit's end living with that old hobo, what's his name with the cowboy hat? I don't want you driving an automobile in your cups, dear, not in this weather."

"If you don't mind my asking, Auntie Vi, who –"

"Oh, don't worry, Joseph. They won't know you. They're just a bunch of strays I feed on occasion. I don't even remember who you knew and who you...perhaps you're right. But Joseph, I doubt if anyone would even recognize you."

"I appreciate the invitation, Vi, I really do..."

"You need to get out of your cave, Joseph. It will do you good to be among people who don't eat their dinner from a tin can and who go to the loo in a proper facility."

He had decided not to chance it. He would stay at home.

But in a weak moment, gazing into the bathroom mirror, he had an idea. He could go as Joseph Eggers, and if anyone recognized him he would claim that he was Joseph Burbidge's older Yorkshire cousin. The older part would work, because up north he had aged a great deal more rapidly than he would have done working for the paymaster's in Castleford or doing a desk job in Edmonton. His face had become permanently ruddy, frostbitten, deeply lined, his neck forever scarred, and ever since his long retreat from the northern claim, he ambled along with a permanent limp. On the other hand, thanks to Hammy Hamilton's dentist in town, he had better teeth than Joe Burbidge ever had.

So, this would be his cover: he was here in Canada because his poor departed cousin had recommended the life out west to him. That's it. He would be popping about looking for resource investments on behalf of his family business. An old associate of poor young Burbidge, a *Mr. Riley, I believe*, had been in the cattle business, and Eggers was at this moment talking to the man about buying some ranchland in the Red Deer Valley. *Of course there's a family resemblance, old boy. Poor Joe's mother and my father, you see, were brother and sister.*

Yes. And Joseph Eggers could wear something that young Joseph Burbidge would never have worn in Edmonton, because young Burbidge, poor chap, had worn nothing but Bernard Cloutiers' enormous castoffs. Yes, he still had time. He would phone Auntie Vi and say he was coming after all. He would go to a men's shop. Henry Singer's. Just the place. He began to sing into the mirror.

Henry Singer has a suit
that'll fit that'll fit that'll fit just you,
Henry Singer, Henry Singer…

He would go right downtown and buy a suit to look like a real sporting chap. Tweed suit and a bowler hat, or the winter equivalent of a bowler hat. A fedora. Jesus, what if someone from seven years ago were to show up at Auntie Vi's? Would she be batty enough to invite them? He returned to the consideration of his togs. Ascot to cover up the scarred throat? No no. Let them see the bloody thing. Of course. But a snazzy new overcoat with a fur collar, something for a worldly chap who would rather die than go up north and poke around for gold. *I'd jolly well catch me death of cold, I would.*

Jolly well catch me death?

Go easy, Joe. Let's not overdo it. Joe Burbidge used to talk too much, didn't he. But young Burbidge was not a secret agent, no. And now Joseph Eggers had a moustache. He didn't exactly *like* his moustache. It was sprinkled with prematurely grey hairs. He was too young for grey hairs. But he was Joseph Eggers now, man of the world. He would be the perfect secret agent, become a good listener and stay sober, yes, and converse in a subdued voice. He would comport himself like a perfect gentleman and deflect the conversation to other people. Maybe just one whisky.

Henry Singer has a fit
That'll suit that'll suit that'll suit just you,
Henry Singer, Henry Singer...

The recently minted Joseph Eggers sighed into the mirror. Just one whisky to get a glow on. Well, perhaps two.

Joe had bought a navy blue 1935 Studebaker. It handled the country roads well enough, it started promptly in cold weather, and it didn't turn heads in the city. The car gave Joe another form of anonymity but little pleasure. Still, the Studebaker seemed to fit his image of the new life.

On the evening of the soirée, he drove the car to Auntie Vi's neighbourhood by the river just after six o'clock and parked near her corner. He crossed the street and walked just past her august building to look down at the frozen river. Already the stars were out and glittering through the cold March air. A pale version of the aurora was flickering downriver to the northeast. Nothing like the aurora up north, but still recognizable.

There now. Another reason to be living here. Where else could he gaze up at the aurora borealis in the middle of a city? And spring, glorious Alberta spring (leafless and mucky, but what the hell) was on its way.

Once again, old half-blind Mr. Lefebvre failed to recognize him in the lobby. Perhaps owing to Joe's newly acquired finery, however, the old man let him through the door with scarcely a hesitation.

Vi greeted him in the hallway wearing a pale pink robe somewhat reminiscent of a Japanese Kimono. Her face was powdered excessively, done up in pale pink, which matched the silk material of her robe, and altogether she struck Joe as a faded rose. Faded but still vital.

"Joseph, you look ridiculous. What is that thing under your nose?"

He reminded her of his new name, and revealed his kinship to the unfortunate young Burbidge.

"I've done a naughty thing, my dear," she whispered. "Cupid Cupid, couldn't help myself. She's a bit young for you but so what, and the poor thing is simply dying of a bad marriage. Or perhaps she's not married at all, just fatefully attached to this fellow. Do be pleasant to her, Joseph. Show a bit of interest or I'll be cross with you. Her name is Barbara something. By the way, Joseph...*Eggers*, you don't look *absolutely* ridiculous. You look very presentable. For you at least."

He entered Vi's living room determined to act subdued yet

confident, a secret agent nursing an unfathomable sorrow, and a perfect gentleman. There were perhaps two dozen in the room, and many of them turned to meet him. *Howdoyoudo*, said Harry something, a tall chap with a rakish moustache; *howdoyoudo*, said a bucktoothed chap who reminded him of someone; and *howdoyoudo* said a pretty woman with a pretentious smile neither hostile nor friendly; and *hi there* from an effeminate man with a mouth full of cold roast beef; and *goot eefning*, said a short artist chap with an impressive mop of blond hair standing next to a lady with a soulful look and a–well well well, and who might this be?

She stood facing the far wall of Vi's living room, hips cocked and arms akimbo, looking at the portrait of a reclining nude, a young lady dressed in a red skirt and ooh, pretty red heels.

"You must be ..." He'd already forgotten the name that Auntie Vi had imparted to him. Was it Caroline? Betty?

"Yes," she said, "I am," and looked up at him with well-contained curiosity.

They both examined the portrait. The model was represented sitting on a rug, ankles crossed, leaning back against a large pillow and staring out through half-lidded eyes at what seemed to be a tedious world. Not a stitch.

"Joseph," he said, and forgot to say Eggers, because he had never gazed into the face of such, such a...her face was familiar, her figure, and for a moment he panicked. *Do I know this vision from somewhere? Does she know me?*

"Have we, have we...ever..." and he glanced at the painting and back at the young woman with a blush. The young woman could not help but smile.

"I say, you're almost as beautiful right there," he said, blush fading, indicating the painting, "as you are right here."

"I don't like the pose," she said with a sleepy pout. "Makes me look too, you know, too...passive? Don't tell Lufty."

She indicated the squat blondhaired painter chap, who was laughing at something Vi had said.

"He's done me before but Vi seems to be all keen on this one."

Auntie Vi approached them in the corner of her living room. Something about Vi's face reminded Joe of his mother. The eyes and nose, perhaps. The way her lips moved to form her words. He had heard not a thing from his mother or the family. For all he knew, his letter had been lost in the mail.

"Oh, Melony," said Vi, not entirely with approval, "I see you two have met."

The young woman named Melony turned to Auntie Vi with a look of tolerant affection.

"This gentleman seems to like Lufty's latest, Vi. That makes one of us." She looked back at the painting, tilting her head. "Can I help with things?"

"Yes, dear. Does your generation know how to make coffee?"

"Haven't a clue," said Melony, and gave Joe a little smile and a wave.

A bit later, Joe found himself peering at the young lady's date (boyfriend? husband? guardian? uncle? father? friend? tormentor?). He was Harry Stohler, a realtor with a neatly trimmed moustache and bounteous black hair combed straight back with disconcerting flare. He stood beside Miss Whatsername, squeezing her right shoulder for a happy snuggle, which in turn seemed to bring out the tedium in her. *Melony.* Her name was Melony. What a lovely name.

"I came back here from Ontario, still in the depths of a depression, to a town," Stohler was saying to several people, "where people sell things to people who buy things. Imagine that." He flashed a startling array of teeth to his listeners. "I started off selling Rollsies that nobody wanted to buy. Rollsies and Bentleys. No luck at all. Couldn't pay a man to buy a Rollsy, not in this one-horse town, so I switched to Caddies and their little cousins and I couldn't beat the customers off with a stick. Perhaps it was timing more than taste, who knows. Something is happening here. You can feel it pulsing. Well, I can. None of that dreary war talk about Europe, or Hitler, or whoever runs the show over there. People simply want to forget the Depression and get on with things. Depression, what Depression? Buy a new car, why not buy a Cadillac while they're at it."

Polite laughter.

"I have, I suppose," said Auntie Vi, "seen less extreme ways of going to hell, for men. Opium dens and dance hall girls and that sort of thing."

They all laughed merrily and little Miss Whatsername laughed hardest of all, wrinkling her nose and revealing for Joe all her ivories and the pink moist glory of her mouth. *(Melony, you ninny. Her name is Melony.)* She caught him regarding her and returned a look of quiet appraisal.

Harry Stohler did not quite get the joke, but his momentum was almost too strong for him to notice. Again, he squeezed his date (wife? niece? daughter? concubine? young friend?) with absentminded familiarity. She wore no rings on her left hand. Melony.

"Anyway, I got bored with selling Caddies. Got a realtor's license, bought into a real estate firm, and now it's office buildings and houses night and day."

"Really," said Joe. "I might be house-hunting myself. Are you part of this enterprise, Melony?"

She shook her head and then shrugged, which meant no and maybe yes. "I help Harry once in a blue moon," she said. "I mostly do modeling and I'm taking art classes."

She yawned or faked a yawn. Her lips were the same tulip red as her skirt and her shoes. She detached herself from the clutch of Oilcan Harry and sauntered off in search of her handbag.

"You remind me so much of your cousin," said the smiling woman next to the bucktoothed chap. "Poor Joseph. We read about him in the papers."

"And you are?" said Joe.

"Maisy," she said.

He tried hard not to swallow, failed, and thrust his glass to his lips.

"Maisy Schuman. You both have the same way about you, the same smile. I don't know, or maybe it's the voice. It's like talking to Joe's father. I never met his father but you know what I mean?"

"Well, you see, my mother and poor Joseph's father were –"

"Elliot, doesn't he remind you of Joe Burbidge?" she said to the bucktoothed man, but he was listening to the young woman beside him. Joe thought he recognized the fellow. The jeweler bloke.

"Well, yes. Poor Joseph," said Mr. Joseph Eggers, lurching back into character. "He must have left lots of friends behind, do you think?"

"Joe, I hope you don't mind me calling you Joe," Maisie said, cocking her cigarette by the side of her face. She was a drink or two past tiddly. "But I think he was sweet on me. Joseph Burbidge, I mean."

Maisy Lipscott. Now Maisie Schuman. She looked older and her voice had gone low like a foghorn, but the sparkle, the fun in her–that had not gone away.

"How long ago did you–"

"It might have been, oh, five or six years ago," she said. "He was a favourite with Vi. She mothered him. A funny fellow, your cousin. With that nervous energy? Kind of innocent? Talk your head off? Always on the go? No one could have imagined him going up there and finding all that gold. Let alone getting himself...well, you know. It was all over the papers. About his big find and his death. We all felt very sorry when it happened, Mr. Eggers. Feels so long ago."

Maisy seemed, for a moment or two, lost in time, and then she recovered. She was looking at his neck.

"Say, that's a nasty looking thing."

"Birth mark," he said. "Tends to act up when I'm drinking."

"Oh, where's my manners? Joe, this is Lady Barbara."

She and Lady Barbara laughed merrily, and Joe wondered if this new face had been part of Vi's soirées circa 1932. He jerked his eyes around to see where the bucktoothed chap had gone. Elliot Schuman.

"I mean," said Maisie, "this is my friend, Barbara Beasley."

A pretty young woman in a wool jumper with a high neckline and a bobbly thing around the neck like a bolas glanced up at Joe with a look of slight expectation. Perhaps he reminded her of every man she'd ever known. She was pretty and tall and elegant but she seemed to be resolutely stuck in display mode. Barbara? Oh dear, wasn't this the one Vi had mentioned to him? He could not be sure. Oh, yes, he could.

"Lady Barbara is one of my oldest friends and she is a direct descendant of Oliver Clomwell."

"Clomwell?"

Again, the sprinkle of laughter from Maisie and Barbara.

"Oh, Maisy Schuman, you fibber."

Barbara returned her attention to Joe and resumed her look of mild expectation, fingers demurely intertwined below her waist. Joe looked down at her. Into his second glass of whisky, he sent a prayer of deliverance. It was answered by Oilcan Harry, who burst upon them with a joke about a talking cow.

"So now it's real estate," said Joe.

"And you say you're in the market?" said Harry.

"I'm looking for a castle on the river. Nothing too fancy, no moats or anything."

"Ha ha ha. Is it Joseph Eggers or can I call you Joe? How about a nice old English manor house in the crescents, quiet as a grave, nice double lot, gas-heated garage, lots of trees in the back. And out front, Joe, out the front door, a view of the mighty North Saskatchewan."

Joe had to look away. Slick though he was, intrusive and full of himself, Harry Stohler had at last caught his attention. He turned back to the man, they ambled over to a corner of the living room next to some of Vi's statuettes, and Joe asked him if he could see the house.

"What, you mean this week?" said Harry. "I'm out of town this week. Are you serious? Vi said you were just over from England or something."

"Right now," said Joe, "the opportunities are here. I'm looking to stay here and be what you might call the Canadian arm of our family business. Their man in the great Dominion and all that."

While Stohler talked to him, he found himself, once again, face to face with the painting of the young woman, and he had to ask Stohler to repeat himself.

"She'll show you in and show you around and I'm sure–"

"Who?" said Joe.

"Melony. Sometimes she doubles as my girl Friday. Got a great eye for the visual stuff. Make a great...a great...oh, what do they call them these days?"

"Interior decorators?" said Melony.

"Oh," said Stohler, "there you is, Daisy Mae."

"WHAT DO YOU WANT?" Melony said, a day later, gazing around from the driver's seat of a small grey Austin, looking anywhere but at Joe. "I mean, with this house. What did you see when you went inside?"

"Reminds me of England, I suppose. Looks almost old enough to have some history, that sort of thing. A place where I can take me leisure, go for walks. Quiet place. That sort of thing."

"Well, let me ask you," she said, patiently, "what do you *imagine*, in the future, when you see this place?"

"I am a bachelor," he said, breathing in the faint drift of her perfume, "so I can't yet see the kiddies and the wife by the hearth. But hope springs eternal, as they say. In the meantime it would be just me alone, a drink after work and a cigar. And...and neighbours who mind their own business. That sort of thing." He paused long enough to catch her eyeing him. "I'm grooming myself to be a man of mystery."

"A lot of house for just one man," said Melony.

"I want a lot of house," he said.

They had seen the house top to bottom, and it had charmed him so thoroughly that he almost said yes to it after five minutes of the tour. The trees were everywhere up and down the street and in the back yard, and he could imagine their leafy glory every summer morning when he had his breakfast on the patio. He sat beside Melony in the Austin on the verge of committing, but before he could say anything, she suggested that they leave the car and walk around the crescent to get a look at the neighbourhood.

"This is the ugliest time of year in Edmonton, so if you can stand the neighbourhood now, you'll love it when the real spring comes."

He followed behind her and watched the fabric of her coat sway.

"Where do you work?" she said. "Short drive from here?"

"I don't exactly…work," he said. "My intention, if I stay here, would be to look after the family's interests. Mind me kingdom. If I wanted an office, I suppose I could rent one downtown, but I see myself doing most of the business from home. I need a room for my samples, a fairly large –"

"Samples?" she said.

"Geological samples," he said. "Gold samples from here and there. I deal a lot in gold, I suppose you could say."

"My my," she said and peered into his eyes.

She had a penetrating gaze and she was as comely as they come. He had not meant to be quite this candid with her. But his old self kept elbowing its way into Joseph Eggers' mouth. They had reached the path that followed the river valley, and they kept on going, missing the street that would have taken them around the block of his future neighbourhood.

"Melony, for a non-realtor art student or whatever, you're pretty good at this sort of thing."

"I fill in here and there when Harry needs me," she said. "Now, if you remember, that room on the west side, the large bedroom next to the stairwell, could that be converted into an office space?"

"Let's go and have another look," he said, and before they had gone two blocks along the river, they turned around and walked rapidly in the direction of his future house.

He would never forget that walk. Her apparent coolness, the distance between their bodies, the suit she wore, a blue jacket with padded shoulders. *Some day you must show me these samples of yours.* The impression that if he had offered her his hand she would have taken it and walked with him hand in hand all the way back to the house. *Never seen a gold brick?* At the door she dropped the key on the mat and picked it up. He saw that her hand had the jitters, and just before the big front door opened she looked up into his eyes as though to say *if we go through this door everything from here on is irreversible.*

Chapter 13

Knock Wood

HARRY STOHLER WAS TO MEET Joe at his new house, bringing with him an extra set of keys and a surveyor's certificate. Joe passed the time pacing outside the front door and trying to guess if, and if so, how much, Melony had told him. He was hoping for the best, expecting the worst, and steeling himself for an ugly confrontation. Did the man keep a revolver in his car?

When Stohler showed up there were no handshakes, no smiles, just an exchange of items and Stohler's gloomy visage. He looked as though he had not slept in days.

"She likes her eggs in bed," he said.

"What?"

"She likes her eggs in bed, her coffee strong. She likes strong everything, and that includes men. She doesn't suffer doddlers, men who can't make up their mind. She is fond of money, but what the heck. She loves high fashion and pretends she can take it or leave it. She claims to be a true bohemian but that's just a passing fancy. She wants no B.S., from you or me or anyone. She won't tolerate B.S. She came from a broken home. I took her in, family stuff, I'm sure she'll tell you all about it in due course."

He found himself thanking Harry Stohler.

Stohler refused Joseph's hand and instead grasped Joe's elbows and glared at him as he might glare hung-over into a mirror. The two men stood there, eyeball to eyeball, for a very long second or two.

"I want you to be good to her, do you hear that? I don't want to see her come running...all teary-eyed because another...

because another..."

Harry seemed to be trying to bring some authority to his voice but he just couldn't call it up. He was peering down at Joe's shoes. He lifted his hands as though to weigh the extent of his loss and slowly backed towards his car.

"Good luck," he muttered. "You'll sure as hell need it."

THE NEXT MORNING early, Joe summoned Stinky Riley and an old carpenter to begin the alterations to a small room on the third floor. Once the men went upstairs to work he locked the doors and let no one in for the remainder of the day. The work went efficiently and, by early evening, the carpenter went home with a wad of bills in his pocket.

Stinky Riley stayed for a drink and a quick goodbye. Like Joe, he had real estate on his mind. Real estate, cattle, a woman in Patricia, horses, barns, and all the dusty glories of the Red Deer River valley.

"MAY I CALL YOU Mellie?"

"Call me what you want."

They were nestled on the carpet of his new house, and their voices echoed in the empty living room. They were hunkered down, knees up, cracker crumbs on the rug, sipping whisky and from time to time dipping their fingers into a small pot of red German caviar. They had piled some of Joe's old clothes and his goose-down bag on the rug to cushion their rumps. The empty room bloomed shamelessly with caviar and sex. She was exploring the large pink scar on his throat with her fingers. She had a light touch. Beside her on the rug lay a custom-made gold brick that weighed about twenty-five pounds. Because of how she had been sitting, a squarish red outline from the brick had been imprinted on the back of her left thigh.

"Ooh," she cooed. "Does your scar tickle you?"

"Not much. It's a birthmark."

"You must tell me about all your scars," she said. "I've never known a man with such scars. And where did you lose that toe?"

"Bitten off by a jealous lover."

"Hah!" she cried. "The man can joke."

She moved back to a sitting position on the carpet with the gold brick under her knees. Absently she began to scratch it with a fingernail, as though the brick were in need of authentication.

"And you'll keep this baby where?"

"In the library, I think. Prop up the books."

"And who will guard it?"

"No one," he said. "I never even lock my doors."

"Did you just buy this thing?"

"I bought the gold from prospectors. Coarse gold. Just a sideline. I might sell it some day if the price goes up. I had a friend of a friend pour this one for me. Not strictly legal, but it's easier this way. He even does fake ones out of lead. Not like this one though. Real McCoy. Pretty, isn't it?"

"Well, Joseph, we might just need to get you a dog."

"We?"

She smiled up at him with her eyes closed, as though everything had been decided and no man in his right mind would refuse her. She may have been right. Wading between several thoughts, mouth agape, he could only feast his eyes on Melony.

"A very big dog," she murmured, "who bites burglars and does what I tell him."

"We?"

"You and me and baby makes three."

"Your uncle was quite emotional. Sorry to lose you. Seemed like an all right chap, your Harry. I think he must have fancied you."

"Fancied me? He's just upset because he's had another setback. Not losing me, losing some money. I think he might be bottoms up again. The poor man will never learn."

In the midst of a subdued caviar belch, Joe noted how skillfully she had avoided his inference, and then forgot all about it.

"My God, he is in a bad way."

"Mm-hm. Yes, a nice big dog. And," she said languidly, "I'll need a cleaning lady. Cleaning huge houses is not exactly my line."

Again, she smiled up at him, but this time with her eyes wide open, and she seemed to be reading the expression frozen on his face, reading into the heart of him. Perhaps she noticed that his mouth was still open, as though he were fighting off the realization that someone had just shot him.

THEY WERE MARRIED in early August, a small affair at the house with Mellie's sister from Winnipeg and a few friends of recent acquaintance. Auntie Vi came over with her German artist friend, and Hammy Hamilton brought his wife. Stinky Riley brought a present, a bright hideous kitchen clock, but he declined the invitation to the wedding. *Got steers to rassle*, was his excuse.

By mid-August they were steaming out into the Atlantic on a passenger freighter. 1939 had turned out just fine after all, a good year for an escape, good year for a honeymoon and for sailing back to England. Let them speculate about his identity in bloody Edmonton. He was on his way to Great Britain. If all went well, it would be a good year for getting reconnected to the old family. He and Mellie would ambush them. It had to be that way, because how else could he break the news to his mother and his siblings without the story spilling out into the streets? His letter to his mother had clearly gone astray, he was sure of it. He would simply ring up his mother from London and prepare her, by telephone, for an immediate visit. *Mother, I can't stress too emphatically the need for absolute silence. To all but you and the family, I need to remain dead. At least for the next while. Can I count on you?*

Every morning, while Mellie slept in, when he rose to take a turn around the deck and stare out at the ocean, he would rehearse this conversation, with variations. Should he not, instead, phone brother Wallace first? Young Wallace always kept a secret and never let anyone down. Joe was reclining on a deck chair with a mug of tea, gazing out at the grey horizon and a calm silvery sea, and at the gulls that seemed to float suspended, nearly motionless, a dozen feet above the deck.

The man beside him had abandoned his newspaper and he offered it to Joe.

"You chaps ready for the fray?"

The man who addressed him sported a grey, bushy military moustache and wore a tweed jacket, greenish brown fabric, no doubt enjoying its second or third decade of wear. He had explained to Joe that he was a Londoner with family in Halifax. He was a good deal older than Joe but seemed in better condition. His back was straight and he moved vigorously about the deck and the dining room like an admiral.

"What fray are we talking about?" said Joe.

"Can't be sure, old boy, but it looks like your militia chaps are on the move."

The man plopped his finger on a front-page story that suggested something might be in the wind. A militia unit from Halifax had been posted on guard duty. Ever since the Germans had taken over the remainder of Czechoslovakia, Joe had been uneasy about what might pop up on the front page, but these days he found the news easy to dismiss. This story about the Halifax militia could mean almost anything. It was not going to ruin Joe's honeymoon.

"Might amount to nothing at all," the old fellow muttered.

On the fifth page, however, another story did catch Joe's eye. *Alberta Businessman Found Murdered.* Police had been called to an altercation at an east end laundry where they discovered the body of a man bludgeoned and stabbed to death by an assailant who had fled, and who was still at large. The apparent motive was robbery. Morley "Buster" Krahn had been raised on a farm near the town of Hanna in Eastern Alberta, and had become a major entrepreneur, figuring prominently in northern mineral explorations over the past decade.

"Jesus," he whispered. "Murdered. That's it. That's the end."

"I didn't catch that," said the Englishman, who had returned to his deck chair. "End of what?"

"Jesus."

Everything, every bloody thing, had been falling into place. And now this, the last thorn in his side. Buster bloody Krahn. Murdered in a hop house. It was like the ending to a movie.

"End of story."

"Just the beginning if you ask me. You Canadians have no idea. How can you? It's all so hush-hush over there, don't you know. Keep them in the dark, that's what they're up to."

When Mellie came up on deck Joe was still sitting on his chair with the newspaper on his lap. The Englishman rose and gave her his seat.

"What are you staring at? Joseph?"

He smiled at her and she took the deck chair beside him.

"You've got a funny look about you," she said.

He closed up the newspaper and eased it under his chair, nervously clearing his throat.

"If I were a book writer I'd say this was the end of my story. This is where the theme music would rise to a crescendo. Cary Grant holding Katherine whatsername in a warm embrace. Making their big escape."

"The end? What do you mean, Joseph?"

"I was just thinking."

"I'd say this was the beginning. New life, new bride, no more waking to jealous floozies who bite off your toes."

"Hah!" he cried. "Touché."

She looked at her new husband and he gazed back at her. The wind was playing with her hair, which seemed in the last few days to be bleaching in the sun from dark brown to copper. The wind ruffled her up, gave her a ravishingly unkempt look, that and the morning light bouncing off the grey ocean, shining on her face. Nature did her a great deal of justice.

"I was just thinking," he said. "If our lives are like stories, there are these times when the story ends, and it's a tolerably nice ending, you know, like in the cinema. I think I've just come to that moment. My story, not my life. Knock wood."

He rapped his knuckles on the arm of his deck chair. Stamped deeply into the wood of his arm-rest was the number 13. That made no sense. He leaned over to check the arm-rest on Melony's chair. She sat in number 14. Two times seven. Two times lucky.

"End of story," Joe concluded. "All that struggle, all that stuff in the past."

"What stuff in the past? You've never told me about it. Not really."

"Worked like a dray horse," he said.

"Speak real English. What's a –"

"I banged away at the business for six or seven years till I found some success. End of story."

"But who were you...banging with?"

"All sorts of characters. Both sides of the pond. My English associates, my Canadian partners. May they rest in peace. Did you notice the stately old gent who gave you his seat? He's a Brit and he thought I was a Canadian. *You chaps*, he called me. *You chaps*."

"Joseph, you're changing the subject. Who were these people? And while I'm at it, how did you get that spectacular scar? It could not possibly be a birth mark."

"A tight Windsor knot. Dangerous things."

"Why does Vi call you a man of mystery?"

"I spread confusion wherever I go. End of story."

They gazed out at the grey horizon and the silver grey Atlantic. Their life had begun. On August 31, 1939, they would dock in London. The Great Depression would be more or less over. Morley Buster Krahn was dead. Robbed in a hop-house. *I am married to a beautiful woman. End of story. We shall embrace my family and help them out of their muddles. Unload a bag of lolly, travel all over Europe. Paris, etcetera. Have a high old time. Thumb my nose from afar at the Royal Canadian Mounted Police. Visit Castleford, visit the little flat where we were all born. Theme music, Maestro, if you please. Might have to reveal a few things to Mellie. How my mean old stepfather forced me to change my name to Joe Eggers. Poor you, she will say. End of story.*

Chapter 14

Joe Speaks

Pentland Firth, 1939

JOE HAD SUNK INTO a prolonged stupor. The sodden weather was the perfect accompaniment to his mood. All along the coast from Ullapool to Thurso, to Wick and beyond, the winter had been battering the Scottish coast with booming winds and fitful sleet and rainstorms. Today it was raining and blowing once again. With an assortment of enlisted men and officers, he was crossing from John O'Groat's over to Hoy on the *St. Ola.* If Jerry had been waiting for this steamer, and if Joe and his shipmates were to take a torpedo and descend to their final reward, he wondered briefly if he would give half a damn. In the course of a few months, his life had turned to –

"Garbage," someone proclaimed, as though the anonymous voice were part of Joe's lugubrious exchange with himself.

He had been thinking about September in London, his last encounter with Mellie, how he left her at the hotel with a ticket for home. *For God's sakes, talk to me. Why are you doing this? What am I supposed to do?* He tried to be as honest as he could *(I have to do this, Mellie. This is my home. My little brother has already signed up. I'm going to disappear for a while.)* That last bit probably made little sense to Mellie, but it was the truest part of his confession, the least evasive. She had no bloody idea what he was going on about, and they were both weeping like children. *But why now? Why so suddenly?*

He couldn't tell her that he had been assailed by a blind panic.

It started with the chap on the boat. Old school, inquisitive, well informed. Preferred talking with Mellie, who dutifully reported the conversations. *Your husband, Mrs. Eggers, you say he's British? He seems kind of tight lipped. What exactly does he do for a living? Haven't I seen his face somewhere?* It was hard to describe in simple terms, but the man had an odour of Scotland Yard about him. Such questions, day after day. And when war was declared, Joe saw his chance to disappear from his past escapades. She had no idea she was married to a murderer with a relatively new identity. A shady customer. Is that what he was? *Why now? Why so suddenly? Because, because Mellie, as of yesterday, don't you see, you're not safe in London. We are at war.* He'd walked out the door and left her there. Not long after that he felt as though he had fallen into a coal pit that had no bottom. His panic increased, and he rushed back to the hotel determined to tell her the whole pathetic saga. But Mellie was gone. It was like one of his nightmares.

Since then, his life had assumed an unmistakable trajectory, from a peak of success and wellbeing to a chaotic fall from grace to a series of tumbles down the mountain onto a progression of steep ledges. He felt as though he were clinging to one of them now – this boat crossing this nasty bit of water to this bloody bleak island, surrounded by these young rowdies serving His Majesty's Royal Navy. Were he to slip and fall once more, he felt as though he would never climb back up again.

Garbage, someone said, or seemed to say.

His letters from Mellie were getting progressively more terse, as though Joe himself were responsible for this war. His mother was dead in the ground, his newfound wealth did him no damn good at all, his friends were all –

"Burbidge?"

He looked up and beheld a young lieutenant peering at him with amused perplexity. The man was leaning over sideways so that his head was parallel to the floor.

"Excuse me," with lurching heart, Eggers replied.

The lieutenant straightened up but his head remained cocked quizzically to the side.

"Is that you?"

"Benbow?"

"Burbidge, it *is* you!"

"Corporal Joseph Eggers, sir, at your service." He said this louder, and with greater finality, than he had intended.

"Eggers, of course. Eggers. But Joe, your brother, the butcher chap –"

"Wallace."

"He told me that you were…he said you were dead."

Joe lowered his voice to a beseeching mutter. "A bit of a mistake, Allan. I'm afraid it's rather a long story."

Benbow rapped his friend on the shoulder and Joseph moved over, and he sat beside Joe, cradling his kit on his knees. He turned away from the ferry's spattered windows and gave Joe a skeptical look.

"Am I to assume that your status on or below the earth is not up for discussion?"

"I'll put your mind at ease, Benbow. I am not a ghost."

"That's a relief, Eggers. Tedious company, those ghosts. Now, fess up, my friend. What about that long story?"

"Get me drunk and I might reveal a secret or two."

"Let's give that a try, shall we?"

His friend pawed through the contents of his duffel and at last pulled out a tarnished and dented flask. Benbow's presence on the boat, the whisky, the gradual return of their old repartee were like medicine to Joe, and slowly, haltingly at first, as the steamer pushed into the swells, Joe told a tale to his old school chum. He tried not to lean too heavily on the exotic (a few Eskimos, a moderate number of polar bears), and if he went too far into hyperbole, he compensated by underplaying the vital information. He would leave the dark secrets to his journal. *My Life in the Orkneys.* Yes, dammit, he ought to write a journal.

"You mean you actually found some gold?"

"We found some, yes. Sold our claim. Made a bit of money."

From the lee off the Island of Stroma, the ferry lurched and moaned into Pentland Firth and, chugging across the Firth, it took the full blast of the wind and the oily swell from the Atlantic. There was a nervous moment or two before Joe continued with his tale.

"You got lost?"

"Yes."

"How do you get lost in a place without any trees? Ever heard of a compass, Burbidge – I mean Eggers?"

"The problem up there, Benbow, is that there are no roads and there's scarcely a landmark in sight."

Darkness began a slow descent over the channel. The waves diminished as their boat churned close beneath the cliffs towards a scattering of feeble lights. As Joe continued to spin his yarn, Benbow did his best to keep Joe honest.

"You mean, you mean these wolves actually surrounded your tent at night? What did you do?"

"I had an electric torch and a service revolver. If they poked their noses under the flap, I pulled the trigger. Bang bang. End of story."

"Delightful adventure, Eggers. I can remember envying you your Canadian jaunt. I almost wanted to join you."

"Quite the time it was. When I got down to civilization I made up my mind never to go north again. Couldn't wait to get back here. War or no war."

"If it ever ends."

Eggers sipped some whisky and returned the flask to Benbow. As the cliffs fell away, their boat pounded into the widening sound and the sound gave way to a sheltered bay. The town was encrusted with grey-gabled houses built just above the tidemark, and the bay hosted a fleet of small vessels.

"And you're *married?* Blimey. I always thought I might go before you did."

"I recommend it, Benbow. Follow my example and wait for a good one."

"Still. The lassies up here."

"Yes?"

"Hate to be the bearer of bad news, Joe, but they just *love* our uniforms. Don't groan at me. Don't disparage it, Joe."

"Disparage what?"

"You know. The old rumpy-bumpy jig-a-jig."

Joe erupted into laughter, which triggered a fit of coughing.

Benbow was fiddling with his duffel again. "What precisely are you laughing at, *Corporal?"*

"That phrase, Benbow. Haven't heard it in a decade. Good to be back in England, you know? Where blokes like you and me can converse in the King's English."

Benbow closed his eyes and released an approving belch.

Lyness, Island of Hoy, the Orkneys, 1940

EGGERS RELIT HIS CIGAR and stared out at the windblown townscape, puffing listlessly. He frowned at the cigar, butted it, took a deep breath and heaved an impatient sigh. He dipped his pen into the ink well and focused his frown on the nib, as though to demand that it stop dilly-dallying and say the right thing. His mind had been darting back to Yellowknife, to Lucy Castaway, to Heraldene and her little brother, to Isidore and his son, Charlie, and riding north on Shanghai Lil. With a disapproving grunt, Corporal Eggers returned to the present, the pen, the ink well, the letter. His private journal was going nowhere, but he could not give up on this bloody letter.

> *I still think I should be more worried about you,* he had just written, *than you about me. Your sad news beats anything I've seen over here, my dear. It makes me feel helpless. Men can only imagine this sort of thing. We'll have to try again, my dear. Win*

this bloody war and get back home to you and live a normal life. And try again.

You might think I'm still in charge of loading bombs into planes, Mellie, but I've got a new posting. Yes, because my back is buggered up and I have a friend in high places. 1940 full of grim news in the papers but we're still in the game.

He crossed out "my back is buggered up" and added, "I have injured my back."

I threw it out whilst loading a bomb onto a plane. I was showing my men how it was done. Had to go to the rehab unit for a few weeks. Bit of bad luck, I thought, but I was wrong. Best luck to come my way since I got to the Orkneys. I am still on the Island of Hoy, but my job now is writing reports for the local bloody newspaper! That's what I'm doing to win the war! Cub reporter Eggers to the rescue. Officially I am the Royal Navy Liaison to The Orkney Blast. Mostly I edit other chaps' rubbish and write keep-the-home-fires-burning pieces and humourous bits for the troops. See enclosed story on live musical theatre in Lyness. Written last week by Adam Fenwick-Symes–that's yours truly. Didn't know you married a bloody toff journalist did you?

He crossed out "bloke" and inserted "fellow" above, and then he substituted the word "gentry" for the phrase "a bloody toff journalist." Annoying, these perfectly good words that never quite make it across the Atlantic. He always seemed to be caught between two languages. Nevertheless, it was good to be back in the good old UK where people didn't butcher the language like the bloody Canadians. Over here, you could call your mates mates, and refer to wankers as wankers, punters as punters, and a bloke could be a bloke. Eggers knew that he wasn't a punter or a wanker, but he wasn't so sure about this Fenwick-Symes. His latest alias. Navy didn't mind. They were the ones who made him take a pseudonym. Farewell Joseph Eggers. See you on the other side. He would see how well the Mounties tracked this one down. Some days he was sure they were on his trail, that they'd seen through his little caper up north. Some days he was sure they had not, and that since his shipboard honeymoon he had become unduly suspicious. To put it mildly.

I now live in a civilian lodging house about a thirty minute walk from the Lyness Naval Base and a five minute walk from my office at The Orkney Blast. I get to wear my uniform to the office each day but I don't have to put up with mess food or barracks routine. I'm in a safe place all because of a wonky back and an old schoolmate, imagine that. His name is Allan Benbow. He gives me cigars.

You haven't mentioned your favourite policeman in quite some time. Has he paid you any more visits?

He looked up from his letter and stared out the window at the view. A treeless clutter of black streets and dark buildings and a trace of snow, which was already melting away. He sighed, recalling a phrase from his letter. *A normal life.* God, how he yearned for it. It was not normal for an Englishman to be laying low from the Royal Canadian Mounties. Not normal to be living under yet another bloody alias. From Burbidge to Eggers to Knaaker to Eggers again to Fenwick-Symes. Had he missed one? Absolutely not normal to go off on a lavish honeymoon only to find oneself all alone and in the uniform of a British naval rating. To find out that one's family scarcely resembled the one he had left behind. All this insanity just to disappear from the authorities, fight a war, reappear and secure a new passport. Mother in her grave, older brother and sister highly disapproving of Joe. The only one he could talk with was his younger brother Wallace, who had urged him to avoid the artillery, avoid the planes, avoid the infantry and enlist in the Royal Navy. Good old steady Wallace.

He had tried to phone his mother the same day in London when he and Mellie had parted. Some tosser was apparently screening his mother's phonecalls. Scotland Yard? Apparently not. He tried again to phone the house a few days later, and it was Wallace who had answered.

"It's me, Wally. Joe."

"What?"

"Joseph, Wallace. Your brother."

"This...this some sort of joke?"

"I assure you, Wally, I'm no joke."

"Joey? You're talking different. We heard you was murdered. Up in the north of Canada like. It was in the papers."

"A small mistake, Wally. They found a corpse and assumed it was me. I was lost up there but I'm pretty sure I wasn't murdered."

"Well, Auntie Vi put the bug in our ear, like. Maybe you might be pokin about somewhere, she says. We almost believed her, but she is Auntie Vi, so we had to wonder. And you'd stopped writin, Joe. What was we t'think?"

"No postage depots up there, Wally. Not a telegraph office in sight. How did Mum take the news?"

"She's gone of a stroke, Joe. Just last month. Died like a saint." Wallace wandered into other territory. The war. Signing up. Shipping out. Wallace's voice had shifted to automatic pilot.

Joe groaned softly into the phone, and his groan sank into a moan. "Our mum is gone? Wally, she's gone?"

"She was poorly for a long spell. We buried her next to Father. Very sorry, Joe. It was her time."

"I wrote to her...I wrote a letter back before the war began. In the summer. Did you not see it?"

"Mum claimed she'd gotten some letters from you, Joe. She got excited about them each time, but we never found them and we stopped believing her. My God. There might have been a real letter, then. Angie claimed Mum burnt one in the fire. Something about an investigation and the police after you. Mum was...you know, not really herself at the end. She imagined the police might find it. Angie and me, after a while, we just thought she was barmy. Well, Joe, she really *was* barmy most of the time."

"I tried to phone you back then and some imbecile refused to put Mother on the phone."

They tried to figure out who that might have been. One of Angie's fellows? The jealous one? Joe tried to follow up on the mystery, but Wallace was calling to his sister. Something about the Prodigal returned. *He's not dead*, cried Wallace. *Angie, come to the phone. Auntie Vi wasn't crazy after all.*

It tore at his heart to remember Wallace's voice on the phone. What damage would this war do to Wallace's gentle soul?

Joe turned back to his letter. Ever since he'd abandoned Melony in the London hotel, he never really knew what to say to her. The words always eluded him. He could rattle off a five hundred word feature on a visit from Lawrence Olivier, but he did not know what to say to his wife.

Mellie, I miss you more than I can say. I dream about you, I reach out for you in the night. I want a normal life, with you there in the morning.

Then say it, you emotionally retentive self-despising guilt-ridden disaster of a man. Say it.

Chapter 15

Important Stuff

Mayfair, 1943

JOE AWAKENED TO A dishwater sky in London. After breakfast he walked, in uniform, through light rain to a government office in Mayfair. He marveled at the sky where ragged clouds drifted ominously between the smog above and the fog below. A strangely mournful day on which to spend his leave–to become officially de-Burbidged. He found his way to the passport office with a leather case full of Eggers identification, most of which turned out to be unnecessary. He had no birth certificate, of course, but his uniform seemed to carry the day. Name: Eggers, Joseph. Age: thirty-one. Born: Castleford. Rank: Corporal. Parents, deceased. Married, yes, to Melony (née Stohler) Eggers. Etcetera, etcetera. All the information fit to print, a little white lie or two, a little omission here and there, and bingo – he had what Stinky Riley would have referred to as a new brand on his arse.

"Do you have a permanent address, Corporal?"

He gave the woman the address of his family home in Yorkshire and his Canadian address in Edmonton. The woman hesitated, stared at him, tapping a ragged nail on her desk.

"I have a business in Canada," he said.

"So you already have landed status in Canada?"

He nodded and then abruptly shook his head. He couldn't give her Joe Burbidge's reply; he had to give her a reply from Joe Eggers. "No. Actually. No, I don't. But when the war is over, I might well be returning to the Edmonton address."

"I think I understand your uncertainty," the woman replied. "A lot of us are crossing our fingers these days."

He looked around. The passport office was in a dreary old building, austere, poorly lit, but apparently untouched by the bombing. High ceilings, spare furniture. London was rationed to the teeth. It was a different city from the one four years ago, when he had docked with Melony.

He disliked getting into conversations about where he would live when the war was over. He didn't know what awaited him in Canada. He couldn't imagine what sort of a reception he would get from Mellie. The Mounties had probably abandoned the case, or she would have mentioned something to him. The investigators would by now have left his trail and found better things to do. His prospecting partners, Riley and Isidore, would have sent them down the wrong road. And if they were actively looking for anyone, a doubtful possibility, but still, it would be Knaaker Johansen.

"Edmonton," said the woman, staring at her desk. "Of course."

He shot a nervous glance at her.

"There was a man in here," she said. "From Canada. This very morning, renewing his passport. He said he lived in Edmonton."

"What was his name?"

She was flipping through a pile of forms on her desk. "He said he was lunching at the pub around the corner. He has an appointment here this afternoon with my…with my…Now where…"

The old Edmonton connection. He could perhaps live there as anywhere. But just what awaited him in Edmonton? Would Mellie have found a new lover? An old one? *Joseph, why in hell did you sign up in the first place? You keep giving me different reasons.* Could he name even one sure thing to look forward to?

"Money," he muttered.

"Excuse me, Corporal?"

She was so gaunt he wanted to give her a quid for a good meal. She looked as though she were starving. Painfully cheerful smile.

"Nothing," he said. "Did you say there was a pub nearby?"

In the pub, with a pint of bitters, Joe attempted to count his blessings on the Edmonton question. There was his little hoard, his portfolio of stocks with Hamilton. And there was always his favourite hobby. The good old gold. He could continue to buy it from prospectors, under the table, and melt it down and play Midas. There was that. There was good fishing, and Stinky. Would Isidore be there? The man kept disappearing for long periods of time.

Joe looked up from his pint. A large fellow loomed over his table, an older man than Joe. He looked rugged enough to clear out the entire pub.

"Burbidge?" boomed the man in a bearlike voice.

"No," he replied, "I'm –"

"Burbidge. I thought you was bloody dead. What the devil…?" The man pulled up a chair, sat down heavily, and leaned forward so that Joe could see very little beyond the man's broad face. "I kept thinking we'd meet up at Great Bear, or do some prospecting around Yellowknife, have a gargle at the Wildcat. But then I read about your…your…you know."

Joe released a prolonged sigh and shook his head. "What can I say, Tom?"

"Demise. Your demise, Joe. Never had a chance to attend your funeral up there. Pay my respects. And then, when the war started, you won't believe what I read in the paper, Joe."

"Buster Krahn?"

"Yes, Buster, murdered in a house of ill repute. And do you know what I thought, Joe? I can hardly believe I'm talking to you. Do you know what I thought?"

Joe raised both hands to speak but the words would not come. They were nowhere to be found. Which piece of him had the right answer? Young British Burbidge, fresh off the boat? Fellow prospector Joe, rolling in sudden prosperity? Sad Joe, man of many secrets? Corporal Joseph Eggers, stationed in the Orkneys?

"I thought you had been avenged, Joe. Avenged. Perhaps that tall bloke, that Scandahoovian chap. Never liked the man, silent bloke, bad drunk, but perhaps he had avenged your murder, Joe. Or somebody else who loathed Buster like we all did." Tom leaned his calloused hands on the table, heaved himself up, and returned to his corner of the pub. He brought his pint back to Joe's table and sat down again. He explained to Joe that he was in London to talk with some military chaps. British and American brass who wanted to talk about a northern front and northern defence. They were paying Tom to talk with them about northern transportation and survival.

"Did you ever see the grave in Yellowknife?" Joe said at last.

Tom shook his head. "Knaaker, was that his name?"

Joe nodded. "I hope some day, Tom, if ever I'm back in Edmonton, we can have a drink and laugh at all –"

"Laugh? Hm."

"I just meant, Tom, with the war winding down here and there."

"It's gone east on us, Joe. The Ruskies are pushing back, raising hell, and the Yankees are all over the globe, but it's not exactly winding down, is it? It's just starting to get fun."

"Matter of opinion, I suppose. I only meant, Tom, that perhaps some day if I came back to Edmonton, we could have a pint now and then."

"Wouldn't that be nice, Joe. Trotting down to the King Edward for a pint, two old Brits going down memory lane, two old prospectors recounting their triumphs in the North. Wouldn't that...but why do you say *if?* I thought you'd settled down there. Married and all that."

"Nothing lasts forever, Tom."

"What's that supposed to mean? Has she left you for another bloke?"

"No. Not that I've heard of. But Tom, I'm not sure I know how to live there any more. I'm through with the North. I wouldn't go back to prospecting if you paid me."

Tom nodded knowingly, closed his eyes, and took a sip.

"What we did up there, Tom. Finding gold. Surviving the winters. Fighting for our livelihood. Tom, it was…well…a bit heroic, wouldn't you say?"

Tom Payne shrugged his shoulders and gazed at his empty pint as though it were an hour-glass. "Do you know what you are, Joe? You're a bit like me. One of those northern adventurers who went to heroic lengths – your word, not necessarily mine. But heroic lengths to get the job done, and afterward, you see, we didn't die. We both became a bit of a legend, but we didn't die."

Tom stood up, wandered away, signaled to the waiter to bring two more pints. When they were served, he brought his great bulk back to the table and sat down, breathing heavily as though he had just exerted himself.

"Joe, what we need to do, you and I, what we need to do is learn how to live out our lives. Not as heroes or former heroes. You read about them in books, and usually they have to die, don't they. Die with their boots on, as they say in the cinema. You never read books about heroes who grow old and have to live like other men. I'm hoping in me own life that the fun of it, the meaningful stuff of life, Joe, that that's not all over. Did you know I'm getting married?"

"Congratulations, Tom. The meaningful stuff?"

"Do you love your wife, Joe? I hear you saying that you're not sure you want to go back home. That's why I ask. Do you love her? What's her name?"

"Melony. Of course I love her."

"You sound a little ambivalent, Joe."

"It's complicated."

"Well, Joe, you're a special case, aren't you? And…you are dead. And I suppose you'll have to stay dead or you'll be tainted by your deeds, and you might wind up in prison to boot."

"What do you mean by the meaningful stuff?"

"Joe, just ask yourself, what is important in this life? What is really important? What is so important in your life that you'd fight for it?"

"I'd be very happy not to be a shady character any more. The man of many disguises."

Tom Payne eased back in his chair, lit a cigar and took a few meditative puffs. He was staring off at something. Perhaps he was staring at the past, when he was the man who rode a motorcycle in the depths of winter, or the man who wore a blanket up north with a hole for his head.

"That's not exactly what I meant, Joe."

When at last they had finished their pints, Joe looked at his watch. They both stood and shook hands as men sometimes do at the end of a funeral.

"Goodbye, Joseph. Luck and all that."

"Goodbye, Tom."

Thule, 1945

DURING HIS REFUELING STOP, Joe looked up from reading his journal, sat and gazed out the window of the small terminal. The landing strip, and the undulating land beyond the base, reminded him of the Barrens. Too much of the Barrens. He wanted to get on the plane right away and continue his flight, not because of where he was going, but because of what he was leaving behind. This American air base in Greenland, with its bare minimum vegetation and its perpetual summer daylight. England, with the memory of his family in Castleford. That dreary, hesitant cast of mind he'd been dragging behind him over the past five years like a drunken friend.

He returned to his journal. His abandoned memoir, *My Life in the Orkneys*. He turned to a spot midway on the first page.

Monday: Got letter from Mellie. Enough said. Tuesday: Checked out Benbow's favourite Island re: military installations.

No photos, thank you very much. Thursday: Wrote feature on theatre in Lyness for The Orkney Blast. Production for the troops. Hen IV. Olivier played Prince Hal and Beavis Glow III played Falstaff! Beavis from Shacklesbury! He was terrible. Worse than terrible. I didn't know he'd become an actor. Still don't know for sure. Sunday: Weather much improved. Rained 4 to 5 hrs. Tuesday: Wrote back to Mellie. Not once between us has either one used the word 'miscarriage'. Wednesday: Why does anyone write a bloody journal? Later on Wednesday: Ditto. Why indeed. Saturday: Hung-over again. Monday: ETCETERA. Thursday: End of story. Saturday: Tweedy bloke on the ship? He was probably just a retired bloody colonel. Paranoia must run deep in my family. Monday: Dreamt of Isidore last night. We were back inside his tripod tent in a blizzard. Did Charlie do it? I asked him. Isidore replied, What you tink, Joe?

Joe turned a couple of pages to give it a final sampling before he burned the thing.

Friday: Saw Tom P. in pub in Mayfair. Depressing encounter. Doubt if I'll ever see him again. Wednesday: Mellie has lost her child. I have probably lost Mellie. I am lost in a mine-shaft with too many Joes. I have lost myself.

There followed a page of doleful wanderings and unearned resentment. With a sigh, Joe trudged into the jakes, pulled out his lighter, and lit the pages one at a time. There were six of them, done in a resigned looking scrawl. End of a promising literary career.

Chapter 16

The Real Story

THROUGHOUT THE WAR, Joe had had recurrent nightmares that Mellie had disappeared. Usually he had no idea where she had gone, or whether she had been kidnapped or murdered or seduced, but he kept on searching. When he confessed this to her, Mellie said that she had had similar dreams. She remembered one in particular where he had promised to meet her at an art gallery, but he forgot to tell her in what country the art gallery was located, and she kept trying to find him in art galleries all over the world. His version of the dream inspired sadness and desolation. Her version inspired resentment. For several years, right through to the end of the 1940s, they would allude to these dreams almost as though they had occurred in their waking lives, until at last the memory of them faded away.

On New Year's Eve, 1950, Joe and Mellie got all dressed up and went down to the Trocadero with broker Hammy and his wife and a few others. Perhaps it was the booze, Joe tended to blame it on the booze, but just as the chorus of *Auld Lang Syne* was ending, he was watching Mellie belt out the last few words by candlelight, and he succumbed to a compulsion. He could no more stifle his words than volcanoes can withhold their lava. Ignoring the banter of their friends all around them, he leaned over so that his lips were a couple of inches from her ear, and he whispered a monumentally inapt remark.

"I signed up because the police were on my trail."

She frowned at him as though he had decided to pull down his dress pants, then she seemed merely annoyed, and then bewildered by this non sequitur.

"Promise me, Mellie," he went on, "if I tell you the real story, you will never ask about my…my checkered past again?"

She gave him a stern look.

"You have to promise," he said.

Mellie leaned forward, glared at him. "Joe, what in hell are you talking about?"

"Forget it," he said. "Happy New Year."

On New Year's Day, at breakfast, Mellie said, "All right. Tell me the real story. Why, during our honeymoon, in London, when I was about to meet your family, did you sign up and head for the hills?"

"I panicked. Like I said, Mellie, the police were…probably… on my trail."

She nodded and at the same time managed, by closing her eyes, to retain her air of fierce indifference. "This is not exactly news, Joe."

"You have to promise me, Mellie, that you will never reveal any of this –"

"Yes yes."

"And Mellie, if I tell you, please never ask me about…this stuff ever again. Promise."

She sent an ambiguous shrug across the kitchen table, which may have contained a pinch of tolerance. Or its opposite.

"I thought we made a promise to forget that awful time."

"Well, my dear," he said, "I thought I owed you an explanation."

"You owe me an explanation *now? Ten years later?"*

He threw up his hands. "Fair enough."

"A fine way of spending New Year's Day," she said.

"I was trying to come clean. It's hard, you know. For a man to be (he was going to say *honest with a woman*, but he thought better of it)…I thought I owed you…the real story. No more evasions."

Melony's stern demeanor was now edging towards total contempt.

"I'm remembering that big, awkward investigator at our front door," she said. "Dunlap or something. A few months after you signed up in London. If such a visit were to happen, you told me to tell them that you were with an Australian division. End of story."

"It's called a wild goose chase," said Joe. "I asked a similar favour of Stinky Riley."

"You discussed these things with that old tramp but you couldn't tell them to me?"

"Of course I did. He was there. Up north, I mean. He knew... what I did."

She leaned forward and Joe looked down at the linoleum.

"Did what, Joe? What is it? Just tell me."

His gaze remained fixed on the floor. Some words seemed to be grinding up his windpipe, and he had to take a big breath.

"I shot a man who was trying to kill me and steal our claim."

Her eyes and her mouth seemed to open at the same instant.

"In the head. I killed him."

He wanted to tell her more, he had intended to tell the whole sordid tale, how he dealt with the man's corpse, how he switched identities with the man, and why; and how the wolves feasted on the corpse, and where he fled to and how he nearly got himself killed again in the process. But at the words *I killed him*, a trap door seemed to open between them, and the bats and the nattering demons, the creatures of the night he had always harboured, threatened to pour forth. So he sat there and she sat there, and they stared at each other, and just then, the trap door began to close.

Looking back on that moment in the kitchen, Joe thinks occasionally that his brief confession might have had a salutary effect. Possibly.

After the war, things had gone poorly between them. Several years after his return from the Orkneys they still could not quite find each other. Instead of being a young mother with a burgeoning family, Mellie found herself childless. She had a defeated look about her. They blamed their disenchanted state on themselves, on the war, on the miscarriage, on Joe's bearlike morning demeanor, on Mellie's baffling changes of mood, on

Joe's preoccupation with his growing wealth, on Mellie's expensive shopping habits, and on the closed book that was Joe's past. But until the Big Confession (as Joe thought of it), they could not quite find each other. He suspected they felt the same way: their yearnings for each other faded, got replaced, gradually and discretely, by the gestures, the white flags, of endurance.

In February of 1950 a blizzard descended on Edmonton. Joe and Mellie's half of the city went dark with a prolonged power outage. The heat went off and Mellie had to find a torch somewhere in the pantry and light some candles in the living room, where her arthritic grumbler of a husband was playing boy-scout, kneeling by the fireplace intent on lighting the kindling. From his experiences up north, he had always loved lighting fires, and this one blazed as the wind moaned outside and the snow built up on their sidewalks, and no one in the neighbourhood felt inclined to go out and start a car.

Shivering audibly, Mellie directed her husband to drag a sofa in front of the fireplace while she held a candle, imperiously, like Miss Havisham. Mellie snatched up a comforter and some blankets from a large cedar chest in their bedroom. Moving the sofa unassisted, Joe felt a sharp pain in his lower back and groaned a little too loud for Mellie's liking. Nevertheless, they sat together and piled on the blankets and the comforter, and gradually, as the storm moaned and shrieked around their house, Joe and Mellie were warmed by the fire and by the proximity of their bodies to each other.

This would be as close as Mellie ever got to camping in the North, but her plan seemed to work, and he took this process of warming as a sign of affection. He found himself caressing Mellie's elbow. That would be her right elbow, which he had always thought of as a sharp object, but which he now conceded might also be shapely, yes, pretty shapely as elbows go, and she did not withdraw her elbow but dammit all, he never really knew what she wanted from him, it was all too baffling, and to tell the truth, he'd never known, really, what pleasures he might hope for in the night, because how in God's name could they ever find their way back to that early state of shameless bliss? She was so…she was so…

Joe would have been fine with forgiveness. Forgiveness for being away when she had her miscarriage. For being up in the Orkneys for five bloody years. For signing up for the War in the first place. Forgiveness would have seemed enough. Until that night with the wind keening when she showed him some things. What extraordinary bloody intelligence the woman possessed, *women's intuition* they called it in the magazines, but that night she must have seen something in his stuttering entreaties, his bashful attempts at conversation, his swollen silences, and she bloody well decoded him, delivered the goods beyond even what he'd hungered for. She summoned his cacoethes and met these urges with her lips and her limbs all over him; such an eruption, such convulsions, could this be what that Bovary bloke had been hinting at, such re-awakenings as the wind wailed and the fire crackled, such a conspiracy of coinciding lusts – and how could she possibly have known how to make so galvanic his craving body, how to lead him back to the secret places of his yearning, the swollen sources of the flesh erectile from tongue to nipples to the horn of his…his…*bless me*, he heard himself cry out, he had become a pillar of probing wonder and he found her lips and tongue again, the skill of her roving fingers, and he smelled all around him the joyful drift, the rank bloom of love. And then again, probing her probing him, and he groaned in pain and tried to stop her until he stopped wanting to stop her because they were now wandering to a steamy place he had always hoped did indeed exist – *Jeeesuss* – which made her laugh, this husband turned sybarite, turned lothario in her silken tent.

Oh, she was all forgiveness.

He had to feed the fire again. At last they entwined beneath the comforter and fell asleep with a mutual sigh on the sofa. They would do this again but not often enough to feed his habit, and the insanity of their craving slowly devolved into mere lovemaking, mere embracing, and each time their bodies came together, however briefly, they were both reminded of who they had become in February of 1950. And that was the Roman candle that launched the 1950s. Not a bad decade. They went on together by imagining what a normal life might be, not always patient with each other, not always accepting, not always accommodating; they moved in their big house at times fretful and peevish, the barren goddess and the bearlike consort, who nonetheless had both known magic because from time to time they had made it for each other.

He sometimes wondered if Mellie thought about it in that way.

Before the miscarriage, she had wanted to call their son Bancroft, because she thought the name sounded aristocratic. He thought it was the craziest excuse for a name he'd ever heard, but he never said so. Throughout the decade he tried to get her to talk about it, her miscarriage, to talk about what the doctor had referred to as ovulatory distress. Or talk with Auntie Vi, or talk about adoptions, but she never encouraged these conversations, and he turned away from them always with a sense of failure. But throughout the decade, Joe could see Mellie moving ever so slightly beyond the pain of it all, and Bancroft became a familiar character in the movie of their lives, a gentle joke obscuring a misty sadness.

Can't we get a dog? Bancroft wants a playmate.

Where's my other bloody sock?

Bancroft must have taken it.

What's that noise?

Bancroft with his cap gun, shooting bad guys.

Part Three

Joe's People

Chapter 17

Galahad

ON SATURDAYS, TWICE A MONTH, Rennie's mother did the cleaning at Mrs. Eggers' house, and because this was on the weekend and she could not afford to pay someone to watch over her son, she got Rennie to come along and help her. He pitched in by carrying his mother's old carpetbag to and from the bus stop, and he did most of the mopping. Mrs. Eggers' mop was taller than Rennie. Her wash bucket had rollers that came together like the ones in a wringer washing machine. Most days, when Rennie had the bucket to himself, he would pour in some liquid wax to mix with hot water in the pail and mop the linoleum in Mrs. Eggers' kitchen, the main floor bathroom, and what she called her mudding room. After each dunking of the mop, he would step on a pedal to bring the rollers together and pull the strands through the rollers so that the grey water gushed back into the bucket. He liked that part.

One Saturday while mopping the kitchen, Rennie noticed Mrs. Eggers corralling her nephew Rodney and one of his friends, who had snuck into Mr. Eggers' library. The Bancroft room, the lady called it. *Give me that key*, she shouted.

When Rennie finished the kitchen floor he gazed up at the clock, a round wall clock with a rooster on the dial. It always ticked too loud. It was too modern of a clock for this house, which was the closest thing to a castle he'd ever seen. Mrs. Eggers was watching him. She was wearing a turban on her head and a tight green beautiful dress. She looked like a famous person going to a party.

"You're quite the little worker."

He looked away.

"Do you like dogs?"

"Guess so."

"Do you have your own dog?"

"Nope."

"Never had a dog?"

"We had one once but he ran away or something."

"He ran away, did he?"

"His name was Snuffy."

"Well, Rennie, you've just passed the test."

"Scuse me?"

"The dog test, Rennie. How would you like to earn a bit of money walking our dog?"

He asked her if Rodney would mind.

"Rodney? He's only here till the end of August and then he goes back to his mum. Besides," she said from the corner of her mouth, "I wouldn't trust that boy with a pet cockroach."

She was peering into his eyes. He did not like to look at other people's eyes. He preferred to look at their noses because noses were less embarrassing. She had a direct way of observing him, as though he wasn't supposed to be just a ten-year-old kid any more, but a grownup boy with everything figured out. She didn't seem to know that he hadn't figured out anything yet.

She took him into her backyard, and they stood for a moment by a lawn chair where someone had been reading a newspaper. She spotted a weed, hiked up her green dress, and bent down to root it out. The yard was filled with big trees, bushes, flowers, bird baths and statues of bare naked people. She didn't even have a potato patch or a spot for growing vegetables. *The Edmonton Journal* was on the lawn chair. The headline seemed to cry out, *Marilyn Dead.* The dead lady was a modern-type movie star, not like the ones in the black and white movies his mother watched on the TV. He wondered why she was dead. Rennie followed Mrs.

Eggers along a path laid out with stepping-stones, and they passed a beautiful tree with crab apples so big they looked like real apples.

"Here's our Galahad."

The dog was confined in a sturdy pen with its own doghouse, a large plastic water bowl, and a shiny metal dish for dog food. Galahad lay in the shade, panting. He was a husky, about the same size as the wolves in the zoo at Elk Island Park, but not nearly as lean. Rennie could not imagine taking anything that big and fierce for a walk. Mrs. Eggers opened the pen. Galahad stretched, yawned, and rose slowly to his full height, which was higher than Rennie's belt.

"How's my big boy," Mrs. Eggers said to the dog.

Her voice sounded so adoring that her greeting seemed to be coming from someone else. She placed a choke chain clipped to a leash around the dog's neck, and she did a little routine for Rennie's benefit. She walked the dog around in a circle, stopped, yanked the choke-chain, and the dog hunkered down slowly by her side. Another yank of the chain and the dog was up and padding along, stiff-legged.

"Heel," she said, in a soft firm voice, and the dog walked in such a way that his right shoulder was never more than a few inches from Mrs. Eggers' beautiful green dress. Galahad seemed old to Rennie, old and compliant and perhaps a little bored, so that he almost stopped looking like a wolf. She fed him a bone-shaped cookie, which he crunched methodically in his great jaws.

Rennie's instructions were to walk the dog along the crescent where the Eggers lived, a quiet crescent that followed the curve of the river valley. Some of the houses were old and grand, like houses in movies and stories. The ravine was heavily treed and it had a shallow creek that drained into the river. Rennie was to keep to the prescribed route every time out, and under no circumstances was he to go down into the ravine with the dog. Mrs. Eggers reckoned that the entire walk was less than two miles.

"What if he wants to run?"

"Run?" said Mrs. Eggers. "You mean run free of the leash? Is that what you mean?"

Rennie did not know what to say. She waited until he returned his gaze to hers.

"Absolutely not, young man."

HIS MOTHER WAS NOT sure her boy should be walking a great big husky. How would he get to Mrs. Eggers' home every week? (His bicycle in summer, the bus in winter.) How would he get into the backyard, just walk in as bold as you please? (Mrs. Eggers said that was okay.) What if the dog attacked someone? What if it attacked Rennie himself? (Galahad was old and worn-out. He didn't attack people.) What if Rennie's mom needed him to help her at work? (Rennie would walk the dog after he'd helped his mother.)

"Why are you so keen to help this lady?"

"She's payin me. She's payin me two dollars."

"Two dollars? You mean every single time you walk the dog?"

He nodded gravely.

"Just for walking a dog for an hour you get two bucks?"

He could see that the news was not welcome to his mother. It seemed to add a burden to her life. Rennie wondered what would happen if he told his mother that Mrs. Eggers was offering a hundred dollars to walk her dog. Or a thousand dollars. Would that mean worse news or better?

THE FIRST TIME RENNIE walked Galahad, the nephew Rodney came along. He was taller than Rennie, and there was something sly and knowing about him that made Rennie feel inferior to him. They reached the farthest point on the circuit from the Eggers' house, which was marked by a green wooden bench overlooking the ravine and the river. Rodney stooped and unclipped Galahad's leash from the choke chain.

"Wanna see something?"

"What are you doin?"

Rodney touched the old dog on the shoulder and cried *Go!* and the animal launched itself through the bushes and cantered like a great horse down into the ravine. The two boys waited. Something yowled from the bushes below, and then there was silence. It could have been anything. A small dog, a fox, someone's cat.

"Wait," said Rodney.

His mouth remained frozen in the shape of a whisper and his head was nodding in anticipation of something. They waited until Galahad trotted up the slope, panting. For the first time Rennie had ever seen, the dog was wagging his tail. He had some drops of blood on one ear and blood smeared on the side of his thick snout.

"Good boy!" cried Rodney. "Good boy!" He turned around and whispered to Rennie, "Sometimes it's better. Sometimes he brings it back."

"Would he ever hurt anybody?" Rennie said.

"Nah," Rodney replied, confidentially, and he chuckled under his breath. "Not unless they tried to run away. Never run away from him."

Galahad belched and continued to wag his tail.

RENNIE LIKED HIS JOB walking Galahad along the rim of St. George's Crescent. Sometimes he came over on the bus and walked the dog twice a week, and Mrs. Eggers paid him extra for the bus tickets. Sometimes a lady in her front yard or an old man taking a stroll would recognize him on his dog walk and say hello. Contrary to his mother's opinion, Rennie thought that rich people weren't all that bad. They just acted a little different. Especially the old lady, called Auntie Vi, who dropped over sometimes.

Often, when Rennie came to the point on the crescent where Rodney had released Galahad, he was tempted to do the same.

Galahad was a strange dog. You could pat him and he wouldn't wag his tail or respond in any way. He would just endure the patting until the walk resumed. Mrs. Eggers could pat him, and then he'd maybe open his mouth and puff approvingly. But even for this muted response you had to be family. And *still*, Rennie liked his job walking Galahad.

From time to time, he overheard things from his mom and Mrs. Eggers about Mr. Eggers. Apparently he owned mines (or maybe it was parts of mines) and traded for shares of other companies, but he didn't seem to have a real job. Mr. Eggers spent much of his time away on business trips in the warmer months, but unlike Rennie's dad, who had taken off a few years ago, he always came back.

One afternoon in September, a few weeks after he had begun walking Galahad, Rennie arrived alone at Mrs. Eggers' house. He opened the gate to her backyard and walked in. He plodded along past a group of statues and one of the statues moved, and Rennie's heart lurched. A big shabby-looking man was leaning against the shoulder of a naked-lady statue. Rennie could smell him. The frames of his glasses had been broken and mended with scotch tape. The frames had thick lenses. He was holding a stubby cigar.

"You Mizz Mudge's lad?"

He nodded and tried to take the man in. His hair was light brown, the same colour as the plastic frames. It was parted in the middle of his head like the hair on his mother's old-fashioned movie stars. The man's face was reddish-brown and weather-beaten, the lower lip protruding as though he were grumpy or stubborn or just thinking real hard about something, and his coat was an old and tattered canvas thing. If Mr. Churchill had gone off to be a hobo, maybe he would look like this.

"I am Mr. Eggers. Welcome to my castle."

His voice was deep and powerful and it rumbled down at Rennie from a great height. He had a sort of accent. He said some things about the statues, he had names for them all, but his manner was jokey, as though everything in the big back yard was supposed to be funny. Rennie didn't think the statues were very funny.

"And you have come for the noble Galahad."

They went inside so that Mr. Eggers could pay Rennie in advance. He beckoned Rennie upstairs to an office with a large wooden desk and a lot of display cases. The big man rattled through a drawer, collecting some change. There were at least a dozen rocks on his desk and more in the cases. It was messy, and he wondered if his mom ever had to clean it when they came over. And how would she clean it with these rocks all over the place? Each one had a label on it.

"What are the rocks for?" he said.

Mr. Eggers plunked a stack of quarters into Rennie's hand.

"That one over there," he mumbled, "is fool's gold, that's what we call it. That one's copper, got some silver too but you need to squint to see it. That's a small piece of pitchblende over there – that's complicated – and this, my boy, this is the real McCoy."

Mr. Eggers handed Rennie one of the smallest rocks. A label had been painted on it. The writing said GOLD ORE GIANT YELLOWKNIFE NWT 52. Mr. Eggers placed a magnifying glass in Rennie's hand. The rock was about half white and half grey. It looked special, it looked different from the rocks he found in the alleys behind his home or the piles of gravel at construction sites, but he couldn't say how it was different. Between the white part of the rock and the grey part were several flecks of yellow about the size of mosquitoes and smaller glinting bits here and there.

"Is this stuff gold?"

"It is indeed. It's a thing fools like yours truly suffer for. Keep it if you want."

"I can keep this rock?"

"Yes, lad. Mind you don't show it to the wrong fellows. Hide it away. Top secret. Pirate's treasure."

Mr. Eggers flashed a big ungainly smile, and ever so slightly his dentures seemed to shift.

RENNIE WALKED GALAHAD all through the waning light of October and into November. Whenever he got the dog, and Mrs. Eggers was there, she seemed to be measuring him for something, assessing his worth, as though he might be important some day, but not *that* day. Whenever Rennie got the dog when her husband was home, however, the big man marked the occasion with jokes and rambling accounts of life in the North.

One day in early November Rodney showed up in the kitchen. Mr. Eggers was talking with Rennie about digging for gold, and about seeing real wolves and caribou. He even had an Indian friend who talked to the bears. Rennie wanted to know if the bears talked back.

"That can't be," Rodney sneered. "Bears can't talk to people, so how come people can talk to bears?"

Rodney did that all the time, it seemed to Rennie. He would slouch into the kitchen and start scoffing at one of Mr. Eggers' stories, and Mr. Eggers would just clam up. This time Rodney was probably there for one of his extended visits. One weekend in November, when the afternoon light was fading, Rennie was warming himself in the Eggers' kitchen, listening to the ticking of the clock. Rodney wandered in and asked Rennie what he was doing.

"Waitin for the bus."

"Lemme show you something."

Whenever Rodney wanted to show Rennie something, he wore a cunning look, as though he held the key to a world of dark secrets. Once he'd shown Rennie a dirty magazine, and another time he'd shown him Mr. Eggers' service revolver from the war. This time he had a skeleton key in his hand.

"I can't miss my bus," Rennie said.

"This'll just take a sec."

They went to the door of the Bancroft Room and Rodney unlocked it. The light fell in from the hallway. The library was in semi-darkness. Rows of books were stacked high up on shelves, some of them behind glass panels, while others sat on tables and chairs. There were gaps on the shelves where the books were held in place by bricks. Rodney hoisted out one of the bricks, and several books fell on the floor. He swore a streak that was longer than it needed to be.

"Hold this whore," said Rodney, handing the brick to Rennie.

It was so heavy that Rennie almost dropped it on the floor. He strained to hold it up to his belt with both hands, which inspired a chuckle from Rodney. Rennie clutched the brick like a kitten to his chest. Rodney scooped up the books and dumped them back on the shelf. He turned on the lamp that stood on a dusty end table. They sat down together and inspected the brick. It was yellow and shiny like nothing else in the world.

"Is this..."

"Whadyou think, *Rennie?*"

"Holy..."

He thought about the sample rock Mr. Eggers had given him, with its glints of pale yellow. He had hidden it in a sock and stuffed it inside an old rubber boot in his closet.

"C'mere, *Rennie.*"

Rodney went to the door to make sure it was closed all the way. With his foot he slid another brick to block the door from opening. It thundered over the gritty floor. It was just like the first one, only dustier. A bar of gold, a smaller one, was lying on the window ledge.

"This small one is Unc's window stick, like in the summer? To hold up the window?"

It was about six inches long, one inch wide, and made of solid gold. He looked around at the library shelves and tried to count. There were maybe half a dozen bars and about as many large bricks of solid gold. Rodney broke into a deep-down nasal laughter. The gold was not funny, so why was he laughing? He might have been laughing at Rennie, or at his weird uncle, or simply at the gold bricks themselves.

"When they die I get all this," said Rodney.

Rennie hurried outside into the dark, unfastened the front gate and trotted up the crescent towards the bus stop. His supper would be waiting for him several miles away near the centre of the city. All the way home on the bus, when he closed his eyes, he could see gold bars floating, dissolving, re-forming.

THEIR HOME WAS a few blocks west of the football stadium, a cozy little row-house, and according to his mother the rent wasn't bad. It was one in a row of many such structures, which were squeezed between an orphanage at one end and a Presbyterian church at the other. Across the street was a Catholic school.

Rennie's mum was mending socks at the kitchen table when he told her about the gold. She inspected him to see if he was telling the truth, and she almost forgot to be scornful.

"Now what kind of a story is that?"

"What do you mean?" he said.

"How do you know Rodney isn't just playing a little game at your expense? Just laughing at you?"

"He isn't laughin at me."

"How do you know it's real gold and not fake?"

"You've never seen these bricks? In the library? Mr. Eggers doesn't even know how many he has. It's like a...a hobby."

"They lock the library, Rennie. Maybe Mrs. Eggers cleans it."

His mother was never much impressed by the Eggers or anyone else with wealth or eminence. She and her boyfriend, Russell, both agreed on this attitude. They seemed to make a point of being unimpressed. His mom was polite to her clients and as pleasant as she had to be, but she never warmed up to them very much, even when they confided in her or praised her work. *I have no time for that kind of nonsense.* That was her favourite phrase. The nonsense in question varied from the fussiness of her clients to the laziness of other cleaning women to the unreliability of streetcars and buses in her end of town to the countless questions he flung at her.

"And that Rodney," she said. "Heir to a fortune. I have no time for their nonsense."

"What do you mean, their nonsense?"

"Russell has this theory. He says that rich people are secretly in charge of all the laws and all the banks and everything that runs in this country. You'll see."

He asked her what it was that he would see.

"They'll be as nice as can be, and then they'll laugh at you as soon as you're out the door."

"But how can you tell they're laughin at you if you're out the door?"

She gave him a look. "Getting to be a real fixture in that house, aren't you."

He didn't know what a fixture was, but he denied it.

MR. EGGERS SEEMED to have a lot of free time. He said it was like this nearly every winter. "Nothing much to do except mind the shop now and then, take a walk down to Mr. Hamilton's office, squint at the ticker tape, pick up some cigars or a newspaper. Come home and let the Missus boss me around."

Eggers smiled down at the boy. They were walking Galahad together, their breath escaping in white plumes.

"But that's life in the trenches."

"What trenches?"

"Just an expression from the war. I was with the Royal British Navy."

"My dad was in the war."

"Well then. Had a good war, did he?"

Rennie shrugged. This was the first time Mr. Eggers had gone out with him for a dog walk. He had a bad back and a bum hip and a foot with one toe missing. He walked stiff, so they had to go slow.

"Promoted me to a corporal. Didn't like the chap over us, the captain. Forget his name. I got insolent, got demoted. Year later I was corporal again. How's that for a spotty career?"

"How come they –"

"Demoted me? I didn't march in step, you might say. Told my captain that he could shove his la de da swagger-stick up his arse."

Rennie laughed hard and then placed a mittened hand over his mouth. Mr. Eggers was clearing his throat and mumbling to himself. He often did these two things at the same time, as though mumbling to himself was part of the throat-clearing process, or as though clearing his throat inspired mumbling.

"I had a good war. Signed up in 1939 and I was a bit older than the volunteers. They sent me to the Orkneys. Spent more time writing reports and reading other chaps' reports than I did on the battle front. Mellie had to go home and keep the fires burning as they say."

"My dad broke his leg."

"Painful for him?"

"He was chasing a cat up a tree in the night time," Rennie said.

"Sounds exciting. My time on the Orkneys was pretty boring. Just what I needed after all that…just what the doctor ordered. Did you know that I never once saw a German till about the second last year of the war?"

"Boy."

"Lucky, wouldn't you say?"

After a pause, Rennie said, "How do you get the gold?"

"You mean how *did* I get the gold? You'll never catch me prospecting up there any more."

"But how do you know where to dig it up?"

"Well now. First you need fearless partners who can live in the

North. I had a couple of great ones. Both of them a lot brighter than I was. One of my partners flew a plane. They were both tough and determined, good company when the chips were down. If you want to find gold, boy, you can't be a whinger. Got to be a go-getter up there. Know what a go-getter is?"

Rennie knew what a go-getter was.

"Then you get all your gear together in the spring and you plop yourself down on a lake somewhere. You take a sharp little hammer, a rock hammer. It's like an alpenstock with a...with a...it's like an ordinary hammer, see, attached to a railroad spike. Yes, and sometimes for the creeks you need a nice big pan, like a big frying pan only lighter."

He held up his imaginary pan and began to sluice it around, and he rolled his old hips as though he were doing a dance.

"Is that how you got to be a miner?"

"Never was a miner, boy. Don't even *like* mines. I was a prospector. Miners are always looking at the sky, or gazing at the hills, or talking their heads off. Prospectors keep their eyes to the ground, see? No talking, always looking down."

"That's what I'd like to do," said Rennie.

"Well," Mr. Eggers said, meditatively, as though he were talking to someone else, "you might want..."

Mr. Eggers began hockling once more to clear his mighty lungs and to clear his throat, and he started to mumble to himself as though he were in bed having a bad dream. They went on silently for a block or two with Galahad padding along between them, and at last they stood at the green bench where Rodney had released the dog into the ravine.

"Does Galahad ever go for a run down there?"

"Why not?" said Mr. Eggers.

"Mrs. Eggers says not to. He might do something."

"He's a good dog. Won't hurt anyone who behaves himself. Just don't *run* from him, see? He'll think you're up to no good."

"That's what Rodney says."

"He's a good dog. Sleeps inside on his blankie. Keeps the burglars away."

Eggers patted the dog on the shoulder. He began to hockle for phlegm and broke into another great coughing spell. He sounded like a volcano dredging up lava.

"Here, look," he said, grunting as he bent over the dog's collar. He snapped off the leash and turned halfway around towards where Rennie stood behind him.

"See, lad, sometimes you've just got to forget what people say to you. Stop worrying about what they think. That's what go-getters do. They do whatever the hell they want. Just...you know...damn the torpedoes and full speed ahead."

He tapped the dog on the shoulder.

"Go!" he whispered, and Galahad leapt forward just as he had done when Rodney released him.

"Is Rodney a go-getter?"

"Not bloody likely."

They waited, the man and the boy, until both of them started to feel the cold, and at last the dog came back. This time nothing cried out and there was no blood on Galahad.

Against his own better judgment, Rennie told his mother about his walk with Mr. Eggers. He and his mother were heading home from the Eggers' house at dark on the bus. He told her that some day he would like to go up north and pan for gold. Rennie left out the part about letting the dog off his leash.

"That's how Mr. Eggers got all that gold," he said. "With a pick thing about so big and a frying pan?"

"Did he tell you what he did with his wife when he got married?"

"No."

"He took her on a honeymoon and when they got to England, he dumped her. That's the kind of husband he was."

"You mean he just..."

His mother nodded.

"How do you know?" he said.

"I have my sources."

"Was that another lady? The one he dumped on their honeymoon?"

His mother brought her lips together so that her mouth went small and she shook her head. She gazed out the window of the bus at the city flashing by in the cold night, and her reflection seemed to gaze in on them from the outside.

"Then how come they're still married?"

"I would of sent him packing."

"Did Dad do that?"

She gave him a look that did not encourage further inquiries in this direction.

"Seriously," he said. "Is that why you sent him packin?"

"Your father ran off of his own accord. He did not need any encouragement from me. But your good friend Mr. Eggers was a different case. He's an Englishman. I guess he thinks he can do anything he wants. Once he even tried to hang himself."

Rennie began to sag. He had been wondering what it would be like to bring Mr. Eggers home for a visit, like people did, so that his mom could see what he was really like. When Rennie was little she used to bring her boss home, Mr. Schuman. It was fun to have him visit, and Mr. Schuman was nice to his mom. But then Mr. Schuman fired his mom, and he never came to visit any more and she turned all grumpy until she met Russell. Rennie could not quite see Mr. Eggers coming through their front door. Not that he was too big for the doorway, but he was too mighty, his voice too loud for their home. Their home was too brittle. It might shatter like an eggshell and collapse around their ears.

"How d'ya know he tried to hang himself?"

"*She* told me. He's got a big scar right here," his mom said, pointing to her neck. "See what kind of people they are? They don't live like other people and they don't care what they do."

"He's nice to me."

"He's nice to you because he feels sorry for you. Any fool can see that. Those people, the whole lot of them with their expensive clothes and their trips to God-knows-where, they only belong with their own kind."

The darkness outside the bus seemed to drift inside of him and stay there. Weary. That was a good word. The darkness was making him weary. He objected to his mom's version of things but he scarcely had the energy to mount an argument. Besides, they were on the bus and people would hear.

When they arrived home and they'd had their supper, his mother said, "Come here," and ruffled his hair. "You need to realize that the Eggers are not like us, Rennie. They are different. They speak another language."

"What kind of a name is Galahad?" he said.

"Well, Galahad was a knight. You know, a knight in armour with a sword?"

"I know what a knight is," he said. "Sometimes they call them errant."

"Yes. Well, Galahad and the others served the king. They sat around a big table and drank their ale. And one or two of them also served the Queen. Hah." Her voice had gone nasal and jokey and she rolled her eyes up at the kitchen wall. "I forget the Queen's name. But the knights fought some battles and chopped people's heads off and then they all died."

"How come they died?"

She paused to look fondly at him, and he jerked his head away, because he did not want to be her little boy tonight. She didn't seem to notice.

"They just did. And then the well-known knight Rennie the Brave, he up and had his bath and went to bed."

She only knew what she knew, but she didn't know what *he* knew. She didn't seem to realize that Mr. Eggers treated him just like a son. He treated him better than he treated Rodney because Rodney was probably a troublemaker. But Rennie wasn't a troublemaker. He was noble. He was a go-getter.

Mrs. Eggers wore a red winter coat with a brown fur collar, and her face was almost as red as her coat. She walked right up to Rennie, stooped down, and put her face too close to his. She smelled of perfume and cigarettes and liquor. He wondered if she was sad today.

"Hello, Mr. Wonderful," she said and smiled so intensely at him that she seemed to be peering right through his eyes to the centre of his mind. "My husband calls you his special friend."

"Aw."

"Wish you could teach my sister's brat how to be such a gentleman."

He didn't mind the flattery, and he didn't too much mind the smell of liquor and perfume and cigarettes, but he wished she wouldn't lean so close and peer so intently into his eyes. Whatever she was looking for, she was not going to find it. Rennie was just an ordinary boy. It was an ordinary Saturday. He and his mother were there to do their ordinary jobs. Mrs. Eggers didn't seem to realize that everything was just ordinary.

She gave him a folded two-dollar bill and tottered back to the house in her beautiful red coat. He went over to the wired enclosure to get Galahad. Now that she was back in her house, it felt good that she liked him. That feeling stayed with Rennie all the way out to the point by the green bench on St. George's Crescent, and he stood there looking down at the ravine and out at the river with the dog sitting by his side. No one could tell that he did not belong here. No one would know that he didn't own this dog with the name of an English knight. They would just say, There goes that boy again, walking his dog.

He looked down at the dog. Galahad was looking up at him. Galahad was expecting something.

"Damn the torpedoes."

He snapped the leash off the choke chain and whispered, "Go!"

The great husky leapt forward, but at the edge of the ravine he froze and listened. Sniffed the air. Scanned the slope below and began to growl softly. Then Galahad tore down into the ravine, and the trees and bushes seemed to part before him.

There came a startled cry, a boy's voice, then the higher scream of a small girl. Rennie galloped down the slope towards the frantic voices until he saw three children running and stumbling through the bushes. The husky snapped among them, eyes blazing and teeth bared and grinning like a demon.

"Don't run from the dog!" Rennie cried. "Don't run from the dog!"

Chapter 18

Running Away

SOMEONE MUST HAVE PHONED the Eggers. They came in their car not long after the ambulance and the police. A small crowd had gathered. One boy was whimpering. He sat on the ground, bent over, gripping his shoulder. The other one, an older boy about Rennie's size, was already on the stretcher with his trousers ripped and blood seeping from a bandage on his leg. A little girl, maybe a younger sister, climbed into the back of the ambulance. She had been sobbing, but she had no blood on her that Rennie could see. She looked back and spotted him and glared at Rennie as though he was the dog's owner. He turned away from her and wandered in the direction of Mr. Eggers, who was talking with two policemen. It did not sound like a pleasant conversation.

Rennie had a sudden thought: he would run away. He would turn around and sneak down into the ravine and run away and never come back. Never come back for ten years. He would live along the river with the hobos and learn how to trap rabbits. Later maybe he would escape to the far North and live off the flesh of reindeer and seals and things like that. Maybe he'd phone his mother once in a while, or maybe not phone at all, but just write her a letter.

"For goodness sakes," said a lady, "what on earth were these kids *doing* down there?"

"They play down there all the time," said another lady.

"Oh, they *do* do they? Well, they don't live around here, I can tell you that."

"Well, it's off to the pound for that one."

Mr. Eggers led Galahad on his leash past Rennie, and his hand pressed lightly on Rennie's shoulder. He handed the leash to a policeman who led the old husky away to a car.

"What's going to happen to Galahad?" Rennie said to more than one person.

No one answered him. It was like trying to cry out in a dream and people couldn't hear you. Mr. Eggers was frowning in the direction of his Rambler station-wagon.

"C'mon, boy. We'd better get you out of here. Time to face the music."

The music, Rennie knew, would be Mrs. Eggers. She was waiting in the back seat, maybe to receive the dog, but the dog was being driven away to another place, and Rennie wondered if they would ever see Galahad again. What did they do in a pound?

At last he found the courage to look at Mrs. Eggers. "I'm real sorry," he said.

She made no reply and Mr. Eggers drove slowly away from the curb. The three of them must have looked to some people like a grieving family heading home from a funeral.

"Rennie," said Mrs. Eggers, "turn around. Look at me."

He turned around and focused on the top button of her coat. The button was brown and made of bound leather.

"Look at me."

Her nose was red. It was small and pointed like the nose of a rodent, and her face was very fine like she was an aging movie star. He had never seen her look so disturbed. He wondered when it was that she had stopped being beautiful.

"Rennie," she began in a soft voice, "you have let us down."

"I didn't mean to."

"You didn't mean to let the dog off his leash?"

"I mean, I didn't mean to let you down. I didn't know there were kids down in the bushes."

"It doesn't matter who was down there, Rennie. It matters that you broke your promise to me."

He nodded.

"Melony!" Mr. Eggers bellowed. "Don't be so bloody hard on the boy. How could he have known?"

"That's. Not. The point."

Eggers cleared his throat and mumbled an oath behind the wheel. Mrs. Eggers went silent. When they arrived back at their house, Mr. Eggers announced that he was going off to the hospital and then he was going to come home and have a bloody drink.

Rennie found his mother waiting by the front door with her carpetbag and a shopping bag on the ground. Mrs. Eggers walked over to have a word with Rennie's mom. They both looked stricken. At first, Rennie could not hear what Mrs. Eggers was saying. He could see his mother's face illuminated by the light above the front door. Her expression shifted real slow, from frightened to scary. Uh oh.

"You raise a vicious dog, Mrs. Eggers, what do you expect? And what about them boys, Mrs. Eggers? Was it my Rennie attacked them boys? And what happens next time that dog of yours attacks another child? Who will you blame for that?"

"Thanks to your son, Ethel, there won't be a next time," said Mrs. Eggers. Her pointy face was shaking with emotion.

Rennie's mom walked around Mrs. Eggers, picked up her two bags with a grunt, and lugged them over to Rennie. She placed them down at Rennie's boots.

"Come on, Rennie, we have a bus to catch."

He reached for the carpetbag but she handed him the shopping bag. He picked it up and glanced at his mom. She was probably as angry with him as Mrs. Eggers was.

They made their way slowly down the street towards the bus stop, and less than a block from their destination, his mother stopped to put down the carpetbag. She was puffing with anger. He didn't know what to say to his mother. She bent over and picked up the carpetbag. They waited for only a minute or so in the cold for the bus to arrive. It squealed to a stop and he waited for his mother to get on, but she insisted that he go first.

When they were seated near the back of the bus, he said, "I'm sorry."

"Shhh."

His mother was looking down at her galoshes.

"But I didn't mean to –"

She glared at him and then allowed her face to soften, and then she peered out at the night.

"I don't want to talk about it," she said. "I don't want to talk, Rennie. Not here. So. If you'll excuse me."

She pulled down her woolen toque and wrapped her coat more tightly around her and drew in her lips as though to hide them. She darted her eyes to the left and right like people did in the movies. Hunted people or spy people. She looked like an old woman, grim old granny Ethel. All the way home on the bus they stared out at the black winter night.

ETHEL WOKE UP with a sore thigh and a real start. She thought she heard the cops knocking on her door but it was just a dream. She went back to sleep and dreamt that she was still working at the jewelry store with Mr. Schuman. He smiled his warm toothy smile at her, the way he used to smile when they were in love. *You've been a naughty girl*, he said, and she woke up again. She wished she could be back in the store and in love again. Before he fired her. She had to shake her head. There was too much scary stuff banging around in her brain.

The day before, she had been putting away the last of the china. The Eggers' house had remained empty for a long while. Rennie had not yet returned with the dog. And then they all showed up together but no Galahad. Mrs. Eggers was mad as a wet hen. Their silly dog had taken after some kids because Rennie had let it go for a run. Any boy would have done the same. Mrs. Eggers gave her a look she had never seen before. A piercing look, as if she knew everything about her. For Ethel, that was the scary part. Well, well. Ethel would take none of that nonsense, not from that old bitch. Off she went, lugging her carpetbag with Rennie in tow. A lucky thing too or they would have missed their bus. Bye bye, Mrs. Skinflint. So long, it's been good to know ya.

And here she was, early in the morning, dark as pitch outside, listening to the wind. It made her shiver deep down just to hear it blow. And for heaven's sake, this *thing* in bed with her, gouging her in the thigh every time she turned over. She made up her mind to sneak it back before Mrs. Eggers discovered it was missing. Old Mr. Eggers would never notice it gone because he was never one to count the price of anything. But Mrs. Eggers had the eye of a hungry bird. She probably counted up the silverware every time Ethel left her house. But after such a row, how on earth would she ever get back into that house? Mrs. Eggers would as soon sic the cops on her as say hello. Well, well Mrs. Mudge, and what are *you* doing here?

Ethel slouched into the kitchen to make Rennie breakfast but all she had the energy for was a cigarette and a cup of instant. A while later Rennie came in and sat down at the kitchen table with a guilty look on his face.

"Sorry about the dog."

She replied, "Rennie, I'm not up to much this morning. Milk's in the fridge, cereal's where it always is."

While Rennie munched on his cereal, Ethel came to the realization that she needed some expertise.

THE FOLLOWING WEEK, after Rennie had gone to bed, and after she and Russell had had their fun, Ethel said to Russell, "Supposing there was this rich guy with a lot of oh, say...a big pile of gold bricks in his house, right? And suppose this guy wanted to divvy up one of them so's he could sell it. How would he do that?"

Russell sat up in bed and seemed to come to life.

"You got someone in mind?"

"Scrooge McDuck," she said.

"Seriously."

"Rennie used to walk the dog for this Englishman? I've told you about him, the old prospector? Sure I have. Rennie thinks this guy was kind of like his friend. Anyway, he's got this gold brick and he wants to turn it in."

"Turn it in?"

"Cash it in. But he can't, because people would ask questions, right?"

"He needs to cash in a entire gold brick?"

"Just supposing."

Russell looked thoughtful for a moment. He began to poke around beneath the blankets in search of something. He dragged out his underpants, held them up and sniffed them.

"So. Likely he wants a bunch of wafers, eh. Flat, like a letter? Then he could sell them off here and there, without the cops come down on him."

"Exactly," she said.

"Me, I'd go to a goldsmith."

Ethel did not know any goldsmiths. What did men do to divide up a brick of gold? Go to a steel mill and melt the thing down when no one was looking?

"Goldsmith or a jeweler," Russell said, yawning. "Yeah," he added in his deep-down voice, pulling on his shorts, as though he had really laid this one to rest.

Ethel did not know any goldsmiths, but she did know a jeweler. And she missed him. He was widowed but still in the game, and by Ethel's reckoning, he owed her one.

Chapter 19

Life in the Present

"WHAT'S GOING ON in the world?"

"Usual stuff," he says.

"Can you be more specific?" she says.

Her hair is wrapped in a towel, her body in a terry cloth robe, royal blue. She labours over her toenails on the chaise longue, goes slowly with the brush (new shade, *la rose foncée*), pondering like an oil-painter in the final touches of a landscape. He reads the paper standing, shifting his weight from one hip to the other, from the arthritic one to the flexible one, left to right and back again, as though to weigh both sides of the news and find a meaning between the lines.

"Our colonial secretary tells us that...hmmm...we're going to give Kenya her independence."

"Bully for your government."

"Not my government any more."

"What else?"

"Kennedy's at the Vatican, cozying up to the Pope. Kruschev wants to ban...wants to ban nuclear testing..."

"Not a bad idea."

"Except for the underground thingummies. Martin Luther King and a chap named Farmer want to march on Washington and... oh, wait for this...a bunch of your artistically-inclined tribe are going to get medals at the White House."

"Who's getting medals?"

"Chap named Cassals."

"He plays the cello."

"Never heard of him. Chap named Edward Steichen."

"He's a terrific photographer."

"Never heard of him. Contralto Marian Anderson, I've heard of her. Fellow named Wyeth..."

"Andrew Wyeth. You know who he is. Auntie Vi has one of his early paintings."

Joe gazes up from his paper and peers out the screen window. Children in the garden. Girls from down the crescent, pretty little things. An oil executive's daughter and a doctor's daughter. Eight or nine years old. They are paying Rodney a visit, smiling shyly, perhaps catching up on the older boy's adventures in Winnipeg. The girls murmur back and forth as Rodney resumes digging a shallow pit for his Aunt Mellie's new bird-bath. A man is coming to pour a cement pad where he will erect the thing, a mounted copper bowl as big around as a man-hole cover, which might well scare the songbirds away.

Nervous laughter from the backyard.

Framed by the screen window, this scene has the feel of an old-fashioned movie. Little Margaret checking out Rodney's pile of dirt. Little Bethy wanting to help with the digging. Rodney holding the shovel over his head and moving back and forth between the dappled shade and the bright sun, denying little Bethy her chance at the dirt. Summertime. No school for anyone, sunny days, sweet idle boredom. Joseph's gaze drifts into the shimmering pantomime – the bright colours of the girls' dresses against a background of Mellie's flowers; Rodney the nephew, the chosen one, holding court, smiling handsomely today in his new khaki pants; nice doggy Gudgeon back in the shade blinking half-asleep at the children. If Auntie Vi were a painter, this is what she might paint. Life in the present tense.

Even Gudgeon belongs in the sketch. There is no need to put him in the cage. Mellie has saved him from the City Pound to be a watchdog, but Gudgeon is too sociable, too entirely human, to be a watchdog. Does this mean that Mellie has at last let her guard down? Probably not.

Little Bethy is having a lively exchange with Rodney, pointing at him, insisting that he stop doing something. Little Margaret watching in the shade. Bethy turns her back on Rodney, perhaps to whisper and conspire with her friend. The mischievous grin has disappeared from Rodney's face. His eyes have narrowed into a cold and stealthy expression. Bethy turns back towards Rodney. She sees to her horror (to her friend's horror, to Joe's horror) that Rodney is pointing his cock in her direction. Margaret screams first, then Bethy, and Joe roars out the back door like a demented bear.

Rodney spins around to make adjustments.

"I didn't mean to," he says calmly, as though to the dog. "We were just fooling around."

With Joe glaring at his back, Rodney grabs the shovel and leaps up to drive the blade into the ground. He does this commandingly, as though nothing untoward has happened.

"You little fool. Get in here. Put that shovel down. I said get in here."

The boy backs away. He grips the spade's wooden shaft with both hands as though to swing or surrender it. Joe can not tell the boy's intent and he doesn't give a good goddam.

"Give me that shovel you little halfwit."

He advances on the boy, and Rodney's expression coils down from defiance to rage. He winds up like a batsman, his man-sized hands slide together on the handle, and he swings with all his might. Joe is ready for the blow. He wants to feel the incriminating crunch of it. The shovel thuds into his left hip, the arthritic one, and for only the smallest tick of a second, Joe grimaces, then grabs the boy around his thin biceps. Rodney soars in Joe's grasp as the shovel clatters to the ground.

"Don't hurt him!"

The plea comes from Bethy.

"Don't hurt him!" cries Margaret.

Their tears are forgotten and fear has transformed their bright faces. They are now afraid of Mr. Eggers.

"THEN WHY DID HE do it? Did you ask him why he did it?"

"He says they dared him to. Girls are like that."

"That's rubbish. Then why did they scream bloody murder?"

"I sent him to his room. You just settle down. Look at you. Settle down. He's not Jack the Ripper, he's my sister's boy."

"He's a bloody idiot, that's what he is. And you're his partner in crime. You just spoil him rotten because you can see no wrong in your little nephew. Well, he's going to end up in reform school if you don't wake up to who he really is. He picked up that shovel like he wanted to kill me."

"Listen to you. Kill this, kill that. When do you ever spend any time with Rodney? When did you ever try to understand him?"

"I understand a little rotter when I see one. I understand a boy who doesn't respect girls. He needs a proper thrashing. Last week he shoots Gudgeon in the leg with the BB gun. He needs…he needs to learn some discipline. And he can't just go raising the flag whenever he feels like it."

"He's a fatherless boy. He's no sooner out from Winnipeg and you're ready to throttle him."

He turns away from her and heads for the upstairs loo to get an aspirin, limping from pain, limping to exaggerate his pain. He stops and turns around to face her. Mellie's face is the same shade as her newly-painted toenails.

"Yes, you're right," he says. "I am ready to throttle him. And now I want him on the train back to Winnipeg. Preferably with an armed guard."

"Men," she says. "What the hell do they know about anything?"

THE UPSTAIRS LOO has been consigned primarily to Mellie and her vast array of creams, bottles, brushes and pills. He scrutinizes the contents of the medicine cabinet in search of a bottle of aspirin. Already he regrets the fight with Mellie. And his confrontation with Rodney. *He needs a proper thrashing.* Did he actually say that? Sounded like the sort of rubbish Master Crotting would dish out back in grammar school. Worse. Sounded like swill from his step-father, the late unlamented Hugo Eggers. But dammit, the boy needs to learn a lesson. He can't just wave his lad at little girls and pretend it didn't happen.

He wants to yell downstairs to Mellie. *Where is the little fiend now? Outside terrorizing the neighbourhood?*

He grips the newel post at the top of the staircase, sucking to dissolve the aspirin, and he wonders briefly if he is meant to have a domestic life like city men. Perhaps he is better suited to a life of grubby bachelorhood down at Stinky Riley's ranch, helping Isidore to muck out the stable and brand the cows. He hears snatches from wife and nephew. In a gentle, crooning voice, Mellie tells Rodney that he shouldn't go about swinging shovels at Uncle Joe. Nephew murmurs something back.

"It just breaks my heart," she says, "to see you two go at it."

Why is it always the heart? Why does love always reside in the heart? And courage and grieving and purity and God knows what else? Why are all the Hollywood villains deemed to be heartless? The heart is just a muscle that pumps blood. It contracts and it dilates and it is said to be hollow. Mike Pearson, new man for the job of running the country. His admirers call him brainy. Won a Nobel Prize because he has a good brain, but he hasn't exactly been exalted by his people. They're good Canadians, they think he might be a little better than the last chap. But to be loved, adored by a nation, you have to demonstrate the courage of a matinee idol and become a heart-throb like Kennedy.

Melony has more than once accused Joe of being heartless. His pursuit of gold in the North had been a heartless venture. His treatment of Rodney the Idiot was heartless. Her word. As though it's cowardly to confront the little runt with his own crimes. As though it's unfeeling to take charge and set things right. And now his little nemesis is stepping up his crimes, acting like a cuckoo. Better to send him back to Winnipeg to Mellie's imbecile of a sister.

And to think that Mellie has been halfway ready to adopt the boy if her sister gives up on him. Now she will probably deny it. In Joe's never-too-humble opinion, this whim to adopt the boy all goes back to Mellie's miscarriage during his service in the war. *Ovulatory distress*, the doctor said. Joe doesn't like to remember it, that awful time. Mellie's recriminations, her sense of failure.

He considers taking a walk to get himself out of his funk. But his leg and his hip are killing him and he doesn't have the heart for it.

There was a stretch in Joe's life when he still stumped, willingly, out the door and up the crescent with their first dog, old Galahad the Vigilant. One mistake and a one-way trip to the pound. Where is young Rennie now? How he'd worn Joe out with all his questions. He got Joe going, he was good to walk with, all curiosity, easy to be around. Another fatherless boy. Pity, the way it ended. Mellie drove him and his light-fingered mother out of the house like Jesus with a bull-whip.

Best to forget about it.

Joe inspects himself in the bathroom mirror. He looks like hell. The flamboyant scar around his neck seems redder than usual. Faded complexion. He's felt restless and exhausted lately. How can you be both? He's been having bouts of insomnia and the next day he's dizzy, anxious. *You are going to take Gudgeon for a walk and you are going to like it. You are going to show that wife of yours that you're not ready for the bone-yard. Get some colour into those cheeks, get some spring back into your step. Fifty-one years old and you look like you've got a foot in the turf. Put your shoulders back and bloody well start breathing again.*

It works. He pulls on his shoes, dons his Mr. Magoo hat, and as he passes the little den next to the parlour, a children's choir begins to sing from the TV set. Angelic voices. *We are climbing Jacob's ladder.* Sounds as though they really are climbing the blessed thing.

"Where are you off to?"

"Take the dog out."

"We need to have a talk."

"Later. Where is he now, little Fly-Blow?"

"Never you mind."

He rouses the dog from his blanket by shaking the leash. Gudgeon is up and wagging, giving Joe that intense look. *Do you mean it? Now? We're going for a walk?* The dog prances around, claws clicking on the kitchen linoleum. He lets out a high whine and Joe can no longer take the intensity of his gaze. Joe, the old grouch, and Gudgeon, the embodiment of joy. Best of friends, brothers in restlessness.

Outside, Joe limps along at his own arthritic pace and Gudgeon grabs up a stick from the boulevard, crunching it with such savage enthusiasm that it snaps in two. Gudgeon halts to mull over which half to grab and drop at his master's shoes. These decisions are important.

"Not today, Gudgeon."

No tossing sticks. Joe's throwing arm feels unequal to the task. Both of his arms. They've acquired a dull ache, an inflated feel to them that pulses up to his shoulders. The pain turns convulsive. Joe stops walking. He is beset by the dreamy notion that he's going far away and will never come back. He sways, holds one hand against a tree, and his head clears. The dream has lost its grip on him and his arms are once again his own. He bends down and grabs one half of the broken stick and tosses it for Gudgeon.

"What the Christ was that?" he says to the drowsy sky.

Joe and Gudgeon manage to make it around the block before the pain returns. Deep down spasms, as though his arms are pumped with electric particles. He approaches the back porch, wades slowly into the kitchen, and the twinges radiate to his chest, sharp throbs that rip from the sternum all the way down to his arsehole and back, and as the kitchen clock ticks louder and louder, he knows once again that he is going somewhere not of his choosing. His hat falls to the floor.

"Mellie!"

"I'm in here."

"Well get the hell in here," he rasps, clinging to the refrigerator as the waiting dog, the ticking clock, the kitchen, the house, the yard, and the world spin mercilessly around and around.

Chapter 20

Bear to the Bog

HE COULD WALK TO the Royal Alec in less than an hour, wasn't afraid of a little exercise, he was probably the best walker in his whole school, because how many guys did papers every morning before school and how many guys had a mother with no car? Two miles, nice August day? Nothing to it. Although it would be pretty cool if he could soar over all the houses and Seventh Ave and all that traffic and give a big *nya-nya* to the suckers stuck in their cars.

In no time flat he strode up to the information desk, from the information desk to the elevator, from the elevator to the third floor, yeah. From the third floor to a ward that...that was the wrong ward, it was for children, to another ward that was also the wrong ward, and a nurse with a very loud voice redirected him back down to the main floor and to another set of elevators. OK. So he went up to the third floor of the east wing then, and once again began to search for the scary ward. He almost forgot that he was on a hero's misheon, because the stupid hospital was so complicated, who ever heard of *two* third floors, so now he was this blind guy and he had to hear and smell his way to the scary ward. The smelling part was the most helpful, because over and above the farty smells of old people's bodies and the whiffs of yurky canned peas, boiled potatoes, stewed chicken, he could smell the familiar stuff, the cleaning fluids, disinfectants, the bucket-mop-type stuff. He remembered doing Mrs. Eggers' floors and he tried to forget Mrs. Eggers and her pukey jobs and her castle-type house and her dinosaur puke of a guard dog, and at last a nurse directed him to a private room.

Jesus. Mr. Eggers was snoring, toothless as a newborn baby. A tube was attached to his arm and another one came out of his nose. There was no redness in his face, no healthiness, even his nose and his cheeks were pale and he was just lying there lumpy like a dead man.

Rennie approached the bed and only then did he see Mrs. Eggers. Perched on a chair like an owl between the far side of the bed and the window. She looked shrunken up tonight. Giving him the evil squint like he was a pain in the ass, and not just a pain in the ass but just *one* of a thousand different pain-in-the-asses she had to deal with, not even like a major pain in the ass but a zit-sized pain in the ass. She looked smaller and older and not so stylish. But she still had the evil eye, she could still look right into the centre part of his brain. He wondered what she saw there.

"Hi."

No answer. Mrs. Eggers just sent out these dark evil crypto-type rays.

"How's he doin?"

She shook her head.

"Can he sit up?"

"Right now he needs his rest. He needs to be left alone."

"I came as soon as I heard."

"And how may I ask did you hear?"

"The doctor."

"Doctor Callaghan *phoned* you?"

"I thought you knew," Rennie said. "They phoned my mom and she gave me the message. She said it wasn't none of my business but I came anyway."

"If, as your mother said, it was none of your business, why did you come?"

"Because."

Mrs. E sat up in her chair. She looked confused. Maybe a sign that old Renwick had stared her down with his X-ray counter-vision. She stood up and went over to Mr. Eggers. He was beckering her with his finger and even his finger looked old and dead like a bear claw. She brought a glass of water up to his lips.

A nurse came in and smiled at Mr. Eggers. Time for his meds. Whisper whisper. Big secrets in the heart ward. Mr. Eggers needed to be *unhooked.* He peered over at Rennie, and his eyebrows came together like smooching caterpillars.

The nurse went off and Mrs. Eggers said, "Did you ask him to come here?"

"Yes I did, Mellie. Told Callaghan to get someone to call his home."

Mr. Eggers tried to raise his body, and Mrs. Eggers struggled to yank him into a sitting position. He started to cough and he waved her off. The scar on his neck beared itself like a gijantic worm. The hanging scar Rennie's mom told him about. Dark purple and also red. For a second or two he wondered about running away and never coming back.

Mr. Eggers said to Mrs. Eggers, "Don't…hover."

"Joseph, you asked them to phone his home?"

Mr. Eggers ignored her and looked at Rennie, like he just forgot he was fighting hand-to-hand with old Witcho.

"Grown a bit, haven't you. What're you? Twelve, is it?"

"Eleven."

"Last time I saw you, you was a little runt."

Rennie was still a little runt, he knew that, but Mr. Eggers was trying to be nice to him. Rennie just stood there with his hands sticking out of his arms. What could you say to a man with a mansion and his own library and ten gold bricks and an explorer up north? Who's almost halfways dead?

"Still helping your mum are you? Still mopping the floors?"

"I have a job now," he said, hoping that the both of them could see the difference between a duty to your mom and a real job. "I deliver the *Journal* every morning."

"Up in the morning, is it? Get up in the dark, do you?"

"Yup."

"Maybe it's a good thing you came to visit my husband," said Mrs. Eggers. "I am guessing that he has a request for you. Because something went missing from our house last November, and *I* know it, Joseph, whether *you* know it or not."

"Mellie, don't let's rush into things."

Rennie leaned forward.

"My wife does not stand on ceremony."

"Scuse me?"

"She believes in getting right to the point."

"We're very disappointed in you," she said. "We had always thought you were a gentleman."

Mrs. Eggers sat on the side of Mr. Eggers' bed as though to show Rennie that they were both solid on the Rennie question and on any other question.

"Mellie," said Mr. Eggers in a raspy voice, "I'm going to ask you to leave us alone for a moment. Young Renwick and I are going to have it out and I…I have–"

"I understand," she said, "but I wish you would have told me."

To Rennie's surprise, she left the room without a fight. But she didn't just leave, she went slow and frowny like he'd just told her it was her turn to feed the cobra.

"Howya feelin, Mr. Eggers?"

"Feel like hell," he said. "Rather be up north chewing raw caribou than swaddled in this Christly nuthouse."

"Mom says it was a heart attack."

"Some bloody thing," he mumbled to himself.

Mr. Eggers was looking down at the sheet that covered him as though he had just lost something.

"Can't even make it to the bloody bog."

Without looking up, he said, "Look here, young fellow, I might just have to settle accounts, if you see what I mean, and well…my wife keeps inventories of…you would not believe how thorough she is…of things in our house. She seems to think…

she believes that…that you have something of ours…and she wanted you or your mother to give it back. Last winter she wanted to call the bloody police, you know, and I said over my bloody dead…ha, there's a good one…over my dead body."

Mr. Eggers was gazing at Rennie through his bushy eyebrows.

"Yeah?"

"Now, we both know you're not a bloody con-man, right? We both know that you're not a common criminal, hm?"

"Yes," he said, and he wondered what a con-man did to people.

"Mellie wanted you to arrange its return. If you've still got it. She wanted you…just…to bring it back and that would be the end of it."

Mr. Eggers added a *hmpf.*

"Yeah?"

"You know what I am referring to, don't you."

He knew the day and the hour, and he remembered exactly how he felt. The label on the rock sample read GOLD ORE GIANT YELLOWKNIFE NWT 52, and the 52 was 1952, the year he was born.

"Yessir."

"Does your mom…does…you know. Do you still have it? After all these months? Hidden somewhere?"

"Yeah," he said. "I can get it."

Mr. Eggers eyed him in a super-serious kind of way, officer to private, one hero to another, like man to man, the way one explorer might have looked at another up north when the ships were down.

"Your mother, will she…oh hell, let's send a car to take you home and bring you back."

He smiled at the old man and shook his head. "No, sir, I'll take care of that. I won't even tell Mom."

"We were always the best of friends, Renwick. You know that, don't you?"

"I THINK YOU WERE DREAMING."

She gazed down at him from the foot of the bed, frowning tolerantly, a sour affectionate once-over that one might have offered to a troublesome child. He had no idea what time it was, but there was less bustle in the hallways. People were murmuring somewhere down the corridor from his room. A nurse drifted like a ghost past his door in her all-whites and rubber-soled shoes. A woman's voice purred through the PA asking for a doctor with a long, baffling name.

"What time is it?"

"A bit before eight. It's getting dark out there."

"Mellie, you need to go home and get some sleep."

"I will when I will. What were you dreaming about?"

"My mother's bed."

"Did your parents sleep apart?"

"No, but after Father died, it became known as Mother's bed." A sort of meeting place for Mother and her brood, he recalled, and he wondered if he was going sentimental. "Has young Rennie come back again?"

Mellie folded her summer coat over a chair and took her place by Joe's bedside.

"No, he won't be back tonight. It's too late."

She plucked some pills from her sweater and released a delicate yawn. He closed his eyes.

"I'm not a praying man."

"No, we're not much in the praying department, are we? I gave it a try when I was a girl."

"Me too, centuries ago. Wouldn't know what to say now, would you?"

"We were Catholics. We always knew what to say."

They fell silent, and the nocturnal workings of the Royal Alec hummed and called, whirred and clicked, and in their separate places Joe and Mellie closed their eyes for a catnap.

Eyes closed, Mellie said, "You dreamt about your mother's bed?"

"I'll bet it wasn't much bigger than this one. Say, did you phone Auntie Vi?"

"Yes, yesterday. But how can you dream about a bed?"

"I was right back there," he said with a sigh. "Our little flat in Castleford. Didn't doubt it for a second. Aren't dreams wonderful?"

The dream had mostly faded but not the bed. And then the bed began to fade, and he with it, and he was somewhere up in the Barrens, praying. He didn't want to be there. Someone said *I'm just going out for a minute.*

"Mmh?"

"Did I wake you?"

Mellie was on her feet.

"I'm going down to the cafeteria. What can I bring you?"

"Bring me some tea, would you? And see if you can find us a paper."

She started to leave, picking her way between the bed and a tray stand.

"Hold on," said Joe. "Come here will you?"

She turned and scrutinized him as though expecting combat. She came over to the bed and he took her hand. He'd been thinking about his sequestered existence on St. George's Crescent. How hard, how bewildering that must have been for Mellie. His secrets and his various ways of disguising himself. He'd seen Elliott Schuman on the street more than once. And Maisie more than once. They both seemed to buy his story, that he was Burbidge's cousin. He'd also run into Tom Payne on his way to Hamish Hamilton's office, and Tom had recognized him right away. *Burbidge*, he said. *Good to see you down here.* Before Joe could correct him, and spew out the usual Eggers story, Tom said, *Tired of being dead, are you?* And he walked on down the street.

He peered up at his wife. "You've been a good partner in crime, y'know."

"Thank you."

"When we met? At Auntie Vi's place?"

"Yes?"

"There wasn't that much left of me, Mellie. I was halfway done. I never quite got it back."

As she moved to leave the room she said, "That's your way of looking at it."

WHEN RENNIE GOT HOME from the hospital, he had already decided not to tell his mom about the conversation with Mr. and Mrs. Eggers. He was going to fulfill his misheon without her knowledge. That's what it was. Maybe he would tell his mom later, maybe tomorrow. He did not want to get mixed up in this stuff, but what could you do? Last November he had brought it on himself by letting Galahad go ape-shit in the ravine and those kids got visherated all to hell. Their legs, their arms. Getting probably thousands of stitches, it was awful. Rennie had disobeyed a clear set of instructions from Mrs. Eggers, and for this he had to pay his dues, run the gimlet. He never should of listened to shitfuck Rodney about the dog. But that was all water under the...pay the popper ecksetera.

He wanted to ask Mr. Eggers what happened to Galahad, but that wasn't going to happen, was it?

Supper with Mom, what a thrill. Munch munch pass the salt, *Now where are you off to, Rennie? It'll be dark before you know it.*

All the way back to the hospital Rennie wondered about the dog. Nine months without a word from any of them, and then came the call from the doctor's office and off he went to the hospital and there they were again. Looking old. Holding a grudge. And it still didn't make sense. What a nice world it would be if all the adults just sat back and shut their traps long enough to...

Rennie stood at the entrance to Mr. Eggers' room. He craned

his neck to see if old Mrs. Awfulchops was waiting for him. There she was, happy day. He walked in and raised his hand in a Hi sort of way. Mr. and Mrs. Eggers glandered at him with the absolute identical look on their faces. He was sitting up in bed with his glasses slidden down to the tip of his nose. Down came the newspaper.

"Well well," said Mr. Eggers.

"Well well indeed," said Mrs. Eggers.

They looked like they were expecting some big miracle to happen. Or maybe like they'd got a cop stowed in the bathroom to leap out and arrest him. He reached into his pocket and pulled out his old sock.

"Here it is," Rennie said.

"Here what is?" said Mrs. Eggers.

Rennie reached inside the sock and pulled out a rock with a label on it. He read them the info, GOLD ORE GIANT YELLOWKNIFE bla bla bla.

"See?"

Rennie handed it to Mr. Eggers and pocketed his old sock. He stepped back and darted a glance at Mrs. E. They both peeped at him, mouths open, like Rennie was some kind of a talking martian octopus.

Mr. Eggers, he raised up the rock for Mrs. M to see. He wore a smirky-type smile.

"He doesn't know what the bloody hell we're talking about!"

Mr. Eggers turned to Rennie. "Come here, boy, right over here. Give me that old sock of yours. Here."

Old Eggers dropped the gold sample into the sock, rolled it up and thrust it into Rennie's hand.

"I gave it to you, boy. It's yours. You earned it, by Harry. Put it away."

The old guy grunted, pushed himself up in his bed, and he was blinking over at Mrs. Eggers. Rennie almost forgot that Mr. Eggers was a millionaire with a mansion and a library and ten gold bricks and adventures people never talked about.

"Does this look like a felon to you? Is this your candidate for the jailhouse, lovey? He doesn't know what the bloody Christ we're talking about."

Mrs. Eggers started to ease up a bit. She was not happy but at least the old talons were out of sight. She turned to Rennie.

"Your mother seems to have forgotten to tell you something."

"Yeah?"

"She seems to think that I can't count to ten."

"You mean…like…"

"Last November," said Mrs. Eggers. "The last time she cleaned for us. Tell her that."

"Tell her what?"

"Tell her I can count to ten."

"Is this got to do with Galahad?" said Rennie.

"Rennie," said Mr. Eggers, "you did nothing wrong. You didn't bite those children, did you?"

"No, but –"

"Then you did nothing wrong."

Mr. Eggers' face was flushed, he started to rouse himself, he wasn't quite the same guy he'd been earlier in the day. He gave out a mighty moan and heaved the old legs to the side of the bed and eased the old feet onto the floor. He had nine toenails and they were all yellow.

"Rennie," he growled, "give us a hand."

Mrs. Eggers was now standing. "Joseph, don't you dare."

Mr. Eggers reached out his gnarly hands to Rennie, they both gave a tug, and up came the old guy in a crouch.

"Joseph Eggers, you sit right down, do you hear me?"

"This boy was born to disobey, my dear," said Mr. Eggers.

"Which one?" she said.

Mr. Eggers was concentrating like anything as Rennie led him away from the bed.

"In there," Mr. Eggers grunted. "Off to the bog with us."

"Just tell your..." Mrs. Eggers began. "Just tell your mother I can..."

They managed it like a circus show. An old dancing bear and his keeper, Rennie going backwards, Mr. Eggers shuffling side to side, his paws clutching Rennie's hands, and when Mr. Eggers farted, Rennie said sorry to Mrs. E.

She was standing there when he returned from the bathroom.

"You want me to tell my mom that she can count to ten?"

"That I can count to ten," said Mrs. Eggers.

"You want me to tell my mom that you can...ohhhhhhhhh, no."

"Exactly," she said.

Chapter 21

The Gift

THE LIGHT WAS RETURNING to Edmonton, grudgingly it would seem. At the end of January there was enough light in the sky to delay the appearance of Venus until after suppertime. This faint signal reminded Joe that February was almost upon them, and, not to labour the obvious, this meant that March would be next. A Chinook had drifted in from the mountains. Throughout the city, like figures liberated from a snow-dome, children had begun to burst from their enclosures and forage the streets of Edmonton in a rush to make the first sticky snowball of 1964.

Tick tock, tick tock, clicked the kitchen clock. Self-important sound. It probably thought it had been enlisted in the changing of the seasons.

When Melony returned to the house, Joe was pacing slowly up and down beneath the massive moose antlers in the front hall in his worn black overcoat and tired-looking homburg. Weather be damned. Joe was strong enough to keep his appointment.

"All dressed and battle-ready," he said.

She gazed at him and dug her keys from her purse. Mellie would drive and then wait for him in the car. She was not happy about this appointment, but Joe had managed to outflank her. He rarely got this determined about anything these days, and she must have seen that he was immoveable on the Rennie Question. He followed her out the door, and arm-in-arm they penguined their way over the icy walk to the car. The warmth from the chinook was welcome to his prematurely aging bones. The hospital seemed like a distant memory.

"You could come in and be sociable," he said.

"I would ruin your little gambit. I'd sooner spit on her carpet."

"Well, that's one way of looking at it."

Mellie braked at the light. She turned to glance at him, and she seemed to want him to look her in the eye.

"I know what you're up to and I do not approve," she said. "Neither does Auntie Vi."

"What am I up to?"

"You want to smooth things over," she said. "Smooth things over so that you can leave that boy something when you toddle off."

"Toddle off?"

"When you pass away, Joseph. As though he were your son and heir."

"You talk too much, Mellie."

"Thank God you had the sense to take them all to the vault."

He smiled inwardly, because he had not quite lived up to that promise. Not yet. Maybe never. "Where you can go down to the bank and gloat over them any time you want."

"Don't you think I won't," she said. "Somebody has to check on them."

"You think they're going to walk away?" he said.

"I don't trust banks. And I like to look at them. From time to time. Is that so hard to understand?"

"Every man, late or soon, sits down to a banquet of consequences."

She gave him a familiar frown. "What the hell is that supposed to mean?"

"Dunno. Might mean something."

They motored past a Presbyterian church and Mellie parked in front of a row of old brick row-houses. The dwellings had a worn, besieged look. Something about them reminded Joe of his childhood home in Castleford. He glanced back at Mellie, who was at the wheel, staring straight ahead with a sullen look. He climbed the steps to the outside door and knocked. Rennie's mother opened the door, peered down at him from the stoop.

"Ethel," he said, and extended his hand. "How long has it been?"

"Mr. Eggers."

She took his hand and raised her eyes to look him over. Her gaze was about as warm and expressive as that of a statue in winter.

"Call me Joe."

From the small exertion of climbing out of the car and mounting the steps of the tiny row-house, Joe was puffing. Bright pulsing floaters drifted across his eyeballs. He felt at a disadvantage. He shed his overcoat and followed Ethel into a cluttered kitchen where she sat him down at a yellow Formica table. The great waft of a thousand meals and a million cigarettes greeted his nostrils, and again he pondered his childhood home in Castleford. The kitchen, something worn and claustrophobic about the kitchen.

"Is this to do with my Rennie?"

Her hand was shaking as she poured the tea, and shaking as she placed the cup before him. Good. Advantage Eggers.

"I'd call it a settling of accounts."

Joe paused to look inquiringly into Ethel's eyes and she looked back at him as though she were watching an ad on the television screen. She sat across from him, lit a cigarette, and rattled the pack at him.

Joe declined. "Have to take care of the old ticker. Doctor's orders."

And how are you feeling these days, Mr. Eggers?

I'll bet you're happy to be out of that hospital.

Mrs. Eggers must be glad to have you home.

Ethel Mudge said none of these things.

"Settle what accounts?"

She gazed at Joseph through a veil of cigarette smoke. Her face remained impassive. Annoyingly so.

"That gold brick," he said, and looked her in the eye as impassively as she had done to him. "I trust it paid a few bills for you? Let's just call it a gift."

"And just who pray tell–"

"We can count, Ethel. We can put two and two together. We decided, Melony and I, not to press charges –"

"Press charges for –"

He held up his hand. "We decided that your son did not need his mother in prison. It's hard enough growing up without a father."

"What would you know about that?"

"I grew up," he said, "in a place like this one, with my brothers and sister, without a father. He died when I was a boy. I still have no idea how my mother managed to feed us and keep her strength up. A gold brick would have come in pretty handy."

"What do you want from me?"

"I can't give your son a father but I can be his uncle. If you'll let me."

"He's already got an uncle."

"Would that be your friend, Russell?"

"I can't believe this. You come over here to my place to sit here all high and mighty and judge me?"

"I am not talking with the police. That would mean at least five years in prison for you, and an investigation of your old boss, Mr. Schuman, and how would any of this help Rennie? I am not talking about you restoring the gold or the money you're getting for it."

"Was it my son told you all this…this bunk?"

"No," said Joe, "it was not. We hired a man to look into the case. A private investigator. He's been quite thorough."

The lie came easily to Joe. He had rehearsed it in his head, and he was ready to flesh out the story should the need arise. His research had been rigourous. A hint or two from Rennie, who had learned a thing or two from Uncle Russell. A sort of confession from Rennie. *She kinda wanted to give it back.* Then there had been Mellie's connection with Schuman, the jeweller who had been Ethel Mudge's boss from away back when. Edmonton still seemed like a small town.

"What do you want from me?"

"Uncles get to spend time with their nephews. And if they get their nephews to do odd jobs, they pay them a good wage. Shoveling walks, cutting the grass, that sort of thing. I want your permission to spend time with your son. A weekend here, a weekend there, at least one per month. Nothing else. And, as I say, you can think of the gold brick as a gift."

"What exactly are you up to? Is there some monkey business you haven't told me about?"

"Monkey business?"

"You know what I mean."

He smiled dolefully. He had never heard it called that before.

"If I told you there was no monkey business between me and your son, would you believe me?"

She raised her head. Closed her eyes. Clenched her fists. Opened her eyes. Glared at Joe. Pounded the table. Her cup and saucer went flying.

"There, there, Ethel. There, there. Let me help you with that."

MORNING ONCE AGAIN, and a ridge of clouds gathered over the skyline, these ones crinkled like a furrowed eyebrow, as though God was worried. Joe mulled his gleanings from *The Edmonton Journal.* President Johnson wanted the Republicans to remember that they were the party of Lincoln. In other words, pass the Civil Rights bill, you old wankers. The French buying gobs of gold from the Americans, but the price of gold stuck at thirty-five dollars an ounce. If they let gold float it might soar. Or it might not. The Albanian Communist Party, whinging about the new Soviet leadership, calls them Kruschevian revisionists.

"Hah!"

"What did you say?"

"Nothing."

Johnson wanted to cut gold backing for the dollar. Might eventually be a good thing for the Eggers family fortunes. (Sliding door, two floors above where he sat right now, like something out of the cinema. Shhh.) Gold fever, his old addiction. Perhaps a faint residue remained? A guilty addiction? No doubt gold fever was alive and well in Ethel Mudge's place.

Joe arose from his easy chair, struggling to his feet. He climbed the stairs to his office on the second floor and began to pace about, recalling the little flat where Rennie and his mother lived, that old familiar cabbage and ciggy smell of poverty. The stolen brick, poured by Stinky Riley's friend with the foundry to their own specifications, would have weighed in at close to twenty-five pounds. Joe's very first gold brick. By Joe's calculations, it would bring in about fourteen thousand dollars.

When Joe's father died, the money had dried up within a year or so. No gold bricks to speak of, no benefactors. Perhaps Auntie Vi had had been the closest thing to their benefactor. Had he ever thanked her for that? Yet another piece of business to take care of.

On Rennie's first visit of February, Joe got bundled up to take a walk along the crescent, as far as his ticker would allow. He brought Gudgeon along on the leash, and they moved slowly down the front walk of the Eggers' house. He loved to look at houses. Joe now regarded his own home with greater understanding. It was an imposing seven thousand-square-foot Tudor, marsh green and white. It seemed to moan the words, *high on the hog.* But really, it was a brick and stone monument to new world emulation of old world dignity, a well-designed counterfeit. They passed a white-pillared home that looked vaguely Tara-esque. Monstrous thing. They moved slowly past an older Georgian home (friendly people, minded their own business), and then an elaborate mansion done entirely in pale grey Tyndall stone. It was bigger than Joe's house. The owners gave tours to groups of people. The farther away from the Eggers' house they walked, the newer the houses seemed to be, proclaiming the brand new joys of oil money or the rapid growth of a small business – sprawling bungalows with occasional swimming pools in the back yard, Cadillacs and Lincolns in front. Mellie had once driven a Cadillac. Raved about it. Stohler's car. They reached a newly developed neighbourhood with tidier, smaller bungalows that heralded the omnipresence of young middle class families. By this point on the walk, Joe was puffing hard. The weather was turning, the wind was up, and a wall of cloud was moving in from the west.

"How's your mum these days?"

Rennie's gaze remained fixed on the dog. He shrugged.

"I hope I'm not prying, Rennie, but I want you to know, I did not peach on you."

"What's peaching?"

"I mean," Joe replied, chuckling, "I did not betray you to your mother. Besides, you did not come right out and tattle on her. Let's say you were somewhat caught in the middle. Caught between loyalties."

"I guess so."

"Are you getting along with her, is what I was wondering."

Again the boy shrugged. He had become a compulsive shrugger. "She's kinda crabby I guess."

"Sorry about that."

"I just stay out of her way."

Gudgeon whined to get off the leash. Rennie had found a poplar stick and the game was on. He hurled it over the bushes and Gudgeon plowed through the snow in pursuit. From Galahad the Fearsome to Gudgeon the Playsome. A new dog for a new era. A wheel in the solar system had turned and the House of Eggers was still standing at the centre of that system. Well, it was still standing. And Joe Eggers could still walk without precipitating another heart attack. Happy and glum, perhaps more glum than happy. The distressing thing was not that you had to die; it was that you had to go through all this dreary enfeebling stuff first. Joe turned around and the three of them headed for home. It was time for Rennie to chip some ice from their front walk.

ANOTHER SATURDAY, this time in March. Rennie was doing his homework in Joe's office. This had become their weekend routine. To anyone who might have asked, Mellie would say, *The boy who walks our dog is paying us a visit.* There would be a pause for explanations. *Rennie Mudge. He's a little pet. He never had a father and Joe and I know what that's all about. Poor thing.*

As usual, Rennie was surrounded by a great array of geological samples from up north. Joe came into the office now and then to shuffle through some business papers or to make phone-calls. Last month he had given Rennie a little quiz to test his knowledge of minerals. To each rock sample a story was attached. *This bit of quartz comes from the country north of Detah, and a beautiful white wolf kept spying on the camp. This rounded piece of rock is from a stream up around Fitzgerald. That was good fun, let me tell you. This bit of granite is from Sangris. Heraldene's little brother used it for a magic trick. This dark bit of ore is a stone I picked up to throw at a ptarmigan for the pot. Like a true rock hound, I checked out the stone for minerals. The ptarmigan flew away untouched, and all we had for supper was tomato soup and crackers.*

Rennie pointed to one of his glassed-in display cases.

"Is this your magic pebble?"

"Something like that."

Young Renwick waited for an explanation, but Joe did not want to talk about his magic pebble. It was like the pebble in the Bible. Samson and what's her name. Ancient history. Delilah.

"Mr. Eggers, I need to do this social studies project at school? You know, like a history report?"

Rennie gazed back and forth at the collection of rock samples. A late-winter blizzard was blowing in. The wind pounded the house and the snow pelted the study window. Winter was winter again and it was good to be inside. Joe listened to the sound of his wife humming listlessly off key in the kitchen. Joe rambled through his brokerage files, muttering to himself. He'd had a dream about being back in the village of Sangris. Jimmy Norrin was there, and Mayday Medzin. *Are you a rich man?* Medzin had asked him. *How rich are you, Mr. Knocker?* Joe had lied to the man in reply.

"Anyways, I gotta do this report?"

"Mm." Mutter mutter.

"Mr. Eggers, what's the first time you ever found some gold?"

"That would be in the early-to-mid 1930s, in Northern Alberta. I was just barely off the boat."

"Where was the gold?"

"Young man, are you writing this down?"

"Not all of it."

"Are you trying to say that *I* am the subject of your history report? I, Joseph Eggers the First?"

"Yep."

"Bloody reporters."

Clutching his files, Joe eased his body over to a plump chair and collapsed into it with a groan.

"They said I could write about anything that's like...Western Canadian history, right, so I thought I'd write about you. You know, like your rocks and stuff?"

"You want me to reveal all my secrets. You're just like all the other magpies looking for scraps."

"What's wrong with magpies?"

"As I just said, young man, the gold was from northern Alberta."

He coughed and hockled mightily, settled himself more deeply into his chair, reached into the pocket of his maroon smoking jacket, and pulled out a cheap cigar wrapped in cellophane. He fingered the cigar, caressed it without opening it.

"Stay away from these things," he said. "Not good for you."

"Then how come you smoke them?"

"Is this part of your history report, boy?"

"Okay, where 'bouts in northern –"

"Fitzgerald."

"Where's that?"

"North of Fort McMurray."

"Where's that?"

He pointed to a low shelf where he kept his maps and atlases. "Look it up, boy. Don't get me bogged down in details."

Joe began to pick through his brokerage records of the past four years, his glasses perched above the tip of his nose. Broker Hammy had handed Joe over to a younger broker, an eager beaver who spoke both official languages and rang with optimism whenever he opened his mouth. It hardly mattered which broker handled his accounts. He kept on making money hand over fist. The thrill of growing wealthy had diminished, however, and Joe had decided to divest himself of some stocks and private holdings. Among them, a bundle of Cominco shares. Some uranium stock and a big bunch of preferreds from Texaco. *Etcetera.* Hammy wouldn't have liked this purification project of Joe's, neither will the new bloke. Purification? Is that what it was? Joe was not sure. He reckoned that the time had come to stop supporting companies dead bent on exploiting the North. Or something like that. Companies that Mayday Medzin or Jimmy Norn might frown upon, was that it?

The words from the market seemed to fly out of his files with all the urgency of a radio commercial. *Joe, ever since Norman Wells, gotta tell you, there's a lot of oil up there... Joe, you know better than I do, the future of Yellowknife is gold... Now we have this new issue, hang onto your hat... You want in on the ground floor, Joe, the word all over the north is uranium... Joe, you won't believe this, but just north of Yellowknife, they've got more diamonds that you can shake a stick at. Yes, you heard me, Joe. Diamonds...*

The boy was looking up from his notebook, as eager for information as Gudgeon for a stick. "So, what happened?"

Easing off the cellophane that bound the cigar, Joe told the boy about his first discovery. Boulder Creek. A great storm with mudslides and a dislodged boulder that left a crater behind. His first bout with gold fever.

"Well, Reporter Mudge, you got that?"

"Not all of it."

Joe went silent. He knew the dangers of spilling out his past like a runny egg, but he felt the edge, just the edge, of a strange exhilaration, and for a vicarious moment at least, he was connecting with a man he used to be. Joe Burbidge. And he was telling secrets. And what was wrong with that? Were Renwick's classmates going to run to the police just because they heard a story about a prospector? Besides, it felt deeply satisfying to cough up these little stories to someone. And Mellie had always been uneasy about hearing the darkest of his secrets. She wanted to know them but she seemed to recoil whenever he tried to tell them.

"Where was I?"

"You couldn't find this boulder? The one with the fish?"

Eggers lit his cigar. The smoke enveloped his face and he coughed for a moment and gazed through the smoke at his memory. Was he turning into a bloody bleeding heart?

"How big were they?"

"The nuggets?"

"The fish."

"Damned if I know. What do fish have to do with history, boy? Fish are just fish, but gold is big news. Gold is history. Besides, young man, when you are panning for gold, you don't think about fishing, even if you like fishing. You think about gold. Like to try prospecting one day, would you?"

"Sure."

Smiling at the boy, Eggers drew on his cigar and held it aloft with a Churchill sort of flourish.

A SPRING WALK with Renwick the Irrepressible. Renwick the Inquisitor. Small for his age, perhaps not built for the rigours of the north. But for a penny he would tell the boy everything, all the dirt, goddam the consequences. *Everybody, soon or late, sits down to a banquet of consequences.* Was that Stevenson? Kipling? Or was it that teacher from his grammar school? Good old... whassisname. Master Herron.

"My teacher says you can't forget to put in the years," said the boy to Eggers. "I wrote down all this stuff but I didn't get the years."

Eggers and Rennie were taking their first dog walk together since the dark days of February. Much of the snow had melted and the puddles were everywhere, as was the litter, hitherto buried like a scattering of bad memories. They trudged along the crescent, glancing occasionally at Gudgeon, who sniffed every melting patch of dog piss within fifty yards. Yellow on white like gold on quartz. The treasures of squalid April.

Gudgeon commenced to roll around on a patch of something pink and sticky. Rennie grabbed him by the collar and told him *No, no. Bad dog.*

"Get that dog over here. Find him a stick."

The boy found the dog a fallen tree branch and tore off the twigs. He sent Gudgeon flying into the ravine again and again till the dog's pink tongue was wet and hanging. And still, the questions kept coming. The conversation reminded him of times he had spent with Master Herron when he was slightly older than Rennie. Bad old Shacklesbury. Yes, and how well old Herron had listened to Joe's questions.

"And you liked it away up there?"

"I liked it at first. It was all right when the season was on, even better after the mosquitoes and flies died off. And there were actual trees up around Yellowknife. August was nice. Before the big strike we made, I flew over the Barrens. Southeast of Great Bear. Didn't care for it."

Gudgeon had chewed his stick into slivers and the boy was extracting the remains from the dog's mouth.

"That Indian guy? The guy who talked to the bears?"

"You mean Isidore."

Joe was caught staring at the air between himself and the boy. He could almost see old Isidore labouring over his tripod, and Stinky Riley, cursing and squinting at the gauges of his all-metal Junkers. Joe called up the clutter of small shacks in Sangris. And the young men had gone to a dingy death and the older men were looking gaunt, and there was no school, no medical clinic, no church. He tried to conjure up the kindly ex-priest standing next to his cabin. And inside another cabin, Norn and Medzin and a thoughtful group of old Dogrib men. And a bulky young woman, Heraldene, who rose occasionally in Joe's dreams, glowing like a monument, an object of mystery. The real Heraldene was something else again. No longer the silent witness. No longer the healing presence in the tent. Very much the opposite. Now she was a delightfully angry woman. She used to write him occasional notes from Yellowknife, Fort Chip, Tuktuk and beyond. She seemed to toss off each letter with great speed. Enjoyed her new job. She liked to complain about the travel, the politics, the work load. Who or what was he to Heraldene? Her contact with the world to the south? Her contact with a former self? Her first crush?

"This guy, Isidore?"

"What?"

"Is he still alive?"

"He's an old man."

Could you put a man who talked to bears in Cree in a history report? Of course you could. Make for some good reading.

"But is that stuff about talking to bears just a story?"

"I was there. Swear to God."

"But was that all true?"

He nodded to the boy and the boy went silent, gazing at nothing, as though he had just been told that dinosaurs walk the earth. Rennie asked Joe if he was getting tired.

"No, let's keep going. Where were we?"

"Remember that big blizzard you guys got into and the...the thing that saved your lives?"

And on they went. *Was he a crook, this Buster Krahn guy? What's frostbitten like? How big is a lake trout? Did Isidore ever talk to wolves? What about coyotes, did he ever talk to coyotes? When you chop up the rocks and you gather them up and you can see they've got gold in them, like, how much is rocks and how much is gold? Were there slaves at Great Slave Lake? Then how come they called it that?*

"Say, young man, you should be inside the house making notes. Your thingummy, your history report."

"I just have to put in the dates."

"Don't forget Isidore. Saved my bloody life more than once, let me tell you."

They turned around and headed for Joe's house. Gudgeon trotted beside them with occasional stops to sniff some leavings or to gulp down snow.

"The Indians up there, you know. Lots of poverty. Health problems. All we did was use them when we needed them. Never occurred to us that we might be doing them harm."

"Once did you try to hang yourself?"

"Who told you that?"

"What's that scar on your neck?"

"Didn't I tell you?" he replied. "Some chaps tried to string me up. End of story."

"How come they tried to hang you?"

"It was rough up there, boy. A man can make enemies. But I was rescued by a big strong girl by the name of Heraldene."

"A girl?"

"A fearless young girl. She is now a tribal chief. Isn't that something?"

Rennie was frowning. "I didn't know a lady could be a chief."

Joe tried to hockle up a reasonable explanation, but Rennie, thank God, had become engaged in a tugging match with Gudgeon and a new stick. Joe limped by himself up the walk and through the front door. It was time for his nap.

JOE AWAKENED, WONDERING if he still had the old yearning. He laboured all the way up to the third floor, puffing like a steam engine. No one would see him up here, not for a while. He plodded over to the guest bedroom where Rennie usually bunked. He checked the far wall of the room, checked one particular corner and ran his finger over the vertical moulding. His thick old fingernails pried out the moulding, which he tossed on the bed. Beneath the moulding was a recessed handle. He pulled on the small handle and the panel that served as a wall slid on its bearings to the left to reveal a room about the size of a large loo. He pulled a brass chain and an incandescent bulb illuminated the room, the shelves, the small desk in the corner, a few notebooks and photographs, his mortar and pestle, his trusty fieldglasses, his rock hammer, a rusted gold pan and a dozen other tools of his trade. His former trade. A musky old down bag. A worn set of mukluks. Knaaker Johansen's rusted skinning knife. They were displayed on the shelves like artifacts in a private museum. One owner, one visitor allowed.

Joe picked up the skinning knife with both hands and he sniffed it, ran a thumbnail down the blade to dislodge a speck of rust. The knife had lost something of its old totemic power. Today it felt like any old knife.

He could wait no longer. Slowly he turned about and gazed at the other set of shelves. The bright bulb still swayed an inch or two each way, and it made the assembled hoard nictitate back at him with a forbidden opulence, and he felt his breath fill the cavity of his chest, felt the old excitement rising in his gut. The latest tally – five rough bricks and seven burnished bars. He hadn't felt the urge to visit them in a long time. If Ethel had kept her hands to herself, there would have been six bricks instead of five. Six bricks and seven bars, making a total of thirteen. An unlucky number so that's all right. But look at it, *macik'*, you old sinner. This might be the last time.

He took in the majesty of it and his pulse ran robust. From childhood he had read about the lure of gold, the jeweled golden mitres and chalices of the popes, the belief among the ancient Egyptians that gold was the skin of the gods, how the nobility of Russia had sewn gold coins into their clothing when they fled from the Bolsheviks, how the Spanish in the New World had brought down the empires of the Aztecs and the Incas for their gold. As an eight-year-old he had read the story of King Midas as though it were but a triumphant quest for treasure, not a moral exemplum. He had memorized the story of Tutankhamun's golden death mask, and later on, in London museums, he had seen the work of Sumerian and Etruscan goldsmiths.

"O, how mighty thou art."

He heard an echo of his own voice, the sad mimicry in it, but the hair still rose on the back of his neck as though the ursine presence of God were rising to rebuke him in all his vanity and futility. Not the presence of God, not really. Not even the graven image, and not mighty like Isidore's great bear, but the antithesis of the great bear, the antithesis of God, twelve pieces of gold assembled like any miser's hoard amassed in any little mining town carved out of the reindeer moss, the rock and the stunted trees.

Soon, when Mellie goes to see her sister in Winnipeg, it will get hauled away. All of it. If Mellie discovers his little deception, well, he will think of something.

Standing in the corner of the room was a bush rifle. Joe plucked up the gun and raised it to his shoulder, lined up the sights at a photograph on the desk. His aim was shaky. The photo was taken in Yellowknife in the spring of 1938, a few months or so before his big discovery. It was a good time. In the photo he stood next to Isidore Chartrand. Young Joey squints up from the photo into the barrel of Joe's rifle. Young Joey looks lean, eager, unafraid. Half in love with the lady with the camera, tall and slim in those fetching slacks and that wicked smile of hers with her astonishing red lipstick. But soon enough, young Joe and Isidore would say goodbye, and Joe would fly into the Barrens with Stinky Riley, into his greatest of all adventures, and the memory, the savage mortality of it, shook Joe Eggers to the core. Because *goddam it, he doesn't know any of this in the bloody picture, does he.*

He ambled, muttering, out of the room, and he slid the panel and pounded the moulding back in place.

"Joe?" cried Mellie. "Are you up there?"

"Yes, luvvy."

"What are you *doing?"*

"Remembering."

"What?"

"Just remembering."

Chapter 22

Rooster

He opened his eyes. Clammy and sweating again. Mellie peered down on him, scratching a mosquito bite, looking tired. The boy was behind her. Rennie. Why was he here? It was summer. Rennie had finished his whatzit. The history report. Something to do with Mellie's garden? Something to do with the birdbath?

"You were shouting," Mellie said. "First you were singing and then you were shouting."

"I was singing?"

Mellie smiled at him. *"Who's that kno-o-o-cking at my door.* Then you were yelling at someone."

He thought he remembered the yelling part. "What did I say?"

Mellie shot a glance at the boy, who seemed torn between merriment and concern. "You said, *Go back to hell where you came from."*

"But who was I yelling at?"

"I hope it wasn't me," said Mellie.

"The knocker," said the boy.

"The what?"

"You heard him," said Mellie. "You called him the knocker."

"Oh, Jesus."

He spent much of the afternoon flat on his back with his eyes half-closed. A kettle rocked beside the bed on a hot plate, and fumes of Friar's Balsam floated over the bed and up to the ceiling. These days his visitors looked down on him with worried expressions, including Dr. Locke from down the street, who said it might turn into pneumonia.

From their bedroom on the second floor, when the kettle wasn't steaming, he could hear the kitchen clock ticking away his life. He had never been quite so conscious of the kitchen clock before. Auntie Vi had claimed that it was louder than Big Ben. Bloody wedding gift. A bit of revenge from Stinky Riley.

Young Rennie was looking down on him. Joe closed his eyes and pushed out his words slowly. "Haven't seen you in some weeks, Renwick. You and your mom getting along?"

"I dunno," said the boy, the very picture of stoic misery. "I guess so."

"Been busy, have you? Still delivering papers? Good for you, boy. Always wanted a son like you. Know that, Rennie…always wanted a son like you."

"Me too."

"What does that mean?"

"I never got to know my real dad," said Rennie. "Not like you."

"If you had been our son, Mellie would have named you Bancroft."

"Who's that?"

"Just a name." Just a sad old secret.

The boy was looking at the floor. He seemed distracted by Joe's condition, his laboured breathing. Joe gave out a yawn, struggled to heave his body higher up on the pillows, lowered his voice to a rasp.

"Did you know that my real name isn't Eggers? My real name is Joseph Burbidge. Had to change it to escape arrest. I've had to pretend for years that I was my own bloody cousin. And did you know that for my sins, Renwick, my sins, I could have gone to prison for a long time? What do you say about that?"

Rennie gave out a Rennie shrug. How many times had he seen that gesture from the boy? How many unanswered questions lay behind all those shrugs?

"Mellie doesn't know the whole story. If she did, she wouldn't want me blabbing it to you. Family skeletons, you know. But sometimes I think the skeletons are the most interesting part. Wouldn't you agree?"

"You mean like when those guys tried to hang you?"

"Hm. That was complicated."

Joe felt a great temptation welling up, and he could hardly believe what he was going to reveal. Joe Burbidge, or someone else inside him, a stowaway perhaps. Words began to dart out like bats imprisoned too long in a cave.

"I was being harassed. Man named Knaaker. Henchman of Buster Krahn. They wanted...they wanted to get me out of the way. To jump our claim."

He was puffing. He stopped for a moment to catch his breath, and then, caught up in the brutal momentum of it all, he went on, piling detail upon gory detail. Joe's torn-up tent. The freezing wind and unexpected snow. Taking refuge by digging a cave. The nocturnal visit from Knaaker. The man's little gift of dynamite. The head shot that ended Knaaker's life. The exchange of identities. A certain grave in Yellowknife.

"You got that, boy? End of story."

But it wasn't the end of the story. There was more, and it made him wonder at how much he had tried to sweep under the carpet, how much he had managed to forget. The boy scrutinized him for a moment.

"So so so okay. So...this guy was gunna kill you?"

"Yes."

"This guy with the..."

"Yes. Renwick, if you write up another. Another history report, old chap. Could you leave out that bit?"

"I guess I would of shot him too."

"You wouldn't need to shoot him, my friend. You wouldn't need to. Because you'd never put yourself in that impossible..."

Joe began to cough and then his breath came whistling back.

"Think twice, me lad. Before you go running off to find some gold."

"*You* did it."

"That's why I'm telling you. You've got brains. Think about what you might also find. I mean, if you want it too badly. Think about the lengths some men go to."

"To what?"

"To make their fortunes."

"You mean like shooting a –"

"Enough, Renwick. I can't bear to hear you say it."

A shiver scuttled up his legs, and it all came back again. The unbearable stench of it, the ghoulishness, the howling of the wolves, the remorse, the suffering and the feverish bouts of atonement and all the things about the North he had loved and feared and could never return to. And then, as though a stay of execution had been granted, he began to breathe more deeply.

Joe pointed his index finger at a dark object on the dresser. His fingernails had grown long again like bear-claws, and his finger was shaking with impatience. He bade Rennie fetch the object, a billfold stuffed with credit cards, addresses, and notes scrawled to himself. It was made of soft brown leather, worn and scuffed, and it smelled comfortably of Joe's cigars. Alas, a habit no more. Joe extracted a scrap of paper from the recesses of the billfold and handed it to Rennie. There was a name in Joe's handwriting, a box number and a phone number in the village of Patricia, Alberta.

"Some day if you get curious," he said. "Look up old Stinky. Rancher chap. Bush pilot."

"I know."

"Ornery on the outside, maverick on the inside. Ha."

"Can I just hang around and get you things?"

"That's what wives are for."

"Are you gunna be...y'know..."

"I've got me memories, boy."

With his eyes still closed, Joe raised his right hand as though he were about to testify in court.

"Do likewise, boy. Repeat after me. I am Sir Gudgeon."

"That's the dog's name."

"It's more than that, boy. Just say it. To satisfy the whims of an old man."

"I am Sir Gudgeon?"

"Don't stand there gawking, boy. This is serious stuff."

"I am Sir Gudgeon."

"That's better. I promise to learn from the past and live in the present."

"I promise to learn from the...from the past?"

"It means you need to keep up with your history lessons, boy. Read your science books, read everything. Read your brains out. Say it again. I promise to learn from the past and live in the present."

The boy said it in a listless monotone, but he got the words right.

"Say it again, boy. Say it like you mean it. Say it even if you haven't got the slightest bloody idear what it means."

He said it again and it sounded less forced this time.

"Can I open the blinds?" the boy said. "Or turn on the light?"

"No," said Joe. "My eyes can't take the light."

"What does this stuff mean anyway? Like, who was this Gudgeon?"

Joe's eyes remained closed. He made himself breathe once again, slower and deeper. "You know what a martyr is, boy?"

"Yeah?"

"Gudgeon was a great martyr to the mines. Never work down in the mines, boy. No good. Stay on top. My father told me that. And if you ever own a dog or a horse, name him Gudgeon. For me. For good luck."

"But what does this stuff mean? I mean...live in the present and like that?"

"It means throw off your…it means get rid of your…it's complicated. But just go out there, Renwick, grow your bloody wings and fly. Leave home at the earliest possible moment and don't look back. And…and…remember this old bloke."

"My wings?"

"Your wings. And talk to the fellow, talk to my friend, my friend Stinky. Talk to Isidore. You know…on the…and remember…just remember."

The boy stood there focused on the air between himself and the bed. He looked miserable.

"I have been procrastinating. Renwick, my old friend. I have a last request."

"Yeah?"

Joe gave Rennie a pointed look for emphasis. "Are those tears, young man?"

"No."

"We all go, me lad. We just get tired and we pop off. I promise not to pop off…while you're in the room…all right? It's early summer for God's sake. Would I be stupid enough? Traipse off to me ancestors on a beautiful summer's day?"

"Okay."

"I'll go when Mellie gives me her…permission."

"Isn't there anything I can do?"

"Yes, there is. Come over here and just listen. Carefully."

Joe drew a raspy breath and exhaled. How many of those breaths were left to him? A hundred? A hundred thousand? He took another breath, less raspy this time, and once more he relaxed.

"You've checked out our new bird bath, copper monstrosity. Mellie had it installed last year."

"Yeah?"

"On the side of the pad? Are you with me?"

"Yeah."

"Just under the side of the pad. Side facing the house. There's something buried. It's for you. Mellie does not know."

The boy seemed momentarily interrupted from his grief. Nervously he rubbed his face as though he had walked into a cobweb.

"You buried a –"

"Shhh. I've left you a small present for your twenty-first birthday. When you've left your mother's house. Left home for good. Not one day before, got it?"

The boy nodded.

"You need to come over here and dig it up. Under the birdbath. Cement pad. The side facing the house. Remember that."

"Okay."

"Mellie might be here, you never know. And she might not welcome our little excavation. Or she might be dead and gone. Either way, you'll have to do this digging on your own. Find a way into the yard and dig it up, you see?"

"You're going to give me a birthday present?" the boy said, as though he were trying to grapple with a philosophical proposition. He tried for a nervous nibble at one of his fingernails but there was scarcely anything left to chew on.

"Yes, I am, but only when you've left your mother's house and you're out on your own. That's the deal. Can you do that?"

The boy nodded.

"Think of it as a little treasure hunt. Every young man wants to go on a treasure hunt. That's why I went up north."

"But what about Mrs. Eggers? What if she doesn't want me back there sneaking around?"

"I love her dearly, my boy. She'll be the richest widow on the block. She'll probably be off visiting art galleries in Europe. Don't worry about Mellie. End of story."

It was dark outside. According to Mellie, a big rain was coming in. Joe was tired. He closed his eyes and managed a faint smile for

Rennie's benefit. *Grow your wings and fly, me boy.* He fluttered the fingers of both hands in a feathering motion, because after all it was good flying weather. But Rennie was not there. Again he closed his eyes, heard the ticking of the kitchen clock, fluttered his fingers again. Tomorrow he might get out of bed on his own, and the next day perhaps he would take a little totter around the back yard or some damn thing. Cast a secret little glance in the direction of the birdbath.

He fell back into a reverie about Lucy. Nine-toed Lucy. He should have gotten in touch with her, told her about his own bout with amputation. Same toe but the other foot. Lucy Castaway and her formidable mother and a rock with a secret, a rock that launched a treasure hunt. But before he could retrace the path of that adventure, he was off somewhere in a dark cold place, being hauled to his feet and dragged over to a fire, being held as though he were a baby in the arms of a massive young woman. What was her name, he couldn't have forgotten her name. They had just tried to hang him, and she had found him abandoned by his captors, swinging from a tree. She and her little brother. Everdean, was that her name? Haverdean? She crouched between his dangling legs, wrapped them around her great shoulders and lifted him up, and he managed to take a breath like a newborn, like a...and now he was staring at Isidore's nose and the blizzard had enveloped them inside Isidore's makeshift shelter and the pains worried him awake.

Joe called for the boy. Before he knew it, Rennie was there by his bedside, looking down at him as though he were already dead. *Get Mellie*, he said, or tried to say. Get Isidore too. Tell Stinky to bring his plane. Rennie was trying to say something to Joe, a last farewell, a cry to come back? *We still have a trip to take.* A trip indeed. Up north? A journey to where? Was the boy speaking in metaphors?

"It's your story now," he said to the boy.

He opened his eyes. There was no boy. Where had he gone?

To fetch Mellie? There wasn't much time left. His throat was tightening. *Heraldene! That was her name!* Where the hell was Heraldene when he needed her?

He was straining for breath, the rope grew tighter with the pounding of his heart. The pain was pulsing up through the cores of his arms, radiating from both sides into his chest. The pressure increased by slow increments as though he were being crushed in a cave-in. The noose tightened. He let go of something.

He had unloaded it all, hadn't he? His little confession? The little misadventure that was his life? It was out of him now, and that was good. And the story of Isidore with his makeshift shelter? Had he told that to the boy? And Joe and Stinky in the plane? Right on the edge of the Barrens? The place where they made their big find. Wolf Lake or whatever the hell it was called. Remembered it like it was yesterday. Not so well the bad stuff that came afterwards, because that was fading. He remembered the perfection of that late afternoon, when they'd come upon the good quartz and gravel, that sublime drink of rum, a perfect epiphany that he still couldn't understand, that shining moment smoking cigars with Stinky, that exhausted sleep and the howling chorus of wolves. And the gold, all that gold. Melony naked on the carpet. And later by the fireplace in winter when the power went out. And later on a bed they broke together. Was it this one? And then he started to roll backwards, his very soul was rolling backwards in the last of his fever, a slow-motion dizzy tumble through the solar system to his beloved Lucy with nine toes, and her mum and her beautiful rock, and back to Stinky's pack train and night-hawking on Shanghai Lil, and drifting back to the entrance to Auntie Vi's building by the river, the paintings in her parlour, and Maisy's laughter, Maisy and her friend whatzername, and winging back to the storm off Newfoundland that drove the old schooner into the drook, and what in hell was a drook anyway, and what had brought him all the way out here so far from home, so far from bloody Shacklesbury and the sunsoaked moors of

Slaidburn and the slag heaps of Castleford, and the chilly little flat where they all slept together and the sound of the miners at four in the morning marching by their window and back to the place where he was made, the bed to which he toddled in the night to ask his mother and his father to take him outside, out side, side, thide, thigh…

"HE'S GONE," SHE SAID.

Rennie was standing in the hall waiting for his mother to take him home because it was raining too hard to walk. Mr. Eggers was dead. That's what she meant. He would never talk with Joe again. Mrs. Eggers approached him in her kimono and bedroom slippers.

"Sit with me a minute?"

It sounded like a plea and a command both. She helped him off with his jacket and they sat in the breakfast nook and listened to the sound of the kitchen clock and the sound of the rain. She looked too tired for weeping.

"I'm going to get dressed and phone the doctor. I think I shall phone the doctor first, but your mother is coming, your…"

She was beginning to shiver and the shivers turned to shaking.

"Yes, Rennie, she'll be here shortly, so you just sit here, will you, while I get the muddles out of my head?"

"Sure."

"He thought of you as a favourite, you know."

He nodded. He was afraid that she would make him go back in there and say goodbye or something.

"He wanted you to make your way in the world, Rennie. To make something of yourself."

"He said I should be a go-getter."

"That's it. His very words. You don't want to…to…court poverty. Not in this world if you can help it. I came from very poor people, you know."

"No, I didn't know."

"How could you?" she said, tearing up. "But I did. My parents were very poor. I can't say that it was all their fault. But I had an uncle…oh, you don't want to hear about this. Too long ago. Toooo sordid."

"I don't mind."

He did mind. He just wanted to go and not come back for a long time. He didn't even want to come back when he was twenty-one. How could he ever return? Mrs. Eggers was being nice to him but that didn't matter. Every time she said something it was almost too much. The kitchen clock ticked louder than any clock he'd ever heard. Mrs. Eggers glared up at it as though they were both having the same thought.

"My father was badly wounded in the war, the first one, and he and my mother couldn't put two cents together, and the silly fools, they kept on having children. Four sisters I had, and a brother. I was the second youngest. They're all scattered now, who knows where. I was the pretty one…"

Rennie managed to drift away, a thing he did in school when a teacher went on too long about something. He wondered what he would find when he dug up the ground next to the bird bath, which in turn made him think about his money maker. He had clipped out an ad on the back of an *Archie* comic and sent away for it with a money order that cost a dollar twenty-five. The money maker was a small black plastic machine with a knob attached to a roller. You put in a blank piece of paper and turned the knob…*and out comes a REAL dollar bill! You can spend it! Makes $5's, $10's, $20's & more! Mystify your friends! Order yours today!* Rennie discovered, too late, that there was a catch: to bring off this miracle, you first had to supply your own dollar bills to load up the machine. Maybe an eight-year-old would have fallen for this racket, but Rennie was twelve. How stupid could he be? *Something your father would have done*, his mother had said. Would he be any smarter when he turned twenty-one? At least by then he wouldn't have to live with his mother any more.

Mrs. Eggers fumbled a cigarette into her mouth. Rennie roused himself and brought her a blanket from her sitting room and draped it over her shoulders. Her shivering continued. The kitchen clock's ticking filled the silences while Mrs. Eggers inspected her hands, turned them over, checked her nails, turned them back. The rain opened up louder and louder until it turned into a downpour. His mother would probably be late getting here.

Rennie and Mrs. Eggers were both, once again, looking up at the clock, a cheap looking thing with a round face and clear plastic covering, a cartoon rooster on the face.

"Noisy thing," she said. "Piece of junk. He wouldn't let me throw it away."

She gazed at a metal stool in the corner of the kitchen.

"Joseph and I, we should have had children, should have adopted. I know I'm being a bore, Rennie, going on like this. But you never want to be poor. It's not much fun. You must know that already. When my parents passed away, Daddy went first, then Mummy. My youngest sister and I had nothing. And what do girls *do* in hard times when they're all alone in the world? They make choices, you see. And I had my uncle, I was his favourite, Harry was young for an uncle and he had money. The great spender, you see, the great salesman. He went bankrupt ages ago, but back then...you don't want to hear about that. You want to get your education, Rennie, and...and..." She clenched her fist and pounded slowly the palm of her hand. "And take charge of your life. Get your education, get your training, and charge out of the starting gate and get a good job. And never let your family...never let them...drag you down. That's what you need to do, Rennie. Be a man to be reckoned with."

"Sure," he said. "A go-getter."

"That's right, that's the very word. A go-getter."

Her lower lip was quivering and he thought she would break down, but she simply bowed her head and let the clock take over, ticking the seconds away. He made a wish to God. *Make the clock stop ticking.*

"That's what he was, Rennie. A man to be reckoned with. Nothing got in Joseph's way. No task was too big for him. I saw that in him the very minute I met him. I saw the determination in his eyes. Uncle Harry saw it too, and that's when I..."

"Uncle Harry?"

For a moment she seemed to lose track of her story. "That's when I jumped ship."

She was smiling tearfully. She seemed to want to tell him something without saying it. Something about the importance of her life, or a secret he ought to know about. But not now, for God's sake not now. Why did old people go on and on like this?

"Rennie, see that metal stool over in the corner? Let's take that thing down and stop it. You lift the seat and there's a set of steps underneath."

He leapt up and dragged the kitchen table over a few feet to make room, got the stool, placed it beneath the clock, lifted the seat and went up three steps on the stool.

"There's some buttons on the back. Just push the button and put the clock back on the nail. Make sure you push the right button. I'll teach that rooster to run my life."

He lifted the clock off its nail, pressed a button on the back of the clock, and hung it once more on the wall. The ticking had stopped.

"What was I saying? Oh, yes. That's when I jumped ship."

"Yeah?"

"I wasn't even twenty-one. Just before the war. Your father had just come down –"

"My father?"

"Oh, goodness. No, I mean Joseph. He was just back from the North. It was at Auntie Vi's. He'd made his big strike and he swore he'd never go prospecting up there again, but he was at sixes and sevens, I suppose. Not much of an idea of what he wanted to do next. That was a hard life up there. Prospecting. He almost ruined his health. Dead at fifty-three, Rennie. Can you believe that?"

"Boy."

"He looked like an old man," she said, wiping her eyes with a paper napkin she had drawn from her sleeve. "Fifty-three. He outlived his own father by six years, if I remember correctly. Thank God I made him move all that gold out of the house."

"Yeah."

"You know what I mean."

"Yep."

The silence began to feel awkward until Rennie shook free of his cobwebs.

"What do you mean, you jumped ship?"

"Oh, it's just an expression. I didn't mean anything by it, I'm just telling you. You know what? After the funeral I'm going down to the vault. That's where he took the gold bricks last year. To the bank vault."

"You keep em in a bank?"

"Safest place in the world," she replied. "I thought you might be interested. What we did with them."

"Do you know this guy, Stinky Riley?"

"Did *he* tell you about that man?"

"He said I should meet him some day." Rennie looked away. "I dunno."

"Not one of Joseph's more respectable colleagues I can tell you that."

"Weren't they friends?"

Mrs. Eggers sighed. "Up there you had your northern friends, Rennie. You know? Rough fellows who come down here and they don't fit in? They're like bears out of the cave. Mr. Riley was one of those. I wouldn't even have him over. He couldn't mix with our friends. He couldn't even talk without...he had a filthy tongue and a bad temper and he smelled. And he dressed worse than Joseph, he dressed like he was a farmhand or something."

"Yeah."

Joe had told him once that the rooster clock was a gift from Stinky. Rennie was about to point at it when it began ticking again, this time faster than before. They glared at it for a moment, and the second hand began to move counterclockwise, and then the minute hand, and almost imperceptibly, the hour hand, slowly at first, but gaining speed.

"I think," said Mrs. Eggers, "that you must have pushed the wrong button."

She rose to her feet and took a deep breath.

"I'm going to phone the doctor. Rennie, bring that thing down and deal with it, would you?"

He climbed up three steps on the stool, lifted the clock gently off the wall and brought it down. He pushed a different button on the back and turned the clock about to face him. The hands kept spinning, around and around, the wrong way. There was an unearthly shriek and he dropped the clock on the table with a clatter. He picked it up and pushed both buttons, but the clock wouldn't stop shrieking, as though an awakened demon were inside. The rooster. The rooster was crowing. He unplugged the clock, and then it faded, and at last the clock lay quiet in his hands.

Mrs. Eggers was standing at the entrance to the kitchen. "I'll expect you at the funeral, Rennie. He always thought of you as a son, you know. You can bring your mother if you want."

He didn't want to go to the funeral but he didn't know how not to go. She was being nice to him, so he had to go. He didn't want any more of her stories. He just wanted to go home and eat his mother's cooking and see his friends and watch cartoons on tv and never leave home for an entire month. He wanted to make his mother like him again.

"You okay, Mrs. Eggers?"

"Of course I am," she said. "Is that thing dead now?"

"Guess so."

He held up the rooster clock next to his ear to see if he'd broken the mechanism inside. It had gone funny like those clocks in the movies where time passes or time goes backwards. With that kind of clock he could go back and stay there and none of this stuff would happen. Before Mr. Eggers got sick. Before his mother stole the gold brick. He could do another walk with Joe and Gudgeon. Or maybe go back and do another walk with Galahad, only this time he wouldn't let him off the leash.

"You can have it," said Mrs. Eggers. "Joseph would have liked that."

Chapter 23

Thunder

INSTEAD OF LOOKING OLD, tired and stooped over, Mrs. Eggers, at fifty-four, appeared stronger and more confident than she had when Rennie was a boy. Her hair was now long and honey blonde. She wore it pinned back in a roll the way old family ladies did on St. George's Crescent. She dressed as sharp as ever, but not all permed up and stylish like the modern women. She never looked in style but she always looked classy, and he thought that maybe she was drinking less. Mrs. Eggers was off visiting her sister somewhere. She had left Rennie with a hundred dollars to walk the dog as often as he could until her return.

On his twenty-first birthday, Rennie caught a ride over to the Eggers' house and greeted Gudgeon in the backyard. The dog had grown lean and scruffy, and his eyes had gone cloudy. As Gudgeon struggled to a standing position, Rennie wondered if the dog would be up for any kind of a walk. He always had been before, but a day would come…

Rennie lay down his backpack, went into the garden shed adjacent to the doghouse. The shed gave off the toxic stink of *Weed-no-more!* and he frowned at the familiar stink with just a touch of moral superiority. He brought out the square turf shovel. He leaned the shovel against the birdbath and walked over to the back door and knocked. *Hi, I'm Rennie? I'm here to do a bit of edging for Mrs. E., just thought I'd let you know.* If a house sitter asked him what he meant by *edging*, he would point at the shovel and say something vague about long grass. He knocked again. Gudgeon limped over to him and dropped a stick on his running shoe.

"Fetch!"

No one was home. A flaxen August light fell on the heads and shoulders of Mrs. Eggers' statues, enough light for Rennie's job. He had just the flash of a memory – Mr. Eggers leaning against one of the statues.

Standing next to the birdbath, Rennie took hold of the shovel and sank it slowly into the black moist earth. Grass had grown almost a foot tall around the concrete pad. He thought for a second that he could smell the smoke from Joe's cigar, and he brushed the thought away. Methodically, like an eager anthropologist, Rennie went about the shoveling. He had started at the side of the pad that faced the house, and he levered out the turf in a five-inch strip. He laid the turf on the grass. Gudgeon dropped the stick on the turf.

"Fetch!"

Gingerly he scraped at the soil where the turf had been, then went an inch or two deeper with the shovel. His hands were steady but something inside of him was shaking. He sniffed the air for cigar smoke and smelled only the chemical stink from the shed. He encountered some small shards of concrete and a large rounded stone. On the next try he scraped something hard and flat. He went down on his knees, pawed at the soil. Gudgeon dropped the stick on his hand.

"Gudgeon, go fetch!"

Beneath his hands was the top of a grey metal box about five inches wide and less than a foot long. With the shovel he pried up the box. He shook it from side to side, and there came a muffled bumping from within. He unzipped his back-pack and placed the box inside. Down on his knees again, he scraped the soil back into place and smoothed the surface of his excavation. He made a brief bow in the direction of one of the statues. *Thank you*, he said. As the dog blinked up at him, he worked the strip of turf back onto the soil and stamped it down. At last he returned the turf shovel to the shed.

"C'mon, boy."

He shouldered the pack and headed for the front yard. Gudgeon carried the stick in his mouth as they made their way across the street to the footpath that led upriver to the green bench. When they arrived at their bench, the light was dim and Gudgeon had given up on the stick. He lay at Rennie's feet in his familiar state of fatigue. The August air moved up from the river and the ravine, and he breathed it in, the acrid sweet perfume of aspen rot and saskatoons past their prime. After many camping trips in the bush with his friend Glooey, he had become a clean air snob. *Thank you*, he said once more to the Joe on the bench, the Joe in the sky.

Rennie lifted the box from his back-pack and wiped off the dirt. He pushed down on the catch but it wouldn't budge. The box was either locked or rusted shut.

Slowly, he walked the old dog back to the Eggers' yard, headed out to Second Avenue, and caught the bus east. It was the same bus he and his mother used to ride when she was a cleaner and he was nine or ten. The same house, same City of Edmonton bench on a Hundred and Second Avenue. He couldn't help thinking about his boyhood. He couldn't help thinking about Joe, as though the old man was watching him as he waited for the bus. Mrs. Eggers had always been there after Joe died, so he never had to imagine her. She had kept him close over the bad years, when Joe's death weighed heavy on both of their minds, and had kept him close in recent years as well. She got him to do the walks or weed her flower beds or take old Gudgeon for a stroll, and sometimes she just had him in for tea and talked at him. Sometimes she gave him paranoid looks, as though he had stolen her precious jewels or her car or something. She never said anything, but he couldn't help but notice those brief looks from time to time.

He badly wanted to open the metal box, but he made himself wait until he was back home in the basement apartment. His room-mate was watching television and necking with one of the girls who lived down the hall from their apartment, so he took the back-pack into the bathroom, locked the door, and sat on the toilet seat. He almost forgot to breathe. He tried to slow down and be calm. Joe would admire him for being calm. He imagined Joe Eggers sitting hunched over on the rim of the bath tub.

With a screwdriver he pried open the box. Wrapped in a worn tea towel were a magnifying glass, an enamel and gold cigarette lighter, a pewter compass, two rocks, and something in an envelope encased in a plastic bag. The largest rock was a gold sample like the one Joe had given Rennie when he was a boy. This one was flat, about three inches long and less than two inches wide. The label read *Joe/Stinky claim, NWT, '38.* This rock contained more gold. Along the side with the label, the quartz glittered with pale crusts of gold. On the other side of the rock, there was a delicate lacework of gold running down the middle. He expected that the smaller rock would be a nugget, but when he checked it out, there was no gold at all. It was just a small round pebble.

"Holy shit!" he cried out.

Muffled laughter from the bedroom.

Rennie held Mr. Eggers' lucky pebble in the palm of his hand. *Learn from the past and live in the present.* The words should have been inscribed on the old man's most recent tombstone. Rennie left the letter until last. It came with a map scrawled in Joe's shaky hand, with directions to a ranch east of Calgary and north of Brooks. And a photo of young Joe and handsome Isidore standing on a big wharf. And a one-page letter typed on Joe's old Underwood.

Hello, Renwick. I am g essing that by now yo are a yo ng man wondering what to do with yo r life. No advice on that q estion, choose something yo like to do and have f n doing it. Give my love to Mellie. No, better not, she will wonder what the hell yo 're doing comm ning with her dead h sband! I hope yo are faring well and that Mellie's having good time spending all my money. Also hope that by now yo 've stayed in to ch with my friend Stinky. He too has a little birthday gift for yo . If he's still alive! Hah! Let's hope so. Do yo own a car? If not, yo will need to get one to visit Stinky. Go alone and go with a car, my friend. If by now Stinky has popped off, be s re to see Isidore. If Isidore has also popped off, see his wife Loney. And if she is no longer living on the ranch, take my letter to the Patricia Hotel bar and show it to Stinky's friend Elsie. These people will know about yo r little excavation by the bird bath.

Wish I co ld tell yo what it's like being dead. Maybe some other time! Doesn't seem too advent ro s to me. Sometimes a man has his big advent re when he's yo ng, b t perhaps the real story is what he does when he grows old. Not the st ff of best-sellers I s ppose, b t it's the real test of who yo are. Not s re how well I managed that part, b t one of the great chapters of my later life has been getting to know yo , Renwick. Walking the dog and telling stories and trying to keep up with yo r q estions! Yo have a healthy c riosity, a gift for asking abo t things. I think we were good ch ms back then and I hope we still are. Whatever yo do with yo r life, try to think kindly of me. I'll be cheering yo on from wherever it is they stash old prospectors. Best Joe

His room-mate's car was a rattley Ford Fairlane that buffeted under the hood whenever he took it over sixty. Rennie had gassed up the car and placed the map to Mr. Riley's ranch beside him. Stinky Riley, very much alive, told him over the phone that they could meet and have supper at the hotel in Patricia because he was goddammed if he was going to cook on a squelcher like this one. The day was windless and soupy hot. He drove all the way to Brooks with the windows open. When at last he rolled up the powdery road to Patricia, it was late afternoon, and the sun bore a vast copper halo on the southwest horizon. A great legion of clouds was moving in from the southeast.

He had first met Stinky Riley at Joe Eggers' funeral in 1965 and most recently lunched with him three years ago in 1970. He remembered peppering the old man with questions about Buster Krahn, Heraldene and Rusty Regan. Their get togethers and phone calls over a period of eight years had been almost enough to fabricate the illusion that Joe Eggers might still be hovering nearby.

In the last of the sultry afternoon, Rennie pulled up to the Patricia Hotel and saw an old man sitting on a bench outside the hotel in the shade of a big cotton-wood. He was looking wary and he did not offer his hand.

"Not sure I reckanize you, son."

"Been a few years, I guess."

Rennie checked his pockets, pulled out Mr. Eggers' letter, and gave it to Stinky. "I think you're supposed to wish me happy birthday."

The old man read the letter and nodded. "Joey never wrote *me* no typed-up letter."

"Wait a second."

Rennie groped around the back seat of his friend's car.

"Here," he said. "Almost forgot."

He handed the old man a flat boxboard carton. The two of them ambled into the sunlight towards the hotel door. Riley stopped and opened the carton and gawked for a moment. He did not reveal any sign of bewilderment or impatience, nor did he shed his pernickety countenance. He just stared at Rennie's offering, a kitchen clock with a cartoon rooster on the face.

Rennie said, "I guess you could say this is mostly from Mrs. Eggers?"

At last the old man spoke. "Sweet sufferin Christ. If that ain't her to a tee."

They sat in the cool refuge of the hotel bar. The old man seemed to belong in here the way some people belonged to a Legion hall or a service club. The bar was more than half-filled with ranching people, men and women, an aging, talkative bunch. Their tack and stirrups could be found attached to the beams and balustrades, and on every wall their brands had been burned into the knotty pine."Young feller, you ever thought a flyin up to the Barrens? Check out our site?"

"I've thought about it. But work and stuff, y'know?"

"What kinda work?"

"I've started up a business," Rennie said with a self-deprecating smile. "I'm going to corner the market on fridge magnets, I guess."

"What the hell kinda work is that?"

Rennie looked down at his shoes, looked up again, and beheld the old man's confused gape. He didn't like to talk about his new business. It was still pretty fly-by-night and it was hardly the sort of thing he'd be proud to tell Joe Eggers about. But hell, you had to start somewhere.

"I buy stuff at auctions, me and my partner. Cheap stuff. We buy in bulk and store it in a warehouse type thing? And we try to sell it as close to retail as we can? I dunno."

"What're y'gonna do with your life, boy?"

"I don't know. I'm barely out the door."

Rennie gave what his mother referred to as the Rennie Shrug. In resignation, the two men faced each other while the rancher talk murmured lazily around them. Maybe this was what it was like to have a father.

"My mom says I should just get a job and forget about buying and selling. Mr. Eggers told me I should just do what I want and have fun with it. My room-mate, Glooey, he's my partner in the business? He says I should go off to university. I dunno."

"This here friend a yours, why does he say you should go off to college?"

Again, the Rennie Shrug. "I was always good at school."

"What would you take?"

Rennie sighed. "Biology. Zoology mostly. Ecology too, if there's a course in that stuff."

"I run into one a them biologists once. I was out huntin. He made me fill out a form."

Rennie stretched out his arms and yawned mightily. "My room-mate can talk all he wants about going to university. His dad owns a construction company."

"When me an my buddies was kids," said Riley, "we couldn't wait to get outa school. No one ever thought nothin about college."

Rennie looked once more at his shoes and suppressed another yawn. He had lain awake most of the night in anticipation of the drive south.

"I tell my room-mate, I could make more money buying and selling stuff than I ever could as a park biologist."

"You like this work you're doin? Like to go to work every day?"

"Not all the time. I'd rather work outside, I guess. It's great, though, when we can find a customer for our stuff. I mean, we just sold our magnets? Our fridge magnets? Guy in Ontario bought all of them. Now I have some cash and I can take a few days off."

Their conversation drifted into other corners. Mrs. Eggers had gone to London. *(Good fer her.)* Auntie Vi had passed away at ninety-three. *(I wasn't exackly one a her favourite people.)* Rennie's mother wanted him to move back home. *(You got my sympathies, kid.)*

Stinky looked around at the bar, suddenly vigilant, like a look-out who had just been awakened on his night shift. He bought a round and tipped the waitress, who gave him an exasperated look, the look that perpetual listeners will sometimes give to compulsive talkers. Rennie wondered if Isidore, the half-breed guy, had been a compulsive talker up north.

"That's my Elsie. Worships the ground I walk on."

"Stinky, whatever happened to Isidore?"

Riley looked up from his beer. "Son, I am almost eighty-eight years old, you have to speak up."

"What's up with Isidore these days?"

"He had a sad ending. He'd been workin with me, see? With the herd. His wife Loney had passed. Son Charlie and his other kids took off years ago. Isidore headed home from the hotel one night. Fall a 1970. He got sleepy, pulled over by the ditch, got some shut-eye. Well, it was cold that night, so he keeps his motor runnin. Damned if there wasn't a leak somewheres in the vehicle? Bad muffler, mebbe? So Isidore got the carbon monoxide."

"Was he drunk?"

"We all do it, kid."

In the ensuing silence Stinky raised his glass.

"Here's to my friend and partner Isidore Chartrand, the man who talked to the bears. No goddam word of a lie. Saved Joey's life more'n once."

They clinked their glasses to Isidore. Through the screen windows of the bar came an extended roll of thunder.

"Did you ever go back and visit your gold mine?" said Rennie.

"Never."

"How come?"

"It's not my gold mine. I'm no miner, I was a prospector."

Stinky mopped his head with a wrinkled hanky, blinked a few times as though he were getting ready for an afternoon nap, did some aimless observing around the barroom.

"Back then, son," he continued, "gold got nailed at thirty-five dollars a ounce. Now it's more than a hunnerd dollars. Can you believe that?"

"Quite a jump."

Stinky gave him a weary nod. "You should go see that mine. Joey sent me a pitcher once. Great big yella head-frame? Looks like a rocket ship to Mars."

"Go all the way up there to see a mine?" He was wondering about the arsenic and other industrial residues, and how much it would stink down there. And he remembered how Joe had warned him about working underground, and how Joe's own father –

"Why not?" said Stinky.

"I like rocks and all, but I know how devastating a gold mine can be to a tract of wilderness. All that chemical crap? The fewer gold mines the better, as far as I'm concerned. You can't eat the stuff."

"Well, back in the thirties, young man, we couldn't afford no high and mighty opinions like that. Most of us couldn't get a job. Hell, you get lucky, gold is your way outta the Depression. Gold is what bought me a nice spread by the river and more money than I can count. Isidore done pretty well by it too but he mostly just give it away." A pause and a brief yawn. "When I think about the mine at all, I think of it as Joey's mine." Stinky raised his glass. "To my good friend Joey."

"Mr. Eggers."

They cocked their ears with their glasses raised, but this time there was no thunder. The stories returned, mostly from their conversations over the years, and they both tried to calculate how many times someone had saved Joe Eggers' life. They got as high as five if you counted Auntie Vi and began to toast each one.

"Let's raise a glass to Heraldene," said Stinky.

They waited for the thunder. A bolt of lightning flashed at the windows and the thunder followed more quickly than before. Soon they could hear the patter of rain on the tin roof of the hotel bar.

"We need this," said Stinky, peering warily up at the ceiling. "Ranches around here dry as hell."

The old man went still, began to blink, and waited for Elsie to bring their supper. He closed his eyes as though to have a catnap. When their steaks and fries arrived, Stinky Riley seemed to come to life.

As the thunder stuttered off into the hills the rain seemed to intensify into a real rainstorm, and then to ease back into a gentle downpour.

"Can I drive the car back to your place with you, Stinky? No way I want to be on that highway tonight."

"I was just bout to invite you back to stay the night. You can sleep in the bunkhouse. Mebbe you can help me with a chore I have to do."

"Fine with me."

"Happy birthday, son. This here dinner, this is your birthday present, so don't get no fancy notions about a cake."

Stinky seemed caught up by yet another memory. "You know, kid, Joey always wanted to build a place near mine over by the Red Deer River?" He looked down and paused for a moment and then gazed up at Rennie. "I owed that man a whole lot back then and I owe him yet. More than I can ever say."

Stinky sounded tearful, as though he were giving the oath of allegiance, and his voice went lower and softer as he spoke.

"I made that man stay behind, don't you see? I made him guard the claim so's I could get it registered. And Joey done it and he nearly died doin it. He coulda gone to jail for the rest of his life. All because I made him stay back and guard the claim."

Once more the old man raised his glass.

"To my friend, Joey Burbidge."

At first, silence. And then there came a ticking dark flash that dimmed the bulbs in the chandelier above them and a crack of thunder that cannonaded under the tables and made the beer glasses teeter and clink. Every soul in the barroom seemed to jump. The room went dark, and for a moment everyone was silent.

"Holy shit."

"Son of a bitch."

"Jesus almighty Christ."

Riley arose and hauled up his jeans, dropped a silver dollar on the table, and the big coin wobbled heavy in the darkness. They left the bar in two vehicles, and in less than twenty minutes Stinky and Rennie were standing in the rain by Stinky's barn door. The barn had been built on a flat stretch of meadow not far from the house and overlooking a wide, deep valley. They went inside and stood before the empty stalls. The stalls gave off a stale odour from their former occupants, and this odour seemed to belong with the sound of the rain. It was a sad smell and a sad sound. What was the name of the horse that Joe had ridden up north? A woman's name? Stinky lifted a pitchfork from a nail in the wall and motioned Rennie to enter the middle stall.

"What are we doing, Stinky?"

"Over here, son."

He pointed to a hay fork leaning against some stacked boards, and they both began to rake and shovel the straw from the rough wooden floor.

"There's a ring in the corner. See that? Pry er up and give er a tug."

Rennie used his fork to wedge up a thick and rusted iron ring. He hunkered down and pulled on the ring with both hands. He grunted, the wood shrieked, and a hinged section of the barn floor began to lift. He tried to calm himself. He imagined Joe once again, admiring him for being calm.

"All the way, son. That's it. Now, let er drop."

They stared at a pit somewhat larger than the size of a grave.

"What's down there?"

"You can't guess?"

Rennie's hands were in his pockets, and he fingered Joe's round pebble. He shrugged at Stinky.

"There's a steamer trunk down there, fella. Somethin in there I gotta get to. I'm too old for this. So you gotta get down there and open up that bugger."

Dimly he could see the rectangular outline of the trunk, about three feet long and two feet wide. He sat on the edge of the pit and eased his body down into the enclosure. The cool walls of the pit came almost to his shoulders.

"Hasp on that there side. It ain't locked."

Rennie fumbled for the hasp and pulled open the trunk. He gaped up at the outline of the old man hulking above him by the edge of the pit. The beams of a small flashlight fell first on

Rennie's face and then on the contents of the trunk. Small bundles lay side by side, individually wrapped in white cloth, pillow cases perhaps, or torn-up bedding.

"Can I have that flashlight?"

"Yer shaking like a leaf, son. I'll hold the flashlight. Hand me one a them smaller buggers. Go ahead. They ain't rattlers, they won't bite."

Rennie reached in and seized a small bundle, and its prodigious weight told the rest of the story.

"Holy…"

With both hands he passed it to Stinky. The old man was wheezing. He sounded like Joe.

"Mrs. Eggers used to say they were all in a bank vault."

"These babies musta flied off when no one was lookin. Hand me another small…over there. Yeah."

One by one he hauled them out of their enclosure, seven small bundles; and then he heaved up five big bundles, each one more than the weight of a large anchor. At Stinky's request, he heaved up the empty steamer trunk. He clambered out of the pit and lugged it to the old Ford and left the trunk open in the back seat. The two men laid in the swaddled bars and bricks, and Rennie closed up the hasp, padlocked it, and locked the car.

"Why don't we just split them fifty-fifty?"

"I got no use for em, kid. You're the one who needs em."

The night air had turned chilly. Their conversation carried on in Stinky's bungalow, where they sipped whisky at the kitchen table and gazed at the coals in the Franklin stove as though they were viewing an old western on television.

"Hell, you got enough capital there to start yer own prospectin business. I hear tell there's some real finds to be had up around Wolf Lake."

"Finds?"

"Gold, son. The stuff fellers dream of."

"You mean sell all this gold so I can go look for more gold?"

Riley laughed and his laughter turned to gasping.

"What do I do with all this gold? Stinky?"

"Sell it, I guess."

"How?"

"I dunno. That's yer problem. Do it legal, son. Get a license. You and me, we can partner up till it's all gone. Anyone asks you where you got the gold, you say none a yer goddam business. Or tell em your partner Stinky Riley the famous bush pilot is sellin his hoard. Heh. But go careful about it. We can split the goddam taxes if you like, and you take the money and run."

"Why don't you come up to Edmonton and help me out?"

Stinky went solemn for a moment and looked away. "Can't believe it. I just give up a fortune so's a young buck can go get hisself a college degree."

Riley looked up at the kitchen ceiling, took in a deep breath, and the booze proclaimed itself one more time. "Wherever you are, Joey, I hope you're satisfied!"

In the morning Rennie bid the old man goodbye, hopped in the car and headed down the road in a light steady rain. Now and then, through the rear-view mirror, he caught sight of the steamer trunk in the back seat. Before long, he saw the town of Brooks ahead, a scattering of low buildings on the near horizon. He glanced again at the back seat and said, *Thank you, Joe.*

He pulled onto the main highway heading north to Edmonton, floored it until the engine vibrated like a wringer washer, and once more he said, *Thank you, Joe.* He felt as though his insides were vibrating just like the car's engine. Never in his life had he felt this much...what was it...frenzy? Like in Alfred Hitchcock? He kept waiting for the happiness part, but maybe that would come later.

His thoughts began to swarm. If he was ever going to become a somebody, it would not be from selling junk. He would turn over the business to his friend. If Glooey asked questions, he would say he had plans. *What plans? The usual stuff,* he would say. *I'm going to university.* And if his mother said *Why don't you come back home and live here,* he would say *I'll get an apartment near campus.* And if she said, *How can you afford your own apartment,* he would say *I sold my half of the business. End of story.*

Long deep puddles lay in the dips and the shoulders of the highway, and as the miles passed , he would line up a puddle and splash the water all to hell and yell *Yeehaw!* out the open window.

A house. He should maybe buy his mother a house so at least she'd have that instead of living in the row-house. Rough neighbourhood. He hit another puddle and this time the car shimmied from side to side.

"Slow down, Rennie," he said like a father, and turned on the radio.

He rotated the dial with little success until, at last, he got a Sunday gospel hour from somewhere, which was better than nothing. The noise would keep him awake if he started to get sleepy. He grew relaxed, patient, humming along to a gospel tune, a black choir from the south, the one about Jacob's ladder. *Every rung goes higher and higher,* he groaned as he drove through the rain, waiting for that moment when happiness would descend at last all over the world.

END OF STORY

Acknowledgements

My gratitude to the late Tom Payne, one of my boyhood heroes. The stories he told us are not recounted here, but his inspiration was a driving force. To Walt and Dianne Humphries and Ryan Silke for your knowledge of prospecting, your awareness of Yellowknife history, and for passing on your love of the North. A huge thank you to my friend, Dave Margoshes, who reads as perceptively as he writes. To Alice Payne, for *Quin Kola*, her remarkable book, and for nudging me towards the finer points of prospecting in the old days. To the Saskatchewan Arts Board for a grant and the Saskatchewan Writers' Guild for four winter colonies at St. Peter's Abbey. To the Campbell River Museum and the Haig-Brown Committee for a residency during the winter of 2014-15. Thanks to Shaun Bradley for her patient and incisive work in the early going. To John Marlow from The Editorial Department. Thanks also to my brother Peter Carpenter, Ron Dickinson, Bernice Hammersmith, Don Sedgwick, Joseph Naytowhow, Lee Mazurick, Lynne Bell, Sandy Bonny, Robert Horwood, Harriet Hart, Nik Burton, Susan Buck, Will Rogers, Terry Myles, Michael Thomas, Les Coleman, Smudge the Wonderdog, and the late Stan Graber. Many thanks to Leona Theis, consumate writer and reader, for her alert editorial work with this novel. And to John Agnew of Coteau Books who demonstrated his faith in this undertaking. And thank you to Kever for your work as first reader and for everything else. For quite a lot, actually.

About the Author

Photograph by Jerry Haigh

DAVID CARPENTER was born and raised in Edmonton of Saskatchewan parents. He began writing as a translator and reviewer in Winnipeg. He moved to Saskatoon for a teaching appointment at the University of Saskatchewan and began writing his own work. This decision was inspired in part by witnessing a reading by the Moose Jaw Movement and was impelled by subsequent workshops with Robert Kroetsch and Jack Hodgins at Fort San. Carpenter's short stories began to emerge around 1980 with a series of publications in *Saturday Night*. He is a recent recipient of the Kloppenburg Award for Literary Excellence (2015). Currently he is editing Volume 3 of *The Literary History of Saskatchewan*.

MIX
Paper from
responsible sources
FSC® C100212
FSC
www.fsc.org

Printed in November 2017
by Gauvin Press,
Gatineau, Québec